# BLACK SUNSHINE

## S. V. DATE

G. P. Putnam's Sons New York

G. P. Putnam's Sons
*Publishers Since 1838*
a member of
Penguin Putnam Inc.
375 Hudson Street
New York, NY 10014

Library of Congress Cataloging-in-Publication Data

Date, S. V. (Shirish V.)
Black sunshine / S. V. Date.
p. cm.
ISBN 0-399-14946-5 (alk. paper)
1. Governors—Election—Fiction.   2. Political campaigns—Fiction.
3. Politicians—Fiction.   4. Brothers—Fiction.   5. Florida—Fiction.   I. Title.
PS3554.A8237B56   2002         2002024949
813'.54—dc21

Printed in the United States of America
1   3   5   7   9   10   8   6   4   2

BOOK DESIGN BY MEIGHAN CAVANAUGH

For my own brothers, Rajeev and Sanjeev

★

# Acknowledgments

★

Thanks once again to Neil Nyren for his invaluable guidance; to Mary Beth, Orion and Rigel for their continued patience; to Randy Wayne White for his expertise with boats that are able to get out of their own way; to the folks at Penn reels for their institutional memory; and to Gary Adkison for his hospitality. And also for telling me where the lobster holes are.

Important Notice to Mariners: The description in these pages of the northeast channel into Walker's Cay IS COMPLETELY MADE UP and, therefore, should not be used for navigational purposes. The prudent mariner will generally avoid taking sailing directions from a work of fiction, particularly one where the author has been away from the water so long that he barely remembers what he's talking about.

# Prologue

★

It took the first echoing *ba-boom* of thunder for Spencer Tolliver to finally notice the purplish-green wall that had taken up position over the Seven Seas Resort's red-tiled condos on shore. As he watched, a leading edge of wispy cirrus eclipsed the late afternoon sun, instantly robbing the water of its sapphire brilliance.

It would not be long before the dark thunderheads themselves loomed overhead, turning blue sky and bluer ocean into a uniform slate color, and the first cold breath of air came blasting out ahead of the squall. And it would be at that moment, he promised himself, that he would abandon the enormous fish on his line and point the boat back in toward the inlet.

Which meant, he estimated with a glance over his polarized Ray-Bans, he had about ten minutes to tire and boat a monster he had been fighting now for more than an hour. Tolliver gave his rod a yank, got a tug in return that reeled off a few yards more line, and then settled back to wait another minute before going all out.

It was a grouper. That or a snapper. Big bottom fish, darting in and out of a maze of hidey-holes along the coral-and-rock seabed some fifty feet down. He had three feet of wire leader at the end of the line. Three feet of margin. If he let the fish go any deeper into a hole than that, it would simply shake its head a few times until the nylon line snagged and parted with a snap.

Tolliver sighed. This fish had no doubt escaped more than one angler that way in its lifetime, and it was looking more and more like it would escape yet another.

Well, that was fine. There was no dishonor in losing to a smart old fish. And certainly the old saw was still true—a bad day's fishing was indeed better than a good day's work, which in his case was being the comptroller of Florida, and was many times better than a good day's campaign fund-raising, which was what he was scheduled to do later that evening.

There was, in fact, little he disliked more than fund-raising—going around the room, shaking hands, grinning like a fool, thank you, thank you, thank you ever so much. Occasionally the donor would whip out a checkbook right in front of his eyes, postdate it, put pen to paper, then look up to ask him: How much?

Spencer Tolliver always struggled to contain the smart-ass reply: Whatever you think owning a piece of the next governor of Florida is worth.

Technically, with his campaign still unofficial and below the radar, he was collecting commitments, not actual money. It made little difference. Owning a piece of the next governor was what nearly every one of his potential contributors was thinking, particularly those who attended the swanky, black-tie-optional, quail-eggs-and-caviar events that netted the big, six-figure IOUs. It hadn't been as bad during the campaign for comptroller, but that was only because, first, few people had even heard of the office, and, second, even fewer thought he had a chance of winning.

There he'd been, a cranky, old retired Marine general and one-time POW, whiling away his golden years on a Panhandle beach, fishing at sunup and sundown and writing cranky, old op-ed pieces to the local newspaper in the afternoon about corruption in Tallahassee, particularly in the office of the comptroller, the erstwhile watchdog of the rest of state government. Finally the local party boss had suggested he put his money where his mouth was and run against the guy. No one, not even Tolliver, thought it possible he might actually win. The incumbent was going on his fourth term, with a big, fat campaign war chest for a race that few voters paid any attention to. Tolliver decided to run because he believed *somebody* should.

Then, out of nowhere, the FBI and U.S. Attorney swooped down and indicted the guy, and political first-timer Tolliver walked into the office with seventy-two percent of the vote, putting him in charge of regulating Florida banks and brokerage houses, giving him oversight over all state finances, and, most important, giving him a seat on the Florida Cabinet, one of six votes equal to that of the governor in state executive-branch matters.

And it was in that capacity—as a free-thinking Republican on the Cabinet who could not be bought by the special interests, as staunch a defender of Florida's remaining wilderness as the environmental lobby could hope to see—that Tolliver began catching the eye of good-government purists who began a whisper campaign to persuade him to run for governor.

Tolliver had thought about it long and hard. There was a lot about public life that he was not crazy about. Particularly following his experience in the military, where his orders were carried out without discussion, the endless wheedling by the moneyed interests on issues where the Right Thing to Do was as obvious as a flashing neon sign sometimes drove him to distraction. At least once or twice a week, to regroup, he would need the long drive from Tallahassee out to his beach house in Cape San Blas for a soothing hour of surf casting for blues and jacks.

On the other hand, Tolliver had realized, he was facing a rare political opportunity. The incumbent Democrat was retiring after his second term. His lieutenant governor, a decent enough fellow, was nonetheless a bad candidate, and beatable. Meanwhile, among Republicans, only he had successfully run a statewide campaign before. A former congressman, two state senators and the political novice Billings brothers were also interested in running, with the state party chairman openly supporting the Billings boys on the theory that their father's name would make either of them the strongest candidate in the field.

Tolliver had almost bought that argument before his contrariness had gotten the better of him: *He* was the one on the Cabinet, by God, not Percy or Bub Billings. And if party boss Farber LaGrange didn't want him, it was because the electric utilities and Big Oil and Big Sugar and Big Everyone Else didn't want him. And that right there was reason enough to run. Besides, he was a widower whose children were grown. What else did he have to do?

Three weeks earlier he had told LaGrange his decision, that he intended to announce his run for Florida governor on June 1, and if that meant the Party had to endure a primary in September, then so be it. That's what democracy was all about. To his credit, LaGrange accepted it and told him he would do all he could to get the Party behind him. He'd arranged a series of unpublicized meet-and-greet sessions with the big-money set in Sarasota, Naples and Palm Beach, had even arranged for Tolliver to use his fishing boat for a little R&R before his event at Jupiter's swanky Seven Seas Resort.

And a nice little boat it was, Tolliver thought again as he eyed the craft up and down. A twenty-six-foot Robolo with a 225-hp Mercury. He personally would have picked an Evinrude, but what the hell. Beggars could not be choosers. Plus the man had been generous enough to point out his favorite fishing hole. Tolliver knew he had little ground for complaint.

The water around him suddenly lost its remaining color, and Tolliver took off the polarized sunglasses and put them in his pocket. They would not do him much good, particularly once the rain started. He eyed the tall thunderheads approaching from shore with a twinge of nervous energy. It would get wild, once the wind started blowing and the waves started frothing. Wild, he knew, but not particularly dangerous. He was only a few miles offshore. Not enough room for the waves to build quickly. Besides, the big Merc would let him cover that distance in ten minutes, tops. Then, if the wind was still blowing too hard once he made the inlet, he'd drop the hook in the Intracoastal for a while before tucking back into Seven Seas's marina.

Tolliver eased back the rod a bit, preparing for his final attempt to land his fish. He had the butt of the pole resting in its receptacle in the leather harness he was wearing, with the pin pushed through the base to keep it from flying overboard. When the time came and he still hadn't caught the fish, he would simply tighten the drag wheel and walk back a few steps until the eight-pound line snapped, and then turn his attention to getting the boat back in ahead of the worst of the storm.

He'd go to his room, shower and order a room-service sandwich before dressing for the gala that evening. He'd spend the night and maybe get in a half day of fishing in the morning before hitting the road for an Orlando gig the following evening—his twenty-first event in twenty-nine days, bringing him close to the million-dollar-commitment mark that would help cement his lead among potential GOP candidates and, with any luck, keep the rest of them from even filing papers.

Then, with all that grubby money locked in early, he could spend the remainder of the summer and early fall doing what he liked best: the town hall meetings where he'd mingle with regular Floridians, one-on-one, and explain why they should not only vote for him for governor, but also pester their legislative candidates into supporting his broad campaign-financing proposal to take big money out of Florida politics once and for all. Like fishing, he thought with a grin, he could happily talk about campaign finance reform for hours on end.

Perhaps, he realized, he could even do both. . . . After all, the vast majority of the state's population lived within twenty miles of a coast. He could park the RV each night at a nearby beach for a couple hours of daybreak surf casting to start out each morning. He smiled at the prospect, gave another gentle tug at the rod perched on his still-flat belly and, without warning, felt himself nearly knocked over by the blast of frigid air barreling ahead of the squall line. Landward, the resort's tiled roofs had nearly disappeared in sheets of rain, and Tolliver wondered if he'd perhaps underestimated the storm's strength.

Well, no matter. He'd run through spring squalls before, and he'd do so again. There was nothing like driving a boat under a purple sky, wind roaring, lightning flashing all around, icy rain coming more straight at you than down. It reinvigorated the life force, reminded him what it meant to be alive.

He couldn't help the beginnings of a grin as he cranked down the drag on the reel, tightening as hard as it would go. Then, a mere tug on the handle would make the rod bend over and the line sing for a moment before it snapped, like so . . .

But the line didn't snap.

He tugged, then tugged harder, then stepped back from the transom, but the monofilament showed absolutely no sign of strain. His brow narrowed and his lips thinned as he stared at the reel, then tried pulling line out by hand.

Nothing.

The drag was indeed set, but for some reason the eight-pound test simply refused to break, no matter how much force he applied. He reached for his belt for his wire cutters, realized they weren't there, saw them on the port bait well and began moving toward them when the fish hit again and again, bigger than it had all afternoon, yanking Tolliver bodily toward the starboard gunwale, slamming him hard against the rail.

Over and over, it hit, now actually pulling the Robolo through the water, and Tolliver struggled to work the pin free from the base of the rod handle, realized he couldn't against the strain of the fish, tried instead to undo the buckles of the harness attaching him to the fishing pole—which is when he felt the unmistakable tightness of electricity surging through his body, contracting every muscle, locking the breath in his lungs, stopping his heart. . . .

And with Spencer Tolliver's ears unable to hear the roaring wind and the exposed skin on his neck barely registering the first cold drops of rain, the fish pulled yet again and yanked him clean over the side and down into the wind-roiled black water.

## ★ ⟨1⟩ ★

The port cap rail was about half scrubbed when the state car pulled into the gravel parking lot beside the single-wide trailer that served as the marina office.

Murphy Moran knew even before the plain yellow tag with the official lettering came into view that it was a state car, and stood with one hand on the starboard shroud to watch. Like most boat docks in Florida, Blastoff View Marina was on sovereign waters, with the submerged land leased to the boatyard. A code-enforcement officer had been by a couple times previously in recent weeks, once even coming on Columbus Day, a state holiday, and Murphy looked forward to the distraction a confrontation between humorless bureaucrat and humorless scofflaw would bring when he noticed the erect carriage of the silver-haired gentleman who emerged from the passenger seat.

Ramsey, he realized with a wide smile. Only Ramsey.

Of all the high-ranking politicos he had ever known, Ramsey MacLeod was the only one who refused to treat his Highway Patrol driver like a chauffer and insisted on riding in the front seat beside him.

Quickly, Murphy appraised himself, set the plastic bristle brush in his hand on the cabin top, grabbed a torn T-shirt off the dorade vent and ran stained fingers through his hair before returning Ramsey MacLeod's wave.

"Mr. Lieutenant Governor!" Murphy called out, moving quickly to the bow.

MacLeod was already walking down the worn dock, agilely avoiding the spots with the missing planks before reaching out to pump Murphy's hand. "Permission to come aboard, Captain!"

Murphy helped him over the pulpit and Ramsey MacLeod grabbed him by both shoulders and squeezed, gray eyes twinkling merrily, then bent to slip off his loafers. "I know how you yachtsmen are about scuff marks." He glanced around the boat, at the squalid trailer on shore, then affected mock concern. "I don't mean to sound unkind, man, but I thought you were a *Republican* consultant. How come you're living like a Democrat? I thought you had a big boat." He nodded at the half-scrubbed teak rail. "And I figured Republicans had *people* to do that sort of thing."

Murphy shrugged. "I did the math. I didn't have money enough to quit *and* keep *Dark Horse*." *Dark Horse* had been his Hinckley Sou'wester 54, the dream boat he had rarely sailed in the years he'd owned her. He shrugged again. "You wanna retire at forty, you gotta make sacrifices. With *Mudslinger*, I can pay my running costs and living expenses off the interest, never touch the principal."

Ramsey MacLeod took off his blazer and slung it over his shoulder. "Spoken like a true Scotsman."

"I'm Irish," Murphy said.

"Well, we all got our shortcomings," Ramsey said with a wry smile. "Anyway, I admire your fiscal discipline. And you gotta love the name: *Mudslinger*." He pursed his thin lips a moment. "Actually, it was on that matter I came to see you."

Murphy nodded toward the stern and led his guest down the narrow side deck, into the cockpit, then down the companionway into the main salon. MacLeod admired varnished cherry bulkheads, hunched over the chart table and dinette, poked his head over the stainless-steel stove and sink, then ran his fingers over weathered bronze portholes.

"Well, this is cozy," he announced.

"The smaller the boat, the less there is to maintain," Murphy said, with more than a twinge of defensiveness.

"She ain't that small," Ramsey MacLeod said.

"Yeah, she is. Southern Cross 31. Nine-and-a-half-foot beam. Canoe stern. She's small." He pounded the bulkhead, and it gave a solid thunk. "But she's built like a tank. Oversized, redundant rigging. Hand-laid glass in the hull. Anywhere I want to go, she'll get me there."

Ramsey MacLeod nodded, impressed. "And once you get there, will you be able to watch videos?"

He reached into his blazer pocket for a VHS cassette and handed it to Murphy, who opened a cabinet over the starboard settee and popped the tape into a compact combination TV/VCR. It turned on automatically and showed a home video of a boisterous campaign rally, the camera panning over hundreds of people clapping to bass-and-keyboards Euro-tech rock music.

"In case you haven't been following, this is one of my *opponent's* events," Ramsey MacLeod narrated. "Mine don't attract quite as many folks. They got better stuff to do, like rearrangin' their sock drawers."

The camera settled on the stage, where a dozen stuffy, Republican-looking community and business leaders stood clapping and stomping their feet at random intervals, when suddenly the crowd went berserk as a short, curly-haired guy in a golf shirt and khakis came strutting onto the stage, his head doing its own strut, like a hen's, and stood at the microphone with arms outstretched and thumbs up.

"That's my opponent," Ramsey MacLeod said. "Bub Billings."

Bub mouthed "thank you" about a dozen times, then, with head still bobbing, he launched into his remarks and got as far as *My fellow Floridians* before the crowd erupted again and the candidate had to say "thank you" another dozen times. Finally he began again: *My fella*

*Floridians, I am humbled and honored by your energy. If I could bottle it and sell it, shoot, I bet I could give ol' Bill Gates a run for his money!*

Another round of insane cheering, with Bub once again flashing thumbs up, before he settled into his speech: *When I founded Bub's Fine Lawn Furniture in my garage five years ago, I didn't have but two nickels to rub together. But I invested both of them in the business, and you know why? 'Cause I believed that in America, you CAN make a difference. Now my payroll's fifty-seven fine people. Fifty-seven TAXPAYIN' folks like you an' me! Because in America, the business of America is business! And that's an ethic, a . . .* Bub squinted just off camera for a long second . . . *What the . . . What? Oh: para-*dime*. Yeah. Great. Teach me for usin' speechwriters that use fifty-cent words. All right: A para-*dime *that we gotta have instead of the somethin'-for-nothin' culture that encourages the economically disadvantaged to pass their values on to the next generation.*

"Amazing, isn't it?" Ramsey MacLeod said. "Guy can't read a Tele-PrompTer. Turns it into an applause line."

*We CAN take this back, folks. For eight long years, the liberal-media-elite's been runnin' things in Tallahassee, and look what they've given us: the highest unemployment in twenty years, and three-dollar-a-gallon gas. Anyone here like payin' three dollars a gallon for gas?* A resounding "nooooooo!" from the crowd. *Me neither! It's time the regular folk got a chance! Or my name ain't Bub Billings!* Bub smiled and pointed out into the crowd until the applause died down. *Three and a half more weeks, everybody! So keep your eye on the brass ring and get ready to grab the prize, and on November the fifth, we the people are gonna win! Thank you very much!*

Bub ran off the stage, thumbs held high, as the music thumped. Ramsey MacLeod reached around the folding dinette table to hit the stop button.

"And Elvis leaves the building." Ramsey removed the tape and slapped his palm with it a few times. "He does five of those rallies a day. Half the folks in the audience are bused from one to the next like cattle. We suspect they're gettin' paid but can't prove it. He and his handlers ride in one luxury bus. All the press rides in the other. The buses have satellite TV and catered food. After five, the press bus has an open bar.

On my campaign, the press has to squeeze into a rented minivan. They eat McDonald's. Sonny's Barbecue on a good day. Guess which campaign the reporters like covering better?"

Murphy Moran said nothing, kept his arms folded across his chest. He had a feeling where this was headed.

"Pretty much the same story on the fund-raising side. They're raising and spending five dollars to every one of ours. Now, I've been a Democrat all my life. I'm used to getting outspent. But five to one? That's a bit hard to take. Especially from a guy and a campaign like this. Had it been Spencer Tolliver beating the pants off me? I wouldn't have minded so much."

Murphy nodded. "I heard that rumor, too. That he was starting to raise some money. It's a damned shame about what happened."

"Even Percy Billings wouldn't have been so bad. Sure he's an arrogant son of a bitch, but there's no doubt he's worked his butt off his whole life. But I suppose he doesn't poll as well as Bub, and we all know how important that is in the World According to Farber." Ramsey shook his head. "I can't tell you how depressing losing to this one is. Shoot, he didn't take his own life seriously until a couple years ago. He hasn't put forward a single policy objective. His entire campaign is high energy and flashy production. That and three-dollar gas. Like that's somehow my fault."

Murphy shuffled his bare feet on the cabin sole. Like most boats, it was dark teak interspersed with strips of white holly. Like most boats too poor to afford paid crew, it was badly scuffed, in need of stripping down to bare wood and re-varnishing.

"You been paying much attention to the race?" MacLeod asked.

Murphy shook his head. "I've been trying to get *Mudslinger* ready to go down island this winter. Finally. You can imagine how it is: a million things to do, fewer and fewer days left to get them done. Like right now, I'm waiting on a part to fix the VHF, haven't even started to install the SSB. Haven't even taken it out of the box yet—"

"They dragged out 'Mother,'" MacLeod said.

Murphy winced, then let out a long, deep sigh. "Mother" had been

Murphy's brainchild four years earlier, when MacLeod and his boss, Governor Bolling Waites, had run for reelection against a punk real-estate developer from Miami. Murphy had worked for the punk, and "Mother" had been a masterpiece of below-the-belt campaigning, a thirty-second television ad shot in grainy black and white, flashing between the image of an old lady lying in a hospital bed with tubes running in and out of her nose, and stark white lettering explaining how she had developed bed sores and lesions and, ultimately, a fatal infection while negligent nursing home attendants had failed to notice—all on the Waites-MacLeod watch. The only sound was the beeping of a heart monitor that, by commercial's end, became the steady flat tone signifying death. Left out of the spot, naturally, was even a hint of how it had been the Republican-dominated legislature, not Waites and MacLeod, who had refused to fund even a token number of nursing-home inspectors as a sop to the industry that, coincidentally enough, had provided millions for their campaigns.

The ad had been as effective as it was unfair, and had given Murphy's man a solid lead in the polls that Waites had been able to overcome only with a stunning performance in the final debate and a blitz of tens of thousands of last-minute "scare" calls to elderly voters, accusing the Republicans of wanting to repeal Social Security.

"How bad is it?" Murphy asked finally.

"Twenty-one days to the election, and I'm a solid eleven down in the polls. Before gas prices went nuts, I was actually ahead. Gas got to two-fifty a gallon, and I was four points behind. Three bucks a gallon, and I fell to eight points. Now they started running your ad, and suddenly I'm down eleven."

"Their poll? Or yours?"

"Mine," MacLeod said, to Murphy's groan. "Exactly. So it's probably more like thirteen, what with pollsters always shading it on the side of whoever's writing the check."

Murphy stared at the grease- and paint-stained to-do list on the navigation table. More than half the items on it still did not have a check mark against them, and he was quickly running out of weather window. If he wasn't in Georgetown by mid-November, he could kiss the Caribbean goodbye for yet another winter.

Still and all, it was *his* brutal handiwork that was continuing its ruthless destruction long after he'd left the scene. Like an abandoned gill net in the middle of the ocean, indiscriminately killing every swimming thing even after the fishermen had forgotten they had lost it.

"Now I know I ain't the most charismatic candidate to come down the pike. Far from it. But I know state government, and I know how to make it work better," Ramsey MacLeod said. "I suppose that's not near as sexy as making fun of it and running against it. But there it is. That's who I am."

"You don't have to apologize for being decent, Ramsey," Murphy said with a sigh. "I'll do it. I owe you."

MacLeod shook his head. "You *don't* owe me, Murph. Not after how you came around and helped Bolling in the tobacco fight like you did."

"That wasn't to help Bolling. That was because it was the right thing to do. I still owe you."

Ramsey nodded slowly, then cracked a grin. "I guess I can't pretend I wasn't hoping you'd see it that way. All right then. I thank you. I don't mean to drag you out of retirement or anything. I just need a mind like yours to come up with a fresh idea. You know, something . . ."

"Devious?" Murphy offered.

Ramsey grinned again. "Just whatever you can manage. I won't destroy your reputation by paying you or anything. It's not like I can afford your rates, anyway. I'm a Democrat, you remember. Just . . . a new concept, is what I'm looking for." He gathered up his blazer and started to climb the companionway ladder. "I've got a few ideas you could work with. About a dozen different things he's said on the campaign trail—"

"We haven't got time for that. That would take a solid two months, minimum, to build a strategy based on contradictory statements. We've got less than three weeks." Murphy followed MacLeod up into the cockpit, felt the boat list slightly as they walked forward along the port-side deck. "This late in the game, we need a sucker punch."

MacLeod put his shoes on and swung one leg over the stainless tubing of the bow pulpit. "You were thinking . . ."

Murphy thought for a second, opened his mouth to answer before closing it again. "You probably don't want to know."

Ramsey MacLeod stood on the dock and waved at his driver. "You're probably right. But I can tell from that gleam in your eye that whatever it is, it ain't gonna be pretty. Okay then. Bolling warned me it might come to this. So be it. *Alia iacta est.* Go for it. Get me something I can use to kick the snot out of the little twerp." MacLeod took a deep breath, blew it out. "You got yourself a cabin wench yet? For this world cruise of yours? Hey, weren't you seeing that lobbyist for Bell South Wireless?"

Murphy winced, shook his head. "Don't go there, please."

Ramsey MacLeod raised a sympathetic eyebrow. "Sore subject? That's all right. I'm sure the wench issue will take care of itself when you get to one of those islands where the women all go topless. You are planning on visiting some of those islands, aren't you? Well, of course you are." He thought about that and nodded slowly. "Well, I think I'll shut up now, before I talk you out of helping me. Take care, and thanks again."

And with a broad grin, MacLeod turned and walked up the dock to the car, where he carefully hung his blazer in the back seat before climbing in beside his driver.

Murphy watched from the bow as the Crown Victoria bumped down the gravel road ahead of a cloud of dust, then turned to gather up and stow his teak-scrubbing gear before heading to the marina bathroom for a shower.

Clyde Bruno cracked his knuckles impatiently as Grant carefully copied the question off the printed page and onto the back of his hand. Behind him hung a giant banner, "Floridians Meet Bub!" over the Coral

Reef Ballroom, and Clyde was starting to get nervous that the candidate would at any moment stroll on through and start the bull session, leaving Grant and his big yellow name tag that said "Regular Floridian Grant" out in the lobby, still copying.

Clyde said, "Hurry it up," and got a grunt in reply.

He stood, walked to the front window and saw the candidate on a stage set up in the parking lot raising his thumbs skyward triumphantly, the crowd going wild on cue. He turned and walked back to the vinyl seat, sniffed with wrinkled nose at the mildew that managed to overpower both salt air and disinfectant.

There had been a time when such a smell would not even have registered with him, so accustomed was he to the rank mess that was his own trailer-park home. Stale beer, cigarette smoke and mildew were constants, interrupted only during the occasional tropical-storm-induced flood that would leave instead a month-long stench of organic decomposition.

That, though, had been before he'd caught the eye of Petron North America chief Link Thresher during a labor dispute. The boss happened to be in town and took notice of refinery hand Bruno and how he'd sided with the foreman against the rabble with enthusiastic violence, resulting in three concussions, a broken nose and a shattered kneecap. The end result was that the unionizing effort failed, and Thresher had started him on a chain of rapid promotions that quickly put him in the rarefied air of the executive suite with the title: Special Assistant to the President.

Now it was strictly first-class for Clyde Bruno. Company house, company housekeeper, company cook, company car. On the road, it was a room next door to Mr. Thresher at five- and, in extremely rare instances, four-star hotels. No more Holiday Inns, no more Waffle House dinners, no more *mildew*.

Except now, he allowed grudgingly, for the sake of getting the job done to Mr. Thresher's satisfaction. Once again he growled, "Hurry it up," and this time leaned over Grant's shoulder to check his progress.

The goober was clutching the pen in his hand like a carving knife and copying each letter individually in all capitals, and Clyde rolled his eyes and shifted his weight from leg to leg.

Whether Grant was a first or last name he had no idea. The man had simply introduced himself as Grant from the Party. Clyde knew he was on the Party's Goon Squad, the thick-browed gents who were dispatched as the GOP's "observers" during election disputes. He personally wouldn't have chosen Grant for this particular task, but there apparently was not a whole lot of choice. They needed someone the candidate absolutely had not met before, which ruled out pretty much everybody at party headquarters. Grant happened to have been out on assignment during Bub's visit and therefore met the main criterion. Others, like the ability to read and speak . . . well, Clyde had had to make do.

"Got it, boss," Grant proclaimed, handing the pen back.

Clyde Bruno read Grant's hand and nodded his assent. "Okay. Good. Now, you know how this works?"

"I'm a Regular Floridian with an important question," Grant recited. "Mr. Billings—"

"Bub," Clyde Bruno corrected. "He likes to be called Bub. Everyone else will call him Bub. Don't draw attention to yourself."

"Okay, Bub. Bub will ask me if I have a question for him, and I read this."

Clyde Bruno heard a roar outside and saw the candidate bounding down the steps off the stage toward the hotel entrance as rally organizers began shepherding the dozen or so other yellow-name-tagged Regular Floridians in the lounge into the Coral Reef Ballroom. Clyde Bruno reached into the inside pocket of Grant's too-small houndstooth blazer, pulled out the Sony microcassette recorder and pushed the record and play buttons simultaneously, then dropped the recorder back in and patted Grant's jacket.

"You're ready to rock and roll, sport." Then he grabbed the larger man's lapel and caught him with a steely gaze. "Don't fuck this up."

Clyde Bruno turned Grant to face the Coral Reef Ballroom and gave a gentle nudge to get him moving before he ducked into a hallway to avoid the approaching entourage.

In the penthouse suite of the Floridians for a Better Future, the Politics Channel blared on from the corner about the latest national poll numbers from the various congressional races that were expected to be close.

Percy Billings paid it no mind, instead furrowed his still-youthful brow as he dug into the raw data of a different poll, one commissioned by the Party five months earlier following the sudden death of its top potential candidate for governor.

In broad numbers, it showed that likely voters regarded Percy Billings most highly among the remaining field for his intellect, his depth of knowledge and his experience for the job. And yet, just as convincingly, it showed his brother as the most likeable candidate and the one they thought would win with the biggest margin in a head-to-head election against Ramsey MacLeod.

Percy swore inwardly at the data, shaking his head in disgust but not, he allowed, disbelief. It had been this way all his life. No matter how hard he worked, how much he learned, how sincere he was, he would still be measured against his brother and come out poorly in the comparison.

It had baffled him since their youth. Percy had been the straight-A student in prep school. Byron made C's. Percy had gone out west to Stanford and earned a master's and bachelor's together in just four years. Byron had gone to Florida State, had dropped out to "find himself" and eventually finished his single degree with night courses at UCF.

After college, Percy joined Southwest Florida's largest commercial developer and had ultimately worked his way up to senior vice president while at the same time serving on a dozen volunteer boards. Byron worked the line in an Alaskan cannery, drove semis over-the-road, then did two stints as a roustabout on a Gulf oil rig before "settling down" to a series of failed businesses in Brevard County until, at age forty-two, he finally hit upon his one success: a lawn furniture company.

In politics, Percy had served as a county committeeman, then county chairman, then state committeeman and, finally, RNC delegate.

Byron had done nothing. Nada. Zero.

And yet, Percy was reminded with each hourly update, it was his brother, not he, who was cruising toward an easy win as governor of Florida in less than three weeks, in so doing becoming the first son of a governor to himself reach that position.

Percy could only blame what had to be the defective polling data relied upon by state party chair Farber LaGrange. He flipped through the pages to see the numbers for Brevard County again and shook his head: In these tables had to be the proof of the poll's fatal flaw.

How else to explain it? The people of Brevard County knew his brother better than anyone else in the state. They had seen his Launch Café fall flat and his Nerds on the Go Dry Cleaning close after a single month. Bub's Computer Repair had folded even before the grand opening because, by then, even the greenest graduates coming out of Florida Tech were wise to him and would not take a job with a known loser. At one point, Byron had even incorporated as Billings' Space Services to bid on NASA's multibillion-dollar Shuttle Processing Contract. The agency had refused even to respond to his application.

Yet somehow, according to the Party's poll, the public even in Titusville, Cocoa Beach and Melbourne—towns with among the highest education levels in the state—had been snowed by Byron's cute dimple and aw-shucks manner, rating him fifteen points higher in likeability, twelve points higher in trustworthiness and seven points higher in competence than Percy.

Percy read that last bit again and stood to walk over to the plate-glass picture window overlooking downtown Marco Island and, beyond it, the green Gulf of Mexico. A pair of charter fishing boats were heading in toward the cut, coming down off plane as they approached the jetties. Percy sniffed angrily as he stood, hands thrust in the pockets of his khakis, as the boats tied up at the fuel dock and the charter parties disembarked, floppy white hats shining in the sun.

He turned away from the window and stared absently at the television. Higher even in competence. Amazing. Absolutely amazing. It proved again his long-held suspicion that no one ever got elected overestimating the intelligence of the voting public. He snorted again at the poll numbers. Likeability: sure, Bryon was more likeable. Like a big, dumb Labrador was likeable. Trustworthiness: okay, fine. Boy Scouts were trustworthy, too. But competence? On what planet?

In front of the focus group Farber had assembled, Percy had presented a well-reasoned, fully documented Twelve Point Plan for Florida, dealing with everything from the lousy public schools to out-of-control Medicaid costs. What had Byron presented? Nothing. Instead he'd just shown up, talked about integrity and honoring the memory of their daddy and some such other nonsense . . . and the idiots had fallen for it!

Given the focus group, given the polling backing it up, there really wasn't much of a choice, Farber had explained. At the time Percy had sucked it up and taken the news like a man and a brother. After all, what else could he do, other than give Byron a big clap on the shoulder and wish him good luck?

But then, over the months, it had started to rankle inside him, how this wasn't some minor delay, some temporary setback. This was the real deal. The people of Florida were never going to elect *both* of Lamont Billings's sons to the Governor's Mansion. Only one of them would reach that level. If it was Byron, it would never be Percy.

In other words, it would be the same as always. *He* had always been the more dutiful, the more loyal, in short, the better son, but Byron had always been Father's favorite. *He* had always been better-looking, but Byron had dated prettier girls. *He* had always been smarter and worked harder, but now Byron was going to get to be governor.

The whole thing had pushed him to distraction, to the point where it was noticeably affecting his work. He had, inexplicably, missed a buying opportunity for a prime, forty-six-acre tract on the edge of some wetlands outside Fort Myers. A perfect spot for a new strip mall, anchored with maybe a Walgreens, filled in with the usual mix of tanning salon, Laundromat and payday loan outlet, and Percy somehow had let it slip away to their arch competitor from Naples.

It was even, Percy had realized one morning, affecting his golf game. It had been months since he had shot below eighty. One recent Sunday, he had actually been on a pace not to break a hundred when it thankfully began to rain and thunder.

He became conscious that he was hearing the name "Billings," and brought his gaze back from deep space to the television set. The Politics Channel had turned its attention to Florida's gubernatorial race, where political novice Bub Billings was incredibly heading into the final stretch with a double-digit lead over the sitting lieutenant governor, Ramsey MacLeod, for eight years the right-hand man of popular incumbent Bolling Waites.

The TV showed a clip of Bub wading through an affectionate crowd, shaking hands, tousling children's hair, pointing at recognized friends, while the reporter's voice-over filled in Bub's back story, the black-sheep-son-made-good of legendary Florida governor Lamont Billings, the man who'd dragged a redneck legislature into the civil rights era and racial integration, a stance that had cost him his job after a single term. Political observers around the state, the reporter noted, had fully expected another Billings to make a run at the Governor's Mansion someday. Interestingly, nearly all of them had assumed it would be Percy Billings, a Marco Island real-estate developer who for years had worked his way up the Republican Party totem pole.

The blood in Percy's ears hissed, his eyes narrowed and his hands clenched, but he was unable to tear himself away from the set. The reporter continued with the tale of Bub Billings's meteoric rise from small businessman—Florida's Lawn Furniture King—to a mere step away from chief executive of the nation's fourth-largest state, while his brother, in all likelihood, was doomed to fade into political obscurity. . . .

The hiss had become a full-blown roar, darkening Percy's vision, when the phone rang. Percy hunted for the remote, hit the mute button, then grabbed the handset off his desk.

"What," he snapped. But then he heard who it was and his brow relaxed a bit. "How did it go?"

He listened, and his face began to brighten. "*Really* . . . and the tape is clear? Let me hear it."

Percy listened to the phone some more, and a smile began spreading across his face. "Okay, listen: Dub it and keep a copy safe. Got it? Good . . . Let me know how it goes."

He hung up, then turned with an amused glance at the television set, where his brother silently mouthed malapropisms to a packed high-school gym. Percy picked up the remote and switched the set off completely, then moved to the plate-glass window. He took a deep breath, let his face assume a posture of equal parts sorrow and sincerity, and addressed a shrimp boat heading out the cut into the sparkling Gulf:

"My fellow Floridians . . . These are indeed the times that try men's souls."


With one ear listening to Farber LaGrange's latest tirade in his office, Florida Republican Party Finance Director Antoinette Johnson sorted through folders until she came to the one marked "Donors—100k—3Q" and cleared some space on her crowded desk.

It was nearly an inch thick, testament to her success at getting the state's richest individuals and businesses to put their money where their mouths were and fork over substantial sums to put a Republican in the Governor's Mansion after twenty years on the outs. Week after week, she went through reams of donations, inputting them into the database so they could be reported the Friday before Election Day to the state Division of Elections, while simultaneously writing personal thank-you notes to those donors who had given more than $100,000.

This election, she had noticed, that latter task had started to give her writer's cramp. At one point she had run a query and was honestly shocked to learn that the six-figure donors now accounted for ninety-four percent of every dollar the Party collected, up from seventy-three percent when she'd taken the job a decade earlier.

The official line to the media and the watchdog groups was that this was a wonderful thing: The more money the Party collected, the more the free-speech rights of Florida's populace were being expressed, the more joy and happiness would spread across the land.

The only one who could manage that explanation with a straight face was Farber. Of course, the only one who could manage a lot of explanations with a straight face was Farber—everything from solemn attacks on the other party's masculinity to a spirited defense of a Republican Miami city commissioner caught embezzling.

As for Toni, she had a while back concluded that the big money she helped collect was the single most corrosive factor in politics. The big checks came in, and a few weeks or a few months later, the contributors would call for help arranging a meeting with their beneficiaries, who were by then elected officials. Toni would always try to discourage such attempts, but would eventually pass the calls along to Farber, who would quickly and without fail set up the requested meetings. And, a few days or weeks later, a particular person would get appointed to a particular job, or a certain state contract would get awarded to a certain vendor, or an obscure rule or regulation would get waived in an equally obscure permit application.

Toni was fairly certain that these exceptions and shortcuts were not advancing the public good. Being a part of the system that generated them had in recent years worn on her soul—to the point where she had taken to making the occasional photocopy to let a newspaper know about a particularly egregious situation.

The treasonous leaks in the name of good government had at first salved her conscience, particularly in those rare instances when a bad actor wound up losing a contract or, even better, going to jail. Ultimately, though, she had come to accept how little real effect the public disclosures had on the system. It wasn't the extreme cases that made the system corrupt, she had realized, but the everyday acceptance of the little ones: the insurance commissioner who returned phone calls from the insurance company executives but not from the consumers who'd gotten screwed on a policy. The museum grants awarded by the secretary of state that happened to correlate with the largest fund-raisers in her last election. The no-bid contracts let by the Department of Agriculture that went to relatives of the citrus baron whose jet the agriculture commissioner had used on the campaign trail.

It was time, she had told herself that summer, to get out. One last campaign cycle and she would leave politics and Tallahassee for good. Maybe move down to the islands. Find an oceanography lab somewhere that needed a CPA or even an office helper or even, frankly, a janitor. Something that would get her back to the sea again. Something that would let her enjoy life for a while, give her a chance to figure out what she wanted to do when she grew up. She'd always been good with numbers, so accounting had been a natural choice. Politics, though, had not, particularly not Republican politics, and it was time she found something she could make a life out of.

A throat cleared beside her, and she returned from her reverie to a perky little blonde holding out a stack of new mail. Her name was Britney. Or maybe Meghan. She always got the two of them confused.

Toni eyed her up and down, over the skimpy blue sundress and sandals, and with a smile accepted the packet from the girl. Toni checked her tongue as Britney or Meghan sashayed away, casually touching the male employees of the office as she walked and generally creating a stir. Farber called them Victory Hostesses, but Toni thought of the dozen fresh Florida State graduates and nongraduates more as honeybees, the way they flitted around, alluring yet dangerous.

During their first week on the job, she had tried to suggest a professional dress code to Farber: closed-toed shoes and business-length skirts, for starters. Farber had come back with one of his vulgar southernisms that, roughly translated, wondered why in the hell he'd go out of his way to hire a gaggle of sexpots and then make them dress up like old ladies.

Toni had stood steaming in a rage for a long minute before stalking out. There was no reasoning with Farber when he was being an asshole. Besides, the girls' presence in the office was minimal. They'd been hired, as their name suggested, as arm candy for fund-raising events, to meet and greet donors, serve them drinks, help with the setup and cleanup.

Or at least that was what Toni continued to tell herself, despite the rumors of what was actually going on aboard Farber's big sailing yacht, the *Soft Money* . . . that the Victory Hostesses had become more like comfort girls, starting each event wearing little more than a bikini and losing coverage from there. Toni didn't know details and she didn't want to know. That despite the number and size of checks that poured in from *Soft Money* events, every single one of them was written by a male.

Well, it just wasn't her problem. All the girls were of legal age, old enough, if they wanted, to perform in pornographic movies or take jobs at the Mustang Ranch. She sure as hell wasn't about to take it upon herself to become their mother hen and try to protect them from sexual harassment—particularly given the attitude they displayed to every other female who worked at party headquarters.

Still, the whole Victory Hostess thing added to her rising discontent with Farber in particular and the state Party in general. Back when she'd taken the job, the Democrats controlled both chambers of the legislature as well as the Governor's Mansion and five of six seats on the Cabinet. They ran the state like a fiefdom. She personally had little political ideology beyond good government, and had signed up with the Republicans because anything was better than the way things were.

A decade later, thanks to Farber's organizational skill and her financial knack, the situation was nearly reversed: Four of six Cabinet seats were Republican, as were both House and Senate, and the old, popular governor, the Granddaddy Gator of Florida politics, was retiring after two terms.

Yet even before the election that would realize Farber's dream, Toni could sense that Floridians were getting a state government every bit as bad as the one they had methodically voted out of office over ten years. And it was Farber's single-minded drive, she realized, that had brought it about. Instead of winning to make things better, he had become consumed with winning for the sake of winning.

It was an attitude that trickled down from the top, so that freshmen

Republican legislators, flush with victory, would at once forget the constituents who had actually voted for them and instead start sucking up to the special interests that paid their way. Farber saw nothing wrong with it. Toni couldn't find the words to adequately express her disgust.

She sighed and pushed her frustration aside. In less than three weeks, it would all be over. Farber would have gotten what he wanted, and Toni could submit her resignation letter, take her weeks of accumulated leave and sell all her belongings at a yard sale. Then she'd fly down to, say, St. Barts, and start from there. Maybe find a waterfront bar that needed help with its books. Maybe use her off-hours to find a beat-up thirty-footer she could restore, down in the tropics, away from politics. . . .

Twenty-one more days, she thought, then realized she was once again chewing her thumbnail and made a conscious effort to pull her hand away. One of the Hostesses, Tiffany she thought it was, had been so kind as to inform her that chewed fingernails were *not* sexy. The last thing she needed was another grooming lecture from a twenty-year-old bimbo.

With a sigh, she removed the rubber band from the fat file folder representing the week's hundred-thousand-and-up donations, then began filling in her database and deposit slips for the Party's checking account.

She studied a cover letter, entered bank number and $500,000 for the amount, flipped a page, entered bank number and $450,000, flipped another page, entered bank number and $575,000. . . . She stopped, looked at the column for bank number, and realized the three entries were the same. Three checks totaling one and a half million dollars from three different corporations, all coming from the same bank. . . .

She blinked, quickly skimmed through the rest of the folder, found three more big checks from the same commercial bank in Miami from three more contributors. She leaned away from her computer, thought a long moment, then brushed a strand of dark hair behind an ear and moved to the query field and typed in the name of the bank.

Within seconds, the screen filled with a list of twenty-four donations over the past five months, all from the same Miami bank, but every one from a different corporate account. She blinked again, thought for another minute, then toggled over to her web browser, where she brought up the state Division of Corporations and looked up the first name on the list.

She noted the result, then looked up the next and, with a sigh and a nod, looked up the third and fourth and fifth. Then she flipped to an open page of her notebook and wrote down names and addresses and drew arrows between them. For a good hour, she zipped back and forth across first the corporations, then the Securities and Exchange Commission and finally the Dunn and Bradstreet websites. Finally she uncrossed her legs, slipped her feet back into the beige pumps beneath her desk and walked over to her boss's office.

She knocked twice and entered at the grunt to find Farber LaGrange seated at his massive desk scribbling on a yellow pad. She watched the bald spot on the exact top of his big head, where Grecian Formula black strands crossed at regular intervals, waiting for him to finish writing. On the wall behind him were photos of him playing golf with Gerald Ford, welcoming Ronald Reagan at the bottom of Air Force One, fishing with George Bush in Islamorada. On the credenza to the side were assorted saltwater fishing trophies, at least a dozen of them, with the largest one a good four feet tall and topped with a gold-plated sailfish in leaping splendor. Fishing and politics, and Farber played both to win.

"You rang?"

Farber's tanned, leathery jowls reflected his age and time on the water, but the steely blue eyes that stared across the desk were as steady and sharp as a bird of prey's. A hawk's. Or in Farber's case, Toni thought, an osprey's, diving out of the sky at full tilt to snatch up an unsuspecting fish.

She glanced down at her notebook and cleared her throat. "Northstar Consulting of Jacksonville, Harris and Beauchamp of Naples, Interlink Transport of Tampa, Rancourt and Associates in Orlando, Southeast Marine of Fort Pierce, Ronadet Service Corp. in Miami and Island Graphics of Palm Beach. You want to guess what they all have in common?"

Farber LaGrange put on the poker face that Toni knew meant he was about to lie: "I ain't got the foggiest idea," he said, pronouncing it *eye-dee*.

Toni continued to play it straight, glanced back down at her note-book. "Well, as it turns out, they have two things in common. One, they all have given our Party between four hundred thousand and six hundred thousand dollars since May."

Farber said, "You want I should write personal thank-you's to 'em?"

"And two, they all list as their registered agent somebody in Apalach-icola called Goodkind and Sams. Sounds like a law firm, right? Well, that's what I thought, too. But I checked in the Bar Journal, and there's no such law firm in all of Florida. So I ran it through corporate records, and Goodkind and Sams has a registered agent named Clyde Bruno. Isn't that something? You remember Clyde, don't you?"

Farber said nothing.

"He's your fishing buddy Link Thresher's, uh, how should we call him . . . executive assistant? Fixer? Kneecap-smasher? Whatever. It's kind of interesting that ol' Clyde would have the time, given his day job, to manage the affairs of so *many* unrelated companies." She watched for a response, got none, continued. "Except, of course, I suppose it's not particularly hard, seeing as how none of those companies actually *does* anything. No record with the SEC, nothing in D and B. Not even a phone number."

Now Farber cleared his throat, played with the fountain pen in his hands, balancing it on the tip of his forefinger. "I'm just curious here, Toni, if there's any part of what you've described is in any way against the law—"

"Of course, those aren't the only companies for whom Clyde is the named agent. There are, via three other intermediary firms, seventeen more, for a total of twenty-four companies around the state whose sole business seems to consist of giving us an average of five hundred thousand dollars to elect a Republican governor."

Farber nodded and smiled, now. "I'll ask you again, Toni: What Florida statute or Division of Elections rule is either Clyde Bruno or his various companies or the Florida Republican Party violating with these donations?"

Toni tucked the notebook against her chest and crossed her arms. "The whole point of the campaign finance code is to let the public know who gave and who got. We're breaking the spirit of these laws."

"That's why we got all them high-falutin' law*yers,* Toni," Farber laughed. "To find ways to break the spirit of laws without messin' with the letter of 'em. Ain't that right? Now you seem to be concerned that Clyde Bruno, and, I presume by extension, Link Thresher and Petron Oil is givin' all this money to us. Correct me here if I'm wrong, but this is all *soft* money, ain't it? Which means, if he wanted, ol' Link coulda sat there at the top of Petron Tower in Houston and written out a check for the *en-*tire twelve mil in one shot and it woulda been perfectly legal. Am I not correct?"

Toni stood her ground. "So why didn't he?"

Farber threw his arms up in mock surprise. "Fuck should I know? Ask *him!*" He began stacking his appointment book, a PalmPilot and other items from his drawers onto his desktop blotter. "Look, maybe he thinks it's to his strategic advantage for everyone not to know he supports our side."

"That's my point," Toni said. "The law was designed so everyone could know exactly that. He's making that impossible."

Farber straightened, narrowed his eyes. "Not *completely* impossible. You figured it out. Now, Toni, I always said you're a smart gal. It's why I hired you. But seriously, you're not suggesting that there ain't nobody in the entire Democrat Party, in all the media, who can't connect the dots like you just did? Christ almighty, Toni, it's what they get *paid* to do." He grabbed his briefcase from the floor and started packing the things on his desk. "Now if you'll excuse me, I gotta get a move on. Flyin' back out to Titusville tonight. Got fund-raisers on *Soft Money* the rest of the week." He glanced up with a smile. "You might even get a couple more checks from Clyde Bruno companies, if you're lucky."

Toni sighed again, thought of one last protest when the phone buzzed on Farber's desk. He hit a button and the speakerphone's static filled the room.

"What now?" Farber bellowed.

"Thought you'd wanna know," a voice crackled. "MacLeod ducked away from his campaign this morning. Guess who he visited."

"The Pope. I ain't got time for games, Buckin'ham. Just tell me."

"Murphy Moran."

"Hah!" Farber laughed, then shot a wink at Toni. "Ain't heard that name in a coupla years. Thought he slinked away with his tail 'tween his legs after the tobacca fight. Well, too bad for Ramsey. Not even ol' Murph's gonna be able to save his bacon this time. Bucky, hold on just one second." Farber nodded at Toni. "We finished?"

Toni Johnson shrugged, then remembered three other transactions that had caught her eye. "Not unless you can tell me anything about the Clean Gulf Trust."

"Ain't got the foggiest," Farber said, then turned back to his phone. "Bucky, you still there?"

Toni blew out an exasperated breath and headed back toward her desk, shaking her head as she walked. It was a giant game to him, that's all. He knew as well as she did that the chances of anyone catching on to the trick with all those checks in the days left before the election were negligible. It was only because the name Clyde Bruno rang a bell with her that she had been able to figure it out.

As Toni walked, though, resignation rekindled into anger. She had no idea what exactly Petron wanted, but could only assume from their desire to remain anonymous that it wasn't good. She should tell someone, is what she should do . . . is what she *would* do, she decided.

She paged through the corporate search printouts in her notebook, tried to think of who. . . . It was probably too late to get them to anyone in the press. Plus, it was a crapshoot, getting them into the hands of a reporter who had both the ability to do the necessary digging as well as fifteen free minutes at the moment he or she opened the envelope to realize the significance of the documents rather than simply pitching them in the waste bin. And sending it to the Democrats was pointless; anything they said this late in the campaign would be viewed as last-minute desperation. If only there were somebody else, somebody not associated with the Democratic Party, somebody with the savvy to—

And then a wide smile broke across her face as she walked right past her desk to the rear window that overlooked tree-lined Meridian Street, to the high-speed photocopier just beside the window, and pushed the green button to let it start warming up.

With enormous gas turbine engines emitting a low thrum and giant screws churning the Gulf into a swatch of whitewater behind her, the oil tanker *City of Galveston* slid steadily west-northwest toward New Orleans.

Seven hundred feet of black hull streaked with rust stains, she carried a Panamanian ensign on her stern rail and sixty thousand tons of Bahrain crude in her holds. Like most commercial freighters, she was staffed with a bare skeleton crew, with nearly half of the ship's complement unfilled. Like most tramp freighters, the crew that was aboard rarely paid much attention.

On most hours of most days, the six-foot radar antenna that spun atop her superstructure was purely ornamental, collecting data for an empty radio room. Neither radar operator nor radio man made a distinction between on- and off-watch hours, typically spending both in the rec room playing cards and drinking whiskey or in his bunk sleeping it off.

All of which had made the wet-suited man's mission that much easier.

Eighteen hours earlier, as the vessel plowed west through the Florida Straits, hugging the hundred-fathom line to avoid the worst of the Gulf Stream current setting the opposite direction, he had climbed aboard easily, finding no one at the forward lookout station.

The one thing that had worried him the most, that during the daylight hours the aft lookout might notice the thin Kevlar rope he had tied to a fitting near the stern, also never came to pass. On the *City of Galveston,* no one kept watch at all—forward, aft or any other direction.

His first six hours aboard, the wet-suited man conducted a thorough reconnaissance of the vessel, finding a total of eight people aboard as he drew himself a schematic of the engine rooms. Less than twelve hours after he'd come over the rail, the wet-suited man was finished and waiting in one of the tarpaulin-covered lifeboats that hung from davits as a red mid-October sun sank into the Gulf off the port beam.

He lifted his head as the moment grew near, risking detection to watch the final seconds of sunset. Alas, the fiery ball dropped uneventfully into the sea—no green flash—and the wet-suited man ducked back into his bivouac and closed his eyes for some sleep.

Hours later, his dive watch beeped softly six times, and he was instantly awake. He checked forward and aft along the deck, and with two steps was over the rail. He clung to the metal bulwark with one hand, undid a knot and retied it around his waist with the other, and then tossed a waterproof, buoyant tool bag into the darkness before following it in with a dive so clean it barely made a splash.

Twenty minutes later, six small explosions simultaneously rattled the *City of Galveston*'s transmission and engine rooms. Had anyone been monitoring the systems panels, he might have seen and heard the oil pressure alarms. As it was, the chief engineer and his mates were placing bets on one of two Hialeah-bred, Mexican-trained roosters in the main lounge, and it was only a few minutes later, after moving parts in both of the ship's propulsion systems had fused into much larger, nonmoving parts, that anyone noticed all the smoke pouring out of the engine-room hatches.

Ten minutes after that, the wet-suited man finished pulling himself along two thousand meters of line back to a twenty-two-foot Ranger flats boat, stripped of her poling platform and painted black and midnight blue and therefore invisible in the moonless night. There he hooked up one of a dozen twenty-gallon fuel tanks arranged in two rows to the big Evinrude on the stern, then sat on the equipment locker forward of the driver's console sipping from a Thermos of hot coffee he'd swiped from the *City of Galveston*'s galley.

He put a hand bearing compass to his eye every few minutes to check the tanker's progress. Then, when the coffee was gone and he was satisfied that *City of Galveston* was dead in the water, he pulled a rope on the outboard to start it, keyed his destination coordinates into the GPS navigation unit and got the black-and-blue skiff up on a plane and pointed toward Flamingo.

## 2

THE AFTERNOON SEA BREEZE came up without warning, giving purpose to the big white sails that to this point had been up purely for show, and *Soft Money*'s teak deck suddenly canted at a jaunty angle.

Farber LaGrange allowed himself a contented grin as he stood against the mast, gin and tonic in one hand and a fat Cohiba in the other. Twelve and a half nautical miles to the west were the high-rise condos of Cocoa Beach, barely visible now even with binoculars. To the east and north and south was nothing but pure blue ocean, overhead an equally blue sky, and all around him on the deck of his semi-custom seventy-foot Oyster sloop were rich businessmen who had never before given a dime to a political party now writing out checks with a minimum of four zeroes.

And all, Farber knew, because of his Victory Hostesses, his bevy of Florida State hard bodies who were cooing and preening in various degrees of sunbathing attire while their guests prattled on about politics and life and whatever other fool thing happened to fall out of their mouths as they tossed back Farber's liquor and ogled as much bare skin as their individual senses of shame would allow.

He watched a hairy fellow in yellow swim trunks conversing animatedly with the chest of a blond hostess—Britney, Farber believed her name was, or maybe Meghan; he had a tough time telling them apart—as they sat on the low side of the deck, and Farber had to chuckle. He could remember when his finance chief had pitched a fit when he announced he was hiring thirteen new associates for seven thousand dollars a month each for the duration of the campaign. And now, thanks to his Victory Baker's Dozen, his until-then unused yacht had turned into a money-raising machine like no other, bringing in a minimum quarter million dollars per outing.

To date he had had thirty such day sails, which, combined with the Petron money, almost entirely accounted for Bub Billings's enormous financial advantage over his Democratic opponent. And that number, Farber knew, would only increase. Word of *Soft Money*'s fund-raisers had spread through the Republican grapevine across the country, and Farber was now getting more requests for invitations than he could possibly accommodate.

He sighed with satisfaction, happened to glance off the starboard bow and saw a flurry of bait fish activity. He squinted, trying to decide whether it was worth getting his casting rod up from below, when he noticed that the man in the yellow trunks, the owner of Hallandale's biggest pawnshop, was helping Britney or Meghan undo her white bikini top.

"Hey, hey, now," Farber called out until he had their attention. "Y'all know the rules. Topless sunbathing foredeck only. Twenty-five thousand minimum."

Pawnshop man thought about this for a second, then glanced at Britney or Meghan's chest again, and from a pocket of his trunks pulled out a checkbook as they moved to *Soft Money*'s spacious foredeck.

Farber nodded to himself, peered forward to take a quick breast count, tallied fourteen . . . divided by two, multiplied by twenty-five, plus the four Hostesses in the cockpit still wearing full bikinis at five thousand each, plus the two already in the aft deck hot tub at a hundred grand a pop, for a running total of $395,000. And they still had a couple hours on the water before they had to head back in. He was confident at least three or four more of the donors on the foredeck would want upgrades to full nudity, meaning he could reasonably expect two-twenty-five to three hundred thousand more.

He took a long, satisfied puff on his cigar and moved to the windward side, where he sat on the rail, legs dangling overboard, when a familiar twang rang out behind him.

"Permission to sit my ass down, Captain?"

Farber glanced over his shoulder at Link Thresher's bad-toothed grin, and shifted the cigar to his cocktail glass hand to free an arm to welcome the Party's number one contributor. "Hey, hey! Sit your ass down!" Farber commanded, grabbing Thresher's shoulder. "You doin' all right? Been conversin' with some of the Hostesses?"

Link Thresher turned beady eyes behind thick horn-rims forward to admire the upturned breasts and buttocks on the foredeck. "I been conversing. A conversing fool, is what I am. No better conversation on the planet than with a woman that ain't been affected by gravity yet."

Thresher turned his gaze to the cloud-dotted horizon, scratched his bald spot with one finger and cleared his throat. "Actually, I need to yak at you about something."

Farber studied his friend, the pale, skinny legs sticking out from plaid Bermuda shorts, the equally pale arms that emerged from a loose-fitting golf shirt, the pasty face, the wispy remnants of flaxen hair. "You need to get out more. Maybe I'll take you fishin'. Out to the Bahamas. Tongue of the Ocean. Ever been there? They got a drop-off you won't believe, where all the big 'uns hang out. Yellowfin tuna, blue marlin. After the election, we'll go."

"I'd like that. Maybe you can show me how well that Special Edition Petrene fishing line works, huh?" Link Thresher flashed a wry smile, then turned serious again. "Actually, it's about the election I need to talk to you."

Farber nodded slowly. Thresher had flown in from Alaska that morning on one of Petron's Gulfstreams, had called from the air, in fact, to tell them not to leave port without him. "I sorta assumed as much. All right. Let's yak."

"I need to ask you about our candidate," Thresher said. "Is Bub Billings a man of his word? If he tells you something, does he really mean it?"

"Absolutely," Farber said. "That's what makes him such a great candidate. People can tell right away they're gettin' the real deal."

Thresher sighed, kicked the shiny blue topsides of *Soft Money* with the heels of brand-new deck shoes. "I was afraid of that." He stared out at the horizon. "I'm afraid our candidate might not be suitable after all."

"Aw, Christ. Not again," Farber groaned. "What? What's the issue this time?"

"Come on, man. Who are you talking to? There only ever is *one* issue."

Farber LaGrange let Link Thresher's words hang there for a minute, hoping they might go away of their own, but they didn't. "I take it you're sure."

"How long you known me, Farber? Twenty years? Twenty-five? I'm a businessman. I don't fuck around. I got important business up at Barrow I set aside to get back down here. You know how long a flight that is? *Yes*, I'm sure. The words right from the horse's mouth, caught on tape."

Farber sulked awhile in silence. "Six years of groomin', down the toilet," he said finally.

"Six years and about twenty million dollars of *my* money. I don't know how many gazillion pieces of lawn furniture." Link Thresher took a deep breath to calm down. "I understand that. Sometimes you spend a pile of money and a well comes up dry. That's why you drill a whole bunch of wells."

Farber drained the rest of his gin and tonic, tossed his cigar stub out into the Atlantic. "So you understand, we got less than three weeks to the election. I can't guarantee what's gonna happen this late in the game."

Thresher nodded sincerely. "I'm aware of that. It's a consequence I'm willing to risk."

Farber stared glum-faced at the eastern horizon, where over the past half hour a puffy cumulous cloud had grown into a towering cumulonimbus, a thunderhead. "Okay. You're payin' the piper, you get to change the tune. So what, you wanna implement the fallback plan?"

Thresher nodded again. "Aren't you glad now I insisted on having one?"

Farber thought for a moment. "I'll need your goon."

"You got him."

The sea breeze picked up a notch, heeling *Soft Money* over another few degrees. Squeals of excitement went up from the foredeck as Victory Hostesses got splashed by the waves now smashing into the bow.

"When?" Farber asked.

"Soon. Soon as possible. Tomorrow—"

Farber LaGrange glanced up in time to see a stocky young man in khaki shorts and a white golf shirt embroidered with the name *Soft Money* approaching. He hissed at Thresher: "Ix-nay for an eh-cond-say," before nodding at his hired skipper. "What?"

"Sir, the breeze is up to twelve knots. We're overcanvassed. You can see we're starting to heel over quite a bit."

Farber glanced across the boat, where the starboard rail was now only inches above the waves, and then aft, where three Victory Hostesses sat on the uphill side of the sunken hot tub with scared faces and perky breasts left high and dry by the water sloshing out. All over the boat, rich businessmen were spilling their drinks as *Soft Money* tipped beneath them.

He grunted. "Yeah, it looks like we're upsettin' some of the gals. Go ahead and douse the main or reef or whatever you think's best in this sorta sit'ation."

The skipper stared up at the masthead, then out at the thunderhead advancing from the east. "I thought I'd roll up some of the genny and tuck a reef in the main."

"I can live with that." Farber nodded.

"Also, things could get bumpy if we get caught in that squall. You want me to get her in ahead of it?"

Farber checked his watch, then the eastern horizon. "Yeah, go on and head in."

The skipper nodded. "Very good, sir. In that case, what I think I'll do is just point her dead downwind and pop the chute opposite the genny."

Farber said, "Sounds just grand."

He sat and watched with interest as his skipper and crew quickly rigged a spinnaker pole off the port side, hauled a long, skinny nylon sock up to the top of the masthead, and then turned the boat until she was headed directly back toward Cocoa Beach's high-rise condos. On the shout of the skipper, the white-golf-shirted crew activated two electric winches and the nylon sock popped the little bits of yarn holding it together and blossomed into a giant blue-and-white sail emblazoned with the Republican Party elephant in the center and, beneath it, the logo for Southern Toyota. The wind seemed to disappear as *Soft Money* began catching up with and then surging down the two- and three-foot waves to oohs and aahs from the Victory Hostesses.

"Wow," Link Thresher said, impressed. "I didn't know a sailboat could go this fast."

"Neither did I," Farber said. He turned to his friend and lowered his voice. "Okay, then. Tomorrow it is. I'll call a strategy session."

Thresher smiled, clapped his pal on the back and stood to go freshen his Tom Collins. "I appreciate it, Farber. Don't forget that."

"Uh-huh. You understand, don't you, that we're gonna need somewhat more than we'd originally figured, now, for the final weeks. Why don't you show your 'preciation with 'bout five or six more mil?"

Thresher smiled even wider as he moved toward the bar set up in the cockpit. "I'll put Clyde right on it."

Farber frowned at the squall behind them now, then at the condos getting slowly taller off the bow. He cleared his throat loudly: "Gals, we've just crossed back into United States territorial waters. Please dress appropriately." The Victory Hostesses roundly ignored him, so Farber cleared his throat even more loudly. "Let me translate: It is now four-oh-five eastern daylight time. By four-ten, I don't wanna see so much as a single nekkid nipple on this boat!"

Amid a chorus of grumbling, the Victory Hostesses began retying bikini tops and slipping into sundresses.

Murphy Moran twisted the little brass key in the mailbox door, grabbed everything inside and shut it again before breaking into a fast walk down the gravel road to the marina.

He'd gotten the heads-up he'd been waiting for fifteen minutes earlier, as he'd been driving up A1A in Cocoa Beach in the MG, and he needed to get a move on if he wanted to take advantage of it. An evening cruise, his source had said, with the candidate himself on board. *Soft Money* was getting stocked for a rare nighttime excursion.

Murphy smiled as he walked across the mowed weeds that served as the marina office lawn. His "source" was the gangly Haitian steward at the snooty Port Canaveral Yacht Club, whom Murphy had taken the effort to actually talk to a few years earlier when he'd moored his first boat there for a while. Apparently few others had bothered even to give him the time of day, and Rufus had reciprocated with lifelong loyalty. Even now, no longer a member and with a boat so small as to not rate a second look, Murphy could still count on Rufus to notice *Mudslinger* approaching the fuel dock at the neighboring public marina and come running over to help with the lines.

Over the past three days, Rufus had become part of Murphy's spy network, on the lookout for all things related to Bub Billings and his campaign. It was from Rufus that Murphy had gotten key details of *Soft Money*'s fund-raising outings: the dozen or so little pretties in skimpy dresses who stood on deck greeting the guests. The prodigious quantities of liquor that Rufus had to keep hauling out to the yacht. Other sources had filled him in as to the amount of money Farber LaGrange was raising on these jaunts, with some sordid stories about what exactly the generous contributors could purchase for themselves at the various donation levels.

He'd been wondering how he could use the information to Ramsey MacLeod's advantage, when just the previous night he'd gotten a tip from Tallahassee that the Billings campaign was suddenly altering his schedule. Bub was going out on Farber's boat.

At first he couldn't believe it. The one thing that would give MacLeod a fighting chance, and here Billings was about to hand it to him. What was the man thinking? Of course, self-destructing candidates were nothing new. Gary Hart had proven that, and each year there were lesser Gary Harts at the congressional, state and local levels for the entertainment of the electorate.

He stopped by the dockside garbage can and quickly sorted through his stack of mail: a credit card bill, four credit card offers, two renewal offers for the same sailing magazine, and a plain, nine-by-twelve manila envelope with a Tallahassee postmark—his second such missive in two days. Amazing, given that he'd only agreed to work for Ramsey four days earlier.

Murphy tore it open, quickly skimmed the enclosed stack of photo-copied documents. They were corporate record filings and campaign donation logs for some company or companies. Somebody, it was clear, with inside info on Bub Billings was working pretty hard to discredit the man. He stuffed the papers back into the envelope, then tucked the manila envelope and credit card bill under his arm before tossing every-thing else away.

Financial improprieties were all well and good—if he had a few months. He didn't. He had seventeen days. He needed a Gary Hart, not some complicated, hard-to-explain, harder-to-appreciate campaign-financing imbroglio. He wished his anonymous tipster could figure that out, too, and act accordingly. One picture was all he needed: Bub Billings, with a great big smile on his face and a nubile Victory Hostess or two on his lap. The newspaper photo's caption would read: "Repub-lican Candidate Cavorts with Interns," and that would be that. Game, set and match.

He clambered aboard *Mudslinger*, leaned over the open hatch in the main salon to drop the mail onto the dinette table, then moved forward to release the bow lines and spring lines. Carefully he undid the stern lines, coiled them and dropped them over the big wooden hooks on the pilings, then put the already-idling diesel into reverse and grabbed the tiller.

It was only as *Mudslinger*'s bow was already nosing out into the barge canal that he remembered he'd left the handheld VHF in the fiberglass locker on the dock, and his cell phone in the car. His onboard VHF was still waiting on a part and he had yet to install the SSB set—meaning he had absolutely no way to call for help if something went wrong.

Murphy frowned, thought briefly about turning around, then checked his watch and throttled up instead.

Percy Billings stretched as he walked down the air-conditioned corridor at Melbourne Regional, glad to be off the cramped commuter plane at last. None of them, least of all the Brazilian Embrair he'd just been on, was designed for large people, and Percy had spent the entire hour partially hunching his six-foot-five frame into a space with five-foot-ten headroom.

He remembered idly that the governor's plane was not much better, in that respect. It was a Beechcraft Kingair, six seats and all of them designed for petite women. Well, there was nothing to be done about that. The only private planes with large cabins were the Gulfstreams, and then you were talking the $20 million range, even in the used market—a tough sell in a state where a fifth of all students attended classes in "portable" trailers. No way could an appropriation of that size that served a mere handful of elected officials and the Florida State football coach survive the straight-face test, particularly in a slow economy with money tight again—

And Percy realized what he was doing and recoiled in horror. He couldn't even think such things, he knew. His *brother* was about to assume the mantle, not him, he reminded himself. He had to know that with a certainty down to the core of his existence. The coming days were going to be hard enough without— And suddenly he was struggling for air, a forearm around his neck from behind. . . .

"Your eight-track collection or your life," Bub Billings whispered in his ear before releasing him, spinning him around and surrounding him with a bear hug. "How ya doin', little bro?"

As he had always done whenever he was around Byron since he was seventeen, when he had shot up in height and surpassed his sibling, Percy affected a slight stoop that served to diminish the full head's height difference between the two.

"I'm fine, big brother," he said. "I'm fine."

Bub grabbed Percy's garment bag and computer case away from him and started leading him across the concourse toward the short-term parking lot. "Whatcha bring your computer for? We're goin' *sailin'*, for Pete's sake!"

Percy shrugged defensively. "I have to check my e-mail."

Bub made a face at him and blinked twice. "Why?"

Percy shrugged once more, glanced around at the travelers walking past them without interest. "I would've thought you'd be mobbed, getting through here."

Bub surveyed the passersby, shook his head. "Nope. No different than usual. People never recognize me, unless I'm surrounded by the campaign machine." With one hand he grabbed his chin and shook it. "It's this face. It's the face of an average Joe. Nothin' special." He flashed a sly grin up toward Percy. "Unlike you."

Percy forced a smile but said nothing. It had been a running thing between them for years. Percy had gotten their father's aristocratic nose and cleft chin, while Byron had inherited their mother's softer, nondescript features, endearing dimple and curly brown hair.

Bub walked out the automatic doors and across two empty lanes toward the parking lot. "So you got Collier County whipped up in a frenzy for me?"

Percy stood by the passenger side of a Ford Tempo while Bub deposited his bags in the trunk. "Collier's almost fifty-eight percent Republican by registration, sixty-five percent by performance. You're going to win Collier County easily."

"I know I'm gonna win Collier. A Republican Alzheimer's patient who has sex with goats takes Collier over any Democrat. Point is, I need to win big." With his key he unlocked his door and reached across to get Percy's. "I need turnout in Collier, Seminole, Duval and the Panhandle to make up for the ass-kickin' I'm gonna take down in Palm Beach and Broward. Know what I mean?"

"Byron, you're going to win the election. All the polls say so. Even Ramsey's press releases crow about him climbing to within eight points of you. Stop worrying."

Bub cranked the engine and turned on the headlights. "Trust me. I ain't worried. If I don't win, I don't win. I got plenty else to do. It's just that, after all this work, it would be nice to win, is all."

Percy's ears burned. Right there was the attitude that so infuriated him. Why, if it meant so little to him, was he even running in the first place? Why not just go back to his lawn furniture and leave the business of governing to those who were bred for it? He said nothing, instead studied the car as his brother began to drive. "This yours?"

"One hundred percent, fully paid." He put on his turn signal and turned right onto Wickham Road. "Pretty spiffy, huh?"

Percy again said nothing, and Bub watched him for a minute.

"I know: It ain't one of them fancy-schmancy S-U-Vs everyone's drivin', but you know what? I been thinkin' about that. First, with gas at three bucks a gallon, it takes what, seventy-five smackers to fill a tank? And then they get somethin' like eight miles a gallon?" Bub snorted. "Who in hell designed these things? The Saudis? Anyhow, that ain't even my main objection to 'em. What's buggin' me is that with so many of these damn things on the road, a fair number gotta be owned by families holding down two jobs to pay the bills, right? So you got medium household income at forty grand, and you got all these folks buyin' cars that cost near thirty-five grand—what's wrong with this picture? And what happens when the economy goes south and a buncha these people get laid off? They lose their cars is what happens. 'Cause you can bet a dime on the dollar they bought 'em on time, not cash."

Percy resisted the urge to correct "medium" income, sat scrunched up in the car as his brother turned north on I-95 toward Port Canaveral. "That's the free market. People want to buy SUVs, so they buy SUVs."

Bub nodded. "That's right. Free market. So when all them loans go bad and Ford Motor Credit's left holdin' depreciated vehicles worth less than the balance on the notes, and they come cryin' with their hand out, we're gonna tell 'em: Tough noogies. Free market. Shoulda been more careful who you made loans to. Right?"

Percy could no longer hold it in. "Why don't you go join the Green Party or something?"

"Because, little bro, the Green Party ain't gonna win an election for governor of Florida. At least not yet." Bub smiled wide, reached across to muss Percy's perfectly combed hair. "Besides, I'm havin' such fun bein' a Republican."

"Sometimes you don't talk like one," Percy pouted.

Bub scoffed. "I thought we're supposed to be the party of the big tent nowadays. Hell, don't you remember Philadelphia? Black Republicans, brown Republicans, purple-haired, transgendered Republicans . . . I was surprised Jesse Jackson and Cesar Chavez didn't show up!"

"Cesar Chavez is dead," Percy said, recombing his hair with a collapsible brush from his pocket.

Bub banged the rim of the steering wheel. "Well, no wonder, then!"

Percy groaned, and Bub laughed, and then stopped to put an arm on his brother's shoulder. "Listen, man. I know this has gotta be hard for you, after all those years of everyone talkin' about *you* runnin' for governor someday. I just want to tell you, well, the appreciativeness I feel for all your support and agreein' to be finance chairman and all. Thanks, bro."

The breath caught in his throat, and Percy cracked his window, letting in air that carried the pungent odor of saltwater marsh. He inhaled and exhaled deeply several times, until he had regained composure.

"Well, just seventeen more days," Percy said finally.

"Yup. I'll tell you what, I'll be glad when it's over. All the canned speeches, and the nutty rallies and the dumb slogans. It's a wonder anybody wants the job, all the crap, excuse my French, you gotta go through." Bub glanced out the car windows, at the thin layer of cloud overhead. "Whatcha think? We got a cold front comin' or somethin'?"

Percy squinted out the window. Stars were partially obscured by a wispy layer of high-altitude cirrus. Father had bought Bub a home weather station when he was twelve. As usual, Bub had had fun setting up the wind cups and the hygrometer and the other gizmos, but never bothered to learn how to interpret them. Seven-year-old Percy instead became the family weather expert. "Got a little cirrus up there. We may see that line squall I saw on the surface charts earlier. It's associated with a weak trough passing through. The front won't hit us for two or three days still."

Bub chuckled. "Still the weather geek, I see. Well, you oughta have fun on the boat. Bet ol' Farber's got one of them brass barometers and everythin', the kind they're always tappin' with their knuckles in them old sea movies." He drove in silence for a few seconds, his brow creasing. "You got any idea what this meetin's about? Farber said strategy session, but I can't rightly figure what that means. What strategy? We're ahead. We just keep doin' whatever we been doin', right?"

Percy felt his heart rate accelerate again and turned back toward the open window.

"Well, whatever," Bub said at last. "We got a highly paid campaign pollster. I guess it's a waste of money if we don't get a full debriefin' on whatever it is he's pollin'. Me, I'm just lookin' forward to bein' away from the campaign for a day. That and maybe doin' a little fishin'. You figure Farber's gotta have some rods on this sailboat of his. Maybe he can teach me some of his tournament-winnin' tricks." Bub laughed aloud. "Although even catchin' *one* fish for me would be some trick, huh?"

Percy swallowed hard and forced a laugh before turning back toward the breeze.


From her vantage point on the fairgrounds stage, Florida Secretary of State Clarissa Highstreet watched with a serene smile as the King and Queen of the annual Suwannee County Possum Festival waved to the cheering crowd, then began some hayseed variant of a waltz to the hay-seed variant of a polka coming from the band beside her.

She clapped along politely, sneaking a glance at her watch to see how many minutes she had left before her car would be brought around and she could escape to the back seat and a good, stiff cognac. She hated fairs in general, but through her six years in office had come to absolutely loathe the Possum Festival, with its Possum Parade, its King and Queen Possum, its Possum Costume Contest, its Possum-on-a-Stick. . . .

The thought of the delicacy made her shudder, and she debated again whether to claim a stomach ailment when it came time to sample the winner and runners-up of this year's Possum Chili Cookoff.

The food, Clarissa had long ago determined, was the absolute worst part of the job. In the Panhandle, everywhere there was mullet. In the Big Bend and throughout North Florida, there was possum and alligator and all manner of other roadkill. And in Miami was that dreadful Cuban food. Why, she had often wondered, couldn't some part of Florida honor some decent cuisine, like French? Where was the Croissant Cookoff? The Soufflé Jamboree?

The only reason she had even run for the job was that the title and job description sounded vaguely diplomatic. Secretary of State. Keeper of the state seal, chief elections officer, chief cultural officer. Cultural officer, she had assumed, meant gallery openings and wine and Brie and rubbing shoulders with the beautiful people. Maybe a junket to Paris or London now and again. Sort of the minor leagues of ambassadorships, a place to idle until her party retook the presidency and she could get the real thing.

So she'd taken her family's millions, raised millions more from her old Bennington friends long since returned to their homes in Beverly Hills and Winnetka and Shaker Heights, handily beaten the Democratic candidate, and then left her sheltered existence in Boca Grande to move to Tallahassee to become the state's . . . chief mullet and possum officer.

She took a deep breath, smile still frozen in place, and opened her mouth and threw back her head to join in with the crowd's laughter at the emcee's attempt at humor. At least, she thought gratefully, the smiling part was easy now. For the first few years after taking office, she'd suffered nightly mouth cramps from all the smiling she had to do all day. Smiling at library openings, smiling at museum award ceremonies, smiling at 4H festivals. It was, she figured out quickly, more than ninety percent of her job, and it was driving her nuts. She had tried the beauty pageant contestants' trick of Vaseline on her teeth, but even that was giving her cramps. Plus she hated the taste of Vaseline.

The solution had come to her one day as she was, conveniently enough, sitting in the waiting room of her surgeon. She was thumbing through a back issue of *Enhance* when she discovered that it was possible to tighten up the skin around one's mouth to improve one's smile . . . when the idea had simply popped into her head: If it was possible to *improve* a smile through modern science, why not simply *create* one?

Her surgeon had been skeptical at first but ultimately was happy to accommodate her. He was planning to tighten up under the chin a bit anyway, so he was more or less already in the area.

A week later, when the bandages came off—*voila!* World, meet Clarissa Highstreet, the most pleasant, most amiable politician Florida had ever seen. Always a smile, no matter how difficult the topic.

A loud cheer went up in the crowd, as people started to mill toward the stage. The Suwannee County commissioners, the property appraiser and the mosquito control officer who constituted the other VIPs all stood, so Clarissa Highstreet adjusted her mid-thigh skirt to fine-tune the positioning of the upper-thigh slit, wiggled her bra to arrange poke-through placement, stood on three-inch heels—and saw with dread that the Possum Cookoff trays were advancing toward them. She swallowed hard, realizing she should have laid the groundwork for her excuse earlier, should have mentioned to the geezer property appraiser in the cowboy shirt and bolo tie that she'd been feeling unwell of late, some sort of stomach ailment that prevented her from holding anything down. . . .

When, at the edge of the fairgrounds, she saw her salvation: her deputy secretary for scheduling and transportation, Robert, waving at her and holding aloft a cell phone. She waved back, signaled for him to approach. When he started walking, she waved more forcefully, until finally he was running.

He arrived a good half minute ahead of the Possum trays, giving her just enough time to claim an emergency, give heartfelt thanks to her hosts and stride off toward her limousine beside her aide.

"It's about eff-ing time," she snapped when they were out of earshot. "Where the hell did you go?"

"To get gas," Robert reported defensively. "But every place I went was closed. On account of the Possum Cookoff. I had to go clear to the next county."

She slid into the back seat after he'd opened the door, lit a Virginia Slims with one hand and poured herself a goblet of Rémy Martin with the other, said nothing until she had sucked down half the cigarette and the entire drink.

"So were there any real phone calls? Or was that just you improvising?"

Robert pulled the stretch Lincoln off the grass parking lot and onto the county road. "No, there were two. First was the Hillsborough county chairman. He says they've got what looks like a pretty close race in the Second District."

Clarissa Highstreet groaned. This, as it turned out, was her main function in her role as elections officer—getting custody of the machine that could generate multiple dimpled and hanging chads: "spoiled" ballots that would not get counted in the official tally. "How many?"

"He says five thousand will do it." He read from his notepad in the dim light. "Punch position twenty-seven on the hundred-eighty-nine-hole card."

"Fine. Make them up and send them down. What else?"

"Mr. LaGrange called. He says to clear your deck for Monday."

She scrunched her nose, the closest her face could get to a frown now. "Why? What's Monday? I'm supposed to get my nails done Monday."

Robert shrugged. "Wouldn't tell me. Said you'd need to come down to Cocoa."

"Cocoa . . . huh. Billings Headquarters? I wonder why."

Robert shrugged again, kept driving down the dark highway toward the interstate. In the back seat, Clarissa Highstreet finished her cigarette, checked her makeup in a compact mirror, then laid her head in the custom-molded foam pillow built into the headrest and fell asleep for the drive back to Tallahassee.

Standing with knees flexed against the slow roll atop the cabin trunk, Murphy Moran made a concerted effort not to squint as he lifted the big, waterproof Fujinons to his eyes. Squinting through the binoculars was counterproductive. It reduced the amount of light getting through to his retinas, and it was light, even the barest pinprick, that he was searching for. Party boats burned lots of lights, and it had to be out there somewhere.

He blew out his breath slowly as he pirouetted, completing a long, slow clockwise scan of the horizon. He stopped momentarily at a soft blink to the west before realizing it was just the lighthouse at the Cape.

With a long sigh, he let the glasses hang by their straps and walked back to *Mudslinger*'s cockpit. Nothing. Somehow, he'd lost her. Farber LaGrange's seventy-foot, five-million-dollar Oyster, cruising through the night with seemingly every light aboard burning, and he had lost her.

He bent over the engine control panel and pulled out the kill switch until the little Yanmar diesel finally coughed to a halt. Then he collapsed onto a cockpit bench, gazed upward at the autumn constellations overhead. It had cleared up nicely, after the squall. After the god*damned* squall that had forced him to clamber to the mast and drop the mainsail when the wind started knocking *Mudslinger* over on her beam ends. He'd rushed up there, with not even enough time to slip into his foul-weather gear, and consequently had been chilled to the bone by the ice-cold rain. And then, within minutes, it was gone, taking with it every last trace of wind and leaving only an oily roll that made all the loose gear on his boat clatter around.

And oh, yes, when the rain stopped, *Soft Money* was nowhere to be seen. Gone, just like that. He cursed to himself again, shaking his head. The best-laid plans . . .

Everything had been going so well, too. He had left Blastoff View Marina, gotten through the barge canal locks with the sun still shining, early enough to see *Soft Money* still tied up at her berth at the end of Port Canaveral Yacht Club's T-dock. To loiter there could have attracted unwanted attention, so he had motorsailed out against the sea breeze until he was a mile past the stone jetties, and there he'd hove-to—something he needed to practice anyway. He'd reefed down on the main, sheeted about half the genny in tight and then thrown the tiller to leeward and lashed it there—the effect of which was to keep *Mudslinger* pointed generally into the wind and moving nowhere.

Then he'd sat in his cockpit with his big Japanese binoculars and waited. *Soft Money* finally came motoring out at a little past eight, about two hours late and therefore right on time, as far as sailboat departure times went.

His plan was to follow the bigger boat through the night, running dark and hanging far enough back not to attract attention until mid-morning the following day, when, with any luck, the Victory Hostesses would be doing their unclothed sunbathing thing up on deck. And that's when having a sailboat would make all the difference. It had been his experience that naked women on sailboats covered up when a powerboat approached, but merely smiled and waved when another sailboat drew near.

Murphy had always been that other boat, never having had any actual naked women aboard *Mudslinger,* and he was banking on the pattern holding up again, and the Victory Hostesses smiling and waving for him as he got within range of his Nikon and its 400mm lens. One grainy, *National Enquirer*–caliber shot was all he needed. Mere debauchery aboard a boat carrying the Republican candidate for governor would be pretty good in and of itself, but a frame that included both Bub Billings and even one partially nude, college-intern-aged Victory Hostess would change the course of the election.

Seven hours later, instead, he was all alone, with *Soft Money* out there somewhere on the same ocean, hosting whatever illicit thing it was that Farber LaGrange had promised his donors once the vessel was in international waters. His odds of finding it hovered between slim and none. He had no radar aboard *Mudslinger,* so he was limited to a circle with a three-mile radius around his boat that marked his visual horizon. Three miles squared, times pi, meant he could see about twenty-eight, twenty-nine square miles. Out of the thousands in which *Soft Money* could be by now.

He sighed and shut his eyes, thinking how good it would feel to sleep for just a few minutes—when he heard a plastic tumbler rattle against one side of the locker, and then, when the boat rolled back to starboard after the wave passed underneath, rattle back the other way. He groaned aloud, knowing now he would be listening for that sound with each passing wave, growing increasingly irritated with it until he finally had to get up and stuff a towel in the locker to stop it. And then he'd hear a different noise, maybe a book he'd left out, sliding back and forth across the dinette table, and he'd feel compelled to go deal with that, too, and so on and so on. . . .

It was, he knew, the unavoidable friction between a seagoing vessel and a livable vessel. A seagoing boat was shipshape at all times, on the theory that when bad things start happening, they can really go to hell in a hurry, and that a line left uncoiled or a kitchen knife left unstowed will serve to trip you or stab you when it is most inconvenient.

If he truly intended to cross oceans, the thing his dad had talked about for so many years but ultimately had not had the time for, he needed to learn the discipline of an oceangoing boat. No more leaving things undone for tomorrow. No more letting repairs pile up until a convenient time came along to fix them. For example, he should not even have come out the jetties without a working radio and an emergency beacon. It was foolhardy, being offshore without them. If something happened, if the mast came down and the engine wouldn't start, he would be fresh out of luck, doomed to drift up the Gulf Stream and across the Atlantic before hitting land.

Well, never again, he promised himself. He would not leave his marina slip again until he'd gotten and affixed the new VHF antenna at the masthead, until he'd installed the insulators and grounding plate for the SSB set that remained in its box, until he'd bitten the bullet and spent the thousand dollars he'd need for a good emergency radio beacon.

No more day trips up to Canaveral National Seashore, no more wasted afternoons at the used bookstore, no more messing around with the MG's oil leak until he'd gotten *Mudslinger* ready for sea. The car especially was time poorly spent. After one trial season in the Caribbean, he planned to do the real thing, with an Atlantic crossing, the Med as far as Corsica, back across the Atlantic and along the northern coast of South America, a Panama Canal transit and then the Pacific. What good was a car going to do him?

Of course, if he didn't get his act in gear and get at least as far south as the Exumas by mid-November, the Caribbean would be a no-go for yet another year. Which meant he had to hurry up and get this thing done for Ramsey. Which meant, damn it all, he had to come out after *Soft Money*'s floating breast party at least one more time. But that meant violating his most recent vow not to take *Mudslinger* out of her slip until he'd gotten all her communications gear in order. . . .

Murphy sat up, his head hurting, and scanned the horizon once more. Still nothing, not even a freighter or a fishing boat.

He ran his fingers through his thinning hair, then his thickening beard, and tried to imagine what Farber would do. This, as far as his sources knew, was only the third or fourth time he'd run a Victory Hostess fund-raiser overnight, and apparently it was the first time he'd actually had the candidate himself aboard. His sources had told him that LaGrange never let the party hit full swing until the boat was twelve nautical miles offshore, apparently so that whatever happened did so in international waters, technically outside the United States.

Well, if he were Farber, he'd just run north and south along that twelve-mile line, or just beyond it, so as to minimize the amount of time necessary to get out and back. In fact, the most efficient way of doing it would be to get out about fifteen miles into the edge of the Gulf Stream, then sail slowly south against the current. The net effect would be hardly any movement at all over the ground and therefore less distance to run when it came time to head home.

Murphy leaned his head down the companionway, read the coordinates off the GPS's soft blue display, mentally transposed those onto the chart spread out on the navigation table. He was just about fifteen miles off the coast himself. . . .

He thought about that for a minute, his hopes beginning to rise: He was where Farber would be, if he were Farber. Would Farber think the same way? Farber had a paid crew that included a Kiwi skipper. What would his advice be?

Murphy allowed himself a deep breath, then shook his head in defeat. He'd already crisscrossed the water for most of the night, hoping to catch a glimpse of the bigger boat. It would be dawn soon. Farber no doubt would head home no later than noon so his candidate could make his afternoon and evening commitments. What were the odds that he would be able to find *Soft Money* in the next few hours when he hadn't been able to find her all night?

Well, there would be another day, another Victory Hostess party. He'd hit a spell of bad luck, was all. Nothing he could do about it, and he would stop moping.

He bent down between his legs to turn the engine back on to motor home when he stopped, realized he hadn't relieved himself since before the squall. First things first, he decided, unclipping his safety tether from a stainless-steel padeye in the cockpit and attaching it to the nylon strap that ran the length of *Mudslinger*'s starboard side. He picked himself up and swung over the cockpit coaming and onto the narrow sidedeck, then walked forward to the starboard shrouds.

Murphy unzipped the fly of his bright yellow foul-weather bibs, pressed his legs against the lifelines and, with left hand holding onto the aft wire, leaned out over the water. And the flow began, and a sense of relief spread upward from his bladder—

"Make sure you don't fall in, now. Look what happened to me."

Murphy shrieked, stumbled backward and landed in a heap on the cabin top. His heart pounded in his ears as he struggled to stuff himself back inside his overalls. The voice had come from the water, he was certain of it. . . .

"Hey, mister, I do apologize. Didn't mean to scare you. Know how hard it is to stop, once you get started."

The voice was weak but clear. Murphy stood, curiosity overcoming surprise, and peered into the black water . . . until finally he made out a lighter shadow about a dozen yards off.

"Yeah, here I am. Say, I was hopin', once you finish your business, if you wouldn't mind givin' me a lift? I think I'm actually about at the end of my rope."

The voice was oddly familiar, Murphy thought as he scrambled back to the cockpit to plug in the searchlight. He tried to place it, but could not get past the jumble of radio and television political ads he'd forced himself to endure over the past days.

He plugged the big light into its waterproof receptacle, slapped it a few times until it came on, played the beam out over the water . . . and found Byron Ulysses Billings slumped over the top of an old wooden crate.

With one foot up on the cockpit bench, Murphy Moran held the steaming cup of instant coffee to his chest as he scanned the horizon for the red buoy marking the shoal five miles off Canaveral Inlet.

There was still no wind, and the sea had settled to a greasy calm modulated by a gentle groundswell. Gray water and gray sky merged at the horizon. When or from where the layer of low cloud had moved in, Murphy couldn't say. Probably during the two hours he had spent getting the Republican candidate for governor aboard *Mudslinger* and then below into a warm bunk.

The man had been on the brink of exhaustion when Murphy had come upon him and hadn't regained consciousness the whole time Murphy backed and filled his unwieldy boat around to a spot where he could reach down and grab him. With Bub unable to help him, Murphy had finally stripped to his shorts and jumped down into the water, where, unable to pry the crate top from Bub's cramped fingers, he had finally undone the webbing on the hoisting sling and threaded it beneath his armpits.

It was only after he'd gotten him below and pulled off his wet clothes that he glanced out a porthole and realized dawn had come and long since gone during his exertions. And it was only after he'd himself lain down on the opposite bunk and shut his eyes for a few seconds that he realized he couldn't. There would be a massive air and sea search for the man, which he was unable to call off because he had no working radio. Which meant he had to hustle back to shore, as fast as his little twenty-horse Yanmar would let him.

And so he'd picked himself up, thrown on sweats and a T-shirt and climbed back up top, stopping only to switch the TV to the Orlando station that came in the clearest so he could monitor any news.

He was cold, exhausted, hungry and above all else, mad at himself for not having fixed the damned radios. His ultimate justification for not doing so had always been that, after all, it was his own skin he was endangering. It had never occurred to him that he might someday cause others to unnecessarily risk their lives searching for someone who was perfectly safe and sound.

He snorted, shaking his head at it all. Republican gubernatorial candidates and saltwater, he decided, simply did not mix. First Spencer Tolliver, technically even before he was a candidate, now Bub Billings. And Bub would have shared Tolliver's fate, had it not been for Murphy's bladder.

And that right there, the supreme irony of how his role in the governor's race had turned out, was driving him nuts. He'd been asked by one candidate, an old friend, the one who rightly deserved to win, for his help. Instead, somehow, his happenstance rescue of the other guy would generate him yet more positive publicity, in the end giving him an even more lopsided win come Election Day.

The only thing that could possibly save Ramsey MacLeod now was some sort of scandal behind Bub's accident, a smarmy tale behind his falling in the drink. A drunken orgy maybe. Or perhaps if he'd made a pass at a Victory Hostess and she'd slapped him, knocking him overboard.

It was, he knew, too much to ask for. Bub had been completely dressed, had still been wearing a pair of brand-new boat shoes when he'd fished him out. Couldn't have been much of an orgy if he'd been wearing all his clothes.

Murphy snapped himself out of his reverie and quickly checked *Mudslinger*'s vitals. The little diesel thrummed its steady, 1,800-rpm thrum, the electronic autopilot held the tiller steady on the course he'd set, and there was still no buoy visible ahead. He took a quick glance around the horizon and decided to answer the rumble in his tummy and check on his passenger when he heard a voice pipe up over the diesel: "Well, *that's* total ka-ka!"

Murphy blinked and ducked down through the companionway to see Bub, a blanket wrapped around him, staring intently at the little television screen. There, amid snowy reception, stood Florida Republican Party Chairman Farber LaGrange, two of his crew, a rumple-suited police detective and a uniformed coast guardsman. Murphy scrambled below and turned up the set to hear Farber talking: . . . *approximately seven miles off Melbourne Beach when the squall hit us. We had a jam in the furlin' mechanism on the headsail, causing* Soft Money *to heel over excessively. It was at that time that I decided we needed to take the sail down completely, and Bub and I went forward to assist in the dousing of the headsail.*

Farber cleared his throat to gather himself, continued: *If you ain't ever been through a squall at sea, you probably don't understand what I'm talkin' about, but it was ferocious. We were taking solid green waves over the bow. Water was everywhere. More than once, I lost my grip and slid down against the lifelines. Lightnin' kept strikin' the water all around us, rain comin' down as hard as can be. Finally, we got the sail down.* Soft Money *got back on her feet. I was congratulatin' everyone on a job well done, when somebody finally noticed that Bub was gone. . . .*

The Coast Guard guy got to the mike, pointed to a little map showing the box off Melbourne where the search had taken place, and then announced that the Coast Guard had as of an hour ago suspended it, based on the sixty-seven-degree water temperature as well as Farber LaGrange's affidavit of all the lightning strikes. . . .

Murphy puzzled over the map on the little television set. "How could I have found you where I did if you fell overboard way down off Melbourne?"

Bub pointed to the television, mug of coffee in hand, sputtered angrily, then got out: "Biggest loada fool bull-crap—I didn't *fall* offa his G-D boat! I was *pushed!*"

With that, the mug fell out of his hands to the cabin sole, and Bub would have followed hard behind it if Murphy hadn't been there to catch him.

★ ③ ★

THE STRETCH LINCOLN honked twice as it turned into the circular, brick driveway at Port Canaveral Yacht Club. Farber LaGrange turned, squinted and groaned when Clarissa Highstreet emerged from the back seat in miniskirt and matching pumps, permanent smile flashing his way as she walked briskly toward the docks.

He took a final look at the broken stanchion base at the port shrouds, realized there was no way to fix it without a replacement part, and stuck the bent stainless-steel pipe and its attached lifelines back into the wobbly holder before dusting off his hands and rising to greet his guest.

"Yoo-hoo!" Clarissa Highstreet called, climbing up the gangplank. "May I?"

She stepped onto the teak deck in her heels, held out a hand for Farber to kiss, then started examining the polished brass dorade vents, the now-empty hot tub sunken into the aft deck, the wood trim that glowed with a twelve-coats-of-varnish shine. She chattered incessantly as she walked, while Farber squatted to study the little round indentations her stiletto heels were leaving in the wood.

He glanced up to an expectant look. "What?" he asked finally.

"This afternoon," she repeated. "Are we all set for this afternoon?"

She was up to something, Farber realized. No doubt about it. She'd had twenty-four hours to plot and scheme since the announcement of Bub's "accident." It had probably been twenty-four hours too many. "I believe so. Four o'clock. Is there a problem?"

She fingered a shiny chrome porthole on the cabin trunk, leaned back to sit on it and crossed her legs in a sassy way. With her arms behind her holding her up, her chest was thrust out. As usual. And, as usual, she was wearing something that showed off both acres of cleavage as well as the indentations from her nipples, Farber noted.

"No. No problem. It's just . . . well, I hope you appreciate the stretch you're asking me to make with the finding."

Farber squinted at her more severely. "Not much more than you've been makin' these past six years, I would imagine. Certification deadlines. Interpretations of legal votes. Et cetera, et cetera."

"Yes, but those have all been with local offices. Tax collectors, county commissioners. Once in a while, the odd legislative seat. This is different: the highest office in the state." She flicked some hair out of her eyes, uncrossed and recrossed her legs. "No?"

Farber nodded. "How 'bout we cut the bullshit, okay? What is it you want?"

Her permanent smile widened a touch. "Same thing I've always wanted. The ambassadorship to Paris."

Farber said nothing, studied her eyes. They were bright green today, accenting her outfit. "I believe the openin's already been filled."

"I've been waiting six years. Six *years*, Farber. For the first four, it was because we didn't have the White House. Now it's because he already gave it to that old bag from Charleston. A woman only has so much patience." She adjusted her bosom upward. "Besides: Which of us puts a better face on American interests? Old What's-Her-Name? Or me?"

Her breasts seemed to leap up and out of the camisole top. Farber nodded at them. "They new?"

Clarissa Highstreet played with her hair again. "Why, yes! Thanks for noticing. They're D cups, this time. I think these are *just* right. Double O's were too big; C's too little. You like?"

"Absolutely scrumptious," Farber said with a sigh. "Any other additions?"

She puckered her lips. "Just a smidgen of collagen." She stood and turned for him, stroking her derriere. "And got a little bit pulled out here, and the whole thing reshaped."

Farber eyed the skin-tight skirt, the flimsy top. She now had the torso of an exotic dancer and the bottom of a pre-pubescent girl. She looked utterly ludicrous, yet somehow continued to get written up in the state's magazines as some kind of glamour queen.

He realized she was awaiting his assessment. "Good enough to eat," he said at last.

The grin widened again. "I might just take you up on that. Anyway. Back to business. I'd be happy to present and defend whatever it is we need this afternoon. But I think you should take a more pressing interest in having someone from Florida receive one of our nation's premiere ambassadorships. We are, after all, the fourth largest state. He wouldn't be president were it not for us. Maybe you should remind him. Perhaps you should also remind your old pal Link. He does have the president's ear on these matters, no?"

Farber bit back his irritation. For the next several hours, at least, he needed her. After that he could be as blunt as he needed. "I'll see what I can do. In old Mrs. Chesterforth's defense, though, I'd have to remind you that she did single-handedly deliver South Carolina for him in the primary. So he owes her." He saw the creases starting to form on Clarissa Highstreet's brow and began to backtrack. "Of course, he owes you, too. And I'll remind Link, next time I see him."

She took a relaxed breath, stuck her chin skyward. "Good. I know the great Farber LaGrange can move mountains, when he needs to. Maybe I'll lobby Link personally, too, next time he's down for a spin on your little toy." She stroked a piece of teak trim around the companionway as she slid past it. "I might have some, shall we say, tools of persuasion you might lack? Yes, perhaps? In the meantime, I think what I'll do is plan on a cultural affairs office on the Continent. I'll expect your assistance in getting the money in next year's budget."

Farber saw over her shoulder that the club's varnish guy had arrived. "The people of Florida should be honored to have you set up offices overseas." He reached out for her elbow to start guiding her down the gangplank. "Tell you what: I'll even get a bill through changin' the title of your office from sec'tary of state to ambassador of state. Would that be better? Until we can get the real thing?"

She put a heavily pancaked cheek forward for a farewell kiss. Farber held her shoulders, could feel the hard points of her boobs through his golf shirt. She wheeled free and down the gangplank, adjusting her top for the benefit of the varnish guy. "See you this afternoon!"

"Clarissa," Farber called.

She turned, hands on hips and weight impatiently on one foot. The green fabric of her skirt didn't come within a foot of her knee.

"You ain't plannin' on wearin' . . ." he nodded at her legs, "*that* this afternoon, are you?"

She examined herself, frowned. "What's wrong with this? I wear this to Cabinet meetings."

Farber bit his tongue again. She'd also worn it to her last inaugural in Tallahassee. It had been a typical North Florida winter day, a cold wind whipping the skirt around and up as she faced the chief justice. Naturally, she hadn't been wearing any underwear.

"We're still in mournin', is all," he said.

Clarissa Highstreet considered that, then brightened. "I just remembered I have this in black!"

Clyde Bruno eased the rented Mustang convertible up to the refinery gates, flashed his badge at the guard, then drove on in to the parking lot in front of the administration building. He pulled into the spot reserved for the director of operations, grabbed his Stetson off the passenger seat and walked toward the glass doors.

He breathed the air deeply as he walked, smiled at the petrochemical stench of the place. He hadn't been back to Lake Charles in over a year, and, as he did every time he came home and smelled the air, he wondered why he'd ever left.

With big strides, he moved over the linoleum hallway, into the director's office, past the director's protesting secretary and sat behind the director's big oak desk. He lifted his cowboy boots onto the desk's blotter, tilted the Stetson's brim over his forehead and closed his eyes.

He didn't have to wait long before a thin, balding man in a short-sleeve shirt and striped tie walked in, yelling at his secretary to have the car that was parked in his spot towed. Then he noticed Clyde Bruno sitting in his seat, told his secretary, "Never mind," and shut the door behind him.

Clyde Bruno moved the hat back off his eyes and flashed a wide smile. "Greetings."

The director stood with crossed arms and severe frown. "What now?"

Clyde grinned again. The man had been his boss, years ago, before he had started his meteoric rise. Clyde lorded it over him whenever he could.

"Did you hear? They sent a couple of tugs out to go get *City of Galveston*. I figure it'll take them at least six days to get her in. When she does make it in, I need you to take down Number Two and Three again for about a week."

The director shook his head. "This is nuts. You know, for the past six months we've already been down longer than we've been online?"

Clyde shrugged, glanced at the calendar. "In exactly fifteen more days, we won't have to worry about it anymore. No more interruptions. I promise."

Clyde smiled wide again, but the director wasn't soothed. "I just want to make sure that when Houston's sitting down doing reviews and handing out Christmas bonuses, somebody remembers that I'm not a fuckup over here. Production was down on account of I was playing ball."

Clyde pulled a tiny cell phone from his pocket and tossed it to the director, who juggled it twice before grasping it between both hands. "You want to remind Mr. Thresher? Here you go. Number one on speed dial is his direct line. Go ahead."

The director hastily returned the phone to Clyde. "Okay, great. So tell me: Which distributors am I supposed to leave dry? No, wait. Let me guess. Florida again?"

Clyde Bruno flashed a wry grin and gathered his feet off the desk to leave.

With an angry glare, Percy Billings kicked shut the bottom drawer of his brother's desk and slumped back in the office chair.

All over the small office were videocassette racks devoid of their contents, emptied stationery boxes, disheveled bookcases. Not one of them had contained the object of Percy Billings's search. He had already been through his brother's bungalow in Merritt Island, room by room, but with no luck. Ditto the Ford Tempo, although he hadn't really expected to find it there.

No, however sloppy Bub had been with most things, he would have been sure to revere this one object, what with all the family lore it represented.

More than a century earlier, there had graduated from the hallowed grounds of the United States Naval Academy a midshipman by the name of Dexter Hewitt Billings. He had ranked within the top five of his class, and had gone on to accept a commission in the Marine Corps. Within two years, he had found himself in Cuba, at the side of a man who would parlay a glorious victory at San Juan Hill into the vice-presidency and then, by chance, the presidency itself.

Captain Dexter Billings had been offered a White House posting, but had declined, preferring instead to return to his native Florida, where he had entered politics himself and, as a state senator, instilled into the fledgling system of state universities an academic rigor that had been lacking. In public speeches, Senator Billings always spoke wistfully about his days in Annapolis, how it was not so much the military history and naval theory that he missed, but the classics. Homer, Ovid, Cicero. And then, later, Chaucer and Shakespeare and, later still, the romantic poets.

Toward the end of his life, retired to the family home in Ocala, Billings, in a solemn moment that was passed down orally through the generations, had given his elder son his Annapolis class ring, as a reminder about honor and duty and public service.

Percy Billings, fifty years later, still was unable to forgive him. What, after all, was so special about the *elder* son? Dexter Billings had had two boys. Why was the younger son automatically inferior because of birth order?

However unfair the reasoning, Dexter Billings's action had established a lasting precedent. His elder son had in turn passed it down to the eldest of his three boys, Lamont Billings, Percy and Bub's father. And Lamont Billings, in his final days, had given it to Bub. Just as through the years he'd given everything of value to Bub, never mind how undeserving he had been. . . .

Percy stopped himself. His brother was gone now. There was nothing to be gained anymore in hating him. And beyond that, he had to admit, the whole thing was not bringing a pleasant feeling, no matter how he tried to spin it. All the justifications were there, from Machiavelli to Nietzsche . . . and still, his insides occasionally kept slipping down toward self-revulsion, a feeling he could only displace by recalling, through the years, all the times he had suffered the unfair rules of primogeniture. Well, now *he* was the eldest *surviving* son, wasn't he? So all the traditions and benefits that had been heaped onto Byron now fell to him.

And it was about friggin' time, too. The son of a bitch never appreciated half the stuff that had come his way through no cause of his own. He was gone and good riddance—

Percy stopped himself again. Charity suffereth long, and is kind; charity envieth not, he reminded himself. He was being uncharitable. That was not a trait The People would find admirable.

He reopened the desk's top drawer, riffed through the papers once more, feeling around in the corners with his fingers. His great-grandfather had not been a large man, and the ring was not a large ring. The one time he'd tried it on, when Father had shown it to them, it barely fit on his pinkie. And he'd only been a teenager then. Surely his hands had grown since, likely making the ring far too small.

Well, that was not a problem. Nothing a good jeweler wouldn't be able to fix. He frowned at the desk, then at the walls, covered top to bottom with campaign posters: Elect Bub! Bub for Guv! And the most simple yet most effective on the campaign trail: Bub!

Bub. As in the acronym for Byron Ulysses Billings. His brother's absurd nickname for himself from grade school that, when it had come time for Farber's focus groups, had let him connect far better with the common folk than Percy could ever hope to.

He sighed, stood morosely. The thing simply was not there. Of course, it was not as if he truly expected to find it there, in his campaign office. He needed to be patient. Patience meant self-suffering. Gandhi had said so. On the other hand . . . what the hell did Gandhi know?

Bub certainly would have kept a safety deposit box. In another couple of days, he would be given the keys to it by the bank and he would have it and all would be well.

Then he thought: What if it wasn't in there? Or what if Bub didn't have a safety deposit box? It's not as if he really needed one. With no wife or kids, he didn't need life insurance or any of that. There wouldn't have *been* any critical paperwork; so why would he have needed a special place to keep them?

What if, he worried again, Bub had been wearing it on the boat and he had simply not noticed it? It would now be at the bottom of the Atlantic, or stuck tight on his bloated and floating body as it drifted with the wind and currents . . . or in the belly of a shark or some other sea beast. . . .

Percy shook the grisly image from his head, straightened at the knock at the door.

"Yes?"

A sincere-looking flunky poked his head in. A College Republican, by the haircut and tie. Percy had been assigned a gaggle of them by party headquarters.

"It's almost time, sir. We need to be leaving."

Percy let his eyes roam around the room a final time, grabbed his jacket from the back of a chair and followed the flunky out.

Methodically, her mind on autopilot, Toni Johnson read figures off an invoice, entered them into the spreadsheet on her computer, then stacked the invoice in an open folder that would be forwarded to Accounts Payable.

Outside the windows was a bright sunny day, but it couldn't break the pall that hung over the Headquarters War Room. The permanent staffers went about their business quietly, the events of the past day not quite registering yet. The volunteers were in open tears, or had simply stayed home.

The suddenness and the permanence had stunned. On Saturday night the campaign was coasting to victory, with a strong candidate, staying "on message" day in and day out, the polls holding steady or growing slightly better each morning. Victory was a foregone conclusion, with party staffers trying to figure out which jobs they wanted in which departments after they took over the government come January.

By Sunday morning, all that was gone. Bub, whom some of the staff had known personally, was no more. The daily polls showed a fourteen-point lead turn into a twenty-point deficit. Party staffers who had been jockeying for particular offices in particular government buildings faced instead the prospect of remaining on the outs for another four years.

And at the highest echelons was a nervous anxiety over the switch they were about to pull. Party lawyers had pored over the election laws, searching for precedent, finding none, ultimately hoping that, in a time of mourning, the people would accept the word of the state's top elections officer as gospel.

Toni herself had passed through something that resembled grief. After all, whatever she thought of Byron Billings, which wasn't much, he hadn't deserved to fall overboard and drown. Or get struck by lightning. Or get struck by lightning and *then* drown. . . .

Curiously, Bub's death hadn't slowed the Petron campaign-fund-raising machine any. To the contrary, the checks from the various Clyde Bruno companies had started coming in even faster, as if in anticipation and approval of Bub's anointed replacement.

And Toni began to wonder to herself: For the checks to have arrived the day after Bub's drowning, they would have had to have been sent at least a day before his death. . . . Could Link Thresher have *known* that Bub was about to be replaced and that the Party would suddenly need many more millions, to sell a new product to a skeptical electorate on just two weeks' notice . . . ?

She cast the idea from her head and continued with her work. The thought was preposterous. Even assuming the cynical worst, what possible difference would it make to Petron which Billings brother was the candidate? Everyone knew their politics were virtually identical.

Toni blew out a sigh. The Party's scheming, its behind-the-scenes conspiring with the secretary of state's office to get the legal interpretation it needed, had soured her even further. The secretary of state was an elected Cabinet officer, after all, not some Party hack. For Farber to corrupt that . . .

She sighed again, flipped another invoice into the Accounts Payable stack and turned to the next one. She read it, blinked and read it again before taking her fingers off the keyboard to pick up the single page and read it more closely: Clean Gulf Trust.

A frown pursed her lips and creased her brow. Clean Gulf Trust, of 564 Water Street, Apalachicola, Florida. Clean Gulf Trust. One hundred thousand dollars due, this time, for surveying services. In her head she went through the list of the environmentalist groups in the state: One Thousand Friends of Florida, Everglades Coalition, Nature Conservancy . . .

But no Clean Gulf Trust. Okay, perhaps it was a new group, or one that she just hadn't heard of. Why, in either event, was the Florida Republican Party paying it for "surveying"? Surveying what?

Toni bit her lip, took a thin folder from her desk and added the invoice to the five already there. She slipped into her pumps, smoothed her skirt and walked toward the copy machine by the window, hit the green button to let it warm up.

She heard a snort behind her, glanced up to one of the new hires, a blue-eyed, dark-haired FSU grad in bright red miniskirt and sandals. One of Farber's latest Victory Hostesses, holding a stack of press releases for photocopying. Toni looked down her nose at the girl's translucent top, and she responded with a petulant smirk.

The machine started making ready noises, and Toni quickly fed the five invoices into the slot, grabbed originals and copies and turned on her heel to head back to her desk.

**W**ith five plastic grocery sack handles entwined in the fingers of one hand, Murphy climbed down scuffed companionway steps and deposited the food on the nav table before noticing that his guest was sitting wide-eyed against the cherry bulkhead.

Murphy smiled, pulled a Campbell's chicken noodle from one of the sacks and set upon it with a can opener. "You're awake."

Bub blinked three times in succession, sat up straighter. "I'm wiped out. Walked up to the marina bathroom for a spell. Damn near passed out gettin' back." He bent his head down to his shirt, wrinkled his nose. "And I smell bad. What day is it?"

"Monday." Murphy poured the can into a saucepan, reached behind the refrigerator to spin a metal valve a few times, then pressed a red button on the gimbaled stove until a burner emitted a ring of blue. He set the saucepan over the burner and leaned back against the fridge. "*Soft Money* left Port Canaveral Saturday night. I picked you up early yesterday. The last eighteen hours you've been sick. Bad sick. Fever of a hundred and four, yesterday. I was getting ready to haul you into Wuesthoff Memorial if it got any higher. Fortunately, it broke overnight." He nodded at the bunk. "That's why your bedclothes maybe don't smell so good. Here, take them off and we'll put on some new ones."

Bub rolled his bare feet down onto the cabin sole, seemed only then to notice that the clothes he wore were not his own. He glanced up, saw his own shirt and trousers laundered and folded neatly on the dinette table. Beside it was the crate top Murphy had pried from his fingers.

Bub flipped it over, read the stamped letters: "*Hecho en Cuba.*" He shook his head and groaned. "I was saved by somethin' that was hecho-ed in Cuba? Now, ain't that just dandy? There goes the Miami vote."

Murphy gave the soup a stir. For the day and a half since getting back into the marina, he had quietly cared for his castaway, all the while following the news reports. From the initial press conference onward, the story Farber LaGrange had put out had been the same: Bub had fallen overboard during a squall about seven miles off the coast of Melbourne.

Murphy had gone back and checked his logbook, and, sure enough, his memory was accurate. The squall had taken place, all right, but *Soft Money,* with *Mudslinger* still in pursuit, had been about a dozen miles off Cocoa Beach—more than twenty miles north. Surely Farber had known where he was when the squall had hit. So why lie? There was only one obvious answer. One that made perfect sense, if what Bub had originally blurted out was true.

"Well, mister, uh . . . I, uh, gotta confess I forgot your name."

"Murphy," Murphy said. "Murphy Moran."

"Murphy Moran," Bub repeated. "Now how come that's familiar?"

"I used to be a political consultant."

Bub nodded. "Well, Mr. Moran, I sure do appreciate your comin' along when you did, and takin' care of me and all. Now I expect I oughta head on out. Got a coupla things I oughta get done. I suppose you'd like to get on with your life, too. Don't need to—" He attempted to stand, sat back down suddenly. "Whoa . . . Maybe I oughta take it a little slower."

Murphy eyed him carefully. Their encounter in the Gulf Stream was the first time he'd seen him in person, and his strongest impression was how little he was. He was a full head shorter than his brother, and a good fifty pounds lighter, with reddish-brown curls and friendly if forgettable features. He was steadying himself again, reaching for his own clothes on the table.

"Is there a bathroom or someplace I can change in? And I appreciate you doin' my laundry for me. Maybe sometime I can buy you a beer or somethin'. I know it don't begin to repay you, but—"

"You said you were pushed," Murphy said, and waited out a long pause as Bub blinked several times in succession.

"Did I?" he asked finally.

"Yes, sir. 'I was pushed,' I believe is the exact quote. You were sitting pretty much right where you are now." Murphy watched as Bub attempted a weak smile, then licked his lips. "You, uh, don't recall things that way anymore?"

Bub managed a version of a laugh. "Shoot, with a high fever and all, I s'pose there's a chance I was, what do they call it, delirious, right? God's honest truth, Mr. Moran? I'm embarrassed to say I was, well, re-lievin' myself over the side, and I guess I was, you know, shakin' off there at the end, when, shoot, next thing I know I'm comin' up for air and watchin' ol' Farber's boat sail off without me."

Murphy glanced at the brass clock on the bulkhead above Bub, asked, "Windward side? Or leeward?"

"Lou who? Sorry . . . I'm ain't followin' you."

"The high side of the boat? Or the low?"

"Oh." Bub thought for a moment. "The low side. Farber told me you can't pee off the high side or the wind blows it back on you. Anyhow, there I was. By the by, you got any idea how hard it is tryin' to tuck your dick back in your pants when you're treadin' water? Trust me: It ain't easy."

Murphy nodded, wondered if Bub could get away with repeating that anecdote on the campaign trail. He studied the dimple and the grinning eyes, decided he probably could. In fact, not only would he get away with it, he could probably tell it at the ladies' auxiliary and pick up votes.

"So that's it? You just head on back to the campaign and pick up where you left off? I suppose you could. You come back, you'd be a hero. Bounce right back to where you were before any of this happened, maybe even pick up five or six points." Murphy let that hang there for a while. "And then, when there's a little downtime, maybe you could get LaGrange to explain how come he told that little fairy tale to the Coast Guard about where and when you went over. Because, I'll tell you what.

That's the reason right there I haven't told a soul about your being here. That thing he did, telling them you went over off Melbourne Beach, that was no misstatement. That was a flat-out, deliberate lie. Period. And if I hadn't happened on you, it would have prevented them from ever finding you."

Bub swallowed, shrugged uneasily. "I suppose anybody can get a little flustered, in a crisis-type situation."

Murphy gave the soup a final stir and turned off the burner. He glanced at the clock again. "Okay. Tell you what. Have a cup of soup. Oh, and uh, there's something I'd like you to watch with me on the TV."

"I'll take you up on the soup," Bub said. "Don't generally watch much TV, though."

"Trust me. You won't want to miss this." Murphy grabbed the remote, flicked through the channels and found CNN, just as Farber LaGrange walked to a podium set up in front of a row of flags, followed by Secretary of State Clarissa Highstreet and Percy Billings. Murphy turned the sound up.

"Hey! That's my campaign headquarters," Bub said.

On the tiny television screen, Farber LaGrange cleared his throat impressively and began: *Good afternoon, ladies and gentlemen. Let me make this brief. As I said yesterday, we in the Republican Party, like everybody else in the State of Florida, grieve terribly for the loss of Bub Billings. He would have made a first-class governor, and he was a first-class human bein'.* LaGrange paused to wipe his eye. *Please 'xcuse me. It's okay, we'll have plenty of time to grieve later. What brings us here today is the campaign at hand. As everybody knows, in exactly fifteen days, the voters of Florida choose a governor for the next four years. I truly believe that had Bub not been tragically taken from us, he would have been that governor. Nevertheless, we are faced with a problem. It is too late for us to recall all the ballots that have already been printed, and go through the entire process of choosing another Republican candidate. So I, in my capacity as party chairman, have petitioned the sec'tary of state for an interpretation of state law. Without further ado, the sec'tary of state of the state of Florida, Ms. Clarissa Highstreet.*

Camera motor drives whirred and strobes flashed as Clarissa Highstreet strode forward in a low-cut blouse and black skirt, while a flunky quickly affixed a Great Seal of Florida to the front of the podium, then unstuck it and repositioned it several times until it was finally on straight. When that was finished, Clarissa Highstreet broadened her ever-present smile for the cameras.

*Greetings. I have been petitioned by one of the major parties of Florida as defined by Chapter Ninety-nine, paragraph one-twenty-one, parens 'b', Florida Statutes, to permit a replacement of candidates following the closing of the filing deadlines.* She smiled again as still more cameras whirred and flashed. *Pursuant to the authority vested in me by Article Four, Section Four of the Florida Constitution and Chapter One-oh-two of Florida Statutes, I hereby substitute Byron Ulysses Billings with Percy Coleridge Billings for candidate for governor on the upcoming general election ballot. All votes recorded for Byron Billings on Election Day shall be construed as votes for Percy Billings.*

A murmur went up among the gathered press. Several voices shouted out different permutations of the same question: Which particular law was she citing?

Clarissa Highstreet flashed a smug grin at first one camera, then another, and leaned forward slightly, thereby offering viewers at home a better angle down her blouse. Finally she stared straight at the CNN camera: *The Constitution gives me plenary authority to determine the procedures for naming statewide candidates for office.*

Several reporters insisted: Which specific law?

Clarissa Highstreet shrugged happily. *No specific law in any way limits the power granted by the Constitution. Thank you! I'll take no further questions.*

She backed away from the mike, in the background adjusted herself to pose for additional still pictures while Percy Billings moved forward. He stood there for a few long seconds, slightly hunched toward the microphone, his hands clasped together, his lips clenched, his eyes exuding sadness and, on cue, a single tear.

*My fellow Floridians,* he began, voice quavering. *These are indeed times that try men's souls. It is with heavy heart that I speak to you today. . . .*

Murphy became aware of a low gurgling noise, thought at first a bilge pump had come on, until he glanced beside him. Bub was kneeling upright on the settee, his face red as he glared at the television set. The noise was coming from deep in his throat somewhere, emerging despite jaws that remained clamped together.

*. . . have always believed that the Lord works in mysterious ways. He needed my brother for a reason, I'm convinced, and left me here for a reason. Well, here I am, and I will do His work. As Paul wrote to the Corinthians: But by the grace of God I am what I am.* Percy leaned forward toward the cameras. The sorrow had left his face now, replaced by a smug confidence. *Let me explain my vision of Florida. It is a vision where the best decisions are those that come, not from on high in Mount Tallahassee, but from our own communities and neighborhoods and churches and synagogues. It is a vision where a world-class education system makes sure no child is left behind, and a state government does less, but does it better. As your governor, I will be a listener. I want to listen to you, and base my decisions on what my bosses, you the people, have to say. And when I decide, I will be firm, in the knowledge—*

Bub lunged forward at the television power button. For a minute he glared at the tiny bright dot that remained on the dark set. Murphy stood frozen, finally moved to put an arm around Bub.

"Jesus, man—"

"Sailorman, you seem to have a pretty good understandin' of Florida politics. Tell me: Is he gonna win? And if so, what, short of my comin' out and tellin' my story, can we do to make sure he doesn't?"

Murphy poured some soup into a bowl, grabbed a large spoon from the drawer and pushed both across the dinette table to Bub before sitting down across from him. "There's something I need to tell you."


**B**ub slurped up soup and gulped down swallows of milk as he listened to Murphy's explanation, finally licked the spoon and laid it beside the empty bowl.

"So let me get this straight: You were followin' *Soft Money* to get pictures of me philanderin' with naked interns. Which is how come you happened to be out where you could find me."

Murphy nodded. "In a nutshell. As a favor to Ramsey MacLeod."

Bub thought about this. "So I suppose I owe my life to Ramsey MacLeod. A guy I've spent the last coupla months basically comparin' to Satan. Good. Perfect. That helps sort everythin' out. The guy who's supposed to be runnin' my campaign instead takes me out on his yacht and has me shoved overboard, and the guy who's runnin' against me instead winds up savin' my ass."

Murphy wrote on a notepad: *"Soft Money,"* and underneath it he wrote: "F. LaGrange." He tapped his pen on the paper. "What exactly was the point of going out the other night?"

Bub snorted. "To throw my ass overboard!"

"No. I mean, the ostensible reason. What he told you when he called."

"Oh. Strategy session," Bub said. "Go over the latest pollin'. Figure out the final week's schedule. Never got to any of that, though. They pretty much threw my ass overboard straight off. Had a coupla beers and sayonara."

"Who did?" Murphy asked again.

"Well, all of us, I guess. We were all drinkin' beers," Bub said.

Murphy shook his head. "No. *Who* threw you overboard?"

Bub shrugged. "I don't know."

"No idea at all?"

"I got pushed in the back on a dark night. Now, how am I s'posed to know who done it?"

Murphy drew a line back and forth underneath *"Soft Money"* on his notepad, decided to try one more time: "You know, we could call Channel Nine in Orlando right now. They've got a bureau in Cocoa Beach. You come out, explain what happened, and boom, Percy's candidacy is over before it starts."

Bub sat silently, arms folded.

"I know," Murphy said. He had already tried going down this path, to no avail. "You don't want to do that. You care to tell me why?"

Bub glanced up at the deckhead, then out a porthole. "A man's got his pride, Murph. It's bad enough I gotta see myself as a victim, let alone for everybody else to see me that way. Besides, it'd be my word against Farber and his minions. Everybody'd think I was a total nut. They'd ask, 'Why on God's green earth would the party chairman want to knock off his own candidate for?' And all I'd be able to do is shrug and look stupid. No, sirree, Bob. Please, can we try it my way? There's gotta be somethin' hinky behind this, right? We just find out what it is, get it out in the open, and Farber and Percy lose without the whole world knowin' I'm a sap."

Murphy considered this awhile. "All right. Forget about the pushed overboard part. How about this: We drive over to the Coast Guard station right now, have the TV and newspapers meet us there, and tell the world that I happened to pick you out of the Gulf Stream and you're grateful and lucky and ready to hit the trail again. I figure by now you'd get an eight-point bounce in the polls." Murphy tilted his head and bit his lower lip. "Of course, Ol' Secretary Big Boobs just replaced you on the ballot. We'd have to sue to get you back on there. But surely the state Supreme Court will see it our way."

Bub perked up. "You think they would?"

"Well, maybe not. Anytime you try to undo the discretionary decision of an elected officer, you're looking at an uphill fight. But we'd definitely have the court of public opinion on our side." Murphy fell silent a moment, blew out a breath. "Of course, we're ignoring the fundamental issue of your party chairman disliking you to the point of having you killed, aren't we? I'd call that pretty desperate stuff, even for Florida. Which means we can't rule out the possibility they'll try again."

Bub looked up. "You think they would?"

Murphy took a deep breath before answering. "Honestly? I can't think of a good reason why they *wouldn't*. If they were desperate before, they'll probably be even more desperate when they find out they failed. We could get you security out the yin-yang. You know, Secret Service–caliber stuff. It'll cost a bundle, but your campaign can afford it. Plus it's just you, by yourself. It would be a whole hell of a lot harder if you were married with kids, the logistics of it all."

Bub blinked, opened his mouth to speak, closed it again and then thought for a long minute. "You know, Murph, the more I think about it, the surer I am I wanna do it the way I originally said. Lay low, figure things out, then get it all out in the open in the days before the election. I wanna be governor, sure. But I don't want it bad enough to take a sniper's bullet in the head." He nodded decisively. "If we can make sure Percy loses, I think that right there oughta be enough to declare victory and go home."

Murphy tapped his pen on the notepad. "Well, I can't say I blame you. All right. We'll try it your way."

"Thank you," Bub said.

"Okay," Murphy sighed. "What time was this? That all this happened?"

Bub closed one eye, remembering. "I'm thinkin' it was maybe ten o'clock? About two hours after we left the marina. We were drinkin' beer, first up on deck, where they got all those winches."

"That would be the cockpit."

"Right, the cockpit. Then, after a while, we all went downstairs in the main room." Bub waved his hand around at *Mudslinger*'s interior. "Kinda like this, only bigger."

"The main salon."

"Right," Bub agreed. "So there we are, drinkin' beer in the main saloon. He had Heineken and Beck's. Me personally, I'm a Budweiser man. That or Miller. So I was havin' Heineken. I guess I was finishin' up my second one, which is about my limit, now that I'm a grown-up. Anyhow, I ask 'em where the bathroom is, and they tell me to go back upstairs and pee over the side like everybody else."

"Who is *they*?"

"They is Farber. He said if I used the bathroom there was all these valves and pumps I had to open and close, and it would be a lot easier if I went up top. It wasn't a big deal to me. I'd seen where the other fellas had been goin', up beside the mast, where them wires come down to the deck."

"The shrouds," Murphy said.

"Okay, shrouds. That's what Farber called 'em, too. He said be sure to hang onto the shroud. One hand for yourself, one hand for the boat, he told me." Bub grinned. "I thought of a dirty joke to say to that, but I kept it to myself. I been keepin' a lot of jokes to myself since I became a candidate, you understand."

"So you held onto the shroud, unzipped, did your business—"

"I did my business and was gettin' ready to tuck everythin' back in—"

"Wait," Murphy said. "When you were tucking back in, did you let go of the shroud?"

Bub blinked, thinking about it. "Yes, sir, I imagine I did. I didn't think about it till just now, but I guess I did let go of it. I didn't think much of it. I'd gotten used to the rhythm of the boat a little, how it moved with the waves. Anyhow, I had my sneakers against that little lip at the bottom, and my legs braced against those white wires that run between them short metal rods that go all around the deck—"

"Stanchions," Murphy said. "And the wires are called lifelines."

"I pretty much figured there'd be a name for 'em." Bub nodded. "So anyway, there I was, and the next thing is I get this shove, right in the small of my back, right here," he said, twisting an arm behind him. "And over I went. I managed to grab onto one of them stanchion things on the way down, and guess what it did? It came clean outta the deck, is what! I'm draggin' along in the water, holdin' onto this stainless-steel rod for about two seconds before it slips out of my hands. And that, sir, is all she wrote. When I got back up, the little white light at the back of *Soft Money* is already twenty yards off and pullin' away."

Murphy doodled on his notepad, drew the outline of a sailboat, a stick figure in the water behind it, arms outstretched. "When you went up top to pee, who else was on deck?"

Bub thought about the question for a second, then shook his head. "Nobody."

"Nobody? Who was driving?"

"Nobody," Bub repeated. "Farber'd set the autopilot."

Murphy blinked. "Autopilot. Where was his crew?" He watched Bub's blank stare. "Crew? The guys he pays to run his boat for him? They're about twenty-five years old, big muscles, wear matching golf shirts with the name of the boat stitched on them. They all got New Zealand accents."

Bub shook his head. "No. No one like that." Bub grinned. "Which maybe explains all of Farber's cussin' as we left the marina. He banged a coupla pilings, gettin' out. But it evidently was the rest of our's fault, somehow. Once we got out in open water he seemed to do okay. It wasn't like there was a whole lot of work. You know he's got electric winches? You push a button, and the thing turns all by itself. It's the damnedest thing. You watch them America's Cup races on TV, with those boys cranking those things for all they're worth, and here all Farber's gotta do is use his little pinkie."

Murphy licked his lips, tried again. "Okay. There was no crew on board. So who was?"

Bub pondered the question. It was, in various forms, about the fifth time Murphy had posed it.

"Come on, Byron," he coaxed. "Somebody pushed you overboard. It had to be someone on that boat. We're not going to get anywhere until you can remember who exactly was on *Soft Money* that night."

Bub thought another minute, shook his head. "I'm sorry, Murph. And, by the way, call me Bub. Everybody else does. I been meetin' so many dang people, I can hardly place a name with a face anymore. There was a total of seven, maybe eight people. I'm assumin' most of 'em were Party types, the way Farber was talkin' to 'em. There was his chief pollster, Fenton Greene. Him, I recognized. Coupla others from his unit. The media guy was there. The one who coordinates the ad buys. And the scheduler." He shook his head again. "Sorry. There were a coupla folks I just can't place. I know I shook hands with 'em, when I went aboard."

"What about Victory Hostesses? Any of those?"

"Nope. No girls at all. Well, I take that back. The scheduler is a girl."

He raised an eyebrow. "Although with that haircut, and that voice, I think maybe that's just a technicality, if you get my drift. Not that it makes any difference, far as I'm concerned. I believe in the big tent, and she puts together a damn fine schedule."

"How about donors?" Murphy asked. "Any rich contributors you were supposed to impress?"

"Nope. None of them, neither. Which makes sense, if the point was to toss me in the drink. Why have potential witnesses you can't control, right?"

Murphy shook his head in frustration. "Okay, forget *who* for a minute. Let's work on the why. *Why*, after getting you a big lead, after spending all that money, would Farber want to toss you overboard?"

Bub puffed up his cheeks, blew the air out. "Sailorman, I been thinkin' on that since the minute *Soft Money* disappeared into the night. Why? What did I do? And I'll tell you truly: I got no earthly idea."

"You didn't piss him off, somehow?"

"I'm sure I pissed him off a hundred times a day," Bub said. "Forgettin' an important contributor's name. Mispronouncin' a word off the TelePrompTer. Usin' the wrong fork for my salad."

"I mean something serious," Murphy said.

"I know what you mean. And I can't, for the life of me, imagine what it might be. Farber had every opportunity to pick Percy instead of me in the first place, way back in June. God knows Percy was lobbyin' him hard enough," Bub laughed. "Anyhow, he didn't pick Percy. He picked me. I polled better."

Murphy doodled a long, wavy line on his notepad, turning it into a facsimile of the Florida Atlantic coastline. He drew a circle off Cape Canaveral, a second one off Jupiter Inlet. "Well, if there's one thing we've learned, it's that you Republican governor wanna-be's just need to stay the hell away from the ocean."

Bub smiled and then blinked. "Why is that, Murph?"

He tapped at his drawing with his pen. "First Spencer Tolliver drowns on a fishing outing. Now you."

Bub blinked again. "Spencer? Spencer was runnin' for governor?"

"You didn't know? He was collecting pledges. Word was he was getting close to seven figures before his accident."

"Huh. I did not know that." Bub shook his head. "Ol' Spencer. Now there was one decent fella. Hell, I'da voted for him, if he was runnin'." Bub thought of something, looked up. "You suppose Farber killed him, too?"

Murphy tossed the pen down in frustration. "Don't we wish. Unfortunately, Spencer was fishing solo." He rubbed his temples, took a long, deep breath and tried to fathom Bub's dark brown, almost black, eyes. He licked his lips and shook his head: "A ten-minute press conference in front of a TV camera is all it would take. Go out and get the best security money can buy. File a lawsuit against Secretary Maybelline to get you back on the ballot."

"No," Bub said.

Murphy held Bub's gaze for a long minute, stood and stepped to the nav table. He lifted the top and removed three manila envelopes. "Okay, let's see if we can't hit this from another angle."

He sat back down and slid one of the envelopes to him. "I got this anonymously a few days ago." He waited for Bub to open it and start leafing through the pages. "Recognize any of those?"

Bub squinted at the faint lettering on the photocopied pages. "Northstar Consulting, Interlink, Southeast Marine . . . Ron-a-det Service? Whatever the heck that is. No, sir. Can't say I've ever heard of these outfits."

"They all gave the Republican Party an average half million dollars specifically for your campaign."

"Really? Huh. How 'bout that."

Murphy moved to the companionway ladder, sat on the third step, held onto the wooden handrails on the ceiling. "Yesterday I got on the Internet and found the one thing they have in common: They don't exist. Well, they exist on *paper*, in the Division of Corporations filings, but that's about it. No offices. No websites. No *products*."

Bub looked up in honest surprise. "I'll be damned. So you mean somebody created them for . . ."

"For the sole purpose of funneling you money," Murphy finished. "That's right. In that second packet in there; yeah, the one held together by that clip. There's a list of registered agents for all the companies that gave the Party money."

Bub set aside the first stack, picked up the second. "Toby Galloway, Earnest Briles, John Peterman . . . I'm sorry, Murph. I used to be good with names. Once I met somebody, I was able to remember that name forever. Now, I been meetin' so many folks of late, the names been goin' in one ear and right out the other. I just had this goofy grin the whole time, no idea what I'm sayin', meetin' and greetin', pressin' the flesh, thankin' 'em for their support— Whoa . . ."

"What?"

"Clyde Bruno," Bub said. "Now, that name I do remember. For the life of me, though, I can't think of why."

Murphy stepped forward, leaned over Bub's shoulder to look at the page he was studying. A powerful odor hit him suddenly and he took a step back. "Phew-eeee," he said softly.

Bub made a face, stuck his nose down toward his armpit. "I'm right there with ya, buddy. I know. If I don't bathe at least twice a day, I get quite the aroma goin'. I need to hit the showers. Maybe I'll go do that right now. Maybe it'll come to me, about that name, why it's— Aha! Now I remember," he said triumphantly. "Clyde Bruno was the purchasin' agent at Leisure American, that catalog place up in South Carolina. They're my biggest customer. I met him once, way back when I was startin' the company. That first order of his, man, it made my first year."

Murphy took the piece of paper from him. "So he's an employee of the company that jump-started your business. Then he happens to turn up as the registered agent of Goodkind and Sams, which in turn happens to be the agent for at least two dozen companies that are funneling millions of dollars into your campaign."

Bub scratched his three-day scruff. "Where we headed here, Hoss?"

Murphy sat down at the table to think. "Farber decides to have his front-runner candidate in the governor's race knocked off. Why? Well, the obvious answer is that maybe your poll numbers were slipping. Maybe the other side was catching up."

"You think so? I thought I was doin' great," Bub said, a little hurt.

"You were," Murphy said. "I was just being rhetorical. That's the other bit of research I did yesterday. I hacked into the Party's intranet and checked their latest internals. You were up by fourteen, up two in the previous week. Three-point-five sampling error."

Bub let this sink in. "So I was winnin'. In fact, I was openin' up on my lead. But Farber wanted me out anyway. I see your point. Okay, so where do we start?"

Murphy reached on a shelf behind the nonfunctioning radio to grab a AAA book of maps for the Southeast. "Remember what Deep Throat told those reporters about Nixon?"

"Follow the money," Bub said.

Murphy nodded, grabbed his car keys. "Let's go."


Against the night glow of downtown Jacksonville across the St. Johns River, the largest petroleum tank farm in the state appeared as a series of squat, dark silos on the horizon. There were twenty-two, total, arranged in rows with common piping to accept and dispense via both river and highway, with each containing thirty million gallons of gasoline meant for distribution to Northeast and Central Florida.

Because of the summer-long problems at refineries in Louisiana, the tanks were only half full, with trucks continually filling up to satisfy the unquenchable thirst of six million residents and their seven million automobiles, pickup trucks and SUVs.

As supplies had shrunk, though, profits had held steady, with prices at every level rising to make up for the diminished volume. The tank farm's operator, Suwannee Southern, in fact was expecting a convoy of trucks from the Midwest to deliver two hundred million gallons to take advantage of Florida's three-dollar-a-gallon prices.

The decision had created some dissension within the ad hoc cartel that controlled the state's gasoline distribution. Producer Petron had quietly tried to dissuade Suwannee Southern from bringing in any outside gas, at least until mid-November. Suwannee, partially owned by competing oil producer Mobil, had refused.

Beyond the weed-covered lot, a freighter loaded with Nissans slid slowly westward along the river toward Jaxport, the main commercial shipping dock. As it approached a bend in the channel, it emitted a warning blast on its horn.

Almost simultaneously, a white light flared in a small building that housed the controls to the tank farm's piping network. Another flared at the base of the tank nearest the river. Within seconds, the four tanks beside the water exploded in a hot, bright *whoosh* that blew out the windows and set off the car alarms of every Sentra, Maxima and Pathfinder on the deck of the freighter.

And seconds after that, the explosions and fires spread to every tank at Suwannee's cyclone-fenced facility.

Soon the wailing of fire engines competed with the car alarms, as trucks and men from a dozen companies converged upon the scene. And as the sirens warbled and the horns blared, no one paid much attention to the dark blue Karmann Ghia with the personalized tag "BLCKTIP" and a longboard strapped to the roof that pulled out from a side road and drove the speed limit in the opposite direction.

★ (**4**) ★

FARBER LAGRANGE STEPPED OUT of the elevator into the penthouse suite of what had been the Floridians for a Better Future, but which days earlier had instantly transformed into the Percy Billings for Governor headquarters. His massive brow creased as he took in the big Percy Billings for Governor banners, the giant Percy Billings for Governor yard signs, the simply enormous Percy Billings for Governor four-color posters.

"Farber! I'm so glad you came."

Farber grunted, pulled his hands out of Percy Billings's grip. "Uh-huh. I'll bet. Where can we talk?"

Percy led the way past dozens of campaign workers, each decked out in Percy Billings for Governor regalia, from the ordinary T-shirts, buttons and hats to the more novel suspenders, ties and cowboy boots.

"I call it Percy Gear," Percy said, opening the door to his corner office.

Farber grunted again, walked over to the picture window overlooking Marco Island and the Gulf. "Shut the door, please."

Percy complied, waited for Farber to speak, finally moved forward to the window and saw the big Grady-White sportfisherman entering the cut that had captured the party chair's attention. "It belongs to Rupert McMahon. The director of Southwest Fidelity? I can get you out on it, if you—"

"I know Rupert. The boat's called the *Tiffany III*. He's on his third wife, too. Every one of 'em named Tiffany. I suspect it's a job requirement. Not that there's anythin' wrong with that. He writes us good, solid checks. Checks with five zeros in 'em." He turned and sat at Percy Billings's desk. "I never been up here before. Nice digs."

Percy nodded. He stood slightly hunched out of deference. "Thank you, Farber. That means a lot, coming from you. As Aquinas wrote in *Summa Theologica*—"

"Much nicer digs than they got up in the Capitol, you understand. Yeah, it's a corner office, but it's on the ground floor. Any snot-nosed kid that wants can press his face up to the window, see what you're doin'."

Percy straightened to full height. "I understand, Farber. And I want to tell you that I'm ready for the challenge." He blew out a half laugh. "And it's not the size of the office, or where it is. It's the responsibility, and serving the people. And, Farber? I just want to thank you, personally, for turning to me when, you know, it became obvious you needed—"

"Aw, can it," Farber growled, leaning back in the tan leather chair. "I got a hunch I know how come ol' Link Thresher soured on your brother as fast as he did. But what the hell. It's not like I give a rat's ass who lives in the Governor's Mansion so long as they got a capital 'R' after their name."

Percy swallowed silently, said nothing.

"Now, you do understand what it is our benefactor requires, correct?"

Percy pretended not to understand, finally nodded his head ever so slightly. "Florida gets a new state motto: A day without Gulf of Mexico crude is like a day without sunshine."

"Good. I'm gettin' tired of re-jiggerin' the whole damn shootin' match for a new candidate." He reached into his back pocket, slowly unfolded a sheaf of papers and put on a pair of reading glasses. "Got our first poll numbers back. Thought you might be interested."

Percy Billings took a visitor's seat across his own desk, leaned back, tried to relax. "I'm glad you brought those. I'm curious to see how the new ad is doing. I really like it. It's solid, a good biographical—"

"Ramsey MacLeod forty-nine, Percy Billings thirty-nine, undecided twelve. Six hundred forty-one likely voters over two nights, three-point-five sampling error." Farber LaGrange looked over the top of his glasses. "How you like them apples?"

Percy shook his head, blinked, reached for the sheaf of papers. "There must be some mistake. Perhaps these don't reflect the new ad? Surely that's it. It's only up in four markets right now—"

"Percy Billings, you big, dumb shit. What are you, book smart and people dumb?" He watched Percy's face, utterly blank as he read the poll results for himself. "You don't get it, do you? The people of this state genuinely *liked* your brother. You may not understand it, or maybe you're too jealous to understand it. Remember Ronald Reagan? Not exactly the brightest bulb on the porch, but folks didn't care 'bout that. He knew how to talk to 'em. Could connect with 'em."

Farber rose to go stand in front of the window again, peered down to where the Grady-White had tied up at a fuel dock. A guy in a red ball cap and shorts was waving his arms, describing something to a passerby onshore. Finally the guy reached down into a giant ice chest, lifted out a long, skinny fish and, with some effort, held it chest high.

"Wahoo. Looks about fifty, sixty pounds, too. Damn fine eatin'." He turned to face Percy Billings, arms crossed. "Now you listen up, and listen up good. I ain't got time here to be teachin' Politics 101, okay? So here's the facts: The voters of Florida liked Bub. They evidently don't like you. How do I know this? The day we announced you were takin' his place, your numbers shot up almost as high as Bub's had been. 'Cause they initially assumed you, bein' his brother, would be similar to him in key respects. Then you start runnin' your ad tellin' everybody how smart you are and how you're gonna fix everythin', your ten-point plan for this and fifteen-point plan for that, and usin' all your bullshit management-seminar jargon about 'countability and measurin' outputs and all that crap, and suddenly, guess what? Ol' Ramsey MacLeod don't look so bad after all."

"That's not fair," Percy protested. "Ramsey MacLeod is pitching the same, tired ideas the Democrats have been pitching for years. The people want a change. One week is all I need. The ads *will* work, I promise you. . . ."

Farber glared until Percy sat back down. "Just shut up and listen, for once in your life, okay? Ramsey MacLeod is a damned fine administrator and a decent guy. He's just a lousy campaigner. And *that's* what we're takin' advantage of. So here's the game plan: From now until Election Day, I don't wanna see any more 'Percy Billings for Governor' crap. We're changin' it all to 'Billings for Governor.' I don't wanna see any more of your bio ad. We're gonna go heavy on the attack ads against Ramsey again, and any ad that happens to use footage of you has gotta have footage of your brother, too."

Percy slumped in his chair as Farber continued.

"I got a new slogan I expect to see on billboards, bumper stickers and yard signs around this state by the end of the day: 'Percy . . . for Bub's sake.'" Farber nodded slowly. "I think you're gettin' the pi'ture, finally. The I'm-the-smarter-Billings-brother shit ends, and the Bub-woulda-wanted-me-to-win shit begins."

Percy made a pained face, but Farber put up a hand as he began walking toward the door. "Don't wanna hear it. This is what the people want, and this is what we're gonna give 'em." He pulled open the door and leaned back for a final word. "Remember: You're a humble substitute for your brother. Nothin' more. Nothin' less. Now, if you'll excuse me, I gotta fly back to Cocoa Beach and deal with ol' Sec'tary Highbeams."

The views from the VIP suite were to the north and west, where the late afternoon sun refracted into thousands of sparkles among the tiny wavelets that covered the surface of the Gulf forty feet below.

Link Thresher ignored the vista, concentrated instead on a large-scale relief model of the United States Gulf Coast, from the Dry Tortugas all the way around to Brownsville. In the offshore part, clear glass overlayed either blue, representing plain, useless seabed, or yellow, representing natural gas, or red, representing oil. The red actually ranged through several shades, from reddish-brown, representing heavy crude, to nearly orange, for light, sweet.

In Thresher's hands were half a dozen tiny oil rigs, similar to the hundreds already glued to the model off the coasts of Texas and Louisiana. He played with the plastic rigs, rolling them from one palm to the other as he bit his lower lip.

Finally, he glanced up with characteristic squint toward Clyde Bruno, who lay back in a leather recliner with eyes closed. "Loose ends bug me, Clyde, is all I'm saying. Whether it's lining up a vote on Capitol Hill or buying tribal leaders in a council of elders. If you ignore details, they come back and bite you in the ass."

Clyde Bruno sighed, eyes still closed. He'd spent the previous day arranging a flurry of new campaign contributions to the Florida Republican Party through the usual make-pretend cutouts. The day before that he'd quelled a labor dispute on a rig off Corpus Christi.

"Which loose ends in particular are bugging you, sir?"

"Well," Thresher continued, "I have yet to hear a satisfactory explanation of why it is that Bub Billings would live in a *rented* house. We know how much his business was making. Does it make sense he'd be renting?"

"Perhaps it's a second house," Clyde Bruno offered.

"With rented furniture?" Thresher shook his head. "No. Something's up. We found records showing the utilities were hooked up in his name there in June. Right after Farber picked him. Something's not right."

He shook the miniature oil rigs in his hands like dice, then rolled one out onto the model. It landed on Fort Walton Beach in the Florida Panhandle, and Thresher picked it up and moved it to the closest patch of orange. He planted a second rig over a finger of yellow off Cedar

Key, and then ran the remaining four in a strip of orange-red that ran offshore from Sarasota to Sanibel.

He glanced back up at Clyde Bruno and adjusted his horn-rims. "A grown man furnishing his house from Rooms-to-Go bugs me, Clyde. You know what it says to me? Mistress." He tilted his head to get a slightly different perspective on his model, then adjusted the position of the rig off Port Charlotte a hair to the east. "A mistress here could kill us."

"Sir, he wasn't married," Clyde Bruno explained. "How could he have had a mistress?"

"You know what I mean. Love nest. Married lover. Something bad. Something that could bite us in the ass, if she starts asking questions." He looked from the model, satisfied. "Check into it, would you?"


**M**urphy Moran drove the MG northward through the night, trying to remain two hundred yards behind the big tractor-trailer.

He eased off the accelerator on hills, put his foot back down in the flats. Beside him, Bub kept up a running commentary, stopping only occasionally to munch from a bag of Orange Milano cookies.

"My furniture goes all over the country, not just the Southeast," Bub said. "But my advertisin' people tell me I got a name now: Lawn Furniture King of the Southeast. I can't rightly call myself the Lawn Furniture King of America. Least not yet anyway. And in terms of image, it's better to be the biggest fish in a medium-sized pond than an average old fish in a big pond. Know what I mean?" He removed an empty paper tray, crumpled it, and reached in to get a cookie from the next layer. "It's a lot like politics, I reckon. Image is every bit as important as substance. Maybe more important."

Murphy glanced over at him. Beneath the sodium lights of a passing rest stop, he made out a scattering of white in the reddish whiskers sprouting from his chin. "You have crumbs in your beard," Murphy announced.

"I do?" Bub ran his hands through the week-old growth. "Now, Murph, you never warned me how much itchin' and scratchin' would be involved with this look."

Bub had been on his way up the companionway steps with a throw-away razor when Murphy had had a brainstorm: Leave the beard alone and shave your head. That way no one would recognize you. So far, through three Burger Kings, two Quick Marts and a half dozen toll-booths, Murphy had been correct. No one had registered a glimmer of recognition, in one case even as a television in a corner happened to broadcast a clip of the old, curly-haired, clean-shaven Bub while the new bald and bearded Bub stood at the pay phone, making one of his se-cretive, twice-daily phone calls.

"The price we pay for anonymity." Murphy stroked his own beard. "Besides, after a few months, you get used to it and it doesn't itch so much." He glanced beside him again, saw Bub stick another cookie in his mouth. "You going to eat *all* of those?"

Bub offered him the open bag. "Why? You want one?"

Murphy turned back to the truck ahead, a massive gray affair covered with road grime and slanted block letters: "Piedmont Transport." They had been following it for nine hours now, ever since it had left Bub's fac-tory in west Cocoa that afternoon, in an attempt to pick up on the high-ways the trail they'd lost on paper. According to corporate records, the main office for outdoor products catalog Leisure American was in Scottsdale, Arizona, not Greenville, South Carolina. A subsequent phone call ascertained that no Clyde Bruno had ever worked there. And so they'd camped in Murphy's rattly, 1974 MG, waiting for the truck bear-ing Leisure American's latest manifest to rumble out toward I-95.

"I'm trying to lose five pounds," Murphy said finally.

"I *did* lose five pounds," Bub answered. "And I'm fixin' to get 'em back." He crunched another of the cookies. "You know, I'm surprised nobody's tried to market that as a crash diet yet. Hypothermia and ex-haustion, with a side of high fever."

He finished the last cookie, crushed the paper-and-foil bag and tossed it in a grocery sack he had hung from the back of Murphy's seat as a litter bag. He glanced around in the back seat, ran a hand across the inside of the vinyl top. "Nice wheels you got, Sailorman," he said with a nod. "Lots of character."

"That's right," Murphy agreed. "That's what you want in a car. Character and a leaky crankcase." He glanced over his shoulder to change lanes so he could pass a horse trailer, then slid back into the right lane behind the truck. "I can't wait to go sailing so I can get rid of it."

"Well, Bubba, I'm right there with ya about leakin' oil. Filthy stuff. At least, on land, you can get at it and clean it up. In the water? Forget it. I remember workin' a rig off of Sabine way back when, seemed we leaked as much oil as we shipped out. Me, the young buck, goin' up to the foreman, tellin' him about a bad valve putting a long slick out in the Gulf. Him givin' me the hairy eyeball. Dirty, nasty stuff." Bub paused, considering. "Although, it does occur to me that you could probably get your car fixed, no? 'Stead of carryin' around a little drip pan everywhere?"

"You don't think I've tried? It evidently cannot be done. Never buy a British car, Bub. Not unless you want something that leaks a quart of oil a month as a normal function."

Bub laughed. "Heaven is where the mechanics are British. . . ." He blinked in the darkness. "No wait, I'm tellin' it wrong. *Heaven* is where the mechanics are German, the policemen are British, the lovers are Italian, the cooks are French and the whole thing is run by the Swiss. *Hell* is where the policemen are German, the cooks are British, the mechanics are French, the lovers are Swiss and the whole thing is run by the Italians."

Murphy laughed with Bub. "That's a good one."

"I didn't make it up," Bub confessed. "I saw it on a postcard, in Spain. In Ibiza, actually. You know the Spanish pronounce it ee-*bee*-tha? With a 't-h' sound? It's true. They got that lisp thing goin' for their *S*'s and their *Z*'s."

"You were in Ibiza?" Murphy asked. "I want to sail there, someday."

"Boy, howdy, is it ever some party town," Bub said, shaking his head. "I spent a whole summer there. I still can't remember it." He paused a moment, still shaking his head. "Yessir. One whole summer. Bummin' around, drinkin', findin' all the good parties. Hittin' all them beaches where the women walk around damn near naked."

Murphy smiled to himself. "This after college?"

"Actually, it was more like between college. I kinda took a few years off between my sophomore and junior years. Spent Granddaddy's trust fund. I like to refer to it as round one of my young and irresponsible years. You may have heard of those. There was a long article about 'em, one time."

"Ah, yes," Murphy remembered. *Vanity Fair* had done a piece about the Billings political dynasty in Florida, and how Percy would be the natural choice to follow in his father's footsteps, and how Bub, because of a somewhat checkered history, would have trouble under any sort of prolonged media examination.

"I tell you, that magazine got one part of it exactly, right on the head. I had fun when I was growin' up. Percy didn't. Right there, that more or less explains everythin' that's happened since. That, and the fact I got a dimple and he doesn't."

Murphy said nothing. He had noticed that the few times Bub seemed at all upset was when he saw or heard a campaign ad for his brother. In the last day, Percy had put up a new biographical spot that in particular seemed to get Bub steamed. Apart from that, Bub seemed completely at ease with no longer becoming governor, so long as his brother didn't, either. Murphy didn't fully understand it, but had decided he didn't need to.

"Actually, young Percy's major objection with me was the fact that Daddy continued lovin' me even though I was a screwup. You know, that whole prodigal son thing. It offended Percy's sensibilities. He had the idea that a father's love oughta be proportional and quantifiable, based on the behavior of the child." Bub considered this a long minute. "We're kinda an odd family, I guess. I sometimes wonder what it woulda been like if Daddy'd been an ordinary guy. If he'd had more time to spend with us. If he'd been less a famous statesman and more a guy to wrestle on the floor with. Maybe Percy woulda done better with somebody like that."

Murphy sat in uncomfortable silence. He'd grown up thinking of Lamont Billings as nobility and virtue personified, the governor who sacrificed his future to bring racial integration to Florida. It was somehow . . . voyeuristic to hear about his shortcomings as a father. He stretched his frame in the little sports car, twisting his shoulders to the left, then the right.

"If you're gettin' a crick, I can take over behind the wheel again next time our fearless leader takes a break," Bub offered, then nodded toward the windshield. "In fact, looks like that might be sooner rather than later."

Ahead, the tractor-trailer's right-hand turn signal was blinking, and Murphy slowed and began easing toward the exit. He followed the truck as it turned north on a two-lane highway, then fell back farther twenty minutes later as it turned east down a smaller access road. Then he stopped in front of a dimly lit sign in front of a tall fence. "What did you say the name of your company's best customer was?"

"Leisure American," Bub answered.

The sign read: "Carolina Resins" in big cursive letters. Below it, in smaller block letters: "A Division of Leisure America."

"What do you think? Leisure American, Leisure America. Coincidence?" Murphy asked, then put the MG into gear and followed the road over a rise and pulled over.

Bub stared over his shoulder at the back of the sign, then snapped his fingers. "Carolina Resin! They're my biggest supplier," Bub hissed.

The two wordlessly climbed from the car, walked through some tall grass toward a clump of trees, through which they could see where the tractor-trailer had parked: at a loading dock in front of a hangar-like building of corrugated aluminum lit by randomly placed floodlights. From their vantage point, they could see quite clearly the conveyor belt running from the open payload bay of the truck and up a slight incline into a giant hopper, over which hung a cloud of white dust.

With only the screech of cicadas as competition, the crunching noise of the pulverizer was plenty loud enough to hear even at their distance, and Murphy and Bub watched and listened openmouthed as workmen quickly and efficiently unloaded an entire truckload of Bub's Fine Lawn Furniture and ground it into its original plastic.

Murphy shook himself free first and dragged Bub, still catatonic, back to the MG for the long drive back to Florida.

*Soft Money* punched easily through a small sea, upwind on a starboard tack. Every available bit of cockpit coaming and cabin trunk was occupied by a Victory Hostess in a varying state of undress. Every Victory Hostess was occupied with one, sometimes two, drunken donors, each attempting with varying degrees of subtlety to grope one or more exposed portions of Victory Hostess anatomy.

Farber LaGrange surveyed it all with a grin, keeping his head nodding slightly as one drunken contributor after another approached him to compliment his boat, his girls or both. The outing was already the most successful to date, raising $420,000 in the first two hours. A quick count showed him that nearly half his girls still had their tops on, which meant that total would more than likely double before he had to turn around and head back in.

About the only negative aspect had been Clarissa Highstreet's appearance at the dock with three hard-sided suitcases. He quickly explained to her that Link Thresher had had to cancel, but she was undeterred, insisting that she come anyway, that she needed a nice day on the water to unwind. He had grudgingly given her the owner's cabin.

"So what's a boat like this run?"

Farber brought his eyes to focus on a stocky, red-cheeked donor holding a cheap cigar in one hand and a martini in the other. The owner of a third-tier alligator attraction in Kissimmee. Gator Universe, if Farber remembered right. One where fake Seminole Indians wrestled toothless bull gators, and tourists could, for five dollars extra, toss a plucked chicken into the pit at feeding time.

Farber winked. "If you gotta ask . . ."

"You can't afford it," the alligator man finished. "Touché." He took a sip of his drink and glanced around, fixing first on a blonde in a yellow thong, then on a long-haired brunette in a slinky one-piece. "So which of these honeys would you recommend, you know, for the hot tub experience?"

Farber was about to answer "all of them," when on the opposite side of the mast he noticed a donor, a Lexus dealer from Miami, pulling his swim trunks down and leaning up against the lifelines and grabbing the port shrouds.

"Hey! No peein' off my boat!" Farber shouted, warily watching the stanchion beneath the Lexus dealer edge out of its support bracket. "Go below and use the head!"

He glared until the guy had pulled his trunks back up and headed down the main hatch, which was how he noticed the lacquered hairdo squeezing past on its way up. Clarissa Highstreet's permanent smile glanced around the aft deck, then settled on him as she climbed the remaining steps in high heels and emerged onto the teak planking.

Farber could only stare. She wore a gold lamé swimsuit constructed of strategically positioned triangles and shiny string. The back, Farber saw when she half turned, was entirely shiny string.

"What do you think?" she asked in a sultry tone, spinning all the way around for him. "You like?"

Farber eyed the rock-hard buttocks, then remembered the articles about the semiannual liposuction treatments. "Hubba hubba," he said.

Her smile widened and she tucked a section of hair the wind had loosened behind an ear. "Maybe a little later I'll show you what else I've got. But first I wanted to run something past you. It's about the ambassadorship." She shifted her weight from one foot to the other, and Farber winced, feeling the dimples her stiletto heels were leaving in the teak as if it were his own skull. "I hired a real estate agent in France, and he suggested it might be wise to buy *two* residences. One in Paris, of course, but one along the Riviera. He said summers in Paris are just *dreadful*, and besides: *Nobody* who is anybody stays in Paris during August."

She shifted her weight to the other foot, and Farber winced again. "I almost told him to go ahead and get a summer place, too, when I stopped and thought: Now how is this going to play in the media? I mean, I can just *see* them making a big deal out of it, implying like I've done something wrong. Don't you agree?"

He stared in pained silence at her pampered feet, each toenail perfectly shaped and painted gold, to match her swimsuit. "You know, Clarissa, as pretty feet as you got, you really think you need to be wearin' high heels all the time? I mean, look around at the other girls. You gotta admit they all look pretty sexy, too. And they're all barefoot."

"None of *them*," Clarissa Highstreet said acidly, "has calves like I do. Now, back to my problem. I was wondering if maybe you couldn't help me out with the summer home with party money. Surely the press can't make a big stink out of just the Paris residence, can they?"

She transferred weight again, this time with the side effect of shifting one of the golden triangles and revealing half of a bright pink aureole. Farber stared at it, then saw that Mr. Gator Universe was staring, too, and suddenly more than staring, reaching into a pocket for a tube of sunscreen, squeezing a gob onto his palm and reaching for Clarissa Highstreet's exposed breast.

"Hey, baby! Don't want to sunburn that, do we—"

The slap reverberated like a gunshot, and Farber winced again, this time in empathy for Gator Universe man. He had gone down hard with the blow to the face, and Clarissa Highstreet had immediately commenced kicking him in the groin.

"I am *not* a quote Victory Hostess unquote, understand?" She kicked him again, hard, and got a groan in response. "*I* am the secretary of state of the state of Florida! I am the chief elections officer and the chief cultural officer! I am a voting member of the Florida Cabinet! I, with my colleagues, can grant clemency at any time. *I* have the power of life and death. . . ."

Farber slipped away quietly, mentally deducting Gator Universe's twenty-five grand from the day's haul.


**W**ith enthusiastic rock music still blasting behind him, Percy Billings made his way back toward the campaign bus. He kept the semblance of a smile on his face as he shook hands, signed autographs and kissed babies. He adopted the appropriate graciousness whenever folks offered their condolences.

It was making him sick, and he needed a stiff drink. For the past hour he had listened to the various civic leaders of Dover, Florida, home of the world's largest Strawberry Research Center, suck up to his dead brother. His dead, dumb brother. And then, when it was his turn, *he* had sucked up to his dead, dumb brother.

As per Farber LaGrange's instructions, the campaign had taken a complete one-eighty. Instead of listing his own accomplishments, Percy now lauded brother Bub's homespun wit. Instead of explaining what he would do if elected, he imagined what Bub might have been able to do if that sudden squall hadn't so tragically swept him away.

It was sappy, sentimental mush. And it was working. The first overnight polls showed a clear three-point bump. They were expecting a ten-point swing by week's end and, based on audience reaction at the campaign events, Percy had no reason to doubt it. Which meant, yet again, even in death, his brother was proving that he was the more popular Billings.

All of which was serving to exacerbate the unmistakable feeling that had started bubbling up more and more often in recent days. It was, he could not deny, guilt, and he was no longer able to suppress it.

Every time he heard someone mention Byron's name, it burbled up in his throat, making him feel awful all over again. Certainly, he had known through the months of plotting that he would have to cope with some of this. He had, there was no getting around it, committed fratricide, an activity of which the Lord took a dim view. He had fully expected there to be some issues he would have to work through. He just had not expected them to be quite so painful.

Well, so be it, he decided as he moved slowly across the community center parking lot toward the Billings for Governor bus, decorated in black bunting now to take advantage of Bub's never-higher approval ratings. Byron, and what he had been forced to do to him, that would be his cross to bear, and he would bear it like a man. Once he was in the

Governor's Mansion, he would slowly but surely leave his mark. He would conduct Cabinet meetings with an intellect and sophistication never before seen in Florida. He would work the legislature with a firm yet fair hand, leadership that every editorial board in the state would grudgingly have to admit was the most visionary since, well, his dad.

And then, finally, as he finished his first term and started running for reelection, someone, somewhere in Florida, would become the first to declare that only through the dumb luck of an autumn thunderstorm had Florida been delivered the better Billings brother, the one they should have chosen on their own in the first place.

And he would be vindicated, at last getting the respect he had been due all along, and finally, *finally,* the terrible burden of what he had done would be lifted, replaced with the knowledge that it had happened for the best, that in this case, maybe, the ends really had justified the means, that—

"I just *loved* your brother!"

A hot flash of anger crossed his face as he turned to find a tiny, white-haired granny. She wore a wide straw hat decorated with American flags and a glossy campaign photo of Bub. Percy willed his fists to unclench and accept the folded-up newspaper page advertising the day's rally.

"So did I," he said, forcing a smile as he autographed the ad in a big scrawl.

"Win it for Bub!" the old lady shouted as he walked away.

Percy increased his speed toward the bus. He *definitely* needed a drink. A great, big glass of Glenlivet. He had a good hour until the next appearance at a Wal-Mart in St. Cloud. A couple of Altoids would do the trick, when it came time to go stand next to the village idiots while they praised his brother.

Yup, a great big glass of Glenlivet was calling his name from the back of the motorcoach. He reached out for the handrail at the entrance when he heard a faint groan, then a smack, then a louder one.

He slipped away from his entourage and ducked behind the idling bus, then watched solemnly as his favorite outside consultant to the Party's Goon Squad beat the living daylights out of a protester wearing a pin-striped suit covered with dollar bills to symbolize the special-interest money the Billings campaign was getting. With each smack, a few more dollar bills flew off and floated to the pavement.

Percy watched as Clyde Bruno picked the protester up and heaved him onto the hood of a car. Both men looked nervously around them, then up at the tinted glass windows of the campaign bus, before meandering over to the shade of a kiosk plastered with notices advertising the health and culinary benefits of Florida strawberries.

"Democratic agitator?" Percy asked, nodding at the still-prone protester.

"Common Cause, or some such shit." Clyde Bruno rolled his sleeves back down, picked his suit coat off a bench. "What's up?"

"Got two safety deposit keys yesterday," Percy said.

"And? You find what you were looking for?"

"Stack of papers. Trustee documents. Not what I was looking for. Seek, and ye shall find. Easy for Matthew to say." Percy took a deep breath. "You're *sure* he wasn't wearing it, that night?"

Clyde Bruno tugged at his shirt sleeves to get the proper half inch. They'd been through this several times already. "I'm sure."

*"Positive?"* Percy insisted.

"Positive." Clyde Bruno nodded at the bus. "I think they're getting ready to pull out. See you in St. Cloud?"

Percy nodded disconsolately, walked back around to the entrance as Clyde climbed into a rented Sebring and roared out of the parking lot. Percy patted the bus driver's shoulder reassuringly, then made his way backward, past a clutch of Victory Hostesses fixing their makeup, past the various party flunkys talking self-importantly on cell phones. He glanced out the window, noticed idly that from the row he was passing on the bus, the body of the dollar-bill-covered protester was just barely visible.

In the seat by the window, raptly fixated on her laptop computer, was an attractive woman . . . Toni Johnson, he remembered with an effort. The Party's finance director. Percy looked back out the window, then back at her, when she startled him by looking up.

He flashed a nervous smile and quickly moved to the back of the bus and his private, wet-bar-equipped suite.

*Mudslinger* was a mess. Stacks of paper were on every square inch of horizontal surface, from the dinette table to the cushion on the port settee to the shelf of piloting books over the nav station. Even the steps of the companionway ladder were covered with paper from a variety of sources: documents from the state Division of Corporations spitting from the fax machine in the corner to printouts of Nexis searches emanating from a miniature printer beside the television, to the various missives from Murphy's secret pen pal.

Murphy sat in a pair of cutoffs on the starboard settee, playing with his beard and scowling at the screen of his laptop. At first glance it seemed frozen, but it was not really. It was just excruciatingly slowly downloading an extremely large attachment.

"Damn this dial-up bullshit," Murphy swore. "I should have signed up for the cable Internet. But *noooooo*. After all, I was only going to be here another two months, and there was that hookup fee, and what would I possibly need a fast connection for?"

Bub sat across from him, eyes still wide, palms flat on the dull wooden tabletop. "I'm a tool. A wholly owned subsidiary of Leisure America, whatever in hell that is." He shook his head slowly. "All these years, I was a self-made man. Pulled myself up by my own bootstraps, all that crap. Know how much of that bullshit I spread out on the campaign trail? Self-made man, my ass."

Murphy glanced up over the top of his reading glasses. "Come on, Byron. It's not that bad."

Bub snorted. "Easy for you to say. You ain't the invention of some multinational conglomerate."

Bub had fallen into the funk the moment he had recovered from the shock of seeing fifty-seven thousand dollars' worth of brand-new lawn furniture getting chewed back up into tiny bits so it could be melted and recycled back into four thousand dollars' worth of raw material.

"Unbelievable," Bub repeated, still amazed. "I buy plastic and make it into chairs. They buy the chairs and make it back into plastic. My company grosses fifty grand, nets twenty per load. One, sometimes two, loads a week, fifty-two weeks a year, five years. How much am I in for?"

Murphy tried to think of something to soften that analysis, but couldn't. It was dead on.

"And to what end? For this very thing, right? To have their boy in the Governor's Mansion. Get me elected, then come strollin' in someday with some outrageous demand."

Murphy flicked at the screen on his laptop in disgust. "Nope. Still coming in, whatever it is. If this turns out to be some bullshit junk mail, some get-rich-quick scheme or penis enlargement ad . . ."

That finally pulled Bub out. "What? Penis enlargement?"

Murphy turned to the nearest stack of papers, the ones they'd started to sort through when they'd returned from South Carolina. "Well, why are they still doing it, then?"

Bub blinked twice. "Doin' what?"

"Buying from your company, if all they were doing was propping you up so you would eventually run for governor. Well, now you're dead. Why keep buying from your company? What do they get out of it now?"

"Beats the hell outta me. Regular, ol' inefficiency? Us Republicans are always yappin' about runnin' the government like a business. I guess we need to start specifyin': like a *good* business." Bub moved a stack of papers to lay his head down on his hands, with a forefinger traced a water ring on the dinette table. "You know, on *Soft Money*, all the inside wood was varnished nice and pretty."

Murphy glanced up, annoyed, then returned to a thick annual statement he'd downloaded from the SEC website. "Great. You get me Farber's income stream, and I'll hire some people to do my teak."

"Didn't mean to criticize," Bub said understandingly. "And judgin' from some of your sailin' magazines, I appreciate there appears to be some level of disagreement among you folk over that whole varnish-versus-teak-oil thing, and far be it from me to get in the middle of *that* one. I'm just sayin', as a plain-speakin' man coming to this without any preconceived notions, that it appears, from an aesthetic point of view, anyhow, that maybe varnish holds its look for a longer period of time. And certainly downstairs, outta the sun—"

"Below," Murphy said.

"Pardon?"

Murphy held his place on the sheet of paper with his thumb, glanced up over his glasses. "'Below' is the word *us folk* use to describe the interior of a yacht. Not downstairs. If you're going to talk the talk, you might as well do it right." He saw Bub's look of contrition, waved a hand at him and began to massage his temples with his fingers. "Look, I'm sorry. I didn't mean to snap. We don't have much time and we need to figure this out. Let's run through real quick what we know and what we don't know."

Bub nodded. "Easy enough. This Clyde Bruno fella keeps showin' up in all these dummy corporations that funneled campaign money my way. There was also a Clyde Bruno once worked for my main customer. We ain't sure it's the same Clyde Bruno, but we're assumin' it is, particularly since it turns out my main customer is also my main supplier. And that right there's about the size of it. Somebody went through a whole world of trouble to make me an attractive Republican candidate. And then somebody, probably that same somebody, was payin' out the wazoo to make sure I won."

"And then, for whatever reason, the guy organizing your campaign decides to toss you overboard one night." Murphy put his reading glasses back on. "And, naturally, there's nothing in the public record anywhere about this Clyde Bruno or, for that matter, half of those companies." He picked up a sheaf of papers. "Carolina Resins, for instance. Privately held. One small article in the Greenville paper when it opened. How many jobs it would create, et cetera. That's it."

Bub stroked the hairs that were gradually thickening on his chin. "What if we leaked what we got? Sent out a bunch of packets with this about Clyde Bruno and Carolina Resins?"

Murphy snorted. "And depend on the media to do actual digging? Less than two weeks before an election? No way. We gotta connect the dots for them." He glanced up with a hopeful look. "Of course, if you've changed your mind about going public, well, that would throw a nice, fat monkey wrench in things, wouldn't it?"

Bub considered this awhile, took a deep breath. "I guess I ain't ready to do that."

"I kind of figured that," Murphy said.

"Leaves us at a dead end, don't it?" Bub asked.

The little Toshiba laptop chimed once, and Murphy pushed his glasses back up his nose and stared at the full-color picture that appeared beside the electronic dossier. "Well, perhaps not." He turned the computer so Bub could see it. "Look."

"Clyde Owen Bruno," Bub read. "Campaign consultant. Six thousand a month . . . What the hell? Who sent you that?"

Murphy scrolled to the top of the e-mail. "GOP-Gal seventy-three at A-O-L dot com, whoever that is. I'll give you odds it's the same person sending us all those financial documents. Confirms my hunch it's coming from within party headquarters, huh?"

"GOP-Gal seventy-three . . . You mean there're seventy-two other GOP gals at AOL?" Bub thought about that, muttered: "Wonder if they got some sorta chat room goin'."

Murphy studied the thin nose, the brooding eyes in the dark face. "Kind of looks like a Bruno, doesn't he? So is this him? The guy from Leisure America?"

Bub nodded. "Looks like a newer picture, but yup, that's him. So, what, he's a political consultant now? I'll be damned. Lawn furniture, right into politics. Who woulda thunk it possible?"

Murphy scrolled down the page, reading. "Interesting résumé. Look here: foreman at a coal mine in West Virginia, shipping company in Newark, oil refinery in Lake Charles, Louisiana. Looks to me like a journeyman management thug, no?"

"Good Republican right-to-work attitude," Bub said with a nod. "Kind of attitude made America strong."

"I thought it was the unions that made America strong," Murphy said, still reading.

"Well, one of them. Depends on the crowd you're talkin' to." He pointed to the screen. "What's this here?"

Murphy clicked the down arrow several times till the item was centered. "Seven Seas Resort, marina director, January through May this year . . . Whoa . . . wait a minute." Wide eyed, Murphy shuffled stacks of papers until he found what he was looking for. "Here it is: Leisure America Florida. DBA Seven Seas Resort!"

Bub read the sheet of paper, then the computer screen, then the sheet of paper again. "Help me out, Sailorman. I think maybe I'm fallin' a synapse or two behind, here."

"Seven Seas Resort," Murphy repeated, standing to grab the overnight bag he hadn't yet unpacked. He shut down the computer, threw on a golf shirt, stuffed wallet and car keys into his shorts. He reached up to pull the main salon hatch closed, twisted the two knobs to dog it tight. "May. Remember? A certain somebody died there? Drowned?"

Bub blinked twice, then a third time. "Tolliver!"


They crossed over onto Jupiter Island via the County Line Road bridge, then drove top-down along a narrow road lined with button-woods and palmettos. Little gravel driveways turned off the road periodically, and Murphy carefully kept to the thirty-mile-an-hour speed limit.

"Never been out here before," Bub said. "It's kinda pretty."

"It's kind of rich, is what it is," Murphy said. "Everybody knows about Palm Beach, but some of the oceanfront houses here give old three-three-four-eight-oh a run for its money."

Bub peered down one of the driveways as they passed, trying to catch a glimpse. "So ol' Tolliver was raisin' money here. I'll be a monkey's uncle. Shoot, I didn't even have any idea he was runnin', till you told me the other day."

Murphy glanced over at his passenger, then turned back to the road. "You didn't follow politics much before Farber drafted you, did you?"

Bub shrugged. "No."

"Didn't think so." Murphy slowed to check the name of a cross street, then sped back up. "Fact is, he was not only running, he was winning. He was popular, he had great statewide name ID. If he hadn't drowned on that little fishing outing, he'd be on the verge of being the next governor right now."

"I'll be damned," Bub said again, and then sat thinking for a long minute. "So Clyde Bruno not only worked for the company that subsidized my existence all these years, and then for the Party when it decided it didn't want me around anymore, but it also turns out he happened to work at the place where the original GOP front-runner happened to accidentally die. That death, by the way, givin' Farber the opportunity to recruit me to run instead." Bub puckered his lips, blew out a long breath. "You know, Murph, you don't need to be a big grassy-knoll kinda guy to see a conspiracy brewin' here, huh?"

Murphy said nothing, instead bore right when the road forked and narrowed, then turned sharply to the left and passed beneath a brick archway with a small brass sign reading SEVEN SEAS RESORT and, in smaller letters, MEMBERS ONLY.

He drove past the registration building, halfway around a manicured roundabout, and followed a small green-and-white sign that said MARINA, with an arrow pointing off to the right. Around another bend was a nearly empty brick parking lot in front of a building of weathered gray wood. On either side rose the masts of sailboats tied to the finger piers, and off to the north was a boat ramp and a storage shed. Everywhere there were flagpoles flying the Seven Seas Yacht Club burgee.

Murphy parked in a corner and they emerged from the convertible in time to see an older man in blue sportcoat and khakis escort two expensive-looking young ladies down a pier toward a ninety-foot motor yacht.

"Jesus," Bub said, examining their own shorts and T-shirts. "Don't know if we're quite dressed for this."

"Sure we are," Murphy said, grabbing a Tilley hat from behind his seat and adjusting it on his head. "We're so goddamned rich we don't care what we look like. Come on. It's all in the attitude. Here, put on your cap and sunglasses. You're incognito, remember?"

They strode with exaggerated self-assurance past the yacht club building and around to the main dock, from which sprouted the row of finger piers. Beyond a narrow channel was a thin mangrove island, on the other side of which opened up the Intracoastal.

Murphy said, "Past that marker is the channel for the inlet. Pretty shallow, real tricky in bad weather."

"That's just great, Hoss. I'll be sure to remember that," Bub said. "By the way, is there a game plan here at all?"

Murphy stopped at a fish-cleaning table overlooking a small turning basin. Three pelicans gazed at them lazily from atop their individual pilings. "Snoop around. Find out whatever we can before they throw us out." He motioned toward the fuel dock, where a young blond man in a buzz cut and a crisp Seven Seas Yacht Club golf shirt leaned against a counter in a shelter by the pumps. "Let's start with him."

The attendant glanced up as they walked down the fuel dock, appraised them head to toe with a look that said they had fallen woefully short. Murphy flashed a confident grin, leaned against the outside of the counter and nodded. "Afternoon."

The attendant nodded, glanced down to his paperwork and then back up at them. "Something I can help you with?"

"What do you need to get out of paying the road tax on diesel here?" Murphy asked.

The attendant sneered, turned back to his account books. "What you got?"

"Bertram 670. I'm figurin' I'll need about eight, nine hundred gallons." Murphy watched as the attendant lifted one eye. He let his grin widen a touch. "She's on her way up from Lauderdale."

The attendant, Chip, the embroidered name on his shirt said, shut the book and cleared his throat. "Well, sir, a copy of the Document will suffice."

"Just bought her," Murphy said. "Don't have the Document yet. But surely that's no reason to pay the government an extra hundred bucks, is it? Thanks, I gave at the office."

Chip shuffled some papers. "We can get you a transient membership here for twenty. Then the fuel is technically ours. No county or state road tax."

Murphy nodded knowingly and flipped out a Platinum American Express card. "Now we're talking."

Chip stuck his pen behind his ear and turned to his computer. "Let me just get you set up here. . . . You'll be needing a berth as well, sir?"

"I suppose I will, somewhere between here and Fort Pierce." Murphy turned with a squint out toward the Intracoastal. "Y'all have room?"

Chip checked a dry-erase board behind him that mapped out all ninety-two slips. "Let's see . . . a 670 is seventy feet overall, right? I can get you on the end of the T-dock. That sound okay? Let me get you preregistered."

Bub watched Chip dig through a drawer and pull out some forms. "You a College Republican, Chip?"

Chip handed Murphy the forms and his pen. "As a matter of fact, I am. At the community college. I'm an officer, in fact."

"Thought so," Bub said. "You got that College Republican sort of look."

Chip squinted at Bub. "You seem kind of familiar."

"Aw, shucks," Bub mugged. "Everybody says I'm the spittin' image of Robert Redford."

Murphy shot Bub a look and started filling out the papers. "There's a man I used to do business with, I believe, works here," he said. "If he's around, I'd love to buy him a drink. Clyde Bruno?"

"No," Chip said, still eyeing Bub, who had now moved down the dock. "Clyde hasn't worked here in months. I'm not sure where he's at now."

Murphy watched Chip watch Bub, cleared his throat. "That's too bad. Anyhow. Listen, while we're here, I'm wondering whether you all got any runabouts we can rent. If I wanted to go fishing on the reef without taking the big boat out."

"No. Sorry. Don't rent boats. There's plenty of captains in town that'll take you out on charter," Chip said.

"Huh," Murphy said. "Don't know why I thought you rented boats. . . . Yeah, I know why. Back earlier this year, when what's that fellow's name . . . Tolliver, that's it; Spencer Tolliver drowned while he was out fishing. I thought I remembered reading that was a rented boat?"

"It was a *borrowed* boat," Chip said. "Belonged to the state Republican chairman, who happens to be one of the founding members here. Lent him his gear. Gave him the coordinates to his favorite fishing hole on that reef, too."

On the other side of the mangrove island appeared the tuna tower of a big Hatteras. The VHF on the wall crackled to life, and Chip told the skipper the fuel dock was open and to tie up on the north side.

"It was old Farber's boat, huh," Murphy said when Chip had replaced the radio's microphone. "That figures. I wonder if it's still around. I bet Farber would let me use it. Christ, he better, with all the money I'm givin' him."

The suspicious look Chip had reserved for Bub now came Murphy's way. "When did you say your boat will be in?"

The Hatteras turned into the channel and honked twice as it approached the dock. Chip stepped out from behind the counter. "Excuse me while I take care of these folks."

Bub grabbed Murphy by the arm and started moving him up the dock. "We're gonna have a drink while we finish fillin' out your forms," he announced to Chip's puzzled look.

Murphy waited until they were out of earshot before he unloaded. "The hell were you doing with that College Republican crap?"

"College Republicans scare the bejeezus out of me," Bub confided. "They drive their daddy's Beamers and drink top-shelf liquor and wear ties and talk about welfare moms. You ever seen 'em at a rally? They're like Hitler youth!"

Murphy nodded. "Okay. Fine. You don't have to socialize with them anymore. But why'd you go and piss off Chip? I was so close to getting what we needed. And you come along and blow it."

"What? What were you close to gettin'?" Bub asked.

"The boat that Tolliver used. I wanted to know if it's still around here. If it is, I want to get a look at it."

"Well, what in hell you think I been tryin' to show you?" Bub stretched a finger at the aluminum shed by the boat ramp, at the transom of a Robolo sitting inside on a trailer. "*Soft Money Too*? Ain't that it right there?"

Murphy scrutinized the boat, first from the outside, then, with a quick look out the shed door, from within. He studied the steering console, the big Mercury outboard that was now tilted upward, the trim tabs. He got on his knees and searched the cockpit well.

Bub sat quietly on the driver's seat with sunglasses tucked in the V neck of his shirt. After some time, he cleared his throat. "Perhaps I can be of some assistance, if you tell me what exactly it is we're supposed to be lookin' for."

Murphy moved to the back of the cockpit, stood with hands on hips and stared forward. "Anything out of the ordinary."

"Good. That narrows it down considerably," Bub said.

Murphy moved to the front of the cockpit and stood looking aft. "Here we had a seasoned boater and a strong swimmer drown during a fishing trip. It wasn't his own boat, so that increases the chances for mistakes, true. But I still don't get it. He was within sight of land, for God's sake. And the boat was found in perfect condition that night."

Bub shrugged helplessly.

"You ever fish with Spencer Tolliver?" Murphy asked. "Well, I have. He was big on routine. Always did the same things, the same way. Said that way, if he caught something big, he'd be able to repeat it. He always used a leather harness to hold his rod. Yet he wasn't wearing it when they found his body the next day. Why?"

Bub shrugged again. "Maybe he was done fishin' for the day."

"Okay. But the boat was still anchored," Murphy said.

Bub scrunched his face up, looking around the inside of the boat. "Murph, I'm havin' a fundamental problem with one little detail. As you pointed out, he was all by himself. And if he was all by himself, then I don't see how somebody coulda pushed him over. Now, there's nobody rootin' for a conspiracy here more than me. But I just don't see it."

Murphy opened a storage locker, pulled out a hand bilge pump, two life vests and a coil of dock line. He surveyed the interior of the locker, was about to start replacing the items when he noticed the large tackle box with the engraved initials, SRT.

"Aha! This was Spencer's." He removed it from the locker, opened it and began picking through the lures. "I came up with one theory while we were driving down here: Tolliver had a habit of clipping his rod into his harness with a steel pin. I asked him about it one time he and Farber and I and a couple of others had gone after marlin off Bimini. Spencer joked that it wasn't really sportsmanlike if the man didn't have as much to lose as the fish. Actually, he just loved that rod of his, and didn't want to lose it overboard. Plus, if a big fish really did hit that hard, it would break the line before it could pull a grown man over the side."

Murphy took out a brand-new, polished spoon with a bright blue eye painted in enamel on top and bottom, studied it, then set it on the bench beside him. "Anyway, so I came up with this scenario: He's got some heavy line, like fifty-pound test. He's on the reef so he's looking for bottom fish. Instead, something big, a shark or maybe even a wahoo, hits, while at the same time, he happens to be off balance because of the rising seas. Okay, now he falls overboard and, with that heavy line, he gets dragged along by the fish until he drowns."

Bub considered this. "Well, if you're sellin' it, I suppose I could buy it."

"Only problem is that harness. It's not on this boat, and he wasn't wearing it when they found him."

Murphy fell silent as he went through the tackle box, and Bub began looking around the console, reached forward to press a button on a square LCD screen mounted in front of the steering wheel. He watched as a full-color chart appeared, with the boat's latitude and longitude appearing as a red icon. "Hey, now that's pretty cool," Bub said.

Murphy glanced up from the tackle box. "Electronic chart with a GPS interface. Hooks into your fishfinder, too. For boaters with more dollars than sense. Although I suppose if you're a world-class angler like Farber, the companies give them to you for free. For the endorsement value."

Bub pushed a button and a box appeared on the display. "What's a WP?"

"Waypoint," Murphy said, lifting out the top tray of the tackle box and studying the contents beneath. "It's a programmable lat-lon coordinate for navigation purposes. Like the location of a buoy or something."

"Or a fishin' hole," Bub remembered. "Twenty-nine and ten-point-seven, eighty-four and forty-two-point-one. That it?"

Murphy thought for a moment. "Can't be. We're at about twenty-seven by eighty."

"Oh. Well, how 'bout Way Point Two. Twenty-six and fifty-seven-point-eight by eighty and zero-one-point-nine," Bub read.

"Turn that off, would you? Otherwise we'll forget and they'll figure out we've been snooping around . . . hello!" Murphy lifted from the tackle box a 1950s vintage Penn reel, with a varnished wood winding handle. "Check this out. It's Spencer's favorite reel. It's the only one he ever used, except when he was fly casting. Which I doubt he was doing here."

Bub nodded, then shrugged. "Okay. So that means . . . what?"

"It means," Murphy said, "that he must have been using one of Farber's reels."

Bub nodded, then shrugged again. "Oh. So *that* means . . . what?"

Murphy shrugged, repacked the tackle box. "I don't know. Probably nothing. Farber always uses Petrene line because the company sponsors him. Frankly, I've never found much difference between it and Berkley or any other brand."

Bub switched off the chart display and swiveled in his chair. "Hey, speakin' about things outta the ordinary, you suppose those wires oughta be like that?"

Murphy followed Bub's finger to a junction box on the starboard wall adjacent to a piece of metal trim that ran the perimeter of the cockpit. Bub saw Murphy's dismissive look and threw his hands in the air. "You *said* anythin' out of the ordinary," Bub said. "I was just thinkin', with that wire as frayed as it looks, maybe the juice is running into that there metal strip . . . and if Spencer leaned against it while he was fightin' a fish, the shock mighta. . . . Well. It was just a theory."

Murphy tucked the tackle box back where he'd found it. "Unfortunately, even if that wire is frayed enough, it's still only carrying twelve-volt current. You can't get a shock from that. Here, watch." Murphy licked his finger and reached out to the metal trim. "That's why everyone uses twelve volt on boats. It's not nearly enough to— Ahhhh!"

The shock physically knocked him away from the gunwale and onto his back. Bub was on him in an instant, gently patting his cheeks and checking for a pulse. "Sailorman! You okay?"

Murphy sat up slowly. "Whoa . . . Okay. Obviously. That's not twelve volt." With Bub's help he stood, leaned to peer into the tiny cabin, immediately saw the toaster-sized metal box covered with cooling fins. "Jesus Christ. He's got an inverter on here!" He popped his head back out of the cabin, followed the wiring to a covered electrical socket on the console. "Here. This is what it's for. Goddamned thing's a menace!" He reached back below and turned the main battery switch off. "There. At least we won't electrocute ourselves getting off."

Bub heard the low rumble of diesels, stood up in time to see the Hatteras pull away from the fuel dock. "Speakin' a which, perhaps we oughta think about doin' just that right about now. That big fishin' boat just left. I expect the Chipster will be lookin' for us."

They scrambled out of the runabout and toward the shed door, from where, sure enough, they saw Chip locking up the register and leaving the shelter. Quickly, they walked out and up the path toward the parking lot. At the "hey" behind them, Murphy turned as he walked, waved, pantomimed putting a phone to his ear, then turned again and began jogging across the parking lot.

They climbed into the MG, Murphy digging for his keys when he stopped, pushed open the door and climbed back out. "Almost forgot my oil tray."

Bub groaned aloud. "Enviro-man, how come you just don't buy a car that don't leak oil?"

"Damn it all!" Murphy got up from the pavement. "I forgot to set it down when we got here. I need a rag from the trunk."

Bub glanced over his shoulder to see the golf-shirt-and-shorts-clad figure moving up the walkway. "Hey, Murph, maybe this once you can let it go, huh? Unless you want to explain to the Chipmeister about your big, fancy yacht again. . . ."

Murphy waved at Chip, jumped back behind the wheel, cranked the engine and peeled out.

Clyde Bruno twisted the volume knob as he drove, letting Hank Williams Jr. drown out the road noise as he wound out the convertible on the two-lane highway.

He sang along, enjoying the warm sun as he hit eighty, then ninety. Speed always gave him a thrill, and he definitely needed one after the morning he'd had. First the city utilities office, then the county court-house, going through property records.

It was the worst part of his job, the research. Slow, tedious, boring. Still, Old Man Thresher insisted that he, not the company's marketing department, do it. "Compartmentalizing," he called it. Keeping poten-tially damaging information in as few hands as possible.

Still, it wasn't all bad. And, over the years, it had begun to give him more of a sense of accomplishment when he finally did use the gathered information for its intended purpose, be it delivering an extortion de-mand or beating up a labor organizer or, more rarely, making an anti-drilling activist disappear.

A gravel truck passed in the other direction, and Clyde Bruno tight-ened his grip on the wheel to keep the car from buffeting in the slip-stream and ending up in the oncoming lane. He was doing ninety-five now, with the cars headed the other way going at least fifty-five. That was a hundred and fifty, total. There would be no surviving that. Air bag, no air bag. Would make no difference.

He wondered what it would feel like, a head-on at a hundred and fifty. If it would hurt at all, as the life was crushed out, or if it would just end in a loud bang. It would depend, he supposed, on how exactly his body reacted to the collision. Whether it flew out through the windshield, or got impaled onto the steering column.

He winced slightly at the thought, then wondered whether it might be possible to sabotage a vehicle to cause such a wreck. Excessive speed would be required. Maybe a locking cone threaded onto the throttle cable. Steering could be degraded easily enough, as could braking. Even easier would be tampering with the tires to cause a blowout. The only problem would be an inherent uncertainty as to when and where the accident would happen. Which, in the end, probably made it unreliable as a tool of his trade.

From over Hank's rowdy friends and the roar of the wind, Clyde Bruno became aware of a soft chirping. He reached down to his belt and flipped open a cell phone.

"Bruno . . . What? Wait. Hang on."

Grudgingly he slowed the Sebring down to the speed limit, then lifted the phone to his ear again. "Okay, what? Oh, hi, Chip. How ya doin'?"

Clyde Bruno scowled, trying simultaneously to read the mile marker and listen. "Well, what did he want? Well, no, I don't believe I know anybody like that. A Bertram? No. . . . No, you're right. I'm glad you called."

Clyde Bruno saw the green marker he had been waiting for and, a quarter mile beyond, the unmarked driveway. He slowed to turn off the highway. "I'll come down tomorrow. Got a couple of errands I need to take care of first. . . . Okay, thanks—what? No, he's definitely dead. . . . No, as far as I know there's no more brothers. Just the two. . . . All right, I'll see you tomorrow."

He flipped the phone closed and tossed it onto the seat beside him with a groan. This he didn't need, with everything else he had to get done. Inquisitive strangers. Well, there was nothing to be done about it just yet.

He followed the dirt road through some pine woods, then out into a clearing overlooking a wide floodplain. He stopped when he saw the ranch-style house a couple of hundred yards away, turned the car around so it pointed back toward the highway, and parked.

From the trunk he removed a pair of high-powered Nikons, which he trained on the house and focused. There was no street number, but there was little doubt that this was the piece of property he had researched. Four hundred and seventy acres. Only one improvement, that being a single-story residential structure, approximately twenty-one hundred square feet, on well water and septic tank.

He held the binoculars as steady as he could, noted an older Volvo wagon in the carport, scanned the windows—when the side door opened, from which emerged a heavyset Hispanic woman leading by the hand a young boy. She opened the rear door of the wagon and helped the boy with his belt, and Clyde Bruno focused on the Volvo's tag to memorize it, then hustled around into the Sebring and headed back toward the highway.

He puzzled over the boy and the woman as he drove, realized there was no getting around it: He would need to make a trip up to the state's Bureau of Vital Statistics in Jacksonville to get the answers he needed. But that would have to wait. The more he thought about it, the less he liked the questions young Chip had been asked down at Seven Seas. He would make that a priority.

Clyde Bruno waited for a tanker truck to roar past, then leaped out in front of a minivan loaded with vacationing Ohioans to make his way back to I-95.

Murphy fought the fish long and hard. It hadn't jumped yet, but he knew it would be big. Enormous, even. Over and over, he pulled line in, let it run, pulled in, let it run . . . until he felt himself bump against the gunwale, instantly felt a surge of hot pain course through him, and then the fish ran even harder and tumbled him over the gunwale, down, down, screaming—

He awoke with a start, took several moments to regroup. He was in his own boat, he realized slowly, not a Robolo runabout . . . and the shouting was not his own, but Bub's.

He glanced forward, saw Bub's legs on the foredeck and his torso hanging off the bow beneath the lifelines, and he scrambled up and over the cockpit coaming onto the side deck. Only when he reached the bow did he see the dolphins, a half dozen of them, clicking and whistling and swimming in helix patterns inches ahead of *Mudslinger*'s wire bobstay.

Bub himself was reaching a hand down, trying to pet them, and whooping each time a wavelet splashed his face.

Murphy grabbed his ankles and pulled sharply.

"What the—" Bub sat up with a smile. "Hey, there. You're awake. Did you check out the dolphins? I swear they were kissin' my hand! Did you know they swam like that? Right up close to the boat?"

Murphy checked his annoyance and reached a hand out to the staysail rising from the foredeck. Like the main and the genny, it was full and drawing as *Mudslinger* slid easily southward through aquamarine waters. Overhead, an occasional white puffy dotted an otherwise brilliant blue sky.

"Bub, in that little cubbyhole in the cockpit? You'll find four safety harnesses. If you're on deck by yourself, please wear one."

Bub's face immediately fell. "Boss, I truly am sorry. I won't let it happen again. You're absolutely right. Havin' been overboard once, you'd think I'da learned somethin'. It's just, well, there I was, sittin' here mindin' my own business when all of a sudden I see these guys swimming at us, jumpin'. . . . It's like they're puttin' on a show for us."

A large dolphin leaped from the water just off the starboard bow, did a forward somersault and splashed back in.

"See what I mean?" Bub asked.

Murphy moved forward onto the oak bowsprit, leaned against the stainless steel pulpit and watched sleek gray bodies rise one by one, their blowholes hissing in that moment at the surface, then slipping back down into clear water.

"Atlantic bottlenose dolphin," Murphy said. "One of the smartest animals on the planet. The folks over at Sea World don't actually teach them any tricks. They only bribe them with food to perform on command." He listened to the whistling in silence for a minute. "Figure out their code, and you'll be the envy of every marine mammal researcher from here to Auckland."

Toward shore, a flurry of silver fish jumped from the water and fell back, jumped out again, fell back. As one, the dolphins swung onto an intercept trajectory and sped off.

"Hey!" Bub shouted.

"Bait fish," Murphy said, sitting on the little teak seat mounted atop the pulpit. "Bait fish mean bigger fish. Bigger fish mean dinner. Playing with us is all well and good, but we can't compete with a nice mackerel fillet." Murphy shielded his eyes from the sun, stared at the green coastline four miles away. "Another half hour and we'll be there. You sure about those coordinates, right?"

"Twenty-six, fifty-seven-point-eight north, eighty, one-point-nine west," Bub nodded. "The one thing I know I can do, and that's remember useless numbers. Nolan Ryan's ERA the year he struck out three hundred eighty-three? Two-point-eight-seven. The odometer reading on your car when we got back to the marina last night? A hundred and eighty-five thousand, six hundred fifty-four."

"Well. I'm impressed," Murphy said, laying a hand flat against the curve of the genoa. "That ought to get us real close. I have the same make GPS as Farber's runabout, so that ought to put us within six hundred feet. Then we can sweep back and forth with the fishfinder."

Bub nodded, scratched his head. "And what exactly we lookin' for?"

"I have no idea," Murphy allowed. "It's just that, well, I get the feeling we're somehow missing something. I had a dream, a little while ago, that I was on that runabout, and fishing, and hooked something. I got a shock from that metal strip and got pulled over."

Bub shuddered. "Nasty, huh? Only . . . Well, and let me play devil's advocate here, but all that sounds like an accident, don't it? A frayed wire, a shock, a drowning. An accident."

"Okay, then how did he get out of his harness?"

"Maybe he got out of it in the water," Bub suggested. "Maybe he got pulled over and dragged along, and he finally came to and managed to open the buckles but by then didn't have enough left to get back to the boat."

Murphy shook his head. "I suppose anything's possible. But . . . I still can't see it. Anyway, we're almost there. We'll take a look around, we won't find anything, but at least I'll know we covered all the bases." He closed his eyes, face raised to the sun and wind. "In any event, we got a nice sail out of it."

"Boy, howdy, did we ever," Bub said, glancing at the horizon. "You know what? I really am enjoyin' this. I didn't think I would. That outing on Farber's boat was my first ever on a sailboat, so you can understand how that mighta soured me on the whole experience. But this, man, is this what you're talkin' about doin'? Sailin' off into the sunset?"

"It's something my dad always wanted to do. We'd talked about doing it together, but, well, we just never got around to it. So now that I finally have both time and money, it's something that I need to do. Sailing off into the sunset, in his memory." Murphy pointed toward the eastern horizon. "Actually, Europe's that way, so sailing off into the sunrise."

"Okay, fair enough. Sunrise then. I could see doin' this. I could definitely see doin' this." Bub nodded toward the dolphins, now in the distance. "Yup, this is definitely somethin' I could get into. You're right. This would be the perfect sorta thing, for a father and son to do together. Just," Bub squinted at the horizon, "pass the time together. Watch nature in all her glory. Sunrise. Sunset. Dolphins."

Murphy watched Bub think about that a long minute, through the *caw-caw-caw* of a passing gull. "You miss your dad."

Bub glanced up with a blink. "Yeah, I confess I do. Every minute of every day. He had such . . . high expectations for me. Such big shoes to fill. For years and years, I figured, there ain't no possible way I can fill 'em, so what's the point in even tryin'? It's only been these past few years I realized, well, maybe I could. Too late, of course, to show him. Of course, this most recent little twist, well, maybe it's best he's not around to see."

He sat back down on the bowsprit, legs dangling down, bare feet nearly dipping into the water on each crest. "Before the dolphins came, I was just sittin', thinkin' 'bout my life. I don't know where you are in yours, Murph, whether you've accomplished somethin' you're really proud of, something you think really proves what you're made of. Me, I thought I finally had, with Bub's Fine Lawn Furniture. After all those years of goofin' off, and screwin' up, it was honest-to-God good for my soul to get somethin' right. Then, one day, boom! Come to find out it's all been a setup."

Bub bit his lip, watched a shearwater circle overhead, swoop down into the water and emerge with a small fish in its beak. Murphy stood quietly, one hand around the inner forestay.

"So now what, Murph? Leisure America was thirty percent of my sales. Carolina Resins was my lowest-priced supplier. If they both go away, I'm screwed. Another business, down the toilet. Hell, I might as *well* go off into exile. Take that caretaker's job you were talkin' about. Rat Island."

Murphy smiled. "Rat Snake Cay."

It was a deserted bit of coral in the northern Abacos, home to an oceanography research station under the direction of a friend of his. The friend was searching for a new caretaker to monitor the various instruments, and Murphy had been tempted to volunteer, put the sailing trip on hold for a year or so.

"That's right. Rat Snake Cay," Bub continued. "Me and the rat snakes, takin' the water temperature and countin' bird eggs."

A larger-than-average wave slapped *Mudslinger*'s bow and splashed Bub as high as his chest.

"Hah!" he laughed. "Serves me right for gettin' all mopey. Here, after everythin', I'm still alive. I got my health, I got my family. I got no complaints. Onward!"

Murphy thought about Bub's family, about the brother who was now using Bub's memory for his own ends, and said nothing. From the cockpit came a faint beeping, and Murphy headed back.

"What's that?" Bub asked, getting up.

"The GPS alarm. It means we're within a mile," Murphy said. "I'll go turn on the engine, then we'll get these sails down."


Water was once again leaking into the mask, so Murphy raised his head, pulled the bottom silicone seal away from his cheeks to let it drain, then made the mask snug before putting his face back in the water.

The depth sounder said forty-five feet, on a narrow ridge with seventy-foot water on one side and ninety on the other. But with the afternoon sun sinking and the silt stirred up by the waves, even the coral ridge seemed a whole lot deeper than forty-five. Murphy swallowed hard and continued kicking.

He was most likely looking for a wreck, based on the clutter on the fishfinder's display that coincided with the GPS coordinates Bub remembered from the runabout. That, in and of itself, signified nothing, he knew. A wreck always made for good fishing. It made sense that Farber's secret hole would be over a place where fish liked to hide. Still, it was something, and, after all the trouble of getting down there, Murphy had decided to check it out.

He swam upwind, the occasional wave sending a quantity of water down his snorkel tube, making him gurgle in a slow breath and then force the water out with a powerful blow. For the hundredth time, he wished he'd bought the slightly more expensive, self-draining snorkel at the dive store. For the thousandth time, he wished he'd gotten certified in scuba, and had a tank with him now.

Forty-five feet was not the deepest he'd ever free dived, but it was darn close, and the thought was giving him the willies, particularly with dusk approaching. He once again played with the idea of tucking into Jupiter Inlet and anchoring in the Loxahatchee River for the night, coming back in the pre-noon calm. And once again he rejected the idea. This was already beginning to seem like a wild-goose chase, a lost day with precious few left. To waste yet another on it would be irresponsible.

He blew out another snorkelful of water and continued kicking steadily, scanning the lumps of orange brain coral, the stands of elkhorn, the fan corals waving in the current . . . until finally he made out a shape on the bottom. He slowed his kick to hover over the spot and stared. It was a wreck, all right. An old fishing boat, her booms and rigging long since broken, her pilothouse stoved in. A layer of barnacles and weed covered her from stem to stern, and she lay canting over to starboard, revealing a gaping hole on her port side. An explosion, possibly, although: who knew? There were so many bad things that could happen on a boat, and so many of them catastrophic. Maybe a fuel tank blew up. Maybe they were rammed on a foggy night, or in rough weather.

The thought reminded him that he, too, would be vulnerable to accidents in bad visibility unless and until he bit the bullet and spent the two grand for a radar. Of course, buying radar meant he needed a place to mount it safely, to avoid making himself sterile from the radiation. It also meant installing either a bigger alternator or a separate diesel generator, as there was no way his windmill could supply enough power to run a radar set—which meant it wasn't going to be two grand, but more like three or perhaps even closer to four. . . .

Which was when he noticed the harness, drifting in the current off the bow.

He held his breath, strained his eyes . . . yup, it was a leather harness, the sort Spencer Tolliver wore. And there, still attached to it, was the fishing pole, hanging from the boat's foredeck.

And immediately Murphy deflated as he realized what had happened: Spencer Tolliver, while trying for bottom fish, had instead hooked onto this old wreck, and had eventually fallen overboard after suffering a shock from that short circuit on the runabout, and . . . And then what? Quickly he saw the illogic of it: Tolliver had fallen overboard, recovered from the electrical shock . . . and then had reeled himself forty feet down?

Well, perhaps it wasn't as it appeared. Yeah, that was it: The line was tangled all around and through, and the rod and harness had just happened to drift over the wreck as he had swum over. Well, he'd just have to go down and check it out. He came upright, treading water with his flippers. Bub stood on the bowsprit twenty yards away, and Murphy pointed downward, waited for Bub's okay sign, then hyperventilated with three quick, deep breaths to purge as much carbon dioxide from his bloodstream as he could before flipping over and kicking.

Ever so slowly, the sunken boat grew nearer, through a scattering school of bluestriped grunts, the water getting noticeably dimmer as he descended, kicking, kicking . . . reaching out for the harness, grabbing it—and instantly knowing how Spencer Tolliver had been murdered.

For the harness's buckles were fastened. The body had been released by cutting the straps in the back, where Tolliver himself could not possibly have reached. The harness was still attached to the fishing rod with the pin Tolliver used to keep from losing it. And the line from the end of the pole led not randomly around various coral heads and thence to some snag on the wreck, but around the drum of the anchor windlass mounted on the wreck's bow. An anchor windlass, Murphy saw, that was shiny and clean and had in its cranking mechanism the long lever used to wind in the anchor rode. Except in this case, it had been used to wind in Spencer Tolliver.

Murphy stared and stared, finally sensed he was running out of breath and reached out to grab the harness and rod. It wouldn't budge—of course it wouldn't, Murphy immediately realized. It had dragged a grown man down from the surface. It certainly wasn't going to break with his tugging on it.

With his mouth clenched tight against the air that wanted to burst from his lungs, he reached to his calf, removed his dive knife from its sheath and grabbed a loop of the line and put his blade to it.

It refused to cut.

With hands now shaking, he sawed the serrated blade back and forth, back and forth, but the line still refused to part . . . and the diabolical cleverness of it all became clear. For on the reel Tolliver had used—the reel lent to him by Farber LaGrange—was not ordinary monofilament at all, but rather some . . .

Air—he needed air, and he needed it now. With knife in hand, he turned for the surface, saw *Mudslinger*'s hull far, far above, so, so tiny. He kicked hard, harder, his lungs straining to explode—

He shot through the surface, spat out the snorkel and gulped in air all at once, splashing back, exhausted and panting.

"Thought I was gonna have to come in after you," Bub called. "You all right?"

"Wire cutters," Murphy yelled, still panting.

"Wire cutters?"

"Wire cutters! Below, behind the starboard settee, in the black tool box marked with the white piece of tape."

Bub nodded, then disappeared. Murphy treaded water and looked around. The sun had disappeared behind a large cloud, and he shivered as he surveyed his boat. From his vantage point, he couldn't really see the shore at all, except when he happened to be at the top of a swell, and he imagined seeing *Mudslinger* in mid-ocean, and thought how insignificant she was. He had never crossed an ocean, even back when he owned a much bigger boat and thought of himself as wealthy. Now he would try to cross one in something so tiny. . . .

He shivered again, wishing the sun would come back out. He didn't like diving in unknown waters, period, and he especially didn't like diving in such lousy light. He had noticed several schools of bait fish drift past during his earlier descent. Bait fish meant bigger fish. Bigger fish meant even bigger predators. He liked there to be plenty of light when he dove, so as to minimize the chance of mistaken identity.

*Mudslinger*'s beige hull nearly disappeared in the trough of a wave, and when it came back, there was Bub, holding the wire cutters in his hand. He tossed them at him, and they plunked down in the water a few feet away attached to an oval piece of green foam advertising Barnett Bank. Murphy separated cutters from the key chain, slid his mask back down on his face, took three fast breaths and once more headed downward.

The water seemed even murkier this time, without the sun, and Murphy imagined that he was being watched. Nervously, he glanced around, saw nothing, then shook off his anxiety and kicked even harder. Right in front of him now was the harness and the fishing pole, and he reached out for the line that ran to the anchor windlass, with his wire cutters snipped it about a foot from the end of the fishing rod. Then he noticed a few inches farther down the line where his knife had abraded but not cut it, and he snipped that piece, too, stuffing both it and the wire cutters into the Velcro pocket of his swim trunks, then turning upward toward *Mudslinger*'s hull high above him.

He swam directly at the boat this time, so that he was about halfway home when something heavy bumped his left shin.

He knew it was a shark even before he turned, panic stricken, and saw the dark eye staring at him dully as it passed, then turned, passed him again. He was reaching for his dive knife, desperately trying to remember where he was supposed to stab him—was it in the eye? If so, which eye? Or was it at the intersection of a line drawn between the eyes and another coming longitudinally over the head—

Which is when he realized he was no longer holding the harness and the fishing rod . . . that they were in fact silently spiraling down, down into the ninety-foot-deep canyon on the near side of the ridge. He almost started after them, before he saw the shark notice the harness and turn downward toward it.

In the gloomy water, it looked enormous, a good ten feet, easily, maybe fifteen, and Murphy decided he had fought the good fight and lost, and with lungs once again on the verge of exploding he shot the remaining way to the surface, gulped a breath, and methodically kicked toward the swim ladder, avoiding as best he could seeming like a wounded fish.

He grabbed the bottom rung, yanked off his fins and threw them aboard, and then nearly fell from the metal ladder as a wave lifted *Mudslinger* high. In the next trough, he scrambled aboard with Bub's help, tore off the mask to see a seven-foot wave approaching the bow, the top foot curling into whitewater.

"I been wonderin' what to do," Bub said. "It don't seem like that anchor's gonna wanna hold in this. It's been buildin' since you went down."

Murphy heard the gurgle as the wave passed, and as it did saw yet another one a few hundred yards off. "It must be the swell from Gomez," Murphy said, panting. "It's breaking because of the reef. I'll get the engine started. You get the anchor up."

Bub's eyes grew big. "Gomez. You mean like that hurricane they were talkin' 'bout the other day on the TV? Jeez, it can't get us, can it? Maybe we just oughta get inside here and go up the Waterway?"

Murphy shook his head. "Gomez can't possibly hit us. It's too far north already. It's that next one in the Caribbean we need to watch for, whatsitsname, Helga, Hilda. Either case, I don't want to risk Jupiter Inlet now, or St. Lucie or Fort Pierce or any of the shallow ones, for that matter. The Bahamians call it 'rage on the bar.' It's just like it sounds. Go on, get the anchor up."

Bub started moving toward the bow, then stopped. "Whatcha see down there? How come you needed wire cutters?"

Murphy turned the key, then pushed the starter button until the Yanmar caught. "You're not going to believe it."

WITH ONLY SAUCE LEFT, Bub's spoon finally slowed as he chewed his last three Chef Boyardee raviolis. His thickening beard was dotted with flecks of red.

"Breakfast of champions," Murphy said. He sat across the cockpit, holding before his eyes the seven-inch strand of fishing line he had cut the previous day, the sum total of his salvage. "I'll heat up another can if you want."

*Mudslinger* moved north-northwest in the diminishing wind. They had split the night in four-hour watches, each spending his "on" time at the salon table, sifting through the documents sent by GOP Gal, every five minutes popping up the companionway for a look around.

"They used to serve it in my boardin' school when I was a kid. I'd forgotten how much I liked it." Bub gave up all pretense of etiquette and licked the bowl in long slurps. "Okay, you got about a hundred cans of this, a hundred cans of Hormel chili and five hundred cans of tuna. You gonna eat anythin' else on this expedition of yours?"

"Emergency nonperishables." Murphy played with the end of the strange strand with his fingertips. "In case the stick falls over a week out from Florida, I have six months of rations while I drift across with the current. Your folks send you to boarding school because you were a discipline problem?"

"I became a discipline problem *because* I went to boardin' school," Bub said. "They sent me because it's some crazy Billings tradition through the generations. Ending with this one."

Murphy glanced up over his reading glasses, decided to let it go, returned his gaze to the fishing line. "It's definitely got some kind of core to it. Doesn't feel like wire. Plus wire gets brittle if it's bent that sharply. Kevlar maybe?"

He passed the line across the cockpit. Bub took it, nodded at the eastern horizon. "Look, sun's comin' up."

Murphy turned to watch the red-orange ball peek over the horizon, then begin its steady march across the sky. Instantly, the seascape lost its dawn grays and started taking on greens and blues. "I always love sunrises on the water, especially in bad weather. It's like a renewal of a promise. Nighttime always ends, if you just hang in there long enough."

Bub twirled the strand of line in his fingers. "Kind of shark was it again?"

Murphy pulled off his foul-weather jacket, stretched in the warming rays. "*Big* fucking shark, is all I know. Probably lurking in that wreck, watching me the whole time. The harness and rod fell into ninety-foot water."

"And you couldn't cut this with your knife?"

"Try it, if you want. Stuff is tough."

Bub bent the line into a loop, let it straighten out. "So let's see if I got this straight: Farber comes up with this really devious plan—"

"Or Clyde Bruno," Murphy added.

"Okay, but Clyde Bruno ain't doin' it on his own, right? He's gotta be workin' for Farber—plan to get rid of Spencer Tolliver even before most folks know he's runnin'. Then he gets me to run instead. Then, in my humble opinion what was a really *lame* plan, he gets rid of me and sticks in my brother. Okay. Why? What's the point? With the kinda money the Party can raise, any one of us three coulda beaten ol' Ramsey. And I thought that was the only thing Farber cared about: winnin' the Governor's Mansion so he could retire to his yachts and his fishin' tournaments."

"Fishing tournaments!" Murphy reached across to grab the piece of ersatz monofilament. "Aha! He cheats! Look!" He ducked below, came back up with a small cardboard box. "See? This is real eight-pound test. Farber's line *looks* like it, but it's actually stronger than two-hundred-pound line."

"So any time he hooks a fish, it's as good as his," Bub said.

"Exactly. While the competition is working a fish, tiring it out, old Farber can just crank it right in."

Bub made a disgusted face. "Why, the no-good, unsportsmanlike . . . That really hacks me off! Cheatin'! And it ain't like he needs the money!"

Murphy shook his head in agreement. "Well, good. So if nothing else, we can at least rat out Farber LaGrange as a World Class Cheat." He thought again of the harness and rod, tumbling down into the gloom, the shark angling downward after them. "I had it in my hands, Byron."

"Now, now, don't you go kickin' yourself 'cause you didn't go mano-to-mano with a man-eater," Bub said. "Anyway, after we figure this out, we can get the Martin County sheriff's dive squad down there huntin' for it."

"That's just it: We don't have much time left and, so far, we've got nothing solid." Murphy checked the sails, saw that the trailing edge of the genoa was flapping halfway up. He turned to the winch behind him, pulled the braided jib sheet out of the self-tailing mechanism and let out a few inches until the sail was smooth again.

Bub craned across to squint at the sail. "How'd you know to do that?"

"The leech was luffing," Murphy said.

"Naturally. Leech was luffin'. I shoulda known." Bub sat back, closed his eyes against the sun. "Man, that Farber. He comes across like a good ol' boy, but he's a ruthless bastard, ain't he?"

"Yeah, he is," Murphy said, shaking his head. "Thank God for GOP Gal. Without her, we'd know none of this."

Bub nodded thoughtfully. "GOP Gal, yessirree. I must confess, Murph, I been kinda fantasizin' about what she looks like."

Murphy laughed. "Long, blond hair. Green eyes."

"No way, Sailorman." Bub grinned. "GOP Gal's a dark-eyed brunette."

"Uh-uh," Murphy insisted. "Blonde and green eyes. Plus she's a sailor, and when she meets me, she'll drop everything and go off with me across the Atlantic."

"She's a sailor, all right, but she already owns a boat, and when she meets *me,* she's gonna drop everythin' and take *me* with her."

Murphy laughed. "Get serious. She *hates* you. She sent me all that stuff so Ramsey MacLeod would kick your ass."

Bub considered that. "I suppose you got a point there. Great stuff she was sendin', though. Though I wish she woulda given us the whole picture, not just a bunch of clues. 'Course, she might not *know* the whole picture and was hopin' we'd be able to figure it out." He played with the bit of cored fishing line some more, bending and twisting it into various shapes. "What I wanna know, for instance, is how come Farber's authorizin' all that money to that outfit buyin' up them Gulf leases."

Murphy blinked once, then a second time. "Excuse me? What are you talking about?"

"Clean Gulf Trust," Bub said. "All those documents in that one packet."

"I didn't read it that closely," Murphy admitted. "I saw Clean Gulf and decided they couldn't possibly be a campaign contributor and tossed it aside."

"They ain't a campaign *contributor* so much as a campaign expense. Here, hold on." He popped down the companionway, came back with a manila envelope, passed Murphy six photocopied pages. "See? The Party's transferred five hundred grand to them in the last six months."

Murphy read silently. "Okay. Yeah. Actually, I did skim over this once, when it first came in. But like I said, it didn't make any sense to me. It still doesn't. Does it to you?"

Bub shook his head. "Nope. Not unless maybe Farber was plannin' some ads to show how green us Republicans are. You know: donatin' all this money to the tree-huggers that're buyin' up them oil leases."

"Oil leases . . ." Murphy rapped a finger on the sheets of paper. "Jesus Christ, Area Sixty-seven! That executive order comes due in January again, doesn't it?"

"Area Sixty-seven?"

"It's a huge tract south of Apalachicola. Supposedly it's got, I don't know, billions of barrels of oil and trillions of cubic feet of natural gas, just waiting to be sucked from the ground and sold for gazillions of dollars." Murphy thought about that a second. "But if I remember right, that group, the Clean Gulf Trust, bought title to those tracts last month, didn't they? To protect it from drilling? Plus all those other leases off Tarpon Springs and Sarasota and Naples."

Murphy glanced toward shore, saw the spires of the rocket garden at Patrick Air Force Base on the horizon. "How fast we moving?" he asked suddenly.

Bub leaned toward the speed log. "Four, four and a half knots. It is knots, right? On a boat?"

Murphy leaned over the sides to make sure there were no lines dragging in the water. "It is. And four knots is too slow. We can do six if we turn on the motor. As soon as we get in we've got to hit the road again." He bent to push the starter button until the diesel turned over.

Bub scratched his head. "Where we goin' now?"

Murphy kicked the gear lever to put the engine in forward, then picked up the sheets of paper Bub had given him. "Five-six-four Water Street, Apalachicola."

Clyde Bruno drove the boat back toward shore with scowl frozen in place. Not even getting the little runabout up on plane, and then driving her past the edge of control, to the point where the bow bounced dangerously skyward on the larger waves, made him feel any better.

He would have to explain it to Mr. Thresher, there was no getting around it. The man would want to know. Although what could be done about it now, he had no idea.

The scuba tank rolled on the cockpit floor into his legs, and, annoyed, he kicked at it. What the hell could be done? Where in hell could he begin? He took a deep breath, pushed his sunglasses back up his nose and goosed the throttle another hair.

He had to concentrate, for starters. The items were gone, no doubt about it. Somebody, or somebodies, with a pair of metal shears or wire clippers, had cut the line and taken both harness and rod.

Clyde Bruno had carefully unwound the remaining line off the anchor windlass, crammed the entire bird's nest into a coffee tin when he got back up to the boat, doused it with lighter fluid and torched it. Afterward he had tossed the ashes, the sinker and the hook overboard at intervals.

It was, he knew, a moot point. They had the critical evidence, whoever *they* were. He would have to find them and deal with them. It was that simple.

The green and red markers flew past, and he was soon racing through the inlet, throttling back as he approached the Seven Seas entrance channel. He approached the fuel dock port-to, killed the outboard when he was a few feet away, then tossed the bow line to Chip while walking the stern line ashore himself.

"You be needing this anymore today?" Chip asked.

Clyde Bruno studied Chip carefully. He was pretty sure Chip didn't know anything important, decided he would keep it that way. "Nope. All done. Thanks."

"Alrighty then," Chip said, climbing aboard and heaving the air tank and a mesh bag crammed with buoyancy compensator, mask and fins onto the dock. "All done with these, too?"

"Yup." Clyde Bruno licked his lips. "Tell me about these guys again. You didn't get either of their names?"

"No, sir. Sorry, sir." Chip dropped the scuba equipment behind the counter of the fuel dock office. "They were in their late thirties, early forties, I think. The one was asking questions about buying diesel for a seventy-foot Bertram. The other guy, the short one, he was kind of a smart-ass. He was the one I thought reminded me of Bub Billings a little bit. They took some forms to fill out and said they were gonna go get a drink."

Clyde Bruno nodded as they walked up the dock toward the yacht club office. "Okay. Then what?"

"Then I was topping off Mr. Richardson's Hatteras that had just come in. That took about fifteen, twenty minutes. Then I looked around for them, and I saw them up there, like they were walking out of the dry storage shed."

Clyde Bruno nodded again slowly. The first thing he'd done when he arrived was call a gofer from the local party executive committee to bring a truck and tow Farber's Robolo out to Clewiston. Then he'd called his home office to have someone pick it up from there and drive it out to the refinery in Lake Charles.

"And then what?"

"Then," Chip said, "I started after them. But the faster I walked, the faster they walked. They got into their car and took off before I could even get close."

Clyde Bruno stood, hands on hips, and surveyed the parking lot. "What kind of car?"

"A dark green convertible. They were parked over in that corner." He pointed with his chin, started to walk across the brick pavers.

"What kind of convertible? Like a Mustang? A BMW? A Miata?"

Chip scratched his chin, thinking. "Not big, like a Mustang. Small, like a Miata, but older. I think it actually might have been like a Spyder or something. Sorry I didn't catch the tag."

Clyde Bruno spotted the stain first, a cloverleaf made of three overlapping circles. He crouched down to put his finger in it, came up with a dab, rubbed it between thumb and forefinger. "Thirty-weight. Probably an old MG." He stood, checked his watch. He would need to call in a jet to get him to his meeting on time. "Thank you, Chip. I think that'll be all. Remember: I was never here."

Clarissa Highstreet lifted her left leg out of the hot tub so Marcel, the deputy secretary of state who also happened to be her nails guy, could get to work on her remaining toes.

She read the latest issue of *Cosmo* as she soaked, but thought mainly of her ambassadorship, and how the opportunity for acquiring it was quickly slipping away. She had spent the better part of a week now camped out on Farber's yacht, waiting futilely for Link Thresher to appear at one of the fund-raisers.

Each morning he was advertised to show up. Each afternoon came, and *Soft Money* cast off without him, and Clarissa Highstreet would spend the rest of the day working on her tan and slapping the occasional contributor who mistook her for one of Farber's hired tramps.

She had to admit it did give her a little charge, to be compared to girls half her age whose equipment in its natural state looked the way hers did only after extensive renovations. Still, she could not abide anyone reaching out uninvited to touch the merchandise, and had continued to inflict violence upon those who tried.

To Farber's pleas that she not physically assault those who were paying the bills, she had a ready answer: Get me Link Thresher, and I'll do my business and go away. And he would promise yet again to try and then would ask in humble tones if she needed anything in her continued stay in *Soft Money*'s owner's cabin.

She knew he was only being gracious about her presence because they expected the governor's race to be close, and could possibly need her help disqualifying ballots from Democratic parts of the state. Yet whatever the reasons for his deference, they didn't spoil it for her in the least. What was important was that he was finally treating her with the respect she deserved.

"I've got a corn starting on that heel, Marcel," she called over the magazine.

*"Oui, mademoiselle, "* he said, grabbing a nail file from his kit.

Marcel had been born Jimmie Mark in a low-rent part of Bartow, in rural Polk County, where he had discovered his sexual identity halfway through his years of torment in high school. He had ultimately gone to work for a beauty salon on fashionable St. Armand's Circle in Sarasota, which was where she had discovered him a decade earlier.

She flipped a page to an article titled "Nine Ways to Stand Out at the Topless Beach," thought immediately of the way Farber's Victory Hostesses were so casual about their nudity, and began reading with interest: *"When all the other women are sporting the European look, will you be ready?"*

Truth be told, it had nagged at the back of her mind, the possibility that when Link Thresher finally did show up one day, he would be so overwhelmed by all the young, bare flesh that she wouldn't even be able to get his attention. Only rarely in her life had she needed to use her body for advancement. Generally, her money had been more than enough. Link Thresher, she knew, would be different. He had plenty of money of his own, a huge corporation of his own, a Gulfstream jet of his own.

Her hook would have to be that of a woman of power. A woman of power willing to do all the things he was used to getting from girls he had to pay for. But how would she get to that point if she couldn't even win his attention?

The worry gnawed at her as she read on: *"Number Four: Don't let the brightest objects on the beach be hanging on your chest. Start tanning those puppies long before you need them."*

She glanced downward at the top halves of her own lily-white globes. The article had a point. She had to be irresistible from the first look. What was more sexy: a girl who was clearly comfortable with her own body? Or a woman obviously stripping down for the very first time? She peered over the top of the magazine, saw nobody on the Yacht Club patio, a solitary gardener working in the rose bed by the pool deck.

"Marcel, don't turn around," she commanded, and with one hand undid her bikini top and set it on the teak deck beside the hot tub. She sat up straighter so her breasts were completely out of the water, then looked down at the unfamiliar sight of her bosom in the sunlight. Oh well. In France, topless sunbathing was *de rigueur*. She would have to get used to it.

She continued reading, got to tip number eight: *"Don't be embarrassed if your nipples become erect. Unlike a man, it doesn't necessarily mean anything."*

Clarissa Highstreet regarded her own epoxy-fortified nipples. Well, there was nothing that could be done about that, one way or the other. She continued on to tip nine: *"Get used to men you don't know looking at your boobs. PRACTICE NOW!"*

She glanced down at her chest, up at the back of Marcel's head, back at her chest, then put the magazine down beside her and sat up straighter still.

"Marcel, turn around and look at me!" she ordered.

Marcel did as he was told.

"Well?" Clarissa Highstreet demanded.

Marcel hesitated for a moment, then forced a grin. "Ooooh, la la!"

Clarissa Highstreet smiled, arched her back and enjoyed the rest of her pedicure.

**M**urphy pumped premium unleaded, just under three-fifty a gallon, into the tank. He berated himself for not having paid more attention to the Clean Gulf material earlier. Offshore oil drilling was always Hot Button Issue Number One in Florida, hotter than abortion or gun control or prescription drugs.

If somehow the Republicans were doing something hinky with drilling, no matter how minor, Ramsey McLeod would easily pick up four or five points in the polls. And in the race that was shaping up, it looked like four or five points might well be the difference.

On the face of it, whatever was going on between the Party and Clean Gulf was almost by definition hinky. Five hundred thousand dollars, channeled under the table to a nonprofit environmental group. Why? If the Party wanted to green up its image, then why not hand over the checks at a big press conference?

He glanced at his watch, then at the folded road map on the dash. They were just outside Perry, nearing the halfway point between Alachua, where they'd turned off the interstate, and Apalachicola. There was no fast way of getting to the Panhandle fishing town, and he had decided the scenic route would take no longer than the roundabout path over the interstates.

The thirty-dollar figure flashed past on the gas pump as Bub strolled back from the pay phone after making his daily calls.

"You get through to your secret Lolita okay?" Murphy said, and then: "I can't believe thirty bucks of gas even *fits* in this car."

Bub nodded purposefully. "It's the current administration's fault. Bolling Waites and Ramsey MacLeod, asleep at the switch while gas prices go through the roof."

Murphy shook his head. "Why would the governor and lieutenant governor have any influence whatsoever on the price of gasoline? How does that line even work?"

"I got no earthly idea," Bub allowed. "But it does. Farber told me one time his focus groups were givin' the price of gas as the number one reason to vote against Ramsey. There was even some scuttlebutt I heard sayin' *we* were somehow manipulatin' the price upward. I never understood how, though."

He stretched his arms, adjusted the ball cap on his head, began polishing his sunglasses on his shirt, which was when he noticed the pickup truck at the pump ahead of them. "I don't believe this," he said, pointing. "Look."

The ubiquitous red, white and blue "Elect Bub!" bumper sticker was plastered on the tailgate—right beside a giant Confederate battle flag. Bub glared at it, then saw the big, potbellied guy in the soiled T-shirt and suspenders come strolling out of the mini-mart toward the driver-side door.

Murphy could only watch, mouth open, as Bub positioned himself squarely in front of Bubba.

"Redneck Man, why do you put the Bub sticker next to your racist flag?" he demanded.

The redneck squinted at Bub, as if deciding whether to take him seriously. "It ain't about niggers. It's about my heritage."

"Then your heritage is racist, and I don't believe Bub Billings woulda appreciated your language, or cared for your support," Bub said. His balled fists hung at his sides. "So right now, either the Bub sticker or the flag. One of 'em's gotta go."

The redneck glared at Murphy, then across the gas island at an old black man in a coat and string tie filling up a dusty Ford Fairlane. "What, he put you up to this?" he asked, nodding.

"No, he did not," Bub said. "*I* put me up to this. Now you gonna take that off or not?"

The redneck glowered, until Bub turned his back to him, stepped to the pickup and in a single pull yanked off the Bub sticker, crumpled it up and stuck it in his pocket. "Fine. Next time, don't go assumin' that just 'cause a fella's conservative means he shares your dumbass ideas."

The redneck roared, grabbed Bub by the neck hole of his T-shirt. Murphy scrambled over the gas hose, yelling, just as the proprietor came out of the mini-mart with a shotgun.

"Billy Bob, you set that man down right this second. Get in your truck and get along. Before I gotta call the cops again."

Billy Bob gave Bub one last hateful look, dropped him, climbed into the pickup and roared off in a cloud of dust. Bub picked himself up, adjusted his cap, nodded once to the proprietor and climbed into the car. Murphy hurried to put the hose back, handed the man some bills, then climbed in and cranked the engine.

As he pulled into the street, he watched in the rearview mirror as the gas station owner stood right there staring after them.

"Very smooth," Murphy said finally, after rounding a bend. "I guess that would be your idea of keeping a low profile. Avoiding attention."

"Murphy, all it takes for evil to triumph is for good men to stand around and not do nothin'." Bub brushed dust off his shirt. "Winston Churchill, I believe."

"I see. So should we stop at every house between here and Apalachicola that's got a Confederate flag? Or you think you had your fill for now?" Murphy glanced beside him, then back at the road. "Next time you get in a fight, keep your sunglasses on. And it was Edmund Burke, not Churchill."

Murphy's MG crested the big bridge swooping over the entrance to Apalachicola Bay, and Murphy squinted down over the hood into the late afternoon sun, looking for traffic signs.

"Found it yet?"

Bub flipped the unfolded map over, then back, before giving up and tossing it behind his seat. "Sailorman, you may have good water maps, but your road maps pretty much suck."

Murphy downshifted to slow down as they neared the bottom of the hill. "They're called charts, not water maps."

"I know," Bub said, picking up a photocopy of a Clean Gulf invoice and studying it. "I only say that to yank your chain. Five sixty-four Water Street. Ain't water streets usually called that 'cause they're on the waterfront?"

Murphy frowned, unable to read the name at the first intersection. "I don't know. I guess. Maybe. Well, that's the waterfront right there. So how about we test your theory?"

He moved into the right lane, turned onto the road that ran alongside the river. At the corner was a little green street sign. Water Street. Bub stretched his hands behind his head, fingers interlaced, to crack his knuckles. "And everybody calls me the dumb brother."

Murphy rolled his eyes, glanced at rusting shrimp boats tied behind fish houses to the right, slowed to check a store window on the left, then another, then turned on his left blinker to pull a U-turn. "If you're so smart, how come you didn't tell me to turn left? The numbers are headed the wrong way."

They crossed back over U.S. 98, then checked both sides for street numbers. "Four forty-one," said Bub. "It'll be on your side."

A dead-end sign appeared, and Murphy slowed to a crawl. On the right was a hardware store numbered five fifty-nine and then a lumber-yard with the number five eighty-three. To the left was a tiny, concrete-block seafood store with the faded numbers five-five-six. Beyond it was only a long, weedy lot beside the bay.

"The hell?" Murphy said. "There is no five sixty-four."

"There's gotta be," Bub said. "Here's the copy of the invoice Republo-gal sent you. This is the address that shows through the window in the envelope. It's the same kind we use at the plant."

Murphy waved at the vacant lot. "Well, maybe they moved."

Bub thought a moment. "Well, if they mailed it to this address, and there's nothin' at this address, then maybe it's bein' forwarded by the post office."

"Good," Murphy said, checking his watch. "It is now five minutes to five. Now all we have to do is locate and get to the post office in the next five minutes. Any idea where those are generally located in, you know, old Panhandle fishing towns?"

Bub craned his head to look around the empty street. "Well, let me think here. Gulf Coast, so that means mainly streets runnin' east-west, and then you got the fact that Apalachicola starts with an A, which means . . . Yeah. If you get back to ninety-eight, I bet it'll be down about two blocks, then right."

Murphy squinted at him suspiciously, until Bub shrugged and grinned. "All right, I saw the sign as we were comin' down off the bridge."

Murphy pulled another U-turn, drove as fast as he dared, but got to the post office at three minutes past five. A grandmotherly black lady was preparing to lock the lobby door when Bub said, "Be right back," popped out of the car and jogged up to her with a grin. Murphy stayed in his seat, knowing it was pointless, and then watched in disbelief as she invited Bub inside.

He emerged a few minutes later, the forwarding address scrawled on the back of the photocopied invoice, and climbed back into the car.

"Even gave me directions," he said, pointing the way.

Murphy followed the outstretched hand, shaking his head. "If it'd been me, she would have told me to come back tomorrow morning. And tomorrow morning she would have told me it was confidential, and she couldn't release it."

"It's in the askin'," Bub said. "You make people feel important, then they're usually willin' to help out. No big secret. Make a left up here, then another left at the light."

Murphy waited for a car to pass, then turned onto a narrow, tree-lined lane. He drove for a mile, until they were on the outskirts of town, and saw a new, five-story, glass-and-steel box. He slowed and turned into the parking lot.

"You sure this is right?" Murphy asked.

Above the automatic doors at ground level were the words Florida Minerals Inc. Bub glanced down at his handwriting, back up at the building. "Yup. Thirty-four hundred Brownsville Road, suite five-oh-six. That's what the lady said."

Murphy parked in the far corner beside a blue Karmann Ghia sporting a yellow longboard, and the two walked toward the entrance. "Clean Gulf Trust has got offices in a building called 'Florida Minerals'? That doesn't sound wholesome."

"Can't be that bad, they let a surfer work here," Bub said.

Inside, the air-conditioning instilled a quiet chill, and they moved uncertainly toward a security desk. The uniformed guard glanced up from a bank of black-and-white monitors and offered a bored look. "Help you, gentlemen?"

Murphy nodded once, licked his lips to get the bullshit flowing. "Yes, actually, if you don't mind. We're from the, uh, Ocean Conservancy in Washington, D.C.? Actually, we're on the Conservancy's board of directors, to be perfectly candid, and—"

He stopped at the sudden elbow to his side, turned to see Bub discreetly nodding at the building directory on the limestone column behind the security desk.

"Ook-lay up air-they," Bub sang.

Murphy looked. Atop the big, etched bronze directory was the title: "Florida Minerals Inc., a division of Petron North America." Murphy read that a second and third time, then found suite 506. It was the home of Goodkind and Sams. Its president was Clyde Bruno. There was no other listing for suite 506, nor was there any mention of Clean Gulf.

"Where'd you say y'all was from agin?" the guard asked, this time with pen in hand.

Murphy blinked, then snapped back. "You know what? I'm sorry. We have the wrong address. Well, sorry to bother you!"

They fast-walked back to the car, Bub climbing in over his closed door, Murphy cranking the engine even before he'd pulled his shut. Wordlessly, he pulled back onto the highway, watched the rearview until they were back amid traffic on U.S. 98.

"Whoa," he said finally, letting out a long breath.

"Whoa is right," Bub agreed. "Got enough of the dots connected, boss? *Now* can we send this off to the press?"

Murphy thought it over. "You know what? There's actually one more detail I'd like to nail if we can. Tomorrow's Friday, right? Eight-thirty, sharp, let's be at the state Minerals Leasing office in Tallahassee. See exactly what the Party of Lincoln wants to buy for Petron. What do you think?"

"Sounds like a plan," Bub said.

Murphy shifted and accelerated up the tall bridge. "You want a Holiday Inn? Or a Best Western?"

Bub settled down in his seat, pulled his ball cap over his eyes. "No preference. So long as it's got HBO."


Clyde Bruno drove the company convertible joylessly, scowling at the road, the other drivers, the world in general.

He was a hunted man, and he did not like it. He was used to being the hunter, the one who melted into the background, who did all the legwork and laid all the groundwork so that when the time came, the quarry had absolutely no course of action other than the one Clyde Bruno had prepared for him.

All the self-worth and peace of mind that that brought with it had

vanished in the instant he had descended to the wreck and made his un-
nerving discovery. The evidence he had assumed was safely beyond the
reach of prying eyes had in fact been salvaged, and now no doubt
awaited examination by a grand jury.

On that last point, he had called in all the chits he could think of from
party officials down in the Jupiter area. Seven Seas Resort was at the
northern tip of Palm Beach County, but he knew the wreck was actually
off Martin County. Through the party hacks, he had made backdoor in-
quiries in both jurisdictions: Had anyone brought in anything unusual?
Were the cops looking into anything weird? Anything at all?

Mercifully, the answer so far had been no. And that had given him so-
lace for exactly fifteen seconds, until the obvious question hit him in the
face: So what were they waiting for?

Clyde Bruno couldn't hazard a guess, and that, too, drove him nuts,
as did the fact that he knew so little about them. Guy number one:
medium height, sandy hair, beard, unknown eye color, unknown name.
Guy number two: shorter, slighter build, bald, scruffy beard, unknown
eye color, unknown name. Oh, and resembled Bub Billings.

That last bit had irritated him at first. If there was one person he absolutely knew it wasn't, it was Bub Billings.

And then, later, aboard the company plane back to Apalachicola,
he had started second-guessing himself about even that. How did he
*know*, absolutely and positively, that it wasn't Bub? Stranger things had
happened. . . .

He had downed another shot of Wild Turkey and shaken off the image. Of *course* it couldn't be Bub Billings. The man had gone over the
side twenty miles offshore, in the rapidly moving Gulf Stream, with
squalls all around. That first day, when the Coast Guard had been
searching off Melbourne Beach, Bub would have been sixty miles off
New Smyrna. By now he'd be on his way across the Atlantic, if the
sharks and the crabs and the sea birds hadn't picked him clean yet.

Or, maybe, on the other hand, after the squalls had passed, and the
seas had flattened, there had been a fishing boat, or a sailboat, or a god-

damned cruise ship, for all he knew, and someone had seen a head bobbing in the water, or heard a voice. . . .

He shook his head savagely, inadvertently pulling the wheel so far
left that the car edged into the oncoming lane, forcing him to flip off the
passing, honking driver. Surely, the first thing anyone who picked him
up would have done was call the Coast Guard. Surely, the first thing Bub
Billings would have done was stage a press conference, explaining how
it was that he wound up in the drink.

Clyde Bruno shook his head again. There was no point stewing over
this. The guy who young Chip thought looked like Bub wasn't Bub. He
must therefore be somebody else. And whoever he was, Clyde Bruno
would find him and deal with him. Him and his sports-car-driving
friend, both.

He scowled again, this time at Chip. *Damn* him for not paying closer
attention. That license plate number would have been as good as gold.
Even a partial would have helped. Instead, the kid hadn't even noticed.
Didn't even remember if it was a Florida tag. Just what kind of operative was the Party recruiting nowadays? Standards, he thought, recalling Grant, clearly had gone to hell.

The glass-and-steel tower, at five stories a skyscraper by Apalachicola
standards, appeared on his left, and Clyde Bruno waited for a break in
the cars to slide into the lot. He parked by the entrance in a reserved
spot, made his way in and up to the top floor, then down the long corridor to his corner suite. He pushed every remaining thought about Chip
and Bub and the missing rod and harness from his head and put on his
game face.

The guy he was about to meet with, he wanted to project a certain image. Doubt and worry could not be part of it.

He opened the door to his suite, immediately noticed that his secretary wasn't there, but that the door to his inner office was open. He
strode in quickly, saw a tall, bony man in jeans and T-shirt staring at a
wall-mounted nautical chart of the Gulf of Mexico, the rigs off Texas
and Louisiana marked with different-colored pins.

Clyde Bruno bit back his anger about the man's unescorted presence in his office. "Mr. Romer, I presume?"

Romer turned with a toothy smile. His face was all angles—a sharp, pointed nose, high cheekbones, jutting chin. "Just Romer is fine," Romer said.

Clyde Bruno suppressed a shudder. The guy, as promised, appeared fully capable of sudden and extreme violence. "I've been reading the news articles from Jacksonville and Tampa and New Orleans. It appears you've fulfilled your contractual obligations."

Romer continued smiling.

"Alrighty," Clyde Bruno said. "I can get your final payment in cash, if you'd prefer, or wire—"

"Wire transfer would be fine," Romer said. "Like last time."

Clyde Bruno nodded, sat at his desk, fingered the mouse on his computer, then started typing on the keyboard. Romer turned back to the wall chart, studied the Florida Big Bend waters particularly closely.

Clyde Bruno tapped his fingers impatiently, then keyed in the number two, then five, then four zeroes. He typed some more, then: "I need an account number."

Romer rattled off a ten-digit series, which Clyde Bruno typed in. A few moments later, the confirmation code flashed on his screen.

"Done," he said.

Romer still smiled, pointed at the solitary pin off the Florida coast. "What's that?"

"Do you want the confirmation number?" Clyde Bruno asked.

"I know it's not my business, but y'all aren't planning on drilling off Florida, are you?"

Clyde Bruno stood, tucked his polo shirt back down into his khakis and opened the door. "I'll walk you out."

They said nothing all the way down to the parking lot. Romer pulled open the door to his Karmann Ghia, climbed in and slipped the key into the ignition.

"Your money ought to be in your account within the hour," Clyde Bruno said. "You can check, if you want."

Romer widened his wicked grin a hair. "No need. I know where to find you."

And with that, he was off. Clyde Bruno watched the car pull out onto the highway, the longboard strapped to the top, and this time allowed himself the shudder. The guy made him way too nervous. Hired guns, mercenaries, independent contractors. Clyde trusted none of them, particularly the ones who seemed like they might be even more ruthless than he was. Well, he would never have to work with him again, thank God.

He turned to walk back to the building when his eye caught the peculiar cloverleaf pattern of drips on the concrete pavement. He blinked, stared some more, then knelt, reaching down to dab some oil and rubbing it between thumb and forefinger as unease became something closer to panic.

Clyde Bruno stood, stared down the highway in search of a British roadster, finally shook himself back to reality and pulled out his cell phone to call his boss.

★ ⑥ ★

Percy Billings stood at the plate glass atop the Red Man Tower, watching a throng of two hundred thousand grime-covered rednecks watch a pack of brightly advertised Chevrolets and Pontiacs and Fords make endless left-hand turns around the two-and-a-half-mile track.

He had already given a brief speech extolling the benefits of the Daytona International Raceway on the local economy and of stock car racing in general and then praised his dead brother before he'd dropped the green flag. Now he stood counting the minutes until they could leave.

The crowd in the hot sun roared, and Percy glanced up to see a yellow car fishtailing dangerously near the wall, then regaining control.

"Almost a martyr."

It was Farber LaGrange, Percy saw, come to stand beside him. It was Farber who had earlier advised him that he had to spend a minimum of a half hour intently watching the race, the Enron-Vaseline 400, in order to impress upon the spectators his serious interest in their pastime.

"How do you mean?" Percy asked.

"Keep your eyes on the race. Clap when they clap," Farber ordered. "What I mean is, if he'da gone into the wall and gotten hurt, he'd be a hero, puttin' himself in harm's way for the sake of America and God and everythin'. If he'da gotten killed, then he'd be a legend. And you'da picked up three or four points in the polls, I might add, just by bein' here and goin' down there and consolin' the widow."

Percy watched the cars more closely now, waiting for an accident, asking finally: "Do these people really vote?"

Farber snorted. "Half of 'em don't know how to read, let alone vote. But you gotta love the dem'graphics: white, undereducated, blue-collar, fair-to-middlin' racist. This is our base, and we gotta kiss their ass." Farber half turned, checked out the crowd of party operatives and raceway executives milling around, drinking Tanqueray and Chivas in the air-conditioned box. He edged closer to Percy. "We need to talk."

"You have the latest poll numbers?" Percy asked.

"Yeah, and they ain't good. But I got somethin' else, somethin' more important." Farber leaned closer to Percy's ear. "You and Bub, you're the only two kids, right? There ain't another brother?"

Percy scoffed. "Of course not. What exactly are you suggesting?"

"Don't get huffy with me. Any cousins? Any relative at all who looks like Bub, only bald on top and wears a beard?"

"No." Percy's eyes narrowed. "Why?"

"Not to alarm you or anythin', but there's somebody resemblin' that goin' round the state with this other fella. They are, evidently, investigatin' the demise of ol' Spencer Tolliver. It appears they are also investigatin' Petron North America."

Percy's face locked up, and Farber elbowed him in the side. "You wanna be governor, you gotta learn to take bad news a little better than that. Now don't get all bent outta joint. Thresher's boy is on the case and I'm confident he'll take care of it. But you gotta tell me the truth: Is there any Billings relative who even remotely resembles your brother?"

Percy shook his head slowly, then more rapidly.

"Are you sure?"

"Positive," Percy said.

Farber nodded. "Okay. Well, let me just lay out the facts. I got a call a little while back from our Taylor County executive chairman. Owns a gas station in Perry, and says he had to go out and bust up a fight 'tween this little guy and a local troublemaker. The little guy apparently ripped the 'Elect Bub' sticker off the guy's bumper 'cause it was right beside a Confederate flag decal. He says he got a good look at the little guy. He says it was Bub. Not that he *looked* like Bub. He says it *was* Bub. Based on his behavior, it even *sounds* like Bub."

Percy absorbed this, watching with clenched teeth as the cars buzzed around the near turn, the stragglers following behind in single file. He pictured his brother at a backwoods gas station in the middle of Klan country, saw him jumping a redneck twice his size over some high-minded principle, imagined the redneck throwing him to the ground, beating him to a pulp. But it *couldn't* have been Byron . . . it couldn't possibly . . .

"The odds," Farber breathed, "of goin' overboard, at night, more than a dozen miles off land, no life jacket, no ring, no nothin', and then gettin' picked up by a passin' vessel next mornin' . . . Well, it's my considered opinion that it's more likely he got picked up by space aliens and brought back to land."

"Or," Percy murmured, "he's come back from the dead. The voice of my brother's blood crieth unto me from the ground. I mean, who knows? Does science have an answer explaining what it is a soul is? Is it just a collection of synapses, a series of electrical impulses? Or is it something more? And if so, do we really know it can't survive outside a human body? Maybe that's what God is, a consciousness outside—"

"Stop!" Farber hissed. He glared at Percy for a few seconds, then sighed. "Now you listen to me: The election's just four days away. Don't start goin' fuckin' melodramatic on me now, all right? That was no ghost Jimmy Hawkins seen at his gas station. It was some dude goin' around askin' questions we don't need asked. We're takin' care of it. I just needed to make sure we ain't doin' in a relative who's gonna come back to haunt us."

Percy looked up, eyebrows raised.

"It's a figure of speech, for Chrissake," Farber said. "Now, the poll numbers. I ain't sure what's happenin', but the win-one-for-Bub thing seems to be losin' steam. We dropped two points in the overnights. I don't know, maybe we peaked too early with it."

Percy considered this, considered reminding Farber how he'd never wanted to go with the surrogate Bub campaign in the first place. How, if they'd followed his instincts, they would have a solid lead by now, based not on his dead brother, but on his own merits. He said nothing. "So now what?"

Farber shoved his hands into his pockets and watched the race cars. "It ain't time to panic yet. We still got a coupla tricks up our sleeves. First we got five million wortha advertisin' hittin' the airwaves this weekend, both positive for you and negative against Ramsey. We called around, and we figure that's ten of our ads for every one of theirs. Then, if it's real close, we got our ace in the hole: thirty thousand spoiled ballots we're distributin' to our trusted election supervisors 'round the state. They'll take the place of Ramsey votes, if we need 'em to. Plus we got a freebie down in Palm Beach County. Those morons came up with this crazy-ass ballot design." He dug into his pocket and unfolded a piece of cardboard. "Here. Check this out."

Percy squinted at it, turned the card onto its side. "It looks like some kind of insect."

"Yeah, a caterpillar," Farber laughed. "A boll weevil caterpillar. But look how they stuck the neo-Nazi candidate smack between you and Ramsey. We did a focus group, and it looks like maybe ten percent of Ramsey's elderly votes are gonna go for the Nazi on accident. Now all we gotta do is get ol' Sec'tary Highbeams to distribute them spoiled ballots for us."

Percy blinked. "What's the problem? She's my damned campaign chairman, isn't she?"

Farber shook his head. "She's makin' this play for ambassador to France. Figured out that Link's got the president's ear. I'm afraid she's gonna tie those ballots to gettin' that appointment. But don't you worry 'bout that. I'll work it out."

On the track below, a red-and-blue car glanced off a white car, went sideways, then flipped over, finally spinning to a stop beside the infield. The crowd leaped to its feet with oohs and ahs. Percy prepared to clap, then stopped. "What do I do?"

"Hang on," Farber muttered, leaning closer to the glass. "If he walks away from it, clap. If they call the meat wagon, straighten your tie and get ready to console the widow."

They stared intently for a long minute, until finally the rescue crew yanked a green-coveralled driver out the inverted car's window. He pulled off his helmet and waved gamely to the stands.

"Ah, dang it all," Farber said, applauding. "We can't *buy* a break, can we? Aw, fuck it. Another ten minutes and we gotta roll anyhow, if we're gonna make Jacksonville by four. Just keep lookin' interested for a bit longer."

Farber grimaced, finally acknowledged the presence behind him of Toni Johnson. "What now? Can't you see I'm tryin' to enjoy the race?"

Toni stepped forward. "I'll only be a minute. You need to authorize this," she said, handing him an invoice and a pen.

"What's this?" Farber grumbled.

"Another bill from Clean Gulf Trust. Another two-fifty K. Don't ask me what it's for. I'm just the financial officer."

Farber squinted at her with hard blue eyes. "I already told you to stop worryin' yourself about Clean Gulf. They're a fine outfit. Good as the Audubon Society. Better. From now on, just authorize anythin' they send."

"Yes, sir." She accepted the clipboard and pen back. "Anything else?"

"Yeah. You arrange the caterin' for the Victory Cotillion tomorrow night?"

"Champagne, caviar, truffles, jumbo shrimp, the works," Toni said. "Only the best for our most valued sponsors."

Farber smiled and turned back to the race. "Good. And remember, I need you there. We gotta process them checks A-S-A-P if we expect to use 'em in time for Tuesday."

Percy watched Toni walk away out the corner of his eye, then leaned closer to Farber. "She makes me nervous. It's like she knows *everything*."

Farber glanced back at her. "Toni? Naw, Toni's all right. A bit on the prissy side, sure. All I know is she looks great in a pair of heels and always makes the numbers work out." Farber reached out and physically turned Percy's head back toward the window. "Listen, you just worry about workin' the crowd and lookin' good on TV, okay? Leave the rest to me. Now you'll excuse me while I get back to Link and his boy."

**B**ub Billings pored over a handful of documents, squinting to read the small print, then waved a sheet at Murphy. "Got another one. Twenty-three hundred acres. Number seventy-seven dash three-five-six-two. It's called the Landsdown tract, for reasons that escape me."

Murphy searched the large-scale chart they'd spread out on the table in the cramped room, the one the records clerk at the Offshore Minerals Office had let them use. They'd been at it six hours now, nonstop since eight-thirty in the morning.

"Got it," Murphy said, scribbling in a notebook. "About seven nautical miles west-southwest of Sanibel. Isn't that special? On a clear day, all those rich folks will have something new to look at out on the water."

Bub flipped through the rest of his stack. "Sailorman, is there a reason you boat people always use nautical miles, instead of regular miles?"

Murphy said, "Yes," and returned to his notebook.

"Well, okay, good. I suppose you'll explain it to me sometime, when it's convenient. Unless it's on a need-to-know basis, that kinda thing—"

"Check this out," Murphy said, pointing at the map he'd sketched on his notebook. "Clean Gulf Trust now owns oil and gas leases from the Tortugas, up off the Ten Thousand Islands, Naples, Sanibel, Sarasota, Cedar Key, and around the Big Bend clear out to Pensacola. With all the purchases happening in the last eighteen months."

Bub whistled. "And Petron owns Clean Gulf, so Petron—"

"Is in possession of drilling rights within a stone's throw of just about every single sandy beach on Florida's Gulf Coast. And Petron, through a series of dummy companies, has funneled at least twelve million dollars to the Florida Republican Party, so it can get a governor who won't renew the executive order banning drilling." Murphy thought a moment. "And to make sure it got that kind of governor, its agents killed one candidate and almost succeeded in killing another. Are we hitting all the high points? Making it simple enough for the seven-second sound bite?"

"Simple enough where even I understand it," Bub said, studying the big chart on the table. "Maybe we oughta have a map of Florida like this, marked with all the new oil wells that folks will be able to see from the beach." He leaned down closer toward the chart. "Hey, you know what? All these lease tracts are plain old boxes of dotted lines, 'cept for this one here, which has got this little bitty black triangle off, what is this, St. George Island? Right close to Apalachicola. . . ."

Murphy leaned over the chart. "I have no idea . . . No wait, I remember now. Back in 'seventy-four, the state gave permission for a single exploratory rig. I don't think anything was ever built, though. Here, let me write down the coordinates—twenty-nine degrees, looks like ten, maybe eleven minutes north, eighty-four degrees, oh, about forty-two minutes west—"

"Hold on!" Bub grabbed the notebook from Murphy. "I'll be damned! Those are the same numbers as were on that gizmo on Farber LaGrange's fishin' boat!"

Murphy squinted at the chart, double checked his extrapolation of the position he'd written down. "You sure?"

"Positive! Don't you remember? I'm Useless Numbers Man! Twenty-nine, ten-point-seven, by eighty-four, forty-two-point-one. How could I forget?"

Murphy stood, stared off into space. "If I recall correctly, Esso wanted to build a rig before protests at their gas stations made 'em stop. But Farber's got that waypoint in his GPS . . . why?" He turned to Bub. "I'm wondering if it might be worth our while to delay our press conference another day to check this out."

"You think there's somethin' out there?"

"In our wildest dreams," Murphy said, packing up his notes and pens. "Can you imagine? All the TV helicopters, circling around an illegal rig. It's a lot to hope for. . . . On the other hand, there's gotta be a reason that waypoint is in Farber's GPS."

They returned the stacks of files back to the clerk at the desk and stepped out into a glorious November afternoon beneath a canopy of turning leaves and a crisp blue sky. Bub breathed the air deeply. "You know, Tallahassee really is pretty this time of year, ain't it? It gets real seasons, which the rest of the state misses out on. I woulda liked bein' governor, just to live up here again." They walked down the street to where they had parked. "Hey, we don't gotta drive all the way back to get *Mudslinger* so we can get out to whatever it is, do we?"

Murphy shook his head. "It would take way too long. We'd have to go all the way around Florida to get up here. It would take us a week. I know a place that'll rent us a Boston Whaler in Carabelle."

"Good. Don't get me wrong. I'm really gettin' into sailin' and all, and I love your boat. But it ain't exactly the fast way to China, is it?" They passed someone on the sidewalk, and Bub nodded. "Hey, how ya doin'?"

Five paces later, Bub did a double take, turned, then turned back. "You know somethin'? I know that guy from somewhere. . . ."

Murphy watched uneasily as the man turned into a back alley toward a tall brick building. "I was just thinking the same thing. Jesus, that was close. His name is Grant Hanson—"

"That's it! Grant the Regular Floridian!" Bub exclaimed. "Murph, I remember now where it was I mentioned my views on offshore drillin'. That guy, Grant, *he* asked me about it. It was at one of those regular-citizens-meet-the-candidate deals!"

Murphy stared at the building, shook his head. "Bub, Grant Hanson is no regular citizen. Don't you know who he is?"

Bub scratched his head. "Can't rightly say I do. I remember at that event, he didn't strike me as the sharpest tool in the shed, if you get my drift. Kept lookin' at his hand, when he was askin' his question, like he was readin' it—"

Murphy shook his head again. "Oh, man . . . Bub, I don't know how to tell you this. . . . Grant Hanson works for the Party. In fact, that's the state headquarters right there, the tall brick one. He's on Farber's Goon

Squad, the one that goes out and starts 'spontaneous demonstrations' and that kind of shit during recounts. Before that, he worked for your brother, down in Marco Island. In fact, Percy's the one who got him that job."

Bub stared off into space, a queer smile unable to mask his bewilderment. "Is that right. . . ."

From the alleyway Grant Hanson reappeared, squinting at them beneath a furrowed brow. Murphy gripped Bub's arm, hustled him toward the MG. "Come on. I think he might have recognized you, too."

Bub settled into his seat, still numb, and mechanically fastened his seat belt as Murphy peeled out.

O kay, you got me," drawled the speakerphone set up in the center of the long conference table. "Now you care to explain what in hell was so important to drag me away from an event that's got contributors lined up around the block?"

Link Thresher leaned back in the chair and scowled at the phone. "Well, ex*cuuu*se me, Mr. Hotshot Party Chairman, Lord and Master. Now, me, I come to Tallahassee's George H. W. Bush Republican Center, all the way from the North Slope, *again,* to make this meeting in person. But I suppose *my* time ain't quite as valuable as yours, although, hold on, wait a minute. . . . Yes, that's right: I *am* bankrolling your candidate out the wazoo! Which I suppose *does* make my time more valuable than yours."

Across the table, Clyde Bruno sat restlessly, staring at the phone. Beside him was a researcher from Credit America, Petron's financial services subsidiary. In light of the circumstances, Thresher had waived his "compartmentalization" guidelines, this once.

"Now you'd think if that somehow weren't enough, you'd at least honor our years of friendship," Link Thresher continued. "Maybe even the years of sponsorship Petron has given you as an angler, not to mention, of course, the, ahem, *custom* edition of Petrene eight-pound test on which you've won, correct me if I'm wrong, thirty-five different light-line tournaments in the past six years?"

"All right, all right. You made your goddamn point," the speakerphone conceded. "You want to talk, let's talk. I got an issue I need your help on, anyhow. Okay, go ahead."

Thresher nodded at Clyde Bruno, licked his lips. "You understand, we would've had this nailed down sooner, except for this business about the two gentlemen looking into Tolliver's, ah, accident."

"This is a secure line, if that makes you feel any better," Farber LaGrange said. "And by the by, I asked young Percy about that. He says there is no male relative resemblin' his brother. So go ahead and act accordin'ly. Extreme prejudice or whatever the fuck y'all call it."

Thresher folded his hands in his lap and raised an eyebrow at his researcher. "It's funny you should mention male relative. Brendan?"

Brendan cleared his throat. "Hello, Mr. LaGrange, can you hear me?"

"Just fine and dandy, Brendan."

Brendan cleared his throat again. "Well, sir, it's about the Billings family that lives on a ranch out by the St. Johns River in west-central Brevard County. Mr. Bruno asked for a rundown on them, make sure it wasn't actually Byron Billings's property. Well, it turns out it's not. It does in fact belong to Lamont Billings, as does the Volvo 240 wagon parked on the premises. However, further investigation has revealed a couple of salient facts. One, Lamont Billings is six years old. Two, according to records we were able to obtain, Lamont Billings is Byron Billings's son."

The statement hung heavily in midair, until finally Brendan cleared his throat once more. "Mr. LaGrange, did you get all that clearly enough?"

Another long pause. "Clear as a fuckin' bell, Brendan," Farber said. "Thresher, how long you known this?"

"We found out yesterday," Link Thresher said.

"Jesus Christ, and you wait till now to tell me? Hold on a minute. . . . What is it, darlin'? No, tell him cash, check or credit card only. Tell him this late in the campaign, we really can't make use of women's lingerie. Excuse me a sec." The sound of footsteps, and then a door closing came over the speakerphone. "Jesus Christ! A son? The goddamn bastard lied to us. . . . Gimme a chance to think. . . . Okay, everybody: There will not be *one* word of this to Percy. Understand? He's already talkin' weird 'bout Bub, and I got no idea how he'd react. . . . Killin' your brother is one thing, but a six-year-old nephew? There ain't no goddamn Greek tragedies about that."

Clyde Bruno stared at his hands through the silence. He had spent much of the morning going over the surveillance videotapes from the Florida Minerals Building. All he had seen was the back of their heads. The guard himself had been useless. Two guys with beards. "Scruffy-looking" was the best he could manage. Clyde had fired him on the spot.

From Jupiter, up to Apalachicola, by way of Perry, apparently, they were closing in. He squirmed in his seat and glared at the speakerphone. For the first time in his adult life, Clyde Bruno thought he understood the meaning of the word "fear," and he didn't like it.

"All right. Hold on, before we go off half-cocked: Thresher, Brendan, are we absolutely positive this is Bub's kid? I mean, how come we haven't heard anythin' from him? I mean, a six-year-old kid's gotta have a baby-sitter, right? Or a mom? Well, why haven't we heard from 'em?"

Clyde Bruno couldn't take it anymore. "Because maybe he's not *dead,* like I keep trying to tell you guys!"

"Goddamnit all, we been there, and we ain't goin' back," Farber roared over the speakerphone. "How many times I gotta tell you? Gettin' thrown overboard out in the ocean ain't like gettin' left by the side of the highway. You can't just hold your thumb out awhile and get a ride—"

There was a knock at the door, and Grant Hanson pushed it open, bearing a decanter of coffee and some cups, and proceeded to distribute and fill them for the table.

"Ask your gas station owner," Clyde said. "Ask *him* if Bub is dead or alive!"

"For the last fuckin' time, Bub is *dead,*" Farber said.

Grant perked up. "Y'all talking about Bub the candidate guy? Oh, he's alive."

Farber said over the phone, "What?"

Thresher and Clyde Bruno said together, "What?"

Grant nodded earnestly as he poured coffee. "Oh, yeah. I saw him a coupla hours ago. Walkin' down Gadsden."

Clyde Bruno stood, demanded: "Show me."

Grant led Clyde Bruno and Link Thresher out the side door, around the wood fence shielding the dumpster and onto Gadsden Street to where he'd seen the little sports car parked. Brendan trailed behind half a block, uncertain of how involved to get.

"It was around here somewhere," Grant said.

"Maybe it was the other side of the street?" Clyde offered.

"Nope, I'm sure. It was this side," he insisted.

Clyde wiped the sweat off his upper lip and dry-swallowed. "And you're sure it was Bub Billings?"

"Oh, yeah," Grant said casually. "The guy you had me ask that question to that time? It was him, all right. He even said hi to me."

Clyde made a conscious effort to slow his breathing. "I don't believe this. And it didn't occur to you that you ought to tell somebody you'd seen him?"

Grant looked up, blinked. "Why?" He turned and resumed walking down the sidewalk. "It was either right here or up beside that tree."

And suddenly Clyde noticed a glint of metal on the asphalt, walked off the curb and knelt down. It was an old baking sheet, partially covered by a fresh square of cardboard. And on the cardboard was the familiar cloverleaf. In a trance, Clyde Bruno reached out to the drippings, rubbed the oil between his fingers.

"I don't suppose you know what they were doing here," he said.

Grant shrugged. "Well, they were comin' outta there," he said, pointing down the block at the Division of Minerals Leasing building.

The words weren't out of his mouth before Clyde Bruno and Link Thresher had broken into a jog.

Bub and Murphy stood shoulder to shoulder behind the steering console of the Boston Whaler, skimming easily over dark, nearly flat water. They had rented it from a marina in Carabelle just as it was closing, had pored over the instruction manual for the GPS unit over a fried-shrimp dinner, then had waited a few hours past sunset before setting out down the channel.

Bub had been nearly mute the entire time, barely able to manage a wisecrack about the North Florida propensity to take perfectly good seafood and fry the livin' daylights out of it before drifting back into silent rumination. Murphy had let him ruminate, giving up after one or two attempts to draw him out, and instead concentrated on finding their objective in the moonless night.

In the open Gulf, the afternoon sea breeze had backed into a mere whisper from the east, letting him set the trim tabs, open the throttle and run fast over the wavelets, barely a hint of spray making its way back to them. He had picked up a couple of waterproof, disposable cameras at an Eckerd's, with the idea of photographing whatever they found at first light, then hightailing it back to Carabelle, then Cocoa Beach to call a receptive environmental group to take custody of the evidence and stage their press conference for them.

He checked the dim red glow of the GPS unit, saw that he was within two miles of the waypoint they had punched in and eased the skiff down off plane and back into the water.

"Don't want to make more of a racket than we have to," he murmured in the sudden quiet. "You positive about those coordinates, right?"

Bub grunted, opened his mouth to speak, closed it, opened it again. "You know, just 'cause a man used to work for you, don't necessarily mean you're close."

Murphy squinted at Bub, turned back to his scan of the horizon. "You're right."

Bub stood silently for a time. "I mean, we got no way of knowin' if Percy has said the first word to Grant Hanson since the day he left Marco."

"You're right," Murphy repeated.

"Far as we know, Grant mighta gotten his marchin' orders directly from Farber LaGrange, or even Clyde Bruno. Hell, he mighta been like an agent pro-va-ca-*toor*, planted there by Link Thresher himself." Bub pursed his lips. "Aw, who the hell do I think I'm foolin'?"

Murphy steered in silence. This part would have to come out on its own, he knew.

"Back when we were kids, my dad belonged to a country club for a while, until he quit when they wouldn't let in this doctor friend of his who happened to be Pakistani. Anyway, that's where me and Percy learned to play tennis. He was good, I mean *real* good, but I was wily. He'd hammer that big serve, and whale on his groundstrokes, and I'd pick off the corners and piss him off. Well, one afternoon, we got into this long, long set, thirteen-thirteen, somethin' like that. Finally, I was up a game and it was my ad, and he hit this big forehand, and I wound up like I was gonna slam it right back, and then I hit this dinky little drop shot."

Bub smiled to himself. "He about had a stroke. His face went beet red, and he came after me with his racket. I laughed and ran back to the fence and jumped up on it, and he was still cussin' up a storm and swingin' that racket at me. I finally dropped down to the clay, and he wound up big and swung right at my face. I was back right against the fence, and I swear, Murph, that frame grazed the tip of my nose. Another half inch, and I woulda been in the hospital with a smashed eye socket. I just stared at him, and you know what I saw in his face? Nothin'. Not a goddamned thing. It was scary as hell, that look. I can't even describe it properly."

He took a deep breath.

"It was that same expression I saw two weeks ago. I was down in the water, and he was standin' at the back of the boat, the stern, as you'd probably call it. I saw him and he saw me, and for a half second, I was relieved. But then I looked closer at his face, and there was nothin' there. Just that same, blank . . . nothin'.' "

Murphy waited through a long pause. "So Percy was on the boat."

Bub sighed softly. "Yeah, he was on the boat. I kept thinkin' 'bout that and thinkin' 'bout that, and kept talkin' myself into this idea that he just happened to be there. That he wasn't part of tossin' me overboard, that he didn't know anythin' about that, that he *still* doesn't. But that when he saw me in the drink, his first instinct was: *Now* I can finally get my due. . . ." He shook his head. "I guess a man can do some pretty wishful thinkin', when he's got a mind to. But at the end of the day, he's still my brother. The only one I got. I'm real sorry I lied to you, Murph, but I didn't wanna mix him up in all this other stuff. No, I don't think he oughta be governor this way. But I don't wanna see him go to jail, either."

Murphy kept scanning the horizon. "So you want they should lose the election but not get into any trouble with the police? Bub, they murdered a man."

"*They* did," Bub agreed. "But my brother had nothin' to do with that. Think about it: Who was the beneficiary of that? Sure as hell wasn't Percy. I don't got a problem with lettin' the authorities know about what we found on that boat and what you found underwater. I think the folks that did that need to be punished in a court of law. But as regards what happened to me . . . Well, I'd prefer to deal with young Percy myself."

Murphy said nothing, continued squinting out into the gloom.

"It's a family matter, Murph. Think about how you'd feel if it was your brother."

Murphy nodded to himself. "Which is why we needed something that'll make him lose the election, without putting him in any legal jeopardy. When we started out on this, ten days ago? I figured it would be a tall order. Too tall, probably. But you know what? I think maybe today's your lucky day." He pointed his chin at the horizon. "Look."

Barely half a mile ahead, against the starry backdrop, rose the silhouette of an enormous derrick, high into the night, above a thick, dark platform and four chunky pillars. Bub blew out a whistle, pushed the ball cap back off his head. "Leapin' Jesus H. Christ in a sidecar, would you look at *that!*"

Murphy further backed off the throttle to approach even more quietly. "What is that, an exploratory well?"

"Exploratory, my big, hairy butt!" Bub blew out another whistle. "That, Sailorman, would be a full-scale production rig. Would you *look* at that! How long you suppose it's been out here?"

Murphy shook his head. "I have no idea. All I know is it's illegal as hell. There's no active permit for anything beyond an exploratory well. Why is it dark, you think?"

Bub shrugged. "Probably 'cause no one's aboard. Oil rig hands, or I should say, *awl* rig hands make good money. It don't make any sense to bring 'em out here if they ain't producin' yet. I'm surprised a fishin' boat hasn't wandered into it yet."

Murphy studied the GPS unit. "Well, we're a good thirty-five miles offshore here. It might be too deep for the shrimpers." He checked his watch. "It's coming up on midnight. Sun will be up in about seven hours. We'll take some pictures, then head back."

"What, you mean you wanna just hang out here all night?"

"You want to drive all the way back to shore and then come all the way back out?"

"Actually," Bub grinned, "I'm thinkin' we oughta go on inside! Take a look around, see what there is to see!"


Link Thresher stalked impatiently back and forth in front of the abandoned Signature Flight Services counter, alternately checking his watch and snapping at Clyde Bruno.

"Where the fuck is he?" he demanded again.

Clyde Bruno occupied himself by assembling, then disassembling the automatic weapons he carried in a Spalding baseball equipment bag. The anxiety of not knowing who was after him was gone, replaced now with the serene high he always felt prior to action and violence. The question of how Bub Billings had managed to survive no longer concerned him. He could accept that Bub, in fact, had survived, now that fate was giving him a second chance to take care of it.

They had found the head clerk in the state Minerals Leasing building just as he was closing for the day and, with the help of a friendly Republican budget chairman, gently persuaded him to extend office hours that particular evening. It had taken them a couple of hours going through the dusty archives until they had found the boxes of documents that Bub and his companion had been looking at, and a couple hours after that before they finally tracked down the MG roadster in a marina parking lot in Carabelle.

Bub and his friend had rented a boat, it was quickly determined, which was when Thresher had called in the Petron helicopter from Apalachicola, reasoning that the chopper would give them a lot more speed and flexibility searching open ocean for an eighteen-foot Boston Whaler than would the entire fleet of Petron yachts.

That had been three and a half hours ago. First, the pilot couldn't be found. And then a particular part had to be replaced. But first *it* had to be found. And then the machine had to be gassed up. . . .

Clyde Bruno once again added in his head the hour-and-a-half drive to Apalachicola, then an hour by boat; if they'd followed his advice, they'd be out on the rig by now.

He began: "If we'd taken a boat—"

Link Thresher turned on him, chin quivering and face red. "You wanna trade for a while? Is that what you wanna do? You be the CEO and I'll be the goon? Huh? Is that it? 'Cause I'd be happy to do it! You think it's so easy, making decisions, fine. . . ."

He trailed off at the sound of a distant whirring, moved to the rear door and saw the lights coming in from the west. "Well, it's about fucking time."

The blue-and-green helicopter landed a hundred yards behind the fixed-base operator building, just long enough for Thresher and Clyde Bruno to climb aboard before it rose fast, tilting forward toward the southwest.

★

That there is the crew quarters," Bub explained with enthusiasm. "You got your rec room, your mess. There's big-screen TV. You can watch anythin' you want on the satellite. Football, pro wrestlin'. All the comforts of home."

They had tied up at a floating dock beneath the massive rig, then climbed up a ladder into the structure itself, whereupon Bub had been overcome with nostalgia for his hard-livin', hard-drinkin' days off the Texas coast and had felt compelled to give Murphy the grand tour.

"Oil's dirty work," Bub said, leading the way down another corridor. "Dangerous, too. Lots of big, nasty machinery just waitin' for a chance to chew on your arm."

Murphy grunted, pointing his flashlight left and right at door signs as they passed. "Just how long did you work on that rig?"

"Twenty-one months," Bub said. "Which actually was a little on the long side. You'd be amazed at the turnover. That's actually how come it's such a messy business. At least half the spills are human error, I'd say. Some yutz openin' a valve instead of closin' it. Most of the guys, the rigs make 'em more money than they've ever seen in their whole lives. So, naturally, what they gotta do when they get back to shore is piss as much of it away as possible in the first coupla weeks on beer and bail money."

Bub stopped at a crossing of hallways, pointed his flashlight left and right. "Hmmmm. Let's see. VIP Quarters. How 'bout we check that out. I bet that's where ol' Link Thresher hangs out when he's here."

He opened the door and flipped a light switch to teak paneling, thick, plate-glass picture windows, polished wood floors and, everywhere, gleaming brass. On the walls hung giant framed photos of oil tankers, the Alaska pipeline, a well field on the North Slope. And in the center, on a glass table amid two taupe leather couches, was an enormous relief map of the United States Gulf Coast. From Pensacola clear around to the Dry Tortugas, there stood dozens of tiny model oil rigs, some in black plastic, some in yellow, some in red.

"Well, how about that," Bub breathed. "Murph, I think we found the mother lode! Would you look at this? They're gonna make it look like the coast of Louisiana!"

Murphy patted his pockets. "Damn it all! I left the cameras in the boat. Come on, we need to go back and get them."

Bub frowned at the little oil rigs. "I wonder what the different colors are for?"

"Black is first online, in the next fiscal year," a voice from behind them answered. "Please put your hands on your heads, gentlemen, and turn around slowly."

Bub and Murphy did as they were told, saw themselves facing a menacing speargun in the hands of a tall, angular man in a blue wet suit and black weight belt. Dark wavy hair was plastered to his skull, and bright white teeth shone behind the weapon.

"Yellow is for the following year, and red for the year after that. In general, they're shootin' for light sweet crude first, gas second, heavy crude last. A regular forest of oil rigs. Give Siesta Key that nice Galveston feel," the man told them. "Like you boys don't know all this already."

Murphy blinked. "Whoa, whoa, whoa . . . You're not with Petron? But you think we *are*?"

"Well, who the hell else would you be with?"

"Think about it! Why would we be skulking around like this? Why would we want to take pictures of that model if we worked for Petron?"

The man considered this. "Well, then, you're probably with Shell or British Petroleum. Doesn't matter, either way. I'm afraid y'all picked the wrong time to go skulking—"

"Wait!" Murphy yelled. "Just hold on one second. You've got no more right to be here than we—"

"Randy?" Bub said, then grinned widely, strode toward him with hand outstretched. "Well, I'll be ding-dong-danged! It *is* you! Don't you remember? We met at the state party convention that time in Orlando! What's it been, eight years? Nine? Murph, this here is Randy Romer, one-time junior surfin' champion and the state attorney for Volusia and Flagler counties!"

"Former state attorney. I lost. Who in hell are you?"

Bub swiped the ball cap off his head. "Chrissake. Maybe my name recognition wasn't so good after all. Pretend I got hair and I don't got a beard."

Romer finally lowered the speargun. "Byron Billings? I thought you were dead. . . ."

"Well, that's what ol' Petron North America would like you to think. You know those bastards are fundin' pretty much the entire governor's race? It's true, they got 'bout two dozen dummy companies set up, all over the state, that do nothin' but funnel soft money to the Party. And you know why?" He pointed at the tabletop model. "Right there. The politics of petroleum. Greasy, dirty oil money. Hey, but enough about me. What the hell you doin' here? So you lost reelection, huh? Was it over that porno-tape crackdown?"

Bub turned to Murphy, jerked a thumb at Romer over his shoulder: "See, ol' Randy tried to enforce the obscenity statutes by crackin' down on porno-tape rentals." He shook his head sadly. "You don't gotta be some high-falutin' media consultant to know *that* dog ain't gonna hunt. So they actually voted you out, huh? How bad was—"

"Shhhh!" Romer commanded, finger over his lips. "Listen!"

The unmistakable whirring of a helicopter, at first barely audible, slowly grew louder. Romer pointed at the light switch by the door. "Kill that! Now!"

Murphy flipped the switch, then froze, listening. The chopper's noise grew louder still. "It's coming here, isn't it?"

Romer pulled a flashlight from his belt and broke into a jog. "Let's go."

They ran down one corridor, turned, followed it to the end, then turned again into the room that contained the top of the ladder descending to the floating dock. Romer led the way, his speargun slung over one shoulder.

Murphy realized it as soon as they stepped onto the floating dock: "Where the hell's my boat?"

"Sank it about a half hour ago," Romer said.

"Sank it?" Murphy shouted. "It's a Boston Whaler! It's unsinkable!"

Romer said, "I beg to differ. Come on. Follow me."

The helicopter was visible as well as audible now, a flashing light low on the horizon, and Murphy jogged behind Romer and Bub to the end of the float, where Romer climbed into a low-riding Ranger skiff painted as black as the water.

"Bring that bow line aboard with you," Romer said, cranking the outboard with a single pull. "Come on!"

**B**athed in starlight, Petron Bravo-1 rose tall and just barely darker than the surrounding water, the square helipad on the northeast corner an improbably small target in the gloom.

Link Thresher peered through the helicopter's bubble canopy, Clyde Bruno looking over his shoulder, at the northwest corner of the living structure, the location of Thresher's VIP suite. "Well, there's no light on now," Thresher said. "Maybe you were just seein' things."

Clyde Bruno was adamant. "No, sir. I saw a light. I thought it was coming from your cabin. I may have been wrong about the location, but I definitely saw a light."

Thresher shrugged, hoisted his overnight bag onto his lap and opened a side pocket. "I guess we'll find out soon enough, if you were right." He removed a small metal box, from its top extended a metal antenna, then pushed a button on its front. "Huh. Guess we're still too far away. Get us a little closer, Earl, and I'll get those lights on for you."

Clyde Bruno continued to scowl out the window as the derrick approached slowly from below. He had definitely seen a light, and he was pretty certain it had come from the VIP suite. All his life, he had had twenty-fifteen vision. He could have been a fighter pilot, if his grades had been a little better . . . and he'd gone to college instead of dropping out of high school. He sure as hell didn't *imagine* seeing anything. . . .

Without warning, the helipad lights came on, bright yellow in the darkness. Link Thresher shouted in triumph as Clyde Bruno blinked against the sudden glare—and in that instant, just before he closed his eyes, saw the reflected white water of a wake.

He snapped his eyes wide open, searching the water's surface, until there, not a hundred yards to the east, he saw the white rooster tail in the black water.

"A boat!" he yelled, pointing.

Link Thresher pushed his arm down in irritation. "Damn it, Clyde, Earl's tryin' to land! It's hard enough without your distractions. All right, so you saw a boat. We're over the fucking ocean. I expect we'll see one or two boats."

"This one," Clyde Bruno said, "came out from under the rig."

Thresher's eyes flashed in rage. "Why didn't you say so? Where?"

Clyde pointed, and Earl twisted the collective to follow, with one hand flicked on the powerful searchlight on the bottom of the aircraft, until Clyde Bruno pointed slightly to the left, where a white wake showed cleanly on the water's surface.

"Got 'em," Link Thresher said. "No gettin' away now. . . . Earl, put the light on 'em. Clyde, why don't you slide your door open and fire at will."

Murphy clung to the back of Romer's seat, over his shoulder watched as the chopper swerved left and right, trying to match Romer's swerves. Each time the helicopter's searchlight illuminated the boat, he could hear the *Pop! Pop! Pop!* of bullets striking the surface of the water nearby.

Romer throttled back, pulled the wheel over hard to starboard, then throttled up, just as the chopper dove low and swung over their path. This time he saw the staccato flashes through the helicopter's open rear door, heard the bullets snap past their heads.

"Jesus Christ!" Bub yelled. "They almost got us that time! He's got some sorta machine gun up there!"

Behind them, the helicopter swung across and back, then zeroed in on their course. Romer glanced over his shoulder, turned forward again. "I would say by the sound of it that it's a Heckler and Koch MP5. Standard issue of the German border patrol. Eight hundred rounds a minute in fully automatic mode. It's illegal, of course, to own one like that. Hang on!" He throttled all the way down into neutral, then further into reverse. The skiff shuddered and leaned over as Romer threw the wheel to port as the helicopter overshot the boat with a *Pop! Pop! Pop!* in the water beside them, then quickly throttled back up in forward and scooted off westward.

Murphy watched the helicopter circle around and back at them once more. "Randy, I'll give you this: You're good, but how much longer can we keep this up?"

"Call me Romer," Romer said, and glanced at his dive watch. "I'm thinking about another thirty-five seconds, is all I need."

Murphy blinked, opened his mouth to ask what happened then, when without warning the sky in front of them erupted in a series of white flashes that lit the horizon. The *boom-boom-boom-booooom!* came five seconds later, rolling over them in rapid waves.

Romer throttled back into neutral, and the three of them watched as the oil rig, ablaze now, slowly collapsed in on itself, hissing as red-hot metal touched water, then suddenly sank into the sea. Overhead, the helicopter shot past toward where the rig had been, as Murphy and Bub began shouting questions.

"What in hell?"

"Did *you* do that?"

"I thought we had another thirty-five seconds!"

Romer shrugged. "Obviously I did not synchronize the time precisely." He waited for the helicopter to become a pair of distant lights, then engaged the outboard, spun the skiff around until it was pointed east and quickly got it up on a fast plane.

Earl flew a precise search pattern of expanding squares, while Clyde scanned the surface below and Link Thresher sat and stared at the point in the water where his $300 million oil rig, not quite legal and therefore not quite insured, had recently stood.

They had broken off the chase at the explosions, watching in disbelief as the rig burned, then quickly disappeared beneath the black water without so much as a slick. Clyde Bruno kept playing the scene in his head, again and again: The pillars had all collapsed inward, while the derrick had sheared off at the base and the main structure had gone straight down, the windows all blown out.

Shaped charges, were what they were. Plastic explosives molded into a specific shape to cut through steel like it was butter.

He had worked with a demolitions man once, a former special forces guy from whom he'd picked up a little of the lingo and know-how. Enough to understand that he had witnessed some quality work. Something a true expert in the field might have accomplished. An expert, he thought to himself, like the guy he'd enlisted for the tank farm fires and the disabling of the tanker. . . .

His mouth fell open as he remembered Romer studying the Gulf Coast chart on his office wall, recalled that he had been in his office, by himself, for God-knew-how-long. Recalled that he had even asked him about the pin marking the rig's location. . . .

He glanced over his shoulder at his boss, who was still staring off blankly into space, and Clyde Bruno decided there was absolutely nothing to be gained by sharing his suspicions. If Romer had in fact destroyed Petron Bravo-1, and Romer had been recruited and ostensibly vetted solely by Clyde Bruno, he knew whose hide it would come out of.

On the other hand, what if Romer's treachery was somehow also related to the removal of the fishing pole and harness . . . and with a shudder he remembered where Romer had acquired his demolitions training— as a Vietnam-era Navy SEAL.

In fact, the boat they had been chasing had been black and dark, dark blue . . . yet the boat Bub and his friend had rented had been a plain, vanilla Boston Whaler, white with the little bit of red trim. And there had been three men aboard, not two: Bub, his friend with the MG and now . . . this deadly Romer?

He bit his lip, hard, and redoubled his unblinking study of the water's surface three hundred feet below. His single best opportunity to solve the problem was right now, while they were on a small boat and he had superiority of both air power and firepower.

Clyde Bruno strained his eyes at the oval of water lit by the searchlight, looking for the telltale flash of whitewater or glint of metal, with such fixation that he only realized something was amiss when the oval grew so large that it barely illuminated anything. He glanced up, saw that Earl had broken off the search and was flying due north.

"Where are we going?" he demanded.

Earl tapped the fuel gauge, whose needle now rested on the red sector at the very bottom.

"Don't worry. This ain't over. Not by a long shot. I already got a team watchin' that convertible in Carabelle," Link Thresher vowed, then seemed to remember something. "Tell me again about that house on the St. Johns River. . . ."

★ ⑦ ★

Romer drove in silence, Murphy beside him in the front seat, with Bub perched between them in the back, chattering away about everything that had happened to him and what they'd managed to learn.

"You mean they *killed* Spencer Tolliver?" Romer blew out through his teeth softly. "Damn them all to hell. He was a good man."

Murphy piped up. "You knew him?"

"Not personally," Romer said. "We were both in Southeast Asia at about the same time."

"You were a POW, too?" Bub asked.

"Not exactly. I got captured, once. For about two days." Romer flashed a grin that positively radiated against his dark tan. "I don't do well in captivity."

They had run his boat through the cut between St. George and Dog islands, driving up between the oyster bars into a bit of wood sheltering a sandy beach. Romer had tied the vessel to a tree, then led the way to a blue Karmann Ghia, offered them a ride to Carabelle to pick up Murphy's car.

"How do you like the MG?" Romer asked.

"A blast to drive," Murphy said.

"They leak oil like a sieve," Romer grunted. "Never trust the Brits to build a car. It's like letting the Italians run a government. I know somebody who can do a retrofit, with custom gaskets. Do the environment a favor."

Murphy said, "I'd like that."

They rode in silence for a short time, until Bub finally cleared his throat. "Okay, there's no way I can keep this in anymore. What you do, Romer, blow things up. Is there a big market for that, eco-terrorism wise?"

"Not normally, no," Romer said. "Normally, it's more of an avocation. Kind of like surfing, only louder. This time, there came a client who wanted things done that I might have done on my own. The professional and the personal coincided, so to speak."

"The gasoline tank farm fires!" Bub blinked. "That was you, wasn't it?"

"I have no idea what you're talking about. Destruction of private property, the foundation of our entire socioeconomic system, calls for severe treatment by our criminal courts." Romer grinned wordlessly for a few moments. "Now, as a technical work of art, that's something else entirely. Imagine, if you will, planning and executing something like that while ensuring that not a drop of carcinogenic solvent spilled on the ground. It would involve making certain all the valves in all the pipes were in the correct configuration prior to the explosion. How come nobody in the newspapers points *that* out?"

Bub scratched his head. "All right, call me slow, but when you burn all that gasoline in a fire like that, don't that release all the same pollutants as using it in cars?"

"Even more pollutants, actually, without the benefit of catalytic converters. However, you'll notice that gas in Florida is now routinely three bucks a gallon, occasionally hitting three-fifty. Go talk to your neighborhood Ford and Chevy dealers. SUV sales are plummeting. All those Yukons and Expeditions and Suburbans and Navigators are just sitting there, gathering dust. *That's* the point, right there."

Murphy watched Romer's strong, long-fingered hands on the steering wheel. He drove the car like he drove the boat: fast and with confidence. He also noticed that the car, though old and wearing some surface rust, seemed mechanically as good as new. Better than new, in fact, with a tight, sports-car suspension.

"So what happened tonight, wasn't that hurting the same client who paid you to do the other stuff?" Murphy asked.

"I was hired on the claim they were trying to increase market share. As long as my objectives were met, I have no quarrel with who gets how much of Florida's high-test unleaded sales. Then I started getting suspicious of their *ultimate* objective, and I decided to come back to their office a little later in the evening and research things further. Sure enough, they've got hard plans to build fifty-four rigs along the Florida Gulf Coast over the next three years." Romer shook his head slowly. "Do what you want on land, but don't fuck with my ocean. I believe that's the marina coming up, correct?"

The Karmann Ghia rolled down the hill off the bridge and slowed as they approached the gravel parking lot of the C-Quarters Marina—and then sped right back up again and continued along the highway.

"Whoa, whoa!" Murphy said, pointing. "That was it right there! That was my car!"

"Uh-huh. Did you see the two vans parked either side of it?" Romer checked his rear-view mirror carefully. "I happened to notice them the other day in Apalachicola. They belong to Florida Minerals. So do the goons who were leaning against them."

"Florida Minerals!" Bub sat up straight. "Wait just one minute. . . . How would they know to come after that car? They couldn't of caught more than a glimpse of us out there on the water!"

Murphy stared through the rear window at the marina, finally turned back around. "Unless that chopper coming out tonight wasn't a coincidence. Unless they were coming out there because they knew we'd rented a boat from right here."

He thought for a moment, then looked back at Bub.

"Grant Hanson," they said together.

"You read my mind," Bub said. "He musta seen us walk outta that office!"

"And they must have gone in there and figured out what we were looking at," Murphy finished.

"They're on to us," Bub concluded. "A fact I suppose we mighta surmised when they started shootin' at us. Hey, you didn't give 'em your real name, did ya? At the marina?"

Murphy shook his head. "Uh-uh. The same bullshit name I gave down in Jupiter. Now that I think of it, I bet that Chip put 'em on to it down there. I guess it's time I dropped that identity."

"When you're on the run, never use a fake identity beyond the first encounter with the enemy," Romer declared.

Bub nodded solemnly. "Wow. Good advice. They teach you that in, you know, special ops school or someplace?"

"Spy novels. *Eye of the Needle. Day of the Jackal.*" Romer drove slowly, checking the rearview mirror. "That name, Grant Hanson, rings a bell. I'm not sure why."

"He's a goon," Murphy said. "One of the guys the Party sends out to beat up poll workers. That sort of thing."

"You ever been a poll worker?" Bub asked Romer.

"Now I remember: G-Hanson at F-G-O-P-dot-org. He was on the carbon list of an e-mail that was printed out on Clyde Bruno's desk the other night," Romer said. "Something to do with a house down in Brevard, out on State Road 520."

Bub's eyes went wide, and he grabbed Romer by the arm. "Did you say State Road 520?"

Romer nodded. "Didn't read the whole thing. But, yeah. State Road 520 in Brevard. That I remember."

Bub stared fixedly through the windshield, his fingers gripping the two front seats tight enough to squeeze the blood from his knuckles.

"Bub, you all right?" Murphy waved a hand before his eyes. "Byron?"

Bub snapped out of it, licked his lips and once more grabbed Romer's shoulder. "Mr. Romer, I never before asked a human bein' for a favor as important as the one I'm fixin' to ask you right now: Is there any way I can impose on you to drive me down to Brevard County? Like tonight? Like right now?"

Farber LaGrange finally found the cell phone beneath a pile of catering invoices and fashion magazines on *Soft Money*'s navigation table, answered it on the twenty-seventh ring.

It was Link Thresher, and LaGrange listened with increasing amazement. "Jesus . . . You're *kiddin'*. . . . Gone, completely gone?"

"That's my problem and my shareholders' problem," Link Thresher said over the phone. "*Our* problem is that . . . *he* is still alive."

"You *saw* him?" Farber LaGrange breathed, casting a nervous eye at the closed door to the owner's stateroom. "With your own eyes?"

"It's him, all right," Thresher said. "No doubt about it. He's with that guy with the MG. Guy named Murphy Moran, the tag comes back to. Plus another guy I don't know, although I got a feeling he's the one behind the oil rig thing. Clyde gets real quiet whenever I mention it."

"*Murphy Moran!*" LaGrange glanced around *Soft Money*'s main salon, at the red, white and blue decorations on every bulkhead, at the Victory banners strung between handholds. "Oh, Jesus, we are in deep shit. The man's a political pro. Dropped out a coupla years back to sail 'round the world or some such bullshit. You sure it's him?"

"On the short side? Beard?"

"Christ. It is him." LaGrange sucked in a deep breath. "Okay, here's what's gotta happen. Election's Tuesday: There's even a *hint* of a story gets out that Bub's still alive, we're in trouble. If Bub and Murphy call a press conference, we're fucked. Understand? F-U-C-K-E-D. Like prison fucked. And do not misunderstand me: If it comes to it, I will roll over on you like a fuckin' walrus. It was all your idea. It was your employee actually done the foul deeds. You were the mastermind—"

"Hey, Farber! Just shut up, all right? I got more to lose in this than you do, okay? Trust me: I'm on the case. I'm taking care of it."

Farber LaGrange scratched his chest hair in agitation. He had shown up after an eighteen-hour day on the campaign bus, had stripped down to his boxers, ready to crawl into his bunk, when he had noticed the hairbrushes and makeup cases and eyebrow machine in the head and had remembered that Clarissa Highstreet was still occupying his cabin. He had muttered to himself disconsolately on his way to the forepeak and fallen into a crew berth instead.

"You know where they are now?" Farber asked.

"We've got a pretty good idea where they're headed. You remember. Where we talked about, yesterday," Link Thresher said. "We'll take care of them there. Don't worry. It's under control."

"You been sayin' that now for weeks, and look where it's gotten us."

"Will you *please* just give me a break? Huh? Would you?" Thresher asked. "I just called to let you know that I might be a little late for the Victory Cotillion, is all. Got a couple of details to take care of."

Farber LaGrange shook his head and waved his finger in the air. "Oh, no, you don't. The one detail you *need* to take care of is gettin' your ass over here. That silicone bitch moved onto my boat and vowed she ain't leavin' till she talks to you about Paris."

"Paris?"

"About the motherfuckin' 'bassadorship. I told you 'bout it."

"You did," Thresher agreed. "And I thought I told *you*. It's out of the question. The president's already given it to somebody else."

LaGrange shook his head again. "You cannot tell her that!" he whispered into the phone. "Have you seen the latest polls? This sum-bitch's gonna be a nail-biter. We're gonna need every last vote we can get. We're gonna *need* her help. Look, I don't give a rat's ass whether she actually gets it or not, all right? Thing is: Today, tonight, if she asks to be 'bassador to the *moon,* you gotta promise it to her. Understand?"

"All right, all right. Whatever. I have to run. I'll see you this afternoon."

"Just remember," Farber LaGrange interjected. "Any of this shit gets out, I'll turn state's evidence so fast it'll make your head spin."

With a grunt, Link Thresher was gone. Farber pushed the end button on the phone and stuck it in the teak binocular holder over the nav table, turned to head back to the forepeak when he saw Clarissa Highstreet in the doorway to his owner's cabin, her eyes sleepy but her mouth in full, perpetual smile. She wore a camisole with lace cutouts over her bosom.

"I thought I heard you come inside." She yawned. "What time is it?"

"Oh-dark-thirty." Farber regarded her spike-heeled slippers unhappily. He had just had the entire cabin sole stripped and revarnished. Now it was covered with tiny pockmarks. "On a boat, it's called comin' aboard, not comin' inside. Is there ever a time you *don't* wear heels?"

Clarissa Highstreet glanced down at her calves. "Oh, it's said that I sometimes take them off in the shower." She winked at him lasciviously. "You want to find out sometime? Oh! Look at that! I can see that *some-body's interested!*"

He followed her finger to his crotch, tucked his limp member back through the boxer's fly.

"Speaking of which: I've got something to show you." Without preamble, she pushed the camisole's straps off her shoulders and thrust out her chest. "What do you think?"

He stared at her breasts. They stared back defiantly, rigid, volcano-shaped nipples pointing the way. "Mouth waterin' as ever," he began, then did a double take. "What in God's name's goin' on with your nips?"

She turned from side to side to offer him a profile. "You like? Nipples are back in. The silhouette look. Don't you read *Cosmo?* Last time I was in, I had my doctor . . . inject a little something extra, shall we say."

Farber bent closer, cautiously reached out one finger. "They're sharp!"

"There was a slight problem," Clarissa Highstreet allowed. "Something about the catalyst hardening too soon. I have to have them redone."

Farber shook his head fearfully. "It's all fun and games till somebody loses an eye."

"Oh, stop it. Anyway, I was *asking* about my *tan!*" she protested, pointing to her now brown globes. "I've been working on them for days!"

"Oh. That. The Riviera ain't seen finer," he said, and immediately regretted his geographical reference.

"Speaking of France," she said on cue, "what's the latest on my ambassadorship? What's your buddy Link Thresher say?"

Farber LaGrange didn't hesitate even an instant. "Ain't got the foggiest. Haven't talked to him in a while. Really. Haven't got a clue. Don't know any—"

"You can stop lying at any time," she interrupted. "I know what you think. You think just because I've got nice legs, a great set of tits, that I don't have a brain upstairs. You probably think you can blow me off, make all kinds of promises you never intend to keep, just to get past the governor's election, and then, afterwards, tell me: Oh, well, sorry, we couldn't make it happen. Well, think again, mister man!"

Her outstretched finger shook with anger, her entire body quivering with it, save for her boobs, which remained rock solid steady.

"I know how to read. I know what the polls are saying," she continued. "And it comes to my attention that *I* hold the power here. I have in my custody thirty thousand spoiled punch-card ballots that I have not yet sent out. Oh, and that nutty ballot in Palm Beach? The one that's going to give a chunk of Ramsey's vote to the Nazi? Well, it so happens that I haven't ruled it legal yet. And guess what? Unless and until I have in my hand the appointment letter from the president, those spoiled ballots stay right in my office. And come Election Day, I'll go ahead and rule that Palm Beach ballot illegal and award any votes the Nazi gets to Ramsey MacLeod."

She smiled wickedly, as an afterthought pulled the camisole's straps back over her shoulders. "I believe I've made my point," she said, turning back into her cabin. "You know, I *was* going to offer to share my bed with you. But now? I've changed my mind. Pleasant dreams."

Farber LaGrange squeezed his temples as hard as he could between his thumbs, wondering whether he should simply burst in and strangle her. Then hard, cold reason took hold again. He would wait until after the election.


Romer flew down State Road 520 at close to ninety in the early morning stillness, the little four-cylinder engine running up near the red line and limiting conversation to an occasional shout above the noise.

He had stayed on the back roads most of the way, using the Turnpike and then a piece of the Beeline only, he had explained, because their value as straight shots outweighed the inability to go as fast because of all the cops.

Murphy had just held on for the ride as Romer raced headlong with high beams lighting the way, wondering what could be so important that they needed to risk life and limb like this. He wondered why Bub would have a second house so close to his Merritt Island place. And then he thought about all of Bub's mysterious phone calls, at least one, sometimes several each day, without so much as a word of explanation. And then he thought about Bub's words on the sail down to Jupiter, and his offhand remarks about his family. So that by the time Bub pointed through the early morning mist at the mailbox and Romer turned down the dirt driveway and bumped around and through the dry mud holes, Murphy thought he had it figured out. When he saw the Volvo wagon parked in the carport, he knew he had it figured out.

"Oh, thank God," Bub breathed. "No other cars. You don't know what a relief that is."

Romer stopped the Karmann, and Murphy followed Bub out and shut the door.

"You sure you don't want me to hang around?" Romer asked.

Bub shook his head as he pumped Romer's hand through the open window. "I got it under control from here. I do appreciate your gettin' me home as fast as you did. I owe you, buddy."

Romer flashed his big white teeth and put the car in gear. "My pleasure. Take care."

They watched the car head out the long driveway back toward the highway before turning for the front door. "Home?" Murphy asked.

Bub took a deep breath as he inserted a key into the dead bolt. "Murph, I don't know how to tell you this. I feel like a total asshole. After you saved my life like you did, I shoulda trusted you with everythin'. Fact is, I was ashamed. Ashamed that I'd been tellin' such a great, big, fat lie. Fact is, well, all those phone calls I been makin'? Murph, I been callin'—"

"Your son," Murphy finished. "He's probably still asleep, isn't he? Why don't you check on him."

Bub blinked through a puzzled smile, then headed for a bedroom off to the side. Murphy wandered around the small living room decorated with pictures of Bub and Percy as children, of their father, Governor Lamont Billings, standing in front of the Mansion in Tallahassee, of Bub, his hair already graying at the temples, getting his college degree. He wandered across to the window overlooking the St. Johns floodplain, checked out the bookcase beneath it full of self-help books about personal finance and business accounting and learning disabilities—

"He's still half asleep. Don't know where Marlita is. That's his nanny."

Bub carried a Spiderman-pajamas-clad six-year-old on his hip, the boy's dirty blond head on his daddy's shoulder. Bub sat down in a beige couch, and the boy's hand went to Bub's cheek.

"He's never seen me with a beard," Bub grinned.

"He's beautiful," Murphy said.

"He's my big boy," Bub said, kissing the top of his head. "His name is Lamont Dexter. After his grandpa and his great-great grandpa. Lamont Dexter Billings."

The boy stirred, and Bub whispered, "Lammy? Can you say *¡hola!* to Mr. Murphy?"

The boy made a noise, and immediately Murphy understood why Bub owned so many titles about autism. He felt a lump in his throat as he watched Lamont Dexter continue stroking his father's face.

"Lammy's special," Bub explained. "His mommy used alcohol on a regular basis during her pregnancy. She also used a number of other, not-so-legal substances. I tried to get her to stop, but let's just say I didn't have the moral high ground at the time. Lammy, honey, hang on. This is really hurtin' Daddy."

Bub shifted Lamont on his chest, reached around his neck to pull a gold chain up and out of his pajama top. At the end was a man's ring, which Bub moved so that it lay over Lamont's back.

"When I first realized there was somethin' wrong, I thought maybe

God was punishin' me for . . . you know, for everythin'. But over the years, I come to see how wrongheaded *that* was. I mean, this child can *read*. He can't really talk too good, but he can read. And numbers? Math puzzles?" Bub blew a soft whistle. "So I've come around. If this is punishment, sign me up for more. Lammy's special. I don't like gettin' all metaphysical and stuff, but who knows? Maybe people like Lammy are the only ones who can really see God, you know?"

Murphy watched father and son hold each other. "So he's the one you've been calling every day?"

Bub nodded. "Yeah. He likes to hear my voice. And I like to hear his. Unfortunately, he's used to my bein' outta town. Sales trips and all, and this summer, the campaign. That's what I meant, when I said I was ashamed. See, Farber LaGrange picked me, or at least he said he did, 'cause I appealed to the quote base unquote. Now, I may not be the sharpest knife in the drawer, but even I knew that a single dad with a boy born outta wedlock wasn't gonna appeal to the base too good. So I didn't tell Farber. I figured, after I won, I could get it out then. You know, pretend to adopt him or somethin'." He shook his head in shame and squeezed Lamont tighter. "Yeah. That's right. That's how bad I wanted it. Pathetic, ain't it?"

Murphy thought a moment, blinked. "So he never heard about, you know, your . . . falling overboard?"

"That's the thing. I was worried sick about that. But when I called from the marina pay phone that mornin', that was the first Marlita had even heard about it!" Bub shrugged. "Makes sense, though. As you can see, we ain't got no TV in the house. Don't believe a child oughta be watchin' one. And Marlita, well, her English ain't too good, so she don't read the paper, except for grocery coupons and such. So anyhow, I just told her: No matter what you might hear about me, don't believe it. I'm here, and I'm safe."

Bub glanced over his shoulder at the approaching footsteps. "Speak of the devil! Hey, Marlita! *¡Hola! ¿Cómo 'stas?* Hey, I want you meet a good friend of mine. His name is Murphy Moran. He's the one who saved my life!"

Murphy stood and nodded, and Marlita bowed her head. "It is a plea-sure to meet you, Meester Moran. Señor Billings, I am so glad you are home. . . . There's a man here from the Party. He wanted us to go with him, but I told him I would not until you—"

Clyde Bruno turned the corner into the living room. He held a large handgun in one hand, casually waved it at Bub and Murphy, then cleared his throat.

"Okay, now that we're all here, I need everybody to keep calm. We're all taking a little trip."

Bub glared at him silently and hatefully, covered Lamont with both arms. "How did you get here?" he demanded.

"Chopper. Landed on your patio back there. It was kind of small, but Earl's good." Clyde Bruno squinted at Lamont, waved his gun at him. "What's that on that chain, there? That doesn't happen to be a Naval Academy ring, does it?"

Bub licked his lips and kept his voice low: "Put the effing un-gay in your olster-hay."

Clyde Bruno blinked. "Un-gay?"

"He's barely six," Bub said evenly, stroking his still-drowsy son. "He doesn't need to know about un-gays. Now, you want us to cooperate, you put it away. You want us to make it ugly, you keep on actin' like an asshole."

Clyde Bruno surveyed the room, cockily slid the gun into a shoulder holster. "From what I've seen, none of you strike me as the sort to be carrying. Now, the ring, please. And then we're all goin' on a little heli-copter ride."

Bub gently took the chain from around Lamont's neck, held it and the ring in his hand. "I won't ask why you want this. It's better for my sanity if I don't. I will tell you this: If you so much as look funny at a hair on this child's body, I swear to you on all that's holy, sir, that I will not rest until I've ripped the een-splay from your chest and fed it to wild ferrets. Do I make myself clear?"

He flung ring and chain at Clyde Bruno, who caught them with one hand while frowning at the imagery Bub had painted for him. He shoved them into one jacket pocket, pulled a roll of duct tape out of another, then nodded at Marlita and Murphy.

"All right. I need everyone to lie down on the floor so I can do your hands. I'll start with you two—"

"I've got a better idea," a new voice said from the corridor behind Clyde Bruno. "How about if *you* very gently put the weapon at your feet, then take two steps forward and lie down."

Murphy smiled in relief as Romer, still in wet suit and weight belt, stepped ever closer to Clyde Bruno, speargun in hand.

"Let me explain it to you," Romer continued. "There is a very sharp, stainless steel shaft approximately four centimeters from your neck. Now, when I fire the trigger mechanism, I suppose there is indeed a slight chance that it will somehow miss both carotid arteries, the jugular vein, spinal cord and trachea as it passes through, leaving you relatively unscathed. Personally, I would call it a *very* slight chance. So how 'bout it, punk . . . you feel lucky?"

At Bub's insistence, Romer drove more slowly this time, no faster than five miles over the posted speed limit.

"Those traffic engineers, they ain't dummies," Bub pointed out. "If a curve's posted at forty-five miles an hour, it's because cars goin' faster than that are more likely to tip over. Better safe than sorry."

They were all five piled into the Karmann Ghia, Murphy in the passenger seat, Bub, Lamont and Marlita in the back. Murphy idly fingered the fuel pump valve from the helicopter and the distributor cap from the Volvo that sat on the dashboard. Romer had disabled both conveyances and cut the phone lines to the house in the five minutes it took Bub to install Lamont's car seat in the back of the Karmann.

"You should have let me kill him," Romer said, turning south on Wickham Road. "That pilot, Earl, he's harmless. But that Clyde Bruno . . ." Romer shook his head. "He's going to get out. When he does, he's going to be trouble. And to be perfectly honest with you, he's the sort that needs killing."

"Hey, hey, hey," Bub called from the back. "I told you already: Stop sayin' ill-kay in front of my boy. He doesn't need to be hearin' that. Now, we don't need to be ill-kayin' anybody. Soon as we take our story public, about oil rigs and Spencer Tolliver, Clyde Bruno will be put away for a long time."

Romer grunted, watchfully checking his mirrors as he drove. "I think your faith in our criminal justice system is misplaced. If I told you how many rapists and killers—"

"Hey, hey!"

"I'm sorry: apists-ray and illers-kay. How many of them I had to nol-pros or plead out as misdemeanor batteries because the cops screwed something up or because the only witness was juiced up on crack . . ."

Murphy pointed at the approaching intersection. "Okay, left there."

Romer turned, then turned again at a sign that read "Passenger Terminal" and parked close in at the short-term lot. Murphy hustled Bub, Lamont and Marlita across the drive, through the automatic doors and then ran ahead to the BahamasAir ticket counter. He paid in cash, then led them to Gate E, the last one down, consisting merely of a door opening onto the tarmac, to where the little ten-seat Beechcraft, the Diver's Special, was already spinning its starboard propeller.

Bub hugged and kissed Lamont before setting him on the floor and combing his hair with his fingers. "Now I want you to do what Miss Marlita says, all right? Be a good boy. Daddy will come get you in a couple of days, okay?"

Murphy scribbled on the back of the ticket envelope, then pressed it into Marlita's hands. "When you get there, ask for this man. Tell him Murphy Moran sent you. *¿Comprende usted?*"

"Yes," Marlita said. "I will tell him. Thank you very much, Meester Moran."

Bub gave Lamont one last hug and then put his hand in Marlita's. He and Murphy stood at the big window, watched as Lamont and Marlita were shepherded onto the little plane, as the boarding staircase was pulled inward and the plane taxied out to the runway, then as it sped down the concrete and up into the afternoon sky.

Both men let out breaths of relief, turned to walk back out to the parking lot.

"So where does this Diver's Special go, exactly, Sailorman?" The words were no sooner out of Bub's mouth than he thrust an open palm at Murphy. "Second thought, don't tell me. Less I know, the better."

They crossed the road in front of the terminal. Romer already had the engine running by the time they climbed in. "Where to now?" he asked.

Murphy snapped his seat belt into place. "Blastoff View Marina."

The remaining threads in the duct tape parted with a *snap* that sent his shoulders slamming into the pantry's bottom shelf. Clyde Bruno braced himself for the shower of cans and bottles, slowly scrunched his knees upward until he could pass his bound wrists under and in front of his legs, then finally stood up.

That son-of-a-bitch Romer had bound him well, with wrists strapped together behind his back, then separately taped to his ankles. It had taken him the better part of an hour to find a corner sharp enough to slowly abrade the layers of tape tying hands to ankles. The rest, he knew, would be easy.

Within a few minutes, he had chewed and spat his way through the tape binding his wrists together, then quickly freed his ankles and then, after a few moments of stretching away a neck crick, began pounding on the door panel with a large can of soup.

It took a dozen sharp blows for the wood to splinter, and a few hasty passes with the soup can, Progresso Black Bean, Clyde Bruno could see now, to clear a hole large enough to crawl out. Immediately he went to the kitchen counter where Romer had left watch, wallet and cell phone in a tidy pile, grabbed the little Nokia—only to find that Romer had swiped the battery.

With a curse, he grabbed the phone on the wall—but there was no dial tone. The blinking, caller-ID screen flashed "NO SIGNAL," and Clyde Bruno cursed aloud now, stomped through the family room and out the sliding glass door, jogged across the backyard to the parked helicopter.

Earl was lying on the floor in the back, and Bruno set to work on the duct tape bindings, tossing the torn pieces out the open door.

"Let's go," he said finally, balling the last length of tape and flipping it over his shoulder.

Earl shook his head. "He was in the engine compartment for a coupla minutes. I can't imagine she's gonna fly." He went to the panel, opened it and shut it again. "He broke the primary fuel pump. We're not going anywhere."

"Your phone?" Clyde Bruno asked.

"Took the battery."

Clyde Bruno pounded the side of the craft, letting loose a long string of profanity, when he noticed the VHF radio on the instrument panel. He yanked open the pilot's door, held his breath a moment, then let his finger flip the main power switch. The radio came to life, and Clyde Bruno tossed the handset to Earl.

"Get the VHF operator and get a phone patch. Call Thresher's office. Have 'em send a car. And then get the research unit on the phone. I'm gonna need a few reverse directory lookups," he barked, then jogged back toward the house.

"Where *you* going?" Earl asked.

Clyde Bruno turned to yell in mid-stride, "Just get on the radio, would you!"

We can connect the dots right out to the oil rig," Murphy said. "Of course, then we'll have to explain that no, there *is* no oil rig anymore. Of course, we can say, 'There *used* to be an oil rig, but then this eco-terrorist blew it up just as we were about to check it out.'"

Romer's Karmann Ghia cruised north on the interstate in the late afternoon sun, Romer adhering to the speed limit as convoys of tractor-trailers flew past in the fast lane.

"Sorry to screw up your story line," he said. "I guess y'all have to balance that against the fact that, without me having been out there, you'd both be dead right now."

Bub considered this from his back seat perch. "Man's got a point."

"Well, never mind. Your mere presence is going to throw everything into a tizzy," Murphy said, then turned to look Bub in the eye. "You sure you want to do this?"

Bub nodded once, brow furrowed. "Darned straight. Mess with me, that's one thing. Mess with my boy? Now you gotta go to jail. Period. End of story. And that includes Percy."

Murphy nodded in agreement. "Don't forget, plus we have that stuff about Spencer Tolliver. . . . Of course, I dropped the only piece of real evidence on that into the deep."

"Just because it's in deeper water doesn't mean it's gone. In fact, there's no place for it to go. The current that close to shore is predominantly tidal," Romer said. "Someone with scuba gear ought to be able to find it within a half hour."

"But there's a big shark lives there," Bub pointed out, returning from his reverie.

Romer snorted. "A shark doesn't *live* there. He happened to be there when you were there. Sharks live in the ocean. They're always there. Every time you've ever been in the water, I guarantee a shark's been close enough to sense your presence."

Bub blinked at that thought. "Really? About how close is that, exactly? For future reference."

"Point is," Murphy interrupted. "We still have time to call a press conference today, but just barely, if we want to make the six o'clock. On the other hand, if we do it tomorrow morning, we can spend tonight getting better organized, maybe even blow up some of the key documents to poster size."

"Can we do that?" Bub asked. "Can we wait?"

"Tonight or tomorrow, it throws a giant monkey wrench into the campaign. It'll change everything," Murphy said. "Only question is whether waiting till tomorrow endangers, you know, our personal safety. In which case we ought to grab our evidence off the boat and go to the cops right now, this afternoon."

Romer moved into the left lane to pass a farm truck flashing its blinkers, then back into the right. "Lamont and Marlita are out of harm's way. So it all depends on whether they can trace you to your boat."

Murphy shook his head. "No way. I only moved to that marina two months ago. My driver's license and car tag go to a street address that forwards to a post office box. So does my cell phone. There's absolutely nothing connecting me to Blastoff View Marina."

"Are you positive?" Romer insisted. "Think hard. There's a hundred ways for them to find out these things nowadays. Traffic tickets—"

"No," Murphy said.

"Utility bills—"

"Nope."

"Caller ID. Call tracing—"

"Have only ever used the cell phone," Murphy said.

Romer nodded. "Okay. If you're sure. The last thing you want is to be sitting there on your boat, rehearsing your speech, and then all of a sudden have Clyde Bruno and his goons come clambering aboard with their guns and knives and piano wire."

"I'm certain," Murphy said confidently. "There's absolutely no reason for them to know where *Mudslinger* lives." He turned to the back seat. "Bub? You good with that?"

Bub stared with a half-smile frozen on his face, eyes fixed straight ahead.

"Bub?" Murphy waved a hand in front of his eyes. "Hel-loooo! Byron Ulysses Billings?"

Bub cleared his throat. "That, uh, caller ID thing, Romer. You figure that, uh, works on pay phones?"

Romer said, "Absolutely."

And Bub said, "In that case, maybe you oughta drive a little bit faster."


From bow pulpit to stern railing, beneath scores of signal flags and Christmas lights, *Soft Money* rang with the polite laughter of the now two dozen Victory Hostesses. They milled about in their most elegant cocktail dresses, glasses in hand, faces perfect, hair big and lustrous, nails shiny.

Each and every one of them wore high heels, and Farber LaGrange was beside himself.

From summery sandals to dressy pumps, the one thing in common was the heel. Not one was larger than a quarter square inch where it contacted his precious teak, and LaGrange's head was swimming in calculations: a hundred-and-ten-pound Victory Hostess, times four, meant his poor teak planks were being subjected to . . . *four hundred and forty* pounds per square inch!

He grabbed a passing brunette by the arm. "Hey, Tiff, honey, why don't you take your shoes off, huh? I mean, there ain't nothin' sexier than bare feet, don't you think? 'Specially yours!"

Tiffany pulled her arm free. "Mr. *LaGrange,* you can't go barefoot when you're wearing this kind of dress! This isn't a *sun*dress!"

Farber LaGrange watched in despair as three others walked past, leaving pockmark trails in their wake. He shook his head and grabbed at Tiffany's elbow as she started moving away. "Okay, sweetie-pie, could you at least not put your weight on your heel? Huh? Please?"

A blonde in a white dress passed and he tried again. "Hey, Britney, come on, take your shoes off, would you?" He pointed at his wood planking, uniformly pitted except for the high-traffic areas, which now seemed more pothole than wood. "Please?"

The girl pouted at him: "I'm Meghan." Then she smiled and waved at a friend of hers and skittered off. Farber LaGrange watched sourly as she left yet another trail of indentations behind her. It wasn't so much the cost of replacing the deck that was irking him—he planned to get every dime out of the Republican Party's hide—but the time. Having the whole deck pulled up and replaced would take a solid month. And then, figuring out where the leaks were and fixing all those holes would take months more. And finding skilled boat labor in Florida that wasn't likely to run off halfway through to go on a pot binge, that in itself was always a mean feat.

"I guess hiring the extra hostesses paid off."

Farber LaGrange turned to find Toni Johnson in a white skirt and red, high-collar blouse. She, too, he noticed with a groan, was wearing white pumps, although the heels seemed blessedly more substantial than those the rest of the girls wore. And it was not just his hostesses, he saw with resignation, but the trophy wives of his most generous donors, as well.

"They're ruinin' my deck," he said. "I asked a couple of 'em to take their shoes off. They refused."

Toni Johnson shrugged. "You wanted a semiformal event. Semi-formal means shoes." She nodded at the aft deck, where Percy Billings was holding forth amid a knot of millionaire phosphate miners and strip-mall developers. "Cheer up. Not all the guests are even here yet, and we've already cleared five-point-seven mil. We can't possibly spend all that by the election, so you can probably embezzle enough for a whole new yacht. Put it down as office supplies."

Farber LaGrange looked up in alarm but saw a smile on Toni Johnson's face. She was only kidding. He smiled back in return.

"Listen, after the election, Wednesday, I need to talk to you," she said.

LaGrange sighed. "Aw, jeez. You ain't thinkin' 'bout leavin' again, are you?"

Toni Johnson smiled again, patted him on the shoulder and turned away. "Wednesday. Don't forget."

"If this is 'bout more money, forget it," Farber LaGrange called after her. "We ain't got any. We're broke. Plus we already pay you four times as much as the Dem'crats pay their finance guy."

Farber LaGrange grumbled aloud. When things went to hell, they really went there in a hurry, that was for sure. He got the feeling she was really leaving, and there would be nothing he could do about it. What were the odds he could find another CPA with an intuitive grasp for political fund-raising? And with great legs, to boot . . .

With enormous effort, he put Toni Johnson out of his mind and re-adopted the smile of the gracious host. He momentarily caught Percy Billings's eye and raised his glass in acknowledgment. Five-point-seven million—a hundred-fifty thousand per person, two-fifty a couple. It would easily be the biggest event he had ever engineered.

Now all he needed was confirmation from Link Thresher that their other problem had been taken care of. By all rights, it should have been.

He had spoken with the man some hours earlier, and he had just received a report from his goon that he was in place at the river house and that a car was coming down the drive.

Farber LaGrange felt queasy at the thought of the boy and the nanny. When he'd first been approached about Spencer Tolliver, that had been one thing. That guy had been a dangerous heretic, vowing to ban soft money in campaigns, capping total spending in individual races, all kinds of crazy stuff.

And then it was Bub, and he'd gone along with that, too. Not happily, but he'd agreed. But this, a child and his baby-sitter . . . He shook his head to regroup. This was *not* his fault. After all, if Bub had told the truth, that he was a single dad, Farber never would have picked him to run in the first place. Percy would have been the choice, and none of the rest would have had to happen. So it was Bub's own fault, Farber LaGrange thought with a nod. Yeah—that was it. *Bub*'s fault.

He said it to himself, over and over, and nearly jumped at the hand on his forearm. "So is he here yet?"

It was Clarissa Highstreet, dressed in a red, skin-tight wraparound and matching pumps. "You said he would be here three hours ago."

Farber LaGrange tried to calm himself. She was Problem Number Two that had to be dealt with, and he hadn't been able to brief Thresher. He would need a minute with him alone, when he arrived—

"Is that him?" She pointed at a black Lincoln Navigator pulling up to the head of the circular drive. A tall man in a blue suit and black horn-rims emerged, straightened his tie, began walking toward the dock.

"It *is* him," Clarissa Highstreet murmured, and began adjusting her bosom for most advantageous display. "Now, when you introduce me, remember to point out that I'm the chief *cultural* officer of the state. Got it?"

Farber LaGrange grunted, trying to discern from Thresher's face how things had gone. But the closer he got, the more the knot in Farber LaGrange's belly tightened. Thresher's surface smile, he could tell already, masked some serious consternation.

Link Thresher climbed the bunting-bedecked gangplank, approached LaGrange with a nod. "Farber."

"Hey, there," Farber LaGrange said, heart pounding. "So. How are *things?*" He felt an elbow in his ribs. "Oh, Link, this is Clarissa Highstreet, our sec'tary of state." The elbow hit him again. "Oh yeah, did I mention, she's also Florida's chief cultural officer?"

*"Bon soir, monsieur."* She held her hand out for Link Thresher to kiss it. *"Enchanté."*

Link Thresher looked at her hand quizzically, nodded at her. "Hi there. Farber, can we talk for a minute?"

"Farber tells me you and the president are quite close," Clarissa Highstreet said, wrapping her bare arm around Link Thresher's.

"He's a friend," Link Thresher acknowledged, then turned back to Farber. "Like right now? It's important."

"Actually, I was hoping to get a minute with you myself," Clarissa Highstreet said, drawing herself closer to Thresher, finally grinding her chest into his arm. "Farber may have mentioned. I might be willing to serve in the president's administration myself. I have some . . . *expertise* he might find valuable."

Link Thresher looked down at his elbow, where she held it tightly in her cleavage, then back up at her face. "In a minute, darlin'. Farber—"

"I am not *darlin'.*" She drew back and planted hands on hips, eyes ablaze. "I am the secretary of state, and I won't be put off like this a minute longer!"

Farber LaGrange cleared his throat, reached into the pocket of his linen jacket. "Oh, Clarissa, I plumb forgot I was s'posed to give this to you." He handed her an envelope. "This came to party headquarters today."

The envelope was of heavy bond paper. On the rear flap were the words: The White House. Clarissa Highstreet tore it open, read it, reread it and read it again.

"We can chat about that a little later," Farber LaGrange said. "Now if you'll excuse me, I need to—"

"It's a fake!" Clarissa Highstreet hissed, the permanently turned up lips quivering. "It's a fucking phony! Real White House stationery has a watermark of the presidential seal, you bastard! What do you think, I was born yesterday?"

"Now, Clarissa, we're waitin' on the real thing any day. I just wanted you to have somethin' till——"

"Shut up." She squeezed the bridge of her nose. "Thanks to you, I'm getting a migraine." She glanced up to Link Thresher with enhanced smile. "Mr. Thresher, I apologize we had to meet this way. I'll tell you what. I need to go take a couple of Darvons right now. But if you'll come down to my cabin, I'd like to explain my proposition to you."

She leaned forward to whisper in his ear. "I'm going to slip into something . . . a little more comfortable? Give me a half hour."

And with a final glare for Farber LaGrange, she stalked off toward the companionway hatch. Link Thresher watched her go below, then released a shudder. "Jesus Christ. What the hell's going on with her tits? You feel 'em? They're hard as rock!"

"You don't wanna know. We need her through Tuesday, but after that I'm thinkin' the easiest thing might be to sic Clyde Bruno on her," LaGrange said. "So, what's up?"

Link Thresher's brow furrowed as he turned toward him. "I have no idea, is what's up. I should have heard something hours ago. That's what I was going to ask you——"

A cell phone in Thresher's suit coat began chirping, and he held up a single finger as he answered it. "Yeah . . . Uh-huh . . ."

Farber LaGrange felt a wave of nausea as Link Thresher's already pale features went absolutely ashen in the early evening sunlight. After a few more grunts, Thresher pressed a button and shoved the phone back in his jacket.

The tinkling of glassware was deafening over Thresher's silence, and Farber LaGrange waited an eternity before finally asking, "Well?"

Link Thresher shoved his hands in his trouser pockets. "Well . . . Let's see, where to start. Okay: The guy Clyde hired to help out with the tank farms and the freighter? Apparently he's now working with the other side. And, uh, oh yeah. They got away. All of them. It's okay though. Clyde assures me that they're on top of it. They got the Party's direct-mail folks tracking down some phone numbers as we speak."

Farber LaGrange stood silently, listened to the swing band on the dock strike up another Duke Ellington number. He stopped a passing waiter, handed two gin and tonics to Thresher and grabbed two for himself, downing them in a series of gulps.

"Go ahead and drink up while you can," he said. "My understandin' is that alcohol's somewhat harder to come by in state prison."

Okay, left right there. Before the drawbridge." Murphy pointed. "That's right. The gravel drive."

Romer threw the Karmann Ghia into the turn at speed, letting the rear end skid into the proper direction before gunning the accelerator and bumping along down the road, past a trailer park and into the marina lot. He pulled up to the heavy hemp rope marking the edge of the lot and cut the engine.

Murphy jumped out and ran down the deserted dock toward *Mudslinger*, Bub two steps behind. "I won't be five seconds," Murphy yelled. "I'll grab all the folders, maybe a couple of clean shirts, and we're outta here."

Bub stood on the dock holding *Mudslinger* by her bowsprit as Murphy scrambled aboard, then ran aft to open the combination lock that secured the wooden slats across the companionway. "I'll tell you what. You pass everythin' to me," Bub suggested. "After all this, it would really suck if we dropped it in the water, huh?"

Romer strolled up beside Bub and surveyed the boat from stem to stern, then waterline to masthead. "Southern Cross 31, right?" He nodded. "Nice boat. Clarke Ryder's company up in Rhode Island. Knew a couple who took theirs clear around the world."

"Bub!" Murphy shouted from the main hatch. "Did you see that folder with all the Clean Gulf Trust material?"

"Don't recall lookin' at it since that mornin' sail up from Jupiter," Bub said, stroking his beard. "Unless . . . We didn't take it with us, did we? In the MG?"

"No, we did not," Murphy answered. "We left everything irreplaceable— Ah! Never mind, here it is. Let me just grab a couple of shirts . . ."

Bub shifted weight onto one leg, then the other. "Hey, I don't suppose there's time for me to hit the head, is there?" He glanced toward the rest rooms by the marina office, then at the approach road, where a white van with a blue logo was bouncing along the gravel, leaving a wake of dust in the air behind it. "Huh. I seen that truck somewhere."

"Indeed, you have," Romer said. "It was parked beside the MG up in Carrabelle last night. Hey, Murphy, I believe we have company."

The van pulled around into the parking lot, stopped first beside Romer's Karmann Ghia, then backed up and moved crosswise to block it in. Out one side jumped Grant Hanson, and out the other came Clyde Bruno.

Romer grabbed Bub's arm and dragged him down to the planking and then behind a deteriorating fiberglass dock box. Clyde Bruno and Grant Hanson jogged to the farthest dock and began inspecting each boat in its slip.

"You see that? How they parked?" Bub whispered. "Now, how are we supposed to get out?"

"I get the sense we're not," Romer said, then whispered hoarsely, "Murph! Stay below!"

Clyde Bruno and Grant Hanson moved quickly, boat to boat, then back to shore and down the next dock. "Maybe they'll miss us and leave," Bub said.

"No, that's why they blocked in my car. They know we're here, and they almost certainly know the name of Murphy's boat, if they ran his name from his car tag."

Bruno and Hanson finished B dock, jogged around onto C dock. From the open forehatch beneath his upturned dinghy came Murphy's voice: "What's going on?"

Bub raised his head for a second to study their two pursuers. "Remember the fella on the helicopter? Well, he's back. And he brought that other guy with him, the one we bumped into outside the state mineral office." Bub squinted at the pair, whispered to Romer, "What, you think we can take 'em?"

Romer blinked at him. "Are you daft?"

"I figured, you know, with your SEAL trainin' and all . . ."

"My friend, that training taught me there is a time to fight and a time to run. Insofar as they've got H and Ks slung over their shoulders and what appear to be Glocks in their hands, this I believe falls into that latter category. Murph!" Romer whispered again. "Can you hear me?"

"Five by five. How do you want to handle it?"

Bruno and Hanson finished C dock and started down D. Romer half-turned in his crouch to direct his voice toward the foredeck: "We're going to need your yacht to get out of this. Can you crank the engine?"

"The instant I do, they'll hear us."

"They're almost here, anyway. Tell you what, we'll get the forward lines, you get the aft ones, and I'll give us a shove out of the slip. Then we'll at least be moving."

"Got it," Murphy answered, and disappeared from the hatch.

"What do I do, SEAL-man?" Bub asked.

Romer pointed at a galvanized cleat a few feet down the dock. "Undo the port bow line there. I'll get the starboard one and the springer."

They crawled on their bellies toward their tasks as Clyde Bruno and Grant Hanson walked purposefully down to the end of E dock. Romer broke open the knot holding the starboard spring line to the piling beside the finger pier, then moved to the cleat on the dock to which the starboard bow line was affixed, tugged at it to give himself some slack, then undid it, as well.

"Come on, Bub!" he whispered.

Bub tugged at the rope as it looped around and through the cleat. "Now, what the . . . How the . . . Now, how did this?" He looked up helplessly. "I got no idea how this got like this—"

"There! Mr. Bruno!"

Through a narrow slot between a faded blue Morgan Out Island and a beige Gulfstar stood Grant Hanson, hand outstretched and finger pointed accusingly at Bub. Clyde Bruno grunted and broke into a run back toward shore.

"Murph, we gotta go!" Romer called. "Start the engine!"

"I can't get this knot," Bub repeated.

Beyond his head, at the shoreward end of F dock, Clyde Bruno had pulled the assault rifle off his shoulder and was checking the clip. Romer bent down, bodily lifted Bub up and over *Mudslinger*'s bow pulpit.

"No time," Romer said, then reached to pull his dive knife from an ankle sheath. He glared at Clyde Bruno for a split second, then with a single swipe slashed the remaining dock line holding *Mudslinger* to shore before pushing the boat away from the pier, at the last moment jumping to grab a stanchion and hauling himself aboard.

The diesel roared to life, Murphy immediately throwing it into gear and jerking *Mudslinger* backward out of her slip. Bub and Romer scrambled down the sidedecks for the safety of the cockpit as the crack of bullets began hitting the water around them.

"Hold on," Murphy sang as he swung the tiller hard to starboard, then jammed the gear shift into forward while throwing the tiller across the cockpit to port. There was barely enough room for *Mudslinger* to clear her bow in a single turn, and Murphy could see that it was going to be close.

Bullets splintered fiberglass as *Mudslinger* now lay broadside against Clyde Bruno's weapon, and Murphy shut his eyes, stayed down and hoped for the best. From the bow came a loud clang as an anchor momentarily snagged against a passing piling, then freed as *Mudslinger*'s bowsprit swung past and out toward the channel leading into the barge canal.

Murphy steered from memory as he ducked below the whizzing of bullets, hoping he could hit the center of the channel. Too soon and he would plow into the boat occupying the last slip on G dock. Too late and he would put *Mudslinger* hard on the earthen breakwater that separated the marina from the canal.

"Look out!" Bub yelled, just as a wide-eyed Grant Hanson flew at them from a running start off the deck of a cabin cruiser, his body hitting the topsides with a *thunk* before crumpling into the water with a soft splash.

Murphy threw the tiller to port, lining *Mudslinger* up with the entrance to the marina. He glanced back through the gears of the wind vane to see Clyde Bruno helping his sidekick out of the water.

"Jesus H. Christ in a sidecar, *without* a helmet!" Bub declared. "That

was *too* close! *Damn* our luck! Five minutes earlier and we'da gotten in
and out without any hassle."

"And five minutes later and we'd all be dead. Luck's what you make
of it. Look." Romer nodded just beyond the entrance to the barge canal,
to where the drawbridge over State Road 3 was lifting for a waiting
Bayliner.

Murphy pushed the throttle to the red line and steered for the center
of the bridge.

Toni Johnson dug through face creams, ointments, foundation and
eyeliners with growing exasperation. All she wanted was some plain,
old soap. What was Farber LaGrange's deal, anyway, that he had all this
girl stuff in his lockers but not a single bar of Ivory?

It had to do, she suspected, with the Victory Hostesses. Oh, well. Not
her problem anymore. They were all eighteen and older. The statutory
rape laws did not apply, and even if they did, these girls, from what she
had seen, were not babes in the woods by any stretch.

If they were trading salary and benefits for favors, well, that was between his conscience and theirs. All she wished, as she closed the locker
beneath the sink and stood, was that they could have left the soap out
where normal human beings could find it. Every minute that passed allowed the 1993 Merlot to set ever more securely into the threads of her
silk blouse, threatening to ruin it forever.

She had immediately come below to the head and dabbed it with cold
water, inside and out, but knew that a little soap, right this moment,
would be the difference between saving or tossing out a hundred-dollar
garment. She began searching in the medicine cabinet behind the mirror, was reading the label on a jar of cold cream, when she clearly heard
Farber LaGrange say, "Aw, fuck."

Toni Johnson looked around, startled, and realized the voice had
come down the dorade vent that supplied the bathroom with fresh air.

"You're positive it was him? Couldn't be a mistake . . . Jesus Christ . . ."

She noticed that the party noise had diminished, now that it had been moved under the tent on the yacht club lawn for the sit-down dinner. She rubbed cold cream into the wine stain with thumb and index finger while listening for more.

"I'm sorry, Mr. LaGrange, Mr. Thresher. But we got there a minute too late. It was a pay phone, where the calls were coming from, and it took a while to put a street address to it. As we drove up, Moran's boat was just pulling out of its slip."

Toni's heart skipped and her eyes went wide: Moran's boat! Murphy Moran! Ramsey MacLeod's consultant she'd sent all that stuff to . . .

"Why didn't you take 'em out right there?" asked a voice she recognized as Link Thresher's.

"We tried. We hit the boat, but I don't think we hit them."

Her eyes went even wider, and she hit the light switch, stood directly beneath the vent with ear cocked.

"You've got the only marine asset on the east central coast, sir."

"The what?" Farber LaGrange asked.

"Boat," Link Thresher said. "He means boat."

"I've got several bags of weapons out in the van, sir. Sir, we've got to hurry. The more we wait, the longer start they get."

There was a long pause before Farber LaGrange said, "All right, fine. Go get your shit aboard. I'll go get Percy. I'll be damned if we're doin' this without him."

"Percy? Two days before the election?" Thresher asked. "Is that smart?"

"Think about it," Farber LaGrange said. "If we *don't* have him and things go to hell, you think he'll help us out? Or hang us out to dry?"

Thresher hesitated only a moment. "Go get Percy."

The voices stopped, and Toni crouched in the darkness, trying to make sense of it all: Take them out. Hit the boat, but missed them. Weapons. What the hell was going on? Whatever it was, Percy Billings was obviously in the thick of it.

And it occurred to her that whatever it was, she had very likely played a part, by sending Murphy Moran all that material. . . . And now Farber LaGrange and Link Thresher and their goons were going to chase down Murphy's boat. With bags of weapons.

She felt *Soft Money* rock a little as heavy work boots thumped aboard. A few moments later the big diesel engine in the compartment adjacent to her rumbled to life, and a minute after that, she felt *Soft Money* pull away from the dock and ease out into the light chop of the ship channel.

Very quietly, Toni Johnson took the white pumps off her feet, crammed them into the locker beneath the sink, then unlocked the door to the head.

## ★ ⑧ ★

THE LIGHTS OF COCOA BEACH had finally faded astern before Murphy Moran released his death grip on the tiller and set the autopilot. *Mudslinger* fought her way upwind under motor alone, with a medium-sized wave periodically slapping her bow and nearly stopping them cold. Murphy would watch with resignation as the knotmeter numerals would hover in the 0.4 range for several long seconds, then slowly build back up to about 4.7 before the next wave would come and knock them right back down to near zero again. The instrument beside the knot log, the depth sounder, merely glowed a dim orange around the bullet hole that had destroyed it.

"If we threw up the big genny and the main," Murphy said with a sigh, "we might be able to hit six, six and a half knots in this direction. Of course, the wind is probably going to die completely in about two hours. So by going to all the work of getting the sails up, we'd gain about four nautical miles. Of course, as soon as we get out about twenty-five miles or so, we need to turn off the engine anyway. We don't have much diesel, maybe five, five and a half gallons total. Enough for ten, eleven hours of motoring."

Romer stood on the tiny triangle of aft deck, nearly invisible in his dark wet suit, his legs entwined among the brackets for the steering gear and the windmill, hands holding a pair of rubber-coated binoculars. Bub sat across from Murphy in the cockpit, arms crossed against the settling chill.

"I can't even think straight, I'm so tired," Bub said. "Hey! We didn't sleep last night. . . . Or hardly at all the night before! No wonder we're exhausted!"

"Anything?" Murphy asked, as Romer climbed down from his perch.

"Nope. Two cruise ships came out. A shrimper went in. That's all I saw." He jumped down into the cockpit. "I don't suppose you have radar."

Murphy snorted. "Know how much electricity radar uses? No, I don't have radar."

Romer pursed his lips but said nothing—the same response he'd had when he learned that Murphy had no radio with which to call for help. Murphy, too, thought he could kick himself. His handheld VHF was still, after everything, in the dock box back at the marina. Why he'd ever put it in there, he couldn't even remember anymore.

With a radio, they would have been home free. One call to the Coast Guard on Channel 16, and that would have been it. The frequency was monitored by Brevard County's newspapers and television stations. A single mention of Bub being alive and in trouble, and their pursuers would have had to back off.

Instead, they had motored down the barge canal, constantly scanning the shore for the white van. It had shadowed them across the Banana River causeway, then through the Canaveral locks, past the Port Canaveral Yacht Club where Farber LaGrange's *Soft Money* lay decked out in full party mode, and finally along the stone jetty bordering the ship channel. The whole time, they had assumed that the goons in the van had called back to headquarters to scramble some goons in a boat—the assumption behind their strategy to head out well offshore, then come back in at some other inlet.

"Ain't you tired?" Bub asked Romer.

"I napped earlier. Right after we cleared the jetties," Romer said. "Five minutes of shut-eye and I'm a new man. You guys need to rest. Why don't we start watches? I'll take the first."

Murphy thought about this, watched the knotmeter bounce down to 0.8, slowly climb back to 4. "You sure you're okay?"

Romer nodded. "I think I can handle it. Course: one-zero-five. Watch for enemy vessels. I'll wake you in three hours."

Murphy pointed down the companionway at the GPS unit on the navigation table. "Can you keep an eye on that? Kill the engine when we get to eighty degrees, zero-five minutes west? That's the second line, the longi—"

"I'm familiar with latitude and longitude, thank you."

"Okay. And you just have to keep an eye on these two gauges here." He pointed at the engine's instrument panel mounted on the forward wall of the cockpit well. "See? Temperature and oil press—"

"Murphy," Romer broke in. "I know diesel engines. I know navigation. I know how to sail, courtesy the United States government. Go below and get some rest."

Murphy took a deep breath, nodded, checked his watch and headed down the companionway steps. Bub rose to follow him, stopped on the second step and turned to Romer.

"You ain't gonna slit our throats in our sleep, are you?"

Romer stared back, expressionless.

"Just a joke, there," Bub said, then headed down into the cabin.


She had found, Toni Johnson decided, the absolute best hidey-hole aboard Farber's capacious yacht: a starboard-side sail locker, adjacent on one side to the cockpit well, on another to the navigation station. Lying in relative comfort atop a pile of sail bags, she could eavesdrop on both areas with ease.

"See if you can pay attention. This here's the target, got it?"

"Uh-huh."

It was Farber, trying to teach one of the party operatives, Grant something, how to operate the radar with which they were tracking Murphy Moran's boat. There was Farber, Percy Billings, Link Thresher, Thresher's goon Clyde Bruno and Grant. Five of them, heavily armed and fully intending, she had come to realize, to kill Murphy Moran and a passenger of his, whose name none of them had uttered but of whom they were obviously terrified.

"You line up the track ball, then hit this button. Then this number here is the bearin', and this number here is the range. Got it?"

"Bearing and range. Got it."

"Good. You try."

"Track ball . . . hit this button. Okay: bearing is one-one-zero, range is . . . seven-point-two."

"Very good. Now every ten minutes, you call out the new bearin' and range to whoever's at the helm."

"At the helm?"

"Drivin' the fuckin' boat, you moron. Jesus Christ. Thresher, anythin' on the radios?"

"Not a peep," came Thresher's voice.

"Now ain't that the damnedest thing. . . . Well, keep lis'nin'."

Toni Johnson stilled her breath as she heard Farber's footsteps approach, then continue right past and up the companionway. She rolled over to get closer to the little porthole that opened into the cockpit, slid her hair behind an ear and positioned it right up against the port's mosquito screen so she could hear over the engine noise.

"Don't see them yet," Thresher's goon reported.

"You won't, for a while," Farber said. "They're still a half-dozen miles ahead. We appear to be gainin' on 'em at around four knots. For whatever reason, they haven't tried to call for help. I got no idea why not. But it seems like if they were gonna do it, they'da done it already."

The goon grunted. "We put a lot of rounds in her. I wouldn't be surprised if one or two of 'em didn't knock out the radio."

"That was lucky shootin' then. They'da called for help, and we'da been up shit creek."

There was a brief silence before: "Hey, how long is this whole thing going to take?"

She placed the new voice as that of Percy Billings, listened to Farber's steps cross the cockpit.

"Why, you got somethin' better goin' on?"

"The final weekend of the campaign, as a matter of fact. I've got services at nine different black churches. Then a radio call-in. Then I have a barbecue, and then I'm supposed to do the coin toss at the Jaguars game. If I miss them, people are going to notice."

"Huh," Farber LaGrange said after a pause. "You s'pose they'll notice that more, or less than if ol' Bub Billings were to hold a press conference to announce that he's alive after all?"

Toni Johnson couldn't contain the gasp of amazement. She covered her mouth with a hand and waited for the door to her locker to come flying open. But no one was coming to the door, she realized, slowly exhaling. No one had heard her.

"You know, maybe them ol' Greeks you're always quotin' were on to somethin', huh? Fratricide's a bitch."

"I don't see why you need me aboard," Percy pouted.

"You most certainly do. You're a stakeholder in this, the second-biggest stakeholder, I would say. You wanna share in the rewards, then by God, you're gonna share in the risk," Farber lectured. "Stop worryin', all right? We'll finish up and be back at the dock by ten, latest. We can outrun 'em and outgun 'em. They ain't gettin' away, this time."

"Ten o'clock," Percy grumbled. "Can't we go any faster? What if we put up the sails?"

Toni Johnson listened to Farber hem and haw about it being night, and that it wouldn't make a big difference, anyway, since they could go faster with just their engine than a thirty-footer could with her engine *and* sails together.

She listened as Farber gave the goon instructions at the helm, then climbed back down into the cabin to check on Grant and Thresher, then went back up top, and the whole time her brain sped at fever pitch: Bub! Bub was still alive! Not only was Bub still alive, but Percy and Farber and Link Thresher had conspired to kill him . . . were *still* conspiring to kill him.

She chewed her thumbnail in the darkness as she thought: Seven miles, Farber had said. Closing at four knots. Meaning they would catch them in under two hours. Two hours was how much time she had to stop them. Two hours to figure out a way to let Murphy's boat escape. . . .

The radio! That was it! She would get on the radio, put out a mayday! Then the Coast Guard would be combing the waters, looking for them. But would that stop them? Or just make them even more determined to hurry up and get it done before they were found? Besides, how was she going to get at the radio? Farber had stationed someone there the entire time, from the very minute they'd pulled away from Port Canaveral Yacht Club.

She switched to the other thumbnail, wondering if there were some way to slow Farber's boat down. That would at least give Murphy and Bub a fighting chance by pushing into daylight hours the time when *Soft Money* would catch up to the smaller vessel.

She blinked, then blinked again, recalling Farber's reluctance to put up the sails. And she remembered all the time cards she'd processed with party money for Farber's New Zealander crew, and it dawned on her that Farber almost certainly was not a good sailor. If somehow she could sabotage the engine, she could at least tilt the odds toward Murphy and Bub.

Toni Johnson took a deep breath and slid off the sail bags, moved to the door, put her ear to it . . . heard no one. She cracked the door open, saw a clear corridor. The door to the engine room was around to the left, she had discovered during her search for a hiding place.

She took another deep breath, and with a final glance toward the main salon, opened the door fully and tiptoed out and around toward the rear of the boat, came to a door, opened the latch to the roar of a big diesel, stepped inside and quickly shut it again.

With one hand she found an overhead lamp, flicked it on. In the center of the compartment was the engine, painted a bright red and vibrating as it ran at cruising speed. Along the near wall was a workbench, complete with a pair of steel vises and plastic lockers containing little drawers full of spare parts.

She studied the engine, how it connected to the propeller shaft via the transmission, and remembered her dad, hanging upside down in the port lazaret of their old Cal 40, making the tiniest adjustment to the packing gland to allow exactly one drop of seawater to drip in every minute. Any more than that, he used to warn her and her sister, and the drips could wash away packing and eventually create a dangerous leak. Any less, and the bearing would overheat, seizing up the shaft and damaging it beyond repair.

She watched the packing gland, spinning with the prop shaft, saw the lock nuts for tightening, from the workbench behind her quickly found the correct-size open-ended wrenches. To tighten it, though, she would have to stop the engine, then quickly crank down on the lock nuts before they restarted it.

So she had to stop the engine. She remembered that diesels were not shut off electrically, but had kill switches, to release the compression. Otherwise they would just keep running until they ran out of fuel. She peered around the big, eight-cylinder monster, searching for the cable leading down from the cockpit . . . when her eye fell on the yellow fill cap atop the valve cover.

Toni blinked, stared at it some more, and a grin spread across her face.

She quickly replaced the wrenches in her hand into their proper slots on the rack above the workbench and instead squinted into each of the small-parts drawers. They were made of clear polystyrene to make it easier to see what each one contained, and very quickly Toni Johnson found what she was looking for.

She pulled the drawer out completely, stepped back to the engine, and, with a rag over her palm to protect against the heat, she quickly unscrewed the fill cap. With engine oil splashing out, she poured in the contents of the drawer and replaced the plastic cap.

The crunching and grinding began instantly, and Toni Johnson slipped the drawer back into the parts cabinet, hit the light switch and padded back to her hidey-hole just as the engine finally clattered and shuddered to a halt.

An alarm buzzer went off in the cockpit, followed by a long, anatomically improbable string of curses from Farber LaGrange.


Clyde Bruno fingered the high-pressure metal tubes running to the injectors, checked the air intake manifold, tapped the glass bowl of the primary fuel filter, then turned to Farber LaGrange with a shrug. "Beats me, sir. Diesels really aren't my specialty, but I don't have a clue."

"Motherfuckin' piece of shit," Farber said.

"An air bubble in the fuel line, perhaps? Disrupting flow?" suggested Percy Billings as he paged through a thick, grimy Detroit Diesel repair manual.

"It's getting fuel. It's getting air," Clyde Bruno said. "The starter motor is getting good juice. It's probably not the starter anyway, seeing as how it shut down while it was running."

"*Cock*suckin', motherfuckin' piece of shit," Farber said. "Just had the goddamn thing overhauled this spring. Why in fuck did I pay 'em all that money for? I coulda fucked it up just as good myself."

Percy Billings sighed. "I suppose this means we won't be getting back by ten."

Clyde Bruno scratched his head as he stared at the silent red machine, then squinted at the shiny bit of metal wedged between the block and the alternator pulley bracket. He reached in with thumb and forefinger, plucked it out, held it toward the light.

"What's that?" Farber LaGrange demanded.

"This is a number-six, stainless-steel, one-half-inch, self-tapping screw." Clyde Bruno turned it around in his fingers, brooding, then with the other hand unscrewed the oil fill cap. He peered down into the hole, reached in with two fingers. "And this is another one."

Farber LaGrange took it, wiped away the black oil on the sleeve of his tuxedo shirt. The tip and part of the head had broken off, and the threads on one side were squashed. "That's it? This little thing busted my engine?"

"There might be more in there, but yeah. A couple of those down in the guts would do the job."

Farber LaGrange blinked. "What, you mean it ain't somethin' that belongs in there?"

"This?" Clyde Bruno fingered the sharp end of the screw. "No. It's safe to say diesels don't normally have self-tapping screws inside them."

Farber LaGrange's face grew dark red and his eyes narrowed to slits. "The mother*fuckers* . . . You know much I paid them bastards at Space Coast Marine? All so they can drop parts in my engine? Well, they clearly don't 'preciate who they fucked with. I'll *own* the fuckin' place 'fore I'm done with 'em!"

Percy tucked the repair manual beneath an arm and grabbed Farber's shoulder to shake him. "Farber! Hey, Farber? Hello! We've got a campaign to finish, remember? You've got to get us home. What the hell are we going to tell the press?"

Clyde Bruno stared at the screw some more. "No, I don't see how they could have fallen in way back then. You said your overhaul was this spring, right? If they'd fallen in back then, the engine would have shut down the first time you turned it on. No, this must have been more recent. In fact . . ." He turned to the parts cabinet, quickly opened and shut a few drawers. "Ha! Look at this: You have number-four self-tappers. You have number eight. But your drawer for number sixes is empty."

Farber's rage built again. "Someone sabotaged my boat? Jesus H. Christ . . . all them people traipsin' around. You think we had a Democrat spy?"

"What *difference* does it make! Don't you understand?" Percy said. "It doesn't matter how it happened. The fact is we're now stuck out here, and the election's on Tuesday!"

"Actually, I don't see how someone could have sabotaged it earlier and it only shut the engine down right now." Clyde Bruno looked at the small-parts cabinet, paced the distance to the engine, then the door. "Actually, if I had to guess, I'd say somebody dropped those screws in about thirty seconds before the engine stopped running."

"What?" Percy Billings said.

"What?" Farber LaGrange demanded. "You mean one of us?"

Clyde Bruno shrugged. "Maybe that Democratic spy is still on board. This *is* a big boat."

"A stowaway," Farber LaGrange said with a nod, leading the way out into the main salon. "Well, she ain't *that* big. All right, we search her top to bottom. Clyde, you start on the port side and Grant—you list'nin?—you start on starboard."

"Sir?" Grant said.

"Search, Grant. You know how to do that, doncha? Meanwhile I'll—"

"Sir?" Grant said again.

"What?" Farber LaGrange said finally.

"Thought you should know, sir. That other boat? It was four-point-two miles away a half hour ago, and it's four-point-two miles away now. Does that mean they're not moving, sir?"

Farber pushed Grant aside at the nav table, acquired the target himself, then watched a long minute as the range number sat unchanged. "Goddamnit, son, you're right! They're stopped! Boys, we're back in the game!"

"How so?" Percy Billings said. "Our engine still doesn't work."

"This is how," Farber said, patting Percy's cheek. "They're sittin' ducks. Maybe they ran outta gas, or got tired, or somethin' broke. Either way, they're as good as ours. Clyde, go check your weapons. Grant, Link, Percy: Come with me. We're gonna throw up some sail, catch the last of this breeze."

Percy stood with mouth open. "You want to catch them . . . under *sail* alone?"

"Know how many folks Blackbeard killed and stole from?" Farber LaGrange rolled up his sleeves, reached into a locker behind the nav station for a brand-new pair of fingerless sailing gloves. "You think *he* had an engine? Come on. Time's a wastin'!"

★

The only light below came from a dim LED bulb over the navigation table, a tip Murphy had gotten from *Cruising World* magazine to save both electricity and night vision.

Murphy himself lay on the starboard bunk, curled around the canvas "lee cloth" that protected the occupant from falling out even when the boat heeled in the opposite direction. On the port bunk lay Romer in military repose, mouth set in a grim line, arms at his sides.

*Mudslinger* herself lay quietly in the water, engine off, mast rocking gently back and forth, her aft quarter pointing into the remnants of the wind. Overhead, the sky had cleared completely to reveal the full, mid-autumn canopy that stretched from horizon to horizon.

Jupiter had just risen in the east, with Saturn overhead and slightly to the south, and a bright orange Mars on the verge of setting to the west, right above a dim yellow star that, instead of setting, seemed instead to grow slowly brighter.

Bub Billings had been watching Jupiter and Saturn and Mars as he sat in the cockpit, back against the bulkhead, legs stretched out on the bench, arms crossed against the damp chill. He might have noticed the dim, brightening star because of its proximity to an object he was watching.

Yet by the time Mars dropped below the horizon while the no-longer-dim star not only grew brighter but seemed to retrogress to the south, Bub Billings—head against the compass dome, mouth open and snoring—was not noticing much of anything.

Toni Johnson's heart once again pounded along as she listened to the conversation in the cockpit. They were getting closer, maybe another half mile to go, and Farber was explaining to his crew his plan.

They would pass by close and put as many rounds into the smaller boat as earthly possible, then come around and approach from downwind, with Clyde Bruno and Grant on the bow, ready to board the other vessel. They would make certain there were no survivors, then cut the raw water hose to the engine to scuttle her.

She'd nearly had heart failure when Farber ordered a search of the boat, had held her breath for what seemed like ages while Farber, distracted by Grant's discovery, had marched everyone up top to unroll the genoa and hoist the mainsail to close in on their unsuspecting prey. And once they had dispatched Murphy and Bub, either Farber or Clyde Bruno would sooner or later—probably sooner—remember about the stowaway who had destroyed their engine. Which gave her a grand total of about fifteen minutes to think of a way to save both the other boat and herself. . . .

"Yup, that's them. No doubt about it. Here, wanna look?"

It was Farber, passing the binoculars to Percy Billings, Toni knew. If they were close enough to see them through binoculars on a moonless night, they were within a few minutes of shooting range. ·

"Ah, machinations, hollowness, treachery," Percy intoned. "All ruinous disorders, follow us disquietly to our graves."

Feverishly, she considered her options: She was alone and unarmed. But they were all topside, meaning she was alone with the radios. If she got to the VHF quietly, she might have several minutes to put out a mayday on Channel 16 before she was overheard.

On the other hand, the nav table was directly beneath the companionway hatch, so there was also the chance she would be caught instantly . . . at which point her only recourse would be to bluff, and bluff loudly. She knew Farber pretty well: Would she be able to convince him that she'd already gotten her message out and he therefore had no choice but to give up? Or would he decide, instead, that he had nothing to lose by pushing ahead? And anyway, how well had she *really* known Farber? Would she ever have guessed that his dream for an all-Republican statehouse would lead him to cold-blooded murder?

She shuddered at the thought, just as she heard a loud clatter above her in the cockpit, then the sound of a zipper opening.

"Here we go. Who wants an AK-forty-seven?" Clyde Bruno asked.

"Oh, I do!"

"I don't think so," Link Thresher said.

"I saw it first!" Grant complained.

"Million-dollar donors trump party hacks, is the rule I think we're operating under," Thresher said.

Farber LaGrange said, "I don't fuckin' believe this. Just take a gun, all right? The bigger the bore, the better. We put as many holes in her as we can, as close to the waterline as we can, got it?"

Toni Johnson gasped at the sound of ammunition clips getting snapped into place and rounds getting racked, bit her tongue to stifle a cry.

"Okay, one last time," Farber said. "Y'all get to the bow and get yourselves set. I'll keep us on course so we'll pass within a few yards, then I'll lock down the wheel and come up with you. Got it?"

Grunts of assent, then footsteps climbing up onto the sidedeck and forward . . . and Toni Johnson realized the time for thinking was over, and it was now time to do something, *anything*. . . .

She rolled off the sail bags, opened the door and crept down the corridor. *Soft Money* was rocking, ever so gently, from side to side, and she braced herself against the varnished paneling. She stopped just around the corner from the companionway ladder, right across from the radio. She could see the green LED lights on the channel selector glowing "16." All she had to do was push the transmit button and start talking about Farber and Thresher and Bub and guns and—

"All right," Farber announced. "Here I come."

He reached for his rifle from the bag, slung it over a shoulder and climbed up onto the teak deck. Toni Johnson listened for his footsteps to grow softer before climbing up the steps and poking her head out.

There, on the bow, were all five of them, weapons shouldered at the little sailboat bobbing in the darkness not a hundred yards ahead. Behind her she saw Clyde Bruno's duffel bag, still loaded with guns. She could grab one, creep up behind them, shout, "Freeze!"

And then what? If she told them to throw their guns overboard, would they listen? If they didn't, was she prepared to shoot them?

Ahead, Murphy's sailboat grew ever closer, and Toni Johnson's mouth grew drier. She would have to do it: She would have to grab a rifle, something she hadn't done since Girl Scout camp, and point it at a human, something she had *never* done . . . when she heard the big genoa shudder slightly in the breeze—and she knew exactly what she would do.

She climbed into the cockpit well and moved to the windward winch, found the end of the lazy jib sheet and quickly undid the figure-eight knot that prevented it from escaping, then stepped across the cockpit to do the same to the working sheet. Then she moved to the big steering wheel, loosened the locking knob on the pedestal, and with a glance at the other boat now just a hundred feet away, leaned into the wheel and spun it to port as fast as she could.

The sail began shaking, the mainsail boom whipped across to the opposite side and Farber LaGrange started yelling and pointing as she jumped to the starboard winch, unwound the jib sheet from the drum and let it run through her hands. Within seconds, the giant sail was flapping uncontrollably ahead of *Soft Money* as she turned left ninety degrees and quickly glided away from *Mudslinger*.

From the bow came bright flashes, and Toni Johnson realized with the first *crack* that they were shooting at her. She crouched low, jumped onto the aft deck, skirted the sunken hot tub and dived in one fluid leap over the lifelines and into the dark water.


**B**ub Billings awakened to the sound of gunfire, then watched in awe as Farber LaGrange's big yacht swung within spitting distance before moving away again, an enormous foresail flying ahead of her like a flag.

He listened to Farber LaGrange's shouts about dropping that halyard, no, the *other* fuckin' halyard, then watched in amazement as both of the boat's sails fell: the main in a billowing heap on the deck, the genoa into the water beside them.

He moved aside as Murphy clambered into the cockpit, leaned to slide the gearshift into neutral and push down the starter button until the diesel caught. He watched as Romer sprang onto the cabin top, undid the sail ties and attached the main halyard to the headboard of the mainsail, then as Murphy pushed the gearshift into forward with his toe and took hold of the tiller.

He cocked an ear, blinked, then shouted, "Stop, stop, stop! There's someone in the water!"

Murphy kicked the gearshift back into neutral, joined Bub at the stern rail. Farber LaGrange's cursing still rang clearly over the noise of their idling engine as they scanned the black water.

"Where?" Murphy asked, as suddenly a spotlight beam started sweeping the surface.

Romer stood over them, the light's cord plugged into the receptacle over the companionway. He played the beam back and forth across the hundred yards of water separating *Soft Money* and *Mudslinger*, and Murphy noticed the distance between the boats was not increasing anymore. *Soft Money*'s forward momentum had dissipated. It was only a matter of time before Farber LaGrange got it together and set sail after them.

"Where?" he asked again.

"There," Romer said softly, holding the light on rhythmic splashing amid the waves.

Murphy moved to the tiller, kicked the gear lever into reverse and backed *Mudslinger* toward the dark head slowly moving toward them. With one hand Romer held the spotlight, with the other he undid *Mudslinger*'s horseshoe Lifesling and heaved it toward the swimmer.

"He's got it," Romer announced, and Murphy put the engine back into neutral while Romer pulled the polypropylene line in, arm over arm.

Murphy glanced up at a particularly lengthy string of invective coming across the water, then back at Bub, who now held the spotlight, and Romer, who continued retrieving line, until finally both men leaned over the side and gently pulled the swimmer aboard. Romer listened for breathing, then looked up with a nod.

"How is he?" Murphy asked.

Bub looked up, slightly flushed, and cleared his throat. "*She*'s fine, I think."

"Any line in the water?" Murphy asked.

"All back aboard," Romer reported. "We're clear."

Murphy pushed the gearshift into forward, snapped the autopilot onto the tiller, then stepped over to the side deck where Bub squatted holding his windbreaker around the sodden figure sitting against the lifelines.

Murphy cleared his throat. "GOP Gal, I presume?"


Farber LaGrange stood with hands on his hips and surveyed the soggy and torn genoa that stretched from forestay clear back past the cockpit.

"You people got *any* idea how much this little bit of fabric costs? Anybody here wanna venture a guess?"

Thanks to the unhappy combination of Farber's inexperience and his crew's incompetence, the sun was high above the horizon before *Soft Money*, finally, was moving again. It had taken a solid hour of bungling to get the ruined sail out of the water, then another hour to sort everything out and hoist a new, heavier genoa to replace it, and then a further forty-five minutes to get the mainsail raised and trimmed.

Grant Hanson and Clyde Bruno lay in the cockpit, exhausted from their workout, clad only in their underwear, white boxers for Clyde Bruno, red cotton briefs for Grant. The gruntwork of manhandling the big sails had fallen on them, with Percy Billings sitting disconsolately on the aft deck, Link Thresher standing at the mast with an ironic look and Farber LaGrange at the wheel cussing them all out.

LaGrange, too, had stripped to boxers and wife-beater undershirt, while Thresher and Percy remained in dress shirt and trousers. All five were sweating under a morning sun that hung heavily in a white, summer-like sky. The night's breeze had died completely an hour before dawn, and only now was filling back in from the east.

"More to the point, y'all realize how much speed we're losin' from flyin' such a heavy sail in such light air?"

Only Grant took the query literally, thinking about it for a few long seconds before finally shaking his head. "No, sir. How much?"

Farber blinked his eyes, enraged. "The fuck should I know? It was a fuckin' rhetorical question! Point is we're losin' *somethin'*. The only advantage we got is we're a bigger boat and can go faster, and here we are pissin' it away. Radar says they're headin' southeast at three knots. Now, I know that engine of theirs can push 'em five knots through flat water, so why they're only doin' three I can't even guess. Unless they're in the Stream and we ain't and they're losin' some speed to it. Whatever it is, we gotta take advantage now and get 'em."

He moved to the ripped sail and lifted an edge with his toe. "In the meantime, we're gonna have us a crash course in sailin'. When we get close, they'll try to maneuver away from us, and we gotta hang right there with 'em. We can't have any more of this what's-a-halyard or what-side-is-starboard shit." He turned and nodded at Grant and Clyde Bruno. "This is 'bout as dry as it's gonna get. Go ahead and roll it up and stow it in the sail locker. And on your way back up, bring a coupla books. Grant, you take the *Annapolis Book of Seamanship*, and Clyde, I want you readin' *Chapman's Piloting*."

Farber walked back along the side deck, sat down beside Percy Billings near the stern railing, dangled his pale legs down toward almost iridescent blue water. They sat silently for several minutes, until finally Percy took a deep breath and blew it out.

"How deep is it here?" he asked.

Farber LaGrange shrugged. "Edge of the Gulf Stream. Couple thousand. More."

Percy sat still again, then took another deep breath. "We're in trouble, aren't we?"

"Trouble? Us? Nah." Farber shook his head, recalled Toni Johnson's fine figure scampering toward the lifelines and snapping off a perfect dive into the water, arms extended, toes pointed. "I mean, I hear prison life ain't all that bad. There's plenty of time for weight liftin', and legal-brief writin'. Okay, sure, there's the hom'sexual rapin', but I s'pose we'll get used to that."

"I'm serious," Percy insisted. "We're not going to get away with it. I think about it all, and it's like a bad dream. I mean, what the hell was I thinking? He's my *brother,* for God's sake. Read your Bible, Farber. How many chapters did it take before the Lord came out with the rules on adultery and coveting? Well, you might remember he stuck a mark on Cain's forehead right out of the box, right there in Genesis. Oh, if Father could only see me now. . . ."

"Oh, no you don't." Farber stood and dragged Percy up by an arm. "Now, you listen up, and you listen up good: We ain't got time for any of this maudlin crap, all right? The time for brotherly love ended that night you set Bub up to get thrown overboard. We crossed that there Rubicon, and now there ain't no goin' back, understand?" Farber lowered his tone and put an arm around Percy's shoulders. "We just gotta stay focused, and I'm gonna need your help. They got no radio, they got a boat that's half as fast as ours. This is no contest. By the end of the day, we'll catch 'em and be done with it."

Percy shook his head. "The press is going to be all over me. Two days before the election, and where the hell am I? Gone. AWOL. Man, the Democrats must be going apeshit."

Farber nodded and led Percy toward the companionway. "That is admittedly a problem. I will not deny. But we can cross that bridge when we get to it. In the meantime—"

And Farber's jaw dropped as he caught sight of the shellacked hair, the unmistakable cleavage ascending the companionway steps. Clarissa Highstreet glanced around through sleep-puffed eyes, finally locked on Farber.

"What the hell's going on? Where are we?"

"Oh, Christ. I forgot about her," he muttered under his breath, then smiled wide. "Mornin'!"

"Morning yourself." She scratched her neck, adjusted the straps of her silk camisole and looked around. "What are we doing here?"

Farber waved an arm magnanimously, affected a hearty laugh. "Us? Here? Why, we're just havin' a nice mornin' sail is all." He sucked in air through his nostrils. "Ahh! Nothin' like the smell of salt air, huh?"

Clarissa Highstreet pouted, shifted her weight from one high-heeled bedroom slipper to the other. "Well, *I* like the smell of a fresh pot of

French roast in the morning. I'll be in my quarters. I'd like some sent in, please. And I'd like Marcel to come by. I need my nails buffed."

Farber LaGrange blinked, at a complete loss for words, then licked his lips. "Well, we'll call Marcel. I ain't sure exactly what time we'll get back to the—"

"Farber," Link Thresher called. "I just tried my cell phone. I can't seem to get a signal."

"That's 'cause we're forty miles from shore. You need to be in line a sight—"

"Mr. Thresher!" Clarissa Highstreet said, turning. "Link! *You're* still here. That's wonderful! Listen, I wanted to chat with you for a minute . . ." She touched her hand to her cheek, quickly turned away. "Oh! Well, you just wait right there. Let me just go put on my face, brush my hair, maybe toss on a swimsuit. . . . Don't you go anywhere, I'll be right back!"

Link Thresher stepped off the cabin trunk and peeked down the companionway after her. "Just where does she think I can go, I wonder." He tossed his cell phone at Farber. "I need to make a couple of calls."

Farber pressed the power button, saw the words NO SIGNAL and turned it back off. "Well, we ain't got a satellite phone. Was fixin' to get one, but never got 'round to it. You can call on the SSB, get a marine operator, patch through a land line. Except, of course, everyone on the planet can listen in."

Thresher shook his head. "Not that important. It can wait." He glanced back down the companionway, lowered his voice: "What about, you know, Bub? What if we don't catch them? What if they head toward shore?"

"We'll catch 'em. And if somehow they head back toward land, don't worry. We got that covered, too," Farber murmured. "It's Sec'tary Highbeams I'm worried about. We gotta figure out a way to keep her from findin' out. Jesus Christ, can you imagine what she'd do with *that* kinda leverage? No, we gotta keep her outta the loop."

"How?" Link Thresher asked.

"Beats me. All I know is, we gotta figure out somethin'. She slept through all that commotion last night. Whatever drugs she took seemed to knock her right out. We'll have to get 'em to her again—shhhh . . ."

Clarissa Highstreet ascended the stairs again, this time in a black bikini top, sheer black sarong and three-inch black heels with see-through cutouts over the sides and the insteps. *"Bon jour, monsieur."* She took Link Thresher by the arm and led him forward. "Did I ever tell you I'm fluent in French?"

Link Thresher said, "Is that right?"

"In fact, the locals sometimes mistake me for a native Parisian! You know, I just think it's *so* important for representatives of our nation to know the language abroad. Don't you?"

Farber LaGrange shook his head, then saw Clyde Bruno and Grant coming up the steps, heavy tomes in hand. "All right. Good. We're gonna make sailors outta you boys yet. Now let's see here." He paged through one book, then the other. "All right, 'Boat Handlin' Under Sail' for Clyde and . . . let's see . . . how 'bout 'Parts of a Boat' for ol' Grant? That sounds more your speed, don't it?"


Toni Johnson stretched her legs across the cockpit well and dug into a bowl of tuna with noodles and peas, the product of Bub's culinary creativity and Murphy's dried and canned emergency provisions.

"Tasty," she said, taking another spoonful. "As you can see, I was starved. Thank you."

Bub beamed and shrugged. "Aw, it was nothin'. Just tossed a coupla things together in the ol' galley. Now if ol' Murph had a jar of capers, maybe some portobello mushrooms, now *then* I'da cooked you up somethin' to write home about."

Murphy watched Bub, annoyed that he had managed to turn even their morning breakfast into a competitive tool. He could easily have improved on Bub's creation because he knew where all the spices were stowed. He briefly considered mentioning this, then bit his tongue, deciding it would sound too catty. He already had the edge. It was *his* boat, and *he*, not Bub, was a sailor like Toni. It was *his* plan to circumnavigate that had piqued her interest. *His* yellow Mount Gay T-shirt she was wearing, having come aboard in just bra and panties after shedding skirt and blouse in the water to let her swim faster. Balanced against all that was the fact that it had been Bub, not he, who had heard her shouts for help.

"So you disabled the engine, how?" Murphy asked, turning the conversation back to an area that gave him the advantage in terms of expertise.

"Self-tapping screws in the oil fill."

Murphy winced knowingly. "Ouch. Of course, from our point of view, well done. That's nothing they're going to be able to fix themselves."

Toni Johnson took another bite. "Which means they're limited to their sailing ability. Which, fortunately for us, isn't so great. Farber himself seems a bit shaky, and none of the others knows a halyard from a hawser pipe."

Bub sat silently, brow furrowed, but said nothing. Murphy pressed his advantage. "Okay, so we're better sailors, and, in a pinch, we still have an hour and a half of diesel left. What we have to do is overcome a three-, three-and-a-half-knot advantage."

"More like four knots, I think," Toni Johnson said. "You're, what, twenty-five feet on the waterline? That puts us at six-and-a-half . . . six-point-seven, actually, versus a sixty-foot waterline, that gives them, I guess, almost ten and a half, no?"

"That's right. You're right," Murphy allowed.

Bub blinked. "Now hold on. How can you tell how fast a boat goes just by how long it is? Shoot, look at Jet Skis. Those things go a whole lot faster than a lot of big boats, and they're only, what, five or six feet long?"

"They don't have a displacement hull," Murphy said, barely suppressing a victorious grin.

Toni Johnson nodded in agreement. "A displacement hull versus a planing hull. A boat that can get up and out of the water is limited only by wetted surface area. Boats that sit in the water, like both Murphy's and Farber's, they're limited by the wave they generate as they move. So the fastest you can go is the square root of the length in feet, times four over three, with the answer in knots. The only exception is if the boat is surfing, like down a huge wave."

Bub said meekly, "Oh."

"It's not that complicated. I'll explain it to you sometime," she said, reaching a hand over to pat his knee.

Bub's eyes immediately brightened, and Murphy glanced away in defeat, leaned his head over the leeward rail to check the shape of the big genoa that curved gently back from the headstay. The trailing edge near the top was flapping slightly, and he reached back to tug on the pulleyed line that moved the turning block for the jib sheet backward along the toe rail. He cleated off the line, then checked the sail again. The luffing had stopped.

He stood and scanned the horizon, saw nothing. They were sailing well through the indigo waters of the Gulf Stream, about sixty degrees off the wind at a speed of just over six knots, through one- and two-foot seas that did little to slow them down. As to their destination, well, that was still up in the air. They had so far picked the direction that would let them sail the fastest, but at some point they had to decide where to put in.

Murphy turned back to face his crewmates, saw that Bub was with much interest listening to Toni Johnson explain about the hydrodynamic lift generated by a keel sailing upwind. He glanced down the companionway to check the GPS display, did some mental calculations and waited for Toni to finish her explanation.

"How about Miami?" he asked before Bub could further their conversation. "We could cross the Stream, then head due south like we were going to Bimini, then cut back across and into Miami in the dark."

"No good," Toni Johnson said, shaking her head. "Farber's got fast boats positioned at every navigable inlet from Mayport to Marathon. They know the name of your boat. They know what she looks like. I don't think heading back to Florida is such a good idea."

Bub said, "We just can't let them get away with this."

"Going home's too risky," Toni Johnson said. "These people are ruthless. They were getting ready last night to board you, shoot all of you and sink your boat."

Bub nodded determinedly, cleared his throat. "Folks? I think it's time I had a heart-to-heart with my brother. I know him better than anybody. I think I can talk him down from this."

"How?" Murphy asked. "How will you talk to him, without a radio?"

"We let 'em catch up, then y'all put me out in the dinghy, and I'll talk to him. Face-to-face, man-to-man." Bub glanced at Toni, then Murphy. "He ain't evil, guys. He's self-centered and he can be petty. But that describes most all of us, to a degree. If he sees me, up close, that'll bring home the reality of what they're doin'."

"You don't understand," Toni said, grabbing his wrist. "They've gone too far to turn back now. And even if you could convince Percy, you think Farber and Thresher will listen? Come on! You said it yourself! They've already killed once."

Murphy took a deep breath. "If anyone should go talk to them, it's me. Bub, you've got a son to think about. I haven't got anybody. *I'll* go out in the dinghy and talk to them."

Bub's mouth fell open and his eyes moistened. "You'd do that for me?"

"Son?" Toni Johnson asked. "What son? I didn't know you had a son!"

Bub moved across the cockpit and threw an arm around Murphy's shoulder. "Man, you would, wouldn't you?"

"Hey! Excuse me!" came a shout.

They all looked up, where Romer had climbed the mast to the spreaders and was now pointing behind them with the binoculars.

"Yeah, I don't mean to interrupt the dynamics of your love triangle down there, but I figured y'all would want to know that they're on our ass and gaining!"

Farber LaGrange rubbed his hands and nodded at his two pupils seated on the cabin trunk beneath the big genoa. "Very good. Now, let's run through tackin' again, all right? Okay, so the wind is comin' over the port side, and the sail is out to starboard. Grant, what tack are we on?"

Grant thought hard. "Starboard?"

Farber winced, took a deep breath. "No. That was a good try, but it's port. Whatever side the wind's comin' over is the tack we're on, all right? Okay, so we're on the port tack, and we see the boat ahead of us off our port bow and we want to head toward them. So we . . . Clyde?"

"Tack," Clyde Bruno said, with barely concealed disgust.

"Good. So I take the wheel, and Clyde, you're on the workin' sheet, which is on the leeward side, and Grant, you're on the lazy sheet, which is on the windward side, and I turn the wheel to port, and say 'hard-a-lee!' and as soon as the boat passes through the eye of the wind and the sail starts to luff, Clyde does what? . . . Grant?"

Grant thought another moment. "Release the jib sheet off the winch?"

"*Very* good! And remember what I said about bein' careful with lines on the winch. Never let your fingers get between the line and the winch drum. There's a powerful lot of wind on that sheet, and it'll put a hurtin' on you if you let it," Farber said, then noticed Grant's raised hand. "What is it?"

"If the wind is coming from directly behind us, then which tack are we on?"

Farber LaGrange narrowed his gaze, prepared a caustic reply when a wave smashed into the bow and sprayed all three of them. "Jesus Christ! What in hell's goin' on?"

Clyde Bruno looked around, shrugged. "Just hit a wave. That's all."

"These waves ain't big enough for that to happen," Farber grumbled, then studied the motion of the bow more closely. "We're hobbyhorsin'. Happens when there's too much weight in the ends. Somethin' musta shifted below. I'll go check it out. Meanwhile, Grant, you go check the radar. See how far off they are. Then I want you guys to read your chapters about jibin'."

He walked aft, looking out toward the horizon. The wind had increased, up to twelve, occasionally fifteen knots, but *Soft Money* was a dry boat, and the little two-foot waves should not have been coming aboard. Hell, the boat was barely even heeled over. He rubbed his chin, reminded himself to shave before they returned to the docks. After this chore was taken care of, they still had a statewide political campaign to finish.

Farber LaGrange crouched, about to jump down into the cockpit, when his eye happened to fall on the aft deck and the two heads in the sunken hot tub. He shook his head, with narrowed eye and furrowed brow moved aft, stood in silent amazement for a minute with hands on hips.

Link Thresher and Clarissa Highstreet were sitting across from each other, smiling and chatting amid the whirlpool jets. Clarissa Highstreet had lost the bikini top, and Thresher's eyes darted between her face and the molded half-globes on her chest.

"Hi!" she said. "Farber, you've been complaining all this time about me wearing my heels?" She lifted one expertly sculpted leg up and out of the water, toes pointed to the sky. "Well, I'm not wearing them now!"

Farber grunted, trying to contain his anger. "Do you realize how many gallons of fresh water you just used up? We ain't at the dock, you know. It takes the watermaker an hour to make fifteen gallons."

Clarissa Highstreet smirked at him. "Of course, I doubt you'd notice my *legs* now. Not with the rest of me . . . on display." She jiggled her torso to emphasize her point. Rock-hard breasts and permanently erect nipples kept pointing directly ahead, unmoved, a steady two inches beneath the surface. "You don't have to pretend not to look. I'm used to the attention."

He glanced down and appraised them once more. "I thought boobs were s'posed to float."

She sneered in disgust. "*Some* women's breasts float because they're mainly fat tissue. *I* don't have an ounce of fat on me."

"All praise to modern science," Farber said.

"I'm leaner than a marathon runner. I even have a certificate."

"I'm impressed beyond words." Farber cleared his throat and clapped his hands. "Okay, enough. We gotta drain the tub. Five hundred and fifty gallons, times eight pounds a gallon, makes four thousand, four hundred pounds. Two tons, this far aft, is makin' us pitch up and down too much."

Clarissa Highstreet shrugged. "So?"

"It's slowin' us down," Farber said, his patience thinning.

She shrugged again. "That didn't seem to be a problem a week ago, when you had a boat full of naked Victory Hostesses. What are we, in some sort of race?"

"Yeah, for the gov'nor of Florida, in case you've forgotten." He looked plaintively at Link Thresher, who nodded and reached an arm around her shoulders.

"Listen, I'm getting kinda hot in here. I was thinking of going below for a shower. Care to join me? We could talk about Paris some more."

She blinked, then stretched her plastic grin wide. "Paris? You said the magic word!"

She turned and climbed out of the tub, revealing bronze buttocks bisected by a black strip of fabric before wrapping the sarong around her waist. She stepped into her heels, then looked back at Link Thresher. "Coming?"

He grinned and patted her bottom. "Go on down. I'll be right there."

She sashayed toward the companionway topless, made a show of taking off the sarong and laying it flat on the cabin top to dry, leered at Clyde Bruno as he hurried past, then climbed down the steps.

Farber LaGrange bent and opened a panel in the deck, flipped a switch to drain the tub overboard. Clyde Bruno stopped before him, nodded toward the bow. "I thought you should know. I just saw a sail up on the horizon. They look like they're a couple of miles ahead."

"Skipper!" Grant Hanson chimed in from the companionway. "I have a range of two-point-two miles!"

Farber LaGrange climbed up on the cockpit coaming for a better view. "Chrissake, I see 'em. At this rate we'll be on 'em in twenty minutes." He put his fingers to his temples and squeezed. "Okay, here's the game plan: Grant and Percy stay in the cockpit with me and work the sails while I drive. Clyde, you're on the bow with the weapons. Link, your job is to keep Miss Sec'tary of Bitch belowdecks, though it seems you were pretty much plannin' on keepin' her occupied anyhow."

Link Thresher shrugged apologetically. "You take what you can get.

Plus you know what? Her tits ain't half bad. A little intimidating, sure, but not half bad."

"The best body money can buy," Farber said. "Whatever floats your boat. All right, go on down there, and don't let her come up until I give the all clear. There's a stereo in that cabin. Put in somethin' loud, cover up the noise from up here."

Thresher stretched his neck from side to side, interlaced his fingers and stretched his arms to crack his knuckles. "I'll give her a symphony to listen to, all right. Don't you worry."

"That's right. Put it to her. You go, boy. Just watch yourself with them nips. Remember, we ain't got no eye surgeon aboard." Farber patted him on the back as he went past, then clapped his hands. "All right, boys! It's time to put all our book-learnin' to use. Let's go!"

Ready about!" Murphy shouted, glancing over his shoulder at the big white sail now just a couple hundred yards behind them.

"Ready!" Toni Johnson yelled, her hands clutching the red-and-white braided line where it came off the winch drum.

Murphy threw the tiller to leeward. "Hard-to-lee!"

*Mudslinger* swung into the wind, her genoa went slack, then started to shake. At that instant, Toni Johnson snapped the line off the drum, then ran forward to help the sail around the inner forestay as Romer cranked in on the opposite winch.

Within seconds, the genny was around on the other side, perfectly smooth and drawing well enough for *Mudslinger* to once more accelerate up to six and a half knots.

"Good tack, guys. Back up to hull speed," Murphy announced, then checked back behind him as *Soft Money* similarly swung from port to starboard tack. "Dammit all. They're getting better."

The first few times Murphy had changed course, *Soft Money* had faltered, slowing to almost dead in the water with a fouled jib sheet or backed sail. *Mudslinger* would run off hundreds of yards, on one occasion a full quarter mile, before Farber's boat would get back on her feet and resume the chase.

"Two hundred forty yards," Bub said, letting the range finder drop to the end of the lanyard around his neck. "They hardly lost any ground at all, that time."

Murphy watched the boat behind them. There were three of them in the cockpit, one standing beside the mast. "The more we do this, the better they're gonna get. Even worse, they can point higher upwind than we can."

Toni Johnson leaned against the boom, her toes curled over the edge of the coach roof, watching the faster boat close the gap. Suddenly she clapped her hands. "Okay, so they've learned to tack. Let's make 'em jibe! That might cross 'em up!"

Murphy's eyes widened and he nodded, first slowly, then more rapidly. "Yeah. Let's do it. Quick. Romer, ease sheets!"

The ropes groaned from the friction around the winch drums as Romer uncleated both jib and main sheets, then slowly let them out as Murphy pulled the tiller to windward until *Mudslinger* raced along, broadside to the wind.

They watched as, behind them, *Soft Money* similarly cracked off the wind and matched their course. Murphy licked his lips, saw a larger-than-average wave approaching from windward. "All right, folks, I'm gonna try to spin around using that wave. Prepare to jibe. Bub, remember to keep your head down!"

"Ready to jibe," Toni answered, back in the cockpit.

"Jibe ho," Murphy said, then pushed the tiller in time to turn down the face of the five-footer.

Romer let the main sheet out until *Mudslinger* was heading directly downwind, then rapidly pulled it in to control the boom as it swung across the boat, then let it out as the boat sped off in the new direction—right back across *Soft Money*'s course and about a hundred yards off.

They ducked low to offer smaller targets, then released a collective whoop as the bigger boat's boom swept wildly across her deck, knocking her momentarily on her side, mast on the water, before she popped back up with her bow into the wind, sails shaking uncontrollably.

"Yes!" Murphy said, offering up high fives all around.

"Did they break anything?" Toni asked.

Romer held the binoculars steady for a long minute, then lowered them. "Unfortunately, doesn't look like it. The guy by the mast went over, but he climbed back aboard."

Murphy checked the trim on the sails, turned a few degrees to port to fill the genoa. "Okay, let's take advantage of this and open up a little gap here."

Toni and Romer moved back to their stations, and Bub slid back to his post, lifted the range finder. "I feel kinda nutty askin' this, but . . . did anybody else hear music as we went past 'em?"

"Maurice Ravel," Romer said. *"Boléro."*


Clarissa Highstreet was buck naked and pissed off, standing at the top of the companionway steps screaming at Farber and his crew, asking why the hell couldn't they keep the boat steady. "I hit the roof! Literally!" she hissed. "The fuck's wrong with you people?"

Farber LaGrange spread his palms. "Rogue wave. They happen. Sorry."

"Sorry is right," she snapped. "The whole bunch of you and this stupid boat. Now, I am *busy!* If you expect my help on Election Day, gentlemen, I suggest you *keep this fucking tub on her feet!"*

She turned around and stomped back down the steps. No one said anything for a while, until Grant Hanson offered, "She's scary."

Percy Billings shook his head. "I can't believe I've gotten into bed with her. I have to live with that the rest of my life, an albatross around my neck. A great, silicone-enhanced albatross."

Farber LaGrange turned on Grant, glaring alternately at him and at the smaller boat once again a mile ahead of them. "Why in hell didn't you control the main when we jibed?" he demanded.

Grant Hanson glanced helplessly around the boat.

"The main!" Farber LaGrange shouted. "The big motherfuckin' sail right above your head! You gotta sheet the main in as we go 'round, then let it out again. Otherwise it flies across like it did. Damn near killed us. We're lucky we didn't lose the flippin' rig."

"But we don't have to do that when we tack!" Grant protested.

"That's 'cause the sail ain't fulla fuckin' wind when we tack, is it? The damn boom hardly moves at all when we tack, does it? It's a different story when we jibe. Now, next time we jibe, what are you gonna do?"

Grant stood silently, mouth open, finally shook his head.

"Oh, for-fuckin'-get it," Farber grumbled. "Clyde! Come trade with Grant. I need you in the cockpit!"

Clyde came back from the mast, wet from his dousing and a fresh machine gun slung over his shoulder, and sidled up to Farber at the big, stainless steering wheel. "Sir, I don't know. This is a serious weapon. He could do a lot of damage with it."

"Yeah, well, he *definitely* does a lot of damage here in the cockpit. I think we already proved that," Farber said. "Now go on. You take the starboard winch."

Clyde sighed, unslung his gun and handed it to Grant. "Now you need to be careful with this, all right? It's an Uzi, fully automatic. You can't hold the trigger down or you'll empty the clip in two seconds. Remember to aim, then shoot. Short bursts. Got it?"

Grant Hanson fondled the black steel in wonderment. "Really? An Uzi? Wow!"

**M**urphy gripped the tiller with whitened knuckles, as if they might somehow go faster the harder he squeezed. No one spoke for a long minute as *Soft Money* once again drew within a few hundred yards.

"What if we tried that jibin' thing again?" Bub asked.

"The more we do that, the better they'll get at that, too," Murphy said. "Plus it takes us right across their bow, perfect targets. Plus they don't ever really have to jibe themselves, to follow us. They can just go all the way around through the wind and tack, instead. With their speed advantage, they can afford it."

"How about if we turned the motor on?" Bub suggested.

"We're almost touching seven knots now," Toni Johnson said. "The engine can't really help us. Not with this much wind. What we need is a flat calm. No wind at all, to let us get out of radar range."

Bub's eyes widened. "Is that how they're trackin' us? Radar? Really? Huh. I'll be damned."

"We could turn on the motor and just go straight upwind," Murphy mused. "Only thing is, they seem to be able to sail upwind at nine knots, so they'd be able to short tack right behind us, strafing us as they went. And then we'd run out of gas in an hour and a half, anyway."

Romer put down the binoculars and stood. "Well, there's no need to be completely passive here. Murph, what do you have aboard in the way of combustibles? Kerosene? Alcohol?"

"Both. In the locker behind the stove," Murphy answered. "Why?"

But Romer had already disappeared below. He returned a minute later with two steel tins, an armful of glass condiment jars, a wad of engine rags and the flare kit.

"Bub, Toni, you guys know how to make Molotov cocktails? No? Well, it's easy. Watch me." He began emptying Dijon mustard and tartar sauce overboard, then filling the jars halfway with alcohol and kerosene.

Murphy nodded at the bright orange plastic barrel containing the flare kit. "You can't possibly hit them with that. That only works in the movies."

"I know." Romer jammed a Phillips-head screwdriver through the metal lid of one jar, pushed through a torn strip of cotton rag for a wick. "But *they* might not. Plus, it might get them to open fire when they're still too far. The more rounds we can make them waste, the better."

He unscrewed the barrel and removed the pistol, breaking off the plastic tab in the trigger guard, then loading it with a flare the size of a shotgun shell.

"Plus, who knows? Maybe we'll get lucky." Romer snapped the pis-

tol shut and stepped up onto the tiny triangle of deck behind the cockpit. "Maybe with the waves and the boat rocking, one of them will shoot
themselves in the foot."

Clyde Bruno stood at a winch on one side of the cockpit, Percy
Billings stood at the other across from him, and in between and slightly
back was Farber LaGrange, driving *Soft Money* as she raced across
the wind.

The seas had built to six feet, with the breeze occasionally gusting
now to twenty, and Farber LaGrange couldn't help but whoop.

"God*damn*it, boys, if we didn't just hit twelve knots on that last
wave! We are *kickin'* ass and takin' names!"

Percy regarded him sullenly. "It smells to heaven, what I do now. It
hath the primal eldest curse upon it. A brother's murder. I'm glad *you're*
having fun, Farber."

"Oh, don't go gettin' all Shakespearean on me," Farber said, bracing
one bare foot against the downhill side of the cockpit as a particularly
strong gust heeled the boat way over for a few seconds. "Ain't no
turnin' back now, even if we wanted to, and you know it."

Ahead and just slightly to windward was Murphy's boat, *Mudslinger,*
he could occasionally read on her stern. Farber had to admit she was
pretty, with nice ends and a graceful sheer that gave her a classic look that
his own modern machine would never have. It would be a shame to sink
her. Now that he was getting into sailing for the sake of sailing, a boat
like *Mudslinger* would have been perfect for him and two crew members,
perhaps a pair of the more nautically inclined Victory Hostesses.

"You know, guys, all these years I've owned *Soft Money* and had
Blake and Ian doin' all the work, I never really 'preciated the *romance* of
this, know what I mean? I mean, here we are, no engine, but we could
pretty much sail anywhere on the planet we wanted to. Hell, this boat
could get us around Cape Horn, if we wanted to freeze our asses off.
Ain't that somethin'?"

Percy said nothing and Clyde grunted. Through the companionway came the strains of Wagner's "Ride of the Valkyries," and Farber grinned.

"I guess Sec'tary Highbeams is gonna get rid hard and put away wet. Either that or ol' Thresher is."

A six-footer slapped into *Soft Money*'s side, sending a shower of sun-dazzled droplets through the cockpit.

Farber LaGrange shook his damp head in ecstasy. "Yee-hah, boys! Now *that's* sailin'!"

Clyde cupped his hand to his mouth and shouted at Grant by the mast: "Hey! Keep that thing dry! Don't let it get splashed like that again!"

Grant Hanson nodded at Clyde and made an okay sign with thumb and forefinger, then stuck the gun up his shirt, the muzzle protruding from the neckline just under his chin.

Farber LaGrange squinted and shook his head. "Well, that ain't exactly how it's taught in the NRA assault-weapon safety course, is it?"

"Sir, he's an accident waiting to happen. Look, we haven't had to change course since I've been back here. I really think—"

Clyde's mouth fell open as a bright orange ball streaked from the boat ahead of them in their general direction before arcing off wildly to leeward, followed quickly by a second orange streak, this one curving up and over them.

At the mast, Grant Hanson went into a peculiar dance, struggling to get the Uzi out of his shirt, screaming, "They're shootin' at us! They're shootin' at us!"

The gun finally popped free and Grant found the trigger just as another six-footer jostled *Soft Money* out from under him. The spray of bullets flew upward, forward and around, as Grant screamed and Farber, Clyde and Percy hit the deck as one.

## ★ (9) ★

LYING FLAT ON HIS BACK in the cockpit, Farber stared glumly at the few remaining shreds left of his mainsail and medium-weight genoa, the vast majority of both having already wafted down around him in a flurry of white cloth.

He turned his head to one side, where Percy Billings similarly surveyed the damage, then the other, where Clyde glared hatefully at the mast. "Anybody shot?" Farber asked.

"Not yet," Clyde said, picking himself up, eyes still locked on Grant Hanson.

"I slipped!" Grant Hanson protested, realizing that the blame was about to fall squarely on his shoulders. "They were shootin'!"

"They were shootin' flares," Farber drawled, squinting off at Murphy Moran's rapidly receding sailboat. "That only ever works in the movies. You coulda killed us all, you moron!"

"I'm sorry," Grant said contritely.

Percy picked a T-shirt-sized scrap of sailcloth off the teak deck. One edge was torn at a perforation created by a string of bullet holes. He dropped the cloth, sat beside Farber and blew out a long breath. "You know, maybe this is a sign," he said. "Maybe Bub is somehow blessed, for some inexplicable reason, and we might as well just pack it in and go home."

"It's a sign, all right," Farber agreed. "It's a sign that *that* fool ought not be permitted to handle a firearm again. Ever."

"I said I was sorry." Grant pouted.

"Oh, well, you're sorry. That's different, then." Farber stood up, bracing himself against the motion of the boat, a random tossing about now without the stabilizing effect of the sails. "All right. Spilt milk. Water under the bridge. Second kick o' the mule. All that bullshit. Let's get going. Mr. Bruno, if you would please take Lee Harvey over there and fetch the number-three genoa and the storm main. Let me caution all of you that the smaller our sails, the slower we go, and therefore the greater their chance of escape. So *please* don't rip, tear or mutilate any more of 'em. Okay?"

Grant thought for a while, then raised a hand in gentle protest. "I didn't have anything to do with the last—"

"What the *fuck* is going on now?" screamed Clarissa Highstreet, once more storming up the companionway, this time clad in heels and Link Thresher's boxer shorts.

Farber LaGrange raised his palms innocently. "How do you mean?"

*Soft Money* simultaneously leaned to starboard and dipped her bow, and Clarissa Highstreet's heels slipped on the varnished wood of the ladder. She scrambled to regain her footing on the teak deck as she screamed, "*This* is what I mean! We're wallowing around like— What happened to the sails?"

Farber played dumb, glanced at Percy, looked back to her with a shrug. "Sails?"

"Sails!" She pointed upward. "The big triangular cloth things that are supposed to go there?"

Link Thresher appeared in the hatch, gently tugged at her leg. He had replaced Wagner with some Miles Davis. "Come on back, baby. You know the French just die for jazz? Honest to God, they do!"

"And furthermore," she continued, unmollified, "what were those noises, a minute ago?"

Farber said, "Noises?"

"Shots. Gunshots," she said.

"I'll tell you what. Petron Europe will even sponsor a weekly jazz concert, right at the embassy. How about that!" Link Thresher tugged at her calf again. "Have I told you recently what great legs you've got?"

"Oh, *that!*" Farber grinned. "Well, actually, that was us, takin' the sails down all of a sudden. When they flap around, they can be loud, I'll allow that much. Anyhow, we, uh, well, we had a line out. Fishin'. And we got a hit, and we wanted to bring it aboard, so we—"

"What's that under your shirt?" Clarissa Highstreet demanded.

Grant Hanson affected a who-me? look and glanced around behind him.

"Yeah, you," she said, advancing on him. "There's something fishy going on all right, but I don't think it has anything to do with fish. What in God's name are we doing out here, anyway? Do you realize I was supposed to have both my nails *and* my hair done today?"

She stepped right up to the kneeling Grant, breasts at eye level, and continued her inquisition as he stared slackmouthed. "What, you've never seen boobs before? Now show me what you're hiding. . . ."

She reached for his shirt, he drew back, she pushed forward, the boat lurched, she lurched, and Grant Hanson screamed, "Aaaaeeeee!"

He collapsed to the deck, the Uzi now protruding from his shirt, and clutched at his right eye socket, still wailing. Farber and Percy scrambled to his side, held him steady, and Farber slowly forced Grant's hands apart long enough for them to get a look.

"Aw, Jesus," he groaned, rolling away. He stared up in horror at Clarissa Highstreet. "I can't fuckin' believe it. . . . You really did it! You put his fuckin' eye out!"

Revulsion spread across Clarissa Highstreet's face, overcoming even the surgically fixed smile. She glanced down at her chest, touched a finger to the goopy fluid dripping off her left nipple. "Eeeewww! What the . . . What is this?"

"You dumb bitch!" Farber screamed. "I warned you them things were lethal, didn't I?"

"What is this stuff?" she repeated, flicking her fingers to get it off.

"That's ocular fluid. Eye juice," Farber said, shaking his head. "Aw, Jesus. Haven't you ever squished a fish's eye? This is the stuff that's inside. Christ, you've fuckin' blinded him!"

Clarissa Highstreet's plastic smile was now thoroughly overwhelmed, scrunched past its breaking point into a frown, as she shook her hand wildly, began running in her three-inch bedroom slippers down the spray-slickened deck. "Ocular *fluid? Eye juice?* Eeeeeewwwww! Get it *off*!"

Both Percy and Clyde Bruno jumped back involuntarily as she lunged at their shirts, strands of Grant Hanson's ocular fluid stretched between the fingers of her hand. Her momentum carried her over the lip of the cabin top, her left heel caught in a deck chock for the spinnaker pole, and with a prolonged *eeeeeeeewwwwww!* she tumbled over the port lifelines.

"Clarissa!" Link Thresher shouted, scrambling out of the cockpit and onto the port sidedeck, a pair of great, hairy buns flapping free as his towel fell away.

He leaned overboard beneath the lifelines, arm outstretched, finally came back up, a black, high-heeled slipper in hand. His face was pale. "She's gone."

Farber LaGrange pointed at the nearest life ring mounted on a stanchion. "Enough melodrama. There, toss that to her."

"No, I'm serious. She's really gone." Link Thresher's eyes were wide with amazement behind his black horn-rims. "Not an ounce of fat on her. She went down tits first."

*Mudslinger* continued flying along on a beam reach, the afternoon sun transforming every droplet of spray into a glorious, miniature rainbow.

No one among her crew even noticed. Instead they stood at the mast, heads craned upward, watching Romer perched at the very top surveying the horizon with the Fujinons. Each time a wind gust or a wave heeled the boat over, Romer swung way out over the water to leeward.

"Anythin'?" Bub yelled.

"Nada. Nothing." Romer let the glasses drop to his chest at the end of the strap. "All right, I'm ready to come down."

Inch by inch, Murphy and Toni Johnson let the spinnaker halyard on which they had secured Romer's bosun's chair unwind around the winch drum, easing him back down to the cabin top.

"So far, so good," Murphy said.

"So far," Romer agreed, unsnapping the harness straps. "Keep in mind that in ideal conditions I'd only be able to see about seven miles from up there. And these are hardly ideal conditions. With the boat heeled over like this, I wasn't really at masthead height. And in those moments I was, at least half the times we were in a trough."

"It's that damned radar," Toni Johnson said, arms crossed in thought. "You know, it would have been far more useful throwing a monkey wrench into that than even the engine."

Bub stared astern, shielding his eyes from the sun. "Well, how far exactly can they see us?"

Toni Johnson bit her lip. "It was a Raytheon SL72. I glanced at it earlier in the evening, during the fund-raiser. Two kilowatts. Range of twenty-four miles."

"Okay, we're doin' six and a half knots, so after four hours we oughta be outta their sight, right?" Bub asked.

"That's assuming they stay stopped," Romer pointed out. "There's no reason for them to do that."

"That's right," Toni agreed. "I spent quite a bit of time in Farber's sail locker. He's got about a dozen bags of sails. So far they've only gone through three, albeit the three most useful."

"Okay, so how fast can they go without their three most useful sails?" Bub continued.

Murphy watched a line of cloud on the horizon, turned his face to the wind. It was just as strong as earlier. "With this much breeze? They could put up their storm sails and still go faster than us."

Bub stood silently for a minute, hands on his hips, then pointed up at the aluminum globe bisected with plates dangling halfway up the mast over the starboard spreader. "Then how about we take that thing down?"

Toni Johnson let out a gasp. "Jesus, Murphy, he's right! We've had the radar reflector up this whole time! No wonder they've had such an easy time finding us!"

Murphy's face went flush, realizing the blunder. He shrugged defensively. "Well, it's not like we'd be a stealth sailboat or something without the reflector. The mast itself will show up on their radar."

Bub blinked and scrunched up his mouth. "Sailorman, I thought you told me, back on our trip down to Jupiter, what a crucial piece of safety gear that little ball is. How all them little corners reflect radar waves back to where they came from. As opposed to the mast, which because it's all rounded, don't reflect the waves back very well at all."

Murphy was already at the base of the mast, uncleating the thin, Dacron line that held the reflector aloft. "All right. I fucked up. Okay? I'm sorry."

Toni Johnson squeezed Murphy's arm sympathetically, and for a moment Murphy thought his screwup might have a silver lining, until her fingers suddenly gripped his arm tight.

"Put it back up!"

"What?"

She pointed frantically at the pulleyed line. "Hoist it back up!"

Murphy did so, tied off the line again, then stood with quizzical expression. "Okay. Care to explain?"

"If we just take it down, they'll know it's still us. The next time they check the radar, I mean. If a bright image was eight miles away, and a half hour later a dimmer image is seven miles away, they'll figure out we've just done something to degrade our reflection." Her eyes glimmered with excitement. "What if, on the other hand, they were faced with *two* images on their scope, and they had to choose?"

Murphy thought for a second, then smiled wide as he and Toni scrambled forward to where *Mudslinger*'s sailing dinghy was lashed to the cabin top. Romer's eyes brightened, too, as he climbed down from his perch on the boom and clambered back to retrieve the spare propane tank from its cockpit locker.

Bub scratched his head, watching all the activity. "Somebody wanna let me in on what in heck we're doin?"

Link Thresher sat on the aft deck, pale, skinny legs dangling overboard, arms resting on the vinyl-clad lifelines. He held Clarissa Highstreet's high-heeled slipper in one hand, studied it wistfully.

Farber LaGrange sat beside him and put a consoling arm around his shoulders. "We'll get you a new bimbo as soon as we get back," he said.

Thresher glanced up, annoyed, then turned back to *Soft Money*'s frothy wake. "She wasn't just some bimbo, Farber. She was a real woman." He considered that a moment. "Okay, except for her tits. And her smile. And, I suppose, her ass. But you know what I mean."

"I know," said Farber, who hadn't a clue.

"A woman with a life of her own. A woman of power. A woman full of *joie de vivre*. A woman on the downhill side of forty still willin' to wear a thong in public. Hell, you think I can get my wife to wear a thong? Even in private?" Thresher shook his head sadly. "All she wanted was to be ambassador to France. That, and a good lay now and again. Now she's gone. Poor thing. Water was her downfall."

Farber nodded knowingly, mumbled, "Like the Wicked Witch of the West."

"What?" Link Thresher asked.

"Nothin'," Farber said, and slapped Thresher on the back. "Look at the bright side. Now we don't gotta figure out a way to explain what we were doin'. You must admit, that was gettin' tiresome. Of course, on the downside, now we ain't got someone who can swing a close election our way."

"Well, then, we just have to make sure we don't end up in a close election." Thresher raised the slipper to his lips, kissed it on the instep, then heaved it as far as he could astern. "Good night, sweet princess! And flights of angels sing you to sleep, or however the fuck that goes." He dusted off his hands and stood. "All right. Let's hurry up and finish that son of a bitch. I got Alaskan wilderness to plunder, beaches to despoil, oil to drill. How are we doing?"

Farber pointed to the small triangle of white cloth attached to the mast and the high-cut yankee flying from the headstay. "As you can see, we ain't got much in the way of sail area. As long as we catch up to 'em 'fore the wind dies, it shouldn't be a problem."

Thresher nodded, pointed with his chin at Percy at the wheel. "How's he doing?"

Farber watched Percy with creased brow. "All right, I guess. He's in a deep slide toward depressive. He's talkin' about God and shit. Like God would have anythin' to do with an election in Florida. After we get him installed in the Mansion, remind me to have him put on lithium."

"I thought it was Prozac now. Or that new one, whatsitcalled, Paxil."

"Whatever. I just don't know how much of his bullshit I can take. One minute he's gonna change the world, next minute he's cursed like Cain." Farber shook his head. "I got no idea what he's gonna do when he sees his brother get gunned down, blood everywhere. . . ."

Thresher patted Farber LaGrange's back. "He'll be fine."

"I dunno," Farber said. "He's kinda close to the edge as it is. I don't know how he's gonna make four years in that job, knowin' he had to kill his flesh and blood to get it."

Thresher laughed and opened his fly to pee over the side. "Who cares whether he makes it four years? After he lets that drilling permit through in January, he can go nuttier than a fruitcake, far as I'm concerned."

Farber LaGrange nodded disdainfully. "Yeah, it's all about you, ain't it? Don't give a rat's ass 'bout anybody else. Me, for instance. I gotta make sure we hang onto the House and Senate in two more years, not to mention the presidential race."

"You? I thought you were going to sail off into the sunset with a couple of your Victory Hostesses, cheatin' and winnin' every fishin' tournament around the globe." He shook himself off and tucked himself back in. "I thought this was your *last* election."

Farber LaGrange rocked and leaned with a larger-than-average wave and started toward the cockpit. "What, and let those assholes piss away everythin' I spent all these years winnin' for 'em? Forget it. *I* got Florida an all-Republican statehouse. I'll be damned if I'm gonna let those boneheads lose it again."

He picked up the pair of binoculars, stood on the cabin top and scanned the horizon ahead. "Still nothin'," he grunted. "I better go check on ol' One-Eyed Magellan. Make sure we ain't completely lost yet."

**R**omer unzipped the red duffel bag, and the rest peered in skeptically. The spare propane tank sat in the bottom. Taped to the top, next to the valve, was an assembly that included a small glass light bulb that Romer had filled with salty water and attached with alligator clips and more wiring to a lantern battery. Two small pieces of plywood were lashed around the light bulb assembly, and a gallon-sized Ziploc covered the whole thing, with duct tape holding the open end of the bag to the metal of the tank.

"It's not going to slow the dinghy down," Romer said, nodding behind them, where *Mudslinger*'s eight-foot tender, *Negative Ad*, followed behind them at the end of its painter.

Its sails luffed in the breeze, and from its masthead hung the basketball-sized aluminum radar reflector. Beneath its thwart seat they'd wedged in big Tupperware containers filled with two months' supply of Publix chunk white tuna as ballast. The only thing left was the debate about whether to include the device Romer had whipped up in a half hour of tinkering in Murphy's spare-parts bin.

Romer flipped the duffel over, showed them the big piece of plywood that he'd lashed to the base of the bag. "This is at least as buoyant as the dinghy itself. Plus it'll be three hundred feet behind her. About one wavelength." He pointed out at the diminishing seas. "I doubt it'll even lose a quarter knot."

Murphy and Bub shared an uneasy glance, and Bub scrunched up his lips. "So how's it work again?"

"A bump on the bag, or even a hard jerk on the line," Romer pointed to the light bulb, "crushes this. The electrolytic solution short-circuits the battery, which provides the ignition for the propane that will have collected in this bag. That, hopefully, will detonate the rest of the tank."

Toni, Murphy and Bub stared some more, until finally Bub asked, "So how many people will it kill?"

Romer answered with a flinty gaze. "I might remind you that they've been firing live rounds at us these past thirty-six hours."

"He's my brother," Bub snapped. "It's bad enough he's gotta go to prison."

Toni put a comforting arm around his shoulders, and Romer nodded. "Fair enough. Chances are a hundred to one against it working. Seawater could leak in, which would set it off early. The bag could tear, making it impossible to collect any gas. And then, even if everything works right, remember, it's not like we've poured nails in around it. It's concussive, not anti-personnel. Ideally, they run into it and put a hole in their boat, in which case they get into their life raft and get rescued and, incidentally, leave us alone. Sure, it's a shot in the dark," he concluded. "But why not take it?"

Murphy and Toni said nothing, left it to Bub, who after a time nodded and waved his hand. "All right. Let's do it. Let's put a hole in Farber's boat. That'll teach him to steal an election."

Grant Hanson squinted his remaining eye, opened it wide, squinted again, but the fuzzy blobs on the radar display got no clearer.

He gulped hard, wiped the sweat away with a forearm and gritted his teeth to control the nausea. The pain wasn't so bad anymore, not since Farber had given him three Darvocets from the medical kit, but the ooze that continued to dribble down his check still completely grossed him out. The rocking and pitching of the boat, magnified by being below-decks, was not helping. Nor was the irritating *beep, beep, beep* emanating from the device just behind the radar monitor. All afternoon now, every few minutes, the damned thing kept going *beep, beep, beep, beep, beep. . . .*

He held a hand to his belly, reached out with the other and felt around for a power switch on the beeping instrument, finally flicked it off.

There. That was better.

Now he could focus on the radar, figure out what was going on with the display. The whole trip so far, the radar thing had been easy. There had just been one blob on the screen, and all he had to do was put the lit-tle plus sign over it and click.

Now there were two. Where had the other one come from? It was dimmer than the first one, so maybe it was smaller? Maybe . . . a little fishing boat, like a Boston Whaler or something? But would a fishing boat be out this far? And exactly how far out was "this far"?

He glanced at all the numbers on the GPS readout and wished he had some idea what they meant. One thing he knew: He wasn't about to ask. He'd taken just about all the abuse from Farber LaGrange he cared to, and now he'd even hurt his eye for him.

Grant Hanson patted the gauze gently, once again felt a vague un-easiness. Under the gauze, he felt . . . nothing. Like it was completely gone. But Farber had told him it would get better, that he just needed to keep the patch on for a couple of days.

He shuddered at the memory of how it had happened, at the vision that kept flashing through his head—a great round breast, tipped with a long, hard, menacing nipple. He would never look at a woman's chest the same way, he knew, and he shuddered again.

"Yo! Columbus!" came Farber's voice down the companionway hatch.

"Sir!" he shouted.

"How's it goin' down there?"

Grant almost smiled, touched that Farber cared. "A lot better, sir. It doesn't hurt near as much. The oozing has almost stopped."

"Well, that's just dandy. Glad to hear it. But I meant about the radar. Where are they?"

Grant went sullen again, stared at the radar screen with one eye, squinted, blinked, squinted again. He knew he'd been having spells of double vision earlier. Was he having one now? If so, why wasn't he seeing two whole radar displays, rather then just two blobs on the one display?

"Helloooooo!" Farber shouted.

The boat rolled uncomfortably again, and Grant waded through a wave of nausea before squinting at the display one final time, rolling the track ball onto the brighter of the blobs and clicking.

"Bearing two-three-seven degrees, range six-point-seven nautical miles," he called back.

"Two-three-seven?" Farber yelled, popping his head down the hatch. "You sure?"

Grant reread the display, shrugged. "Two-three-seven. Now two-three-eight."

"Two-three-eight." Farber grinned. "Southwest. Means *they're* goin' west."

Farber straightened and turned away from the hatch. "Guess what, boys! They're runnin' for home! Let's show 'em the way! Clyde, Percy, to your stations. Prepare to ease sheets!"

Grant glanced one last time at the two blobs on the display, now nearly a half screen apart from each other, then clutched his gut and scrambled topside to puke.

Clyde Bruno braced himself against the mast, held the night-vision glasses against his face until his eyes grew accustomed to the green glow. Slowly he swept back and forth across the horizon and settled on an unmistakable triangular shape a few degrees off their port bow.

"That's them," he announced after a time. "No doubt."

Farber LaGrange grunted, waved an angry fist at the sky. The wind had almost completely died. They had thrown up ever lighter sail in an attempt to catch what little of it was left, but to no avail. Very soon it would be gone entirely.

"Goddamn motherfuckin' weather," he cursed. "At this rate we ain't never gonna catch 'em."

"We weren't meant to catch them," Percy sighed. "Typical. He's always been the favorite. First Father, now . . ." He raised his eyes skyward.

Farber snorted in disgust. "Oh, will you please stop tryin' to make this into some fuckin' Greek epic. This is nothin' more than Big, Dirty Oil lyin' and killin' to own the governor of Florida. Nothin' new or grandiose about it."

Percy set his jaw and spoke without looking at him. "Well, perhaps from your point of view. Me, I always had a vision. Believe it or not, I really wanted to make Florida a better place. . . ."

Farber left him chattering to himself, moved forward to where Clyde Bruno and Link Thresher were murmuring.

"We were talking," Thresher said. "I think it's time you call out the cavalry. You know, send a couple of boats out to intercept 'em."

"Any call we make is on an open frequency," Farber said. "Definitely overheard by somebody. Possibly even recorded by the Coast Guard."

"Well, we're fast approaching crunch time. I mean, your people have been selling the family-emergency story all day to the media. What happens when somebody checks out poor, sick Uncle Reginald, finds out he doesn't even exist?"

"They won't. Tomorrow's the election. The press don't do no investigative reportin' on Election Day." Farber stared at the dark horizon, wiped his brow with the back of his hand. "But I'm afraid you got a point 'bout callin' for help. If we don't call, and they get away, we definitely go to jail."

They peered out over the black water in silence, until Clyde Bruno pressed a button on his watch, making it glow blue for a second. "You know, the moon comes up in a few minutes."

"I can't adequately express how much joy that brings me," Farber said.

"When it does," Clyde Bruno continued, "it'll light up their sail real nice against the horizon."

"So what?" Farber asked. "We should sit here and take potshots at 'em from two miles out? We might as well hope that a meteor falls on their head. Or a submarine rises up underneath 'em and sinks 'em."

"I've got something that might work from this range. I've been keeping it under wraps." Clyde Bruno nodded at the forward hatch. "To keep it safe from you-know-who. I'll go get it."

He returned two minutes later lugging a long, black canvas case. He set it on the deck, began removing components and snapping them together. Behind him, a crescent moon rose from the sea, casting a ghostly white light on the rippled water.

"I see them!" announced Grant Hanson, who had joined everyone on the foredeck.

"Bully for you," Farber said.

Clyde Bruno continued putting the weapon together, until finally he hefted a long, dark tube onto his shoulder and sighted through the scope. "Yup, I can see their sail. Clear as day."

"Can I look?" Grant asked, leaning in.

"You most certainly may not," Farber said, pushing him back. "One firearms disaster per cruise is more than enough." To Clyde: "Is that what I think it is?"

Clyde Bruno set the tube down, removed a black missile from the bag and loaded it into the rear. "Rocket-propelled grenade launcher. Powerful enough to take out a T-72."

Farber, Thresher, Percy and Grant watched him shoulder the weapon again, peer through the sight. "How's it gonna home in?" Farber asked. "If they ain't got their engine on?"

"It's not heat-seeking. It's laser-guided." Clyde looked around. "We ready?"

"You got a shot, take it," Farber said.

Link Thresher said, "Hear, hear. Let's finish it."

Keeping his eye on the sight, Clyde Bruno reached for where the battery pack fitted onto the tube, flipped a pair of switches. Two miles away, a bright red dot appeared on white sailcloth. "Target acquired. Got 'em."

All breathing had stopped on the foredeck, and Clyde Bruno's finger settled on the trigger, slowly began squeezing . . . and he stopped, turned to find Grant Hanson standing directly behind the rear of the tube.

"Why don't you move a little?" Clyde Bruno suggested.

Grant Hanson froze. "Which way?"

"Either way," Clyde said, then turned back to his target . . . with knees bent for the boat's motion, carefully moved the red dot back onto the sail . . . squeezed the trigger.

Instantly, *Soft Money*'s foredeck was bathed in warm, yellow light from the flame that shot backward from the tube as, from the opposite end, the rocket *whooooshed* out across the water. Clyde Bruno held his breath, rolling his knees with the boat, keeping the red dot centered on the sail . . . long seconds, and then a white flash obliterated the sail, expanding into a yellow ball, then orange, before dissipating through red.

By the time the *boooom* rolled over them ten seconds later, there was nothing at all left on the horizon. "Target destroyed," Clyde Bruno announced to Grant Hanson's joyful whoops and Farber's claps on the back.

He lowered the weapon, began disassembling it as Link Thresher clapped an arm around a speechless Percy Billings and pumped his fists for him.

"Congratulations," Thresher said. *"Governor!"*


**M**urphy Moran sat rigid, afraid to move a muscle for fear of tampering with perfection.

*Mudslinger* slid northeast in the fading wind under full canvas: big genoa, staysail and main. The steering gear held the boat on course effortlessly and silently, the chain on the tiller nudging it back and forth across the cockpit. Overhead, a clear day had become a brilliantly clear night, the sky littered from horizon to horizon with stars, a sliver of moon coming up just off the starboard bow.

And most important of all, beside him, under an old blanket, hips and knees occasionally grazing his own, sat Toni Johnson, chatting about sailing, about her daddy's Cal 40 she grew up around, and, now, celestial navigation.

"Yet another one of the things I never got around to learning," she admitted. "It just seemed so complicated."

"Actually it's not," Murphy said, grateful for a topic he actually felt comfortable with. "Basic geometry. Imagine you're on the ocean and you've got three really tall lighthouses all around you. If you measured the angles to the tops of each, and you knew how tall they were, you'd be able to draw circles of position around each of them, right?"

"Right," Toni said.

She shifted her thigh, momentarily brushing his, and he consciously stifled a gasp. "Right," he continued with an effort. "And of course the intersection of those circles is your position. Okay, so now instead of lighthouses, imagine three stars. The principle is the same. For every star, at any given moment, there is one and only one point on earth where it's directly overhead, right?"

"Right," she agreed, then, "Oh! I *get* it! And if we measure how far from overhead the star is—"

"We can calculate how far from that one spot on the earth we are. Exactly. For each star, you get a circle of position. Three stars—"

"Gives you a fix!" Toni Johnson cheered, grabbing his hand and squeezing. "My God! I can't tell you how many times I've read the theory in *Chapman's* and never understood it. You're my navigational hero!"

Murphy felt himself blush, tried to control his heartbeat. He hadn't showered in three days now. If he got too worked up, he'd sweat like a pig, and his accumulated aroma would be enough to drive away man and beast alike, let alone someone he was trying to . . .

"It's nothing," he mumbled. "I mean, I've got the theory down. When it comes to actually taking a sight with the sextant, shoot, I make such huge errors—"

"But that's only a matter of practice. The more you do it, the better you'll get." She squeezed his hand again. "Actually, do you have it on board? The sextant? I'd love to give it a try. I've only ever seen one once."

Murphy moistened his lips. This time her hand had stayed on his for several seconds beyond what had been necessary to punctuate her request. "Actually, yeah—"

"Actually," came a voice from the companionway, "how's a man s'posed to sleep with all this sex talk?"

Murphy felt the roar of blood in his ears, opened his mouth to correct him, but then Toni spoke: "Sex*tant*. It's a navigation tool."

"I know," Bub said, climbing into the cockpit. "I was just givin' y'all a hard time."

Toni said, "If you can't sleep, why don't you join us?"

She lifted her edge of the blanket, Bub said he wouldn't mind if he did, and Murphy deflated. He had been slowly working up the courage to ask her if she might consider helping him get *Mudslinger* to the Caribbean, presuming they ever made it home, and once again Bub had wrecked the moment.

She pushed up close against him as Bub slid beneath the blanket on the opposite side, and it occurred to Murphy that he probably was reading far more into their casual physical contact than she had ever intended. She had sat close to him because, well, it was a small cockpit and there was only one blanket.

"No sign of 'em?" Bub asked.

"Nope," Toni said. "So far, so good. It's been six hours now since we lost sight of them."

"Good, good, good," Bub said, leaning his head back on the cockpit coaming. "Beautiful night. Lookit all them stars, would ya? That bunch right there, that's one of them constellations, ain't it, Murph?"

"Orion," Toni Johnson said.

"Orion, yeah, sure. One of them ancient Greek dudes." He pointed. "What's that bright blue star, in the corner?"

"Rigel," Murphy said. "Good navigation star. Right across from it? That red one? Betelgeuse."

"Beetlejuice? Oh yeah, Beetlejuice! Like in that movie? You remember, Murph, with Michael Keaton?"

Toni Johnson exclaimed, "You like that movie? I *love* that movie! All that great Harry Belafonte music: *Jump in de line! Rock you body in time—*"

"*Okay! I believe you,*" Bub said.

They sang together: "*Shake! Shake! Señora! Shake you body line. Shake, shake, shake, señora! Shake it all de time!*"

Murphy sank in defeat. They had, somehow, once again found a common wavelength that he couldn't dial in. He waited until they had finished, climbed up on the aft deck with the binoculars to scan the horizon, then sat back down again and cleared his throat.

"You know, assuming we've shaken them for good, we kind of need to figure out where to go."

They sat silently for a minute, pondering, before Toni Johnson spoke. "Well, Florida is out of the question. Farber has activated every party goon from Miami to Pensacola and every big sportfisherman and cigarette boat he could get his hands on. I wouldn't be surprised if he's got Georgia and the Carolinas covered by now, too."

They sat quietly again, until Bub said, "I sure hope that little asshole didn't get himself killed by Romer's bomb. Although, I was askin' him later, and he said about the only way someone could get seriously hurt was if they were pickin' it up out of the water. Now, knowin' Percy like I do, I'd say the chances of that are slim and none." He nodded at Toni. "Little brother ain't got much use for heavy liftin'."

Murphy himself had stopped worrying about Romer's device. The more he considered it, the more he agreed that it was a complete shot in the dark. He went back to wondering where they could head . . . blinked, thought about it another minute and snapped his fingers: "Bermuda."

"Bermuda?" Toni asked. "You got charts?"

Bub asked, "How far's that?"

"I do have charts," Murphy said, his excitement growing. "They'll never think of it! A nine-hundred-mile offshore passage. It's perfect!"

"Nine hundred miles," Bub repeated. "Well, you got a point there. No way they'll expect that. Only . . . I don't suppose we're gonna make it all the way there in time to fly home for Election Day, are we?"

Murphy sighed. "No. I suppose not."

"So the little bastard's gonna win, after all."

Toni Johnson shook her head and sat upright. "Wait. What are you guys talking about?"

"Gettin' home 'fore the election," Bub said. "I wanted so bad to tell the world what they'd done, about the oil drillin'. Make sure they lost."

"Why?" She shook her head again. "You're *alive!* That's all that matters. *You're* the candidate!"

Murphy and Bub sat in stunned silence, so she continued: "It's still your name on the ballot. You show up alive after the election, the Supreme Court will have no choice but to certify you governor. Clarissa Highstreet had absolutely no authority to replace you with Percy like she did absent a court order, and they know it. Why do you think they're so determined to get you?"

Murphy asked finally, "But that legal opinion she had . . ."

"Total bullshit," Toni Johnson said. "Her general counsel is actually her masseuse. He flunked out of law school after one semester. Didn't you know? I thought everybody knew."

Bub thought for a minute, raised a finger in the air. "So, we take four or five days gettin' to Bermuda—"

"A week," Murphy said.

"A week," Bub agreed. "We take a week gettin' to Bermuda. We fly home. I show up in Florida. I'm the governor?"

"Yup," Toni Johnson said. "No doubt about it. I even overheard Farber and Thresher talking about it on *Soft Money.*"

Bub blinked. "So I come home, I'm the governor, and come January I renew the ban on offshore drillin', and Link Thresher is screwed?"

Toni laughed, a sweet tinkling of glass. "If you wanted, you could sign an executive order kicking Petron out of the state!"

"Well, I'll be damned. Don't *that* put a new spin on things!" Bub stretched his arms overhead, cracking his knuckles. "Well, alrighty, then: Which way to Bermuda?"

Farber LaGrange stood at the bow, hands on hips and scowl on face.

With barely a breath of wind left in her sails, *Soft Money* had taken four hours to cross the remaining two miles, so that dawn was starting to take the eastern sky through a series of grays before Farber and his crew could get their first look at their handiwork. And that first look, Farber sensed immediately, was not promising.

"This is not good," Farber said.

Scattered across the flat water were chunks of scorched fiberglass and foam and, Farber noted with concern, little else. "There oughta be more," he said.

Beside him stood Percy Billings, arms crossed over his chest to help control emotions that swung from euphoria to dread. "How so?" he croaked.

"Mattresses, clothes, paper. Food jars. All kinds of floatin' stuff on a sailboat. But all we're seein' is fiberglass and foam?"

Percy surveyed the black water surrounding them, counted several dozen of the white and beige chunks. "Maybe it all sank," he suggested hopefully. "If she went down fast, wouldn't it all have sunk?"

"I s'pose," Farber drawled. "But what about fuel? A cruisin' sail-boat's usually got gasoline for the dinghy outboard, kerosene for lanterns, not to mention diesel for the engine. There oughta be a slick a mile wide by now."

Percy stroked his arms and shook his head. "Polls open in two hours. What must voters be thinking? The leading candidate goes off on a boat, then his campaign claims he's visiting a sick uncle. . . . Would *you* vote for a guy like that?"

"All this foam. I don't get it. Even if she was a foam-cored hull, that shit'd be fiberglassed in place. Plus it'd be in half-inch sheets, not thick chunks. This," Farber nodded at a passing slab, "looks more like what they put in dinghies to make 'em unsinkable."

Percy glanced up toward the east, blinked in puzzlement. "Check out the sky. Isn't that an odd color? Almost green."

Farber ignored him and turned to find Clyde Bruno. "Hey, you found any bodies yet?"

Clyde Bruno had not, but had come upon a large, sealed Tupperware storage container with barely its lid above the water. It was filled, he saw, with dozens of cans of tuna fish. He was scratching his head over that, the tins stacked before him on the deck in piles of ten, when he noticed the red duffel bag floating some twenty yards off.

Tied to one end seemed to be a thin white line, trailing off into the water. He went to the cockpit to retrieve the binoculars, focused on the bag. It appeared nondescript. Just a regular cylindrical shape, black straps. Nothing unusual about it.

Except for the piece of plywood that it was sitting on. He chewed on that awhile, watching through the glasses. How on earth could a piece of luggage just happen to land on a scrap of wood barely larger than itself, then stay there half the night. . . .

Then he got a glimpse of the lashings holding it on, and that raised new questions. Why would anyone do that? Why tie a bag to plywood?

"I found a rope."

Clyde Bruno turned behind him to see Grant Hanson fishing a line out of the water with the boat hook, turned back to examine the bag. It was still a good ten yards off. If he wanted it, he would need to snag that line that was tied to it. . . . He blinked, turned back to Grant, who was tugging on the line he had found. It was, he noted, the same color and thickness as what was tied to the duffel.

"It's stuck," Grant complained.

"That's because it's running under the boat. It's probably hung up on the keel," Clyde Bruno said, then thought about the bag, the piece of plywood, the line. . . . "Don't!" he screamed, just as Grant Hanson gave a mighty heave.

The explosion brought Farber, Percy and Link Thresher running. Clyde Bruno was stretched flat on the teak, holding his ears and groaning, while Grant Hanson screamed about sharks as he splashed in the water.

Scattered on deck were tiny fragments of red cloth. With a bad feeling, Farber LaGrange leaned over the side and saw the black scorch mark on *Soft Money*'s polished topsides.

"That's the last fuckin' straw," he muttered, turning to the spectacle of Percy and Thresher lifting Grant Hanson out of the water feet first. "You people got any earthly idea what a good Awlgrip job costs? How hard it is to find people with the talent *and* work ethic to polish a hull smooth enough to take a urethane finish? Y'all are really startin' to tick me off! Now: What the fuck happened here?"

Grant was on hands and knees, throwing up seawater, so Farber lifted Clyde Bruno to a sitting position and repeated: "What the fuck happened?"

"What?" Clyde Bruno said.

"Somethin' blew up! What happened?"

"What?" Clyde Bruno said.

Farber LaGrange stood exasperated. "Does *anybody* on this fuckin' boat got a clue what the fuck's goin' on? Where in fuck are the bodies? There oughta be four of 'em!"

"Sharks," Grant Hanson groaned, testing his eye patch. "Sharks musta got 'em."

"And wreckage," Farber continued. "There ain't near enough from a boat of that size. And where's the fuel slick? Where's all the shit from down in the cabin?"

Percy stood and pointed off in the water. "I see something. See? Look: It's their mast."

Farber moved across the deck, muttering, "Now that's *one* thing we *shouldn't* be able to find. Damn thing's made a heavy-gauge 'luminum. Oughta have sunk right off the bat."

"Looks like a mast to me," Percy insisted. "See? And it's even got that round radar reflecting device on it."

Farber saw that indeed it did. He sized up the wooden spar, its length and thickness, the radar reflector tied to the top, and then glanced again at the pieces of foam floating around. White Styrofoam. The sort used to make dinghies unsinkable.

He raised one hand to his face, squeezed the bridge of his nose, then his temples. "Grant, last night, when you were callin' out bearin' and range, was there just one target? Or might there have been two?"

They had pulled open the dinette table to lay out the big, ocean-scale charts, Bub squinting with interest at the pilot chart for the southwest North Atlantic for the month of November.

"What's it mean when an arrow's got all these little sticks on it?" he asked.

Murphy glanced up momentarily, then returned to walking off distances with a pair of brass dividers. "It means we'll probably get our ass kicked. That little number in each corner? That's the average number of gales that particular square of ocean has seen in that month over the last century."

With the wind completely gone and the sails hanging limp, Romer was asleep on the starboard settee, tucked in behind the canvas lee cloth. Toni Johnson had finally crashed out in the forecabin. Nearly fifteen hours had passed since their last encounter with *Soft Money*, and they had cautiously allowed a sense of security to settle in.

"I wish I could talk to my boy," Bub said, gripping the edge of the table as the boat rolled to port, then starboard, then back straight.

Murphy nodded, scribbling some figures on a notepad. "Yeah. I'm sorry. If I'd only hooked up the ham radio, you could talk to him to your heart's content." He blinked once. "Of course, if I'd installed the radio, we could've called for help from back in the barge canal."

"No sense beatin' yourself up. How were you to know you were gonna need *Mudslinger* to foil a murder, bribery, election-stealin' conspiracy?" Bub flipped a page back to October, then forward to December. "Speakin' a which," he continued in a lowered voice, "I was wonderin' about Toni."

Murphy's hand hesitated over the notepad. He forced it to continue. "What about her?"

"You takin' her sailin' with you? When you go off 'round the world?"

"I'm not going around the world, for starters. Just the Caribbean."

Bub nodded. "Okay. Whatever body of water it is you're sailin' on or to in the near future. Are you takin' Toni Johnson?"

Murphy finally met his eyes. "I have not asked her. She has not offered. Of course, I wouldn't—"

"Good," Bub said. "You won't mind, then, if I ask her to be my chief of staff? If I win the election?"

Murphy shook his head. "Chief of staff?"

"Maybe budget director. She's got a head for numbers, don't she? And a pretty one at that. . . ." Bub nodded solemnly. "Not that that makes one iota of difference. In my administration, things are gonna be based on merit."

Murphy said nothing, waited through another roll to port and starboard, then went back to his chart work.

"You don't approve," Bub said.

"What don't I approve of?"

"Me bein' governor. Well, I can appreciate that. Shoot, the only reason you got into this mess was to help Ramsey MacLeod, and here, instead, you wind up savin' my life, and then in the course of investigatin' stuff, you end up puttin' *me* in the Mansion. I can see as how you might feel a little conflicted." Bub took a deep breath. "If it's any consolation, I might tell you that I think I learned a whole lot from all of this. I can also tell you that, if I win, I'm beholden to nobody. I sure as hell ain't beholden to the Republican Party. I think even they'd understand the general principle that once you try to kill your candidate, that candidate ain't necessarily gonna toe the party line anymore."

Murphy still said nothing.

"I'm sorry. I'm babblin'. But this is hard for me, Murph. Back when I was up twenty points in the polls, and everybody tellin' me how good and smart I was . . . Well, shoot. That kinda talk makes you start believin' in yourself. And you know what? I think I can do a decent job. I know I ain't necessarily the smartest bear around. Okay. I've lived with that all my life. But I know right from wrong, and if I got some smart bears around me that I can trust, like Toni and . . . you—"

"Okay, stop," Murphy cut in. "Given the time we've spent together these couple of weeks, Bub, you don't have to sell me on yourself anymore. I didn't know you when you were young. But I know you now, and you're smart, and you work hard. If you end up governor, you'll do yourself and Florida proud. Right now, I'm not concerned about that. I'm concerned about getting us safe and sound to Bermuda's airport and on a flight back home so we can tell CNN and *The New York Times* and everybody else what they did to Spencer Tolliver and they *tried* to do to you. To us. Whether you win the election or lose, we can't let them get away with that. Agreed?"

"Agreed," Bub said instantly.

"So let's take this a step at a time, all right?"

"You're absolutely right," Bub said. "And hell, who knows? Ramsey might just pull this out, and I won't have to worry about it at all." He turned his attention back to the pilot charts, flipped backward and forward. "You know what? It looks like there's actually less gales in December here than in October."

"Equinoctial gales. You get your most violent, sudden storms right around the spring and autumn equinoxes."

Bub considered this, nodded, braced himself against another roll of the boat. "Somethin' to do with the shiftin' of the jet streams, I bet."

Murphy glanced up in mild surprise, then returned to his chart work. "By the way, you don't have to worry about Lamont. He's in good hands."

"I knew he would be. Believe me, I have not feared for his safety. This friend of yours, whoever he is, if you trust him, I trust him." Bub grinned. "You know? You're a good guy. I really mean that. I don't care what anybody says."

Murphy offered a mock smile, jotted a note on the chart and circled it in pencil. "I can tell you where he is, if you want."

Bub held a hand up. "No, no. I haven't known so far, and so far we ain't gotten killed. Let's not jinx anythin'." He nodded at Murphy's chart work. "Sailorman, how come you're doin' all these calculations? I thought your little GPS gizmo made it so you just punch in where Bermuda is and then steer in whatever direction it tells you to?"

"You can, if you just want to go straight rhumb line. That's not the best way of getting there, though. First thing we need to do is get out of the Gulf Stream. Otherwise the first norther that comes through will definitely kick our ass."

"Well, there's definitely no point in that," Bub agreed. "Boy, I tell you what: It sure would suck if, after escapin' the schemes of my brother *and* the Party *and* a huge multinational like Petron, we end up gettin' killed by some stinkin' storm."

Murphy began gathering up the charts. "Well, that's not going to happen. This boat can take a lot of punishment. A whole lot more than we can. If the weather gets bad, we'll just let her take care of us." He stood, then sat back down hard as *Mudslinger* lurched one way, then the other. "Jesus! What the hell *is* that?"

"That," Romer announced, opening his eyes, "is a ten- to fifteen-foot swell. Period of approximately fifty-five seconds." He sat up and swung his legs to the cabin sole. "There's something big out here. Have you got *any* kind of radio?"

Murphy popped his head out the companionway to look for himself. "Nothing. I have a little AM pocket radio. But no batteries."

"Bring it to me," Romer said.

From atop the boom, Murphy stared at water, flat as glass, all the way to a horizon that once every minute appeared slightly more distant as *Mudslinger* rose to the top of a swell. More and more frequently, she would roll first one way, then the other as the wave passed beneath them.

"Funny," Bub said, watching the water. "They don't look ten or fifteen feet."

"That's because the wave is so long. Fifteen feet tall, but a half mile long." Murphy turned and scanned in the opposite direction, then studied the wide swath of cirrus that had invaded from the northeast. "The fact we can feel it at all is not good news. It means it's close enough that the wave still has some steepness to it."

Bub pondered this quietly. "When you say, 'not good news,' like, *how* not good? Just *not good*? Or actually crossin' over into *bad*?"

"Actually *real* bad," Murphy said as, from below, a tinny reggae band came to life.

They both scrambled to the companionway and peered in at the nav table, where Romer stood putting a propane soldering iron, rubber insulation and some crimp connectors back into a plastic tool box. On the table, the radio's cover was off, with wires bound with electrical tape running toward the boat's battery compartment.

"How'd you do that?" Bub asked in wonderment.

"High-school physics: E equals I-R. Voltage equals current times resistance."

Murphy slapped his forehead. "Of course! You put in a resistive load to get the boat's twelve volts down to the radio's nine! *I* should have thought of that! Only . . . where'd you get the right transistors?"

Romer snapped the tool case shut, stowed it behind the bunk and replaced the cushion. "Your depth sounder wasn't going to work with a bullet hole in it anyway."

"I *thought* I heard music," Toni Johnson said, rubbing sleep from her eyes and stumbling over the sail bags stacked on the floor of the cramped forecabin. "Where'd you guys find a radio?"

"Romer built it outta toilet paper tubes and some rusty fish hooks," Bub said.

"That's great," she said. "How's the election going? What's turn-out like?"

Romer tapped the radio with a finger. "This is the only station I could get. I'm assuming it's out of West End or Nassau. Might be able to pick up a big, fifty-thousand-watt station out of Miami after dark."

"Shhh! Shhh!" Murphy said, waving an arm.

". . . . *on dey latest CD,* Groovin' da Moon," came the singsong accent over the radio. "*We go right back to de music after a quick update on Hilda. We got a noon position of twenty-eight degrees, t'irty-two-point-seven minutes north, seventy-six degrees, zero-two-point-eight degrees west, or one hundred and fifty miles north-northeast of Hope Town. Peak winds now at one hundred and twenty-five knots, makin' it a cat'gory-four storm. Dey sayin' dat because of de unusual steerin' currents, Hilda be movin' south-southwest at twelve knots, but de motion is expected to diminish by dis ev'nin', with a turn to de northeast tomorrow.*"

"Uh-oh," Romer said.

"Uh-oh?" Bub asked with alarm. "*You're* sayin' uh-oh?"

"Shhhhhh!" said Toni Johnson.

"*De Hurricane Center in Miami is postin' a hurricane warnin' for de northern Abacos, and a tropical storm warnin' for the southern Abacos, Grand Bahama, Eleuthera and New Providence. To be on de safe side, all marine in-trests should remain in port! Dat means you, Uncle Johnny! Nooo conchin' today! Everybody hang tight today an' maybe dis ting go safely out to sea by tomorrow. Stay tuned, and we get the next update at tree o'clock.*"

The station returned to reggae music, and they all stared at one another in bewildered silence.

"Safely out to sea," Bub said finally. "Ain't that what he said? Safely for who?"

"Where is it compared to us?" Toni Johnson asked.

Murphy quickly walked off the distance on the chart with his dividers. "A hundred and thirty miles northeast. Give or take." He shook his head. "Jesus Christ. Didn't this system supposedly dissipate to nothing last week?"

"What I don't get is," Toni Johnson said, "if this thing's less than a hundred-fifty miles away, how come we're still becalmed?"

On cue, through the companionway hatch came the *wheeep-wheeep-wheeep* of the wind generator starting to spin, then the loud thrum as it swung around into the new wind, the first gust of which blasted into *Mudslinger*'s full suit of canvas and knocked her on her side.

W*hat* Hilda?" Farber LaGrange screamed into the radio handset.

Beside him stood Link Thresher and Percy on one side, Grant Hanson on the other. Clyde Bruno was up top by himself, driving *Soft Money* back toward Cape Canaveral through suddenly wild wind and the sharp, steep waves of the Gulf Stream.

"Hurricane. Hurricane Hilda," came the voice of the Party's chief of operations. "Went from dissipated depression to category-four storm in twenty-four hours. A new record, apparently. Hurricane Center's been putting out warnings all night. Haven't you been getting them?"

"Goddamned, fifty-grand, state-of-the-art communications suite, and a hurricane's gotta kick our ass 'fore we know about it. . . ." Farber LaGrange scanned the nav table instruments, finally squinting at the weatherfax. He flipped the power switch on the front of the unit, at its urgent beeping hit the receive button, then slapped Grant Hanson on top of his head as the machine began spitting out a chart topped with HURRICANE WARNING in bold letters. "Never mind. Our genius weather officer here decided we didn't need no stinkin' weather . . . Holy shit! This thing's right on our ass!"

"That's why I've been calling," the radio said. "That, plus this sick-uncle stuff is starting to wear thin. The press wants to know how come, on Election Day, the candidate isn't even in Florida. Hey, you guys gonna be okay, getting back? You want I should call the Coast Guard?"

"Hell, no, don't call the Coast Guard! Did you lose your mind? How in fuck would we explain the candidate gettin' rescued from a yacht when he's s'posed to be with sick Uncle Reggie?" Farber grimaced. "And watch what you say. This ain't exactly a secure line."

A violent gust heeled the boat hard, pushing Farber and his crew over the nav table. A slash of droplets drove down the companionway, soaking the left half of Percy's two-day-old dress shirt. He took the latest indignity without emotion.

"We'll get home okay," Farber continued. "Now that we got some wind. It's the other . . . you know . . . *party* that I'm concerned about. Any sign of 'em?"

"Nope. We've had every inlet covered around the clock. Nothing."

Farber shook his head and blew out a breath. "All right. After this storm blows over, we need to, uh, redouble our efforts. We can't have the other party making a surprise appearance. Understood?"

"Loud and clear. Oh, we just got the noon exit-poll numbers. . . ."

"And?" Link Thresher yelled, leaning over Farber's shoulder.

"And . . . it's too close to call. Within the margin right now."

"I knew it," Percy breathed. "I knew this would happen. After all this, we're going to lose. Well, serves us right. The gods are just, and of our pleasant vices make instruments to plague us."

"For once in your life: shut up, would you?" Farber said, then to the radio: "Well, we'll be back by tonight. I want you to get a chopper to Cocoa Beach. We'll take that to Orlando Executive. Have a coupla limos there to take us to the Peabody. Got it?"

Another wave slapped hard at *Soft Money*'s hull. Grant Hanson quickly put a hand to his eye patch to protect it from the spray coming down the hatch while Farber spread his shoulders to shield the radio.

"Yes, sir," the voice said. "Oh, I almost forgot. This is for Mr. Bruno. We finally got a lead on that, you know, third party we were discussing."

Farber cast a sidelong glance at Percy, said into the radio, "Hang on." Then, to Percy: "Can you go up and spell Clyde?" He waited for Percy to climb up the companionway before pressing the transmit button. "Go ahead."

"Well, we went backwards and forwards through Orlando International and got nothing," the radio said. "Finally we tried Melbourne. There was a charter that included the, uh, third party that left late that afternoon."

Farber inhaled sharply. "You sure?"

"Positive."

Farber LaGrange nodded at Thresher's grim expression. "Then the third party's been . . . taken care of?"

"Negative, sir. With the storm warning, the two flights that go there a day were both canceled, and we can't get a pilot to take us."

"But you know where they are?"

"Yes, sir. Walker's Cay."

Farber blinked twice at the radio, then at the LCD chart plotter display beside the radar, then at his watch and finally at Link Thresher. "Did you say Walker's?"

"Yes, sir. Walker's. It's located—"

"I know where it is," Farber LaGrange said, his jaw hardening. "Listen. Cancel that chopper at Cocoa Beach. Instead, send a campaign plane over to Walker's as soon as the weather clears. Better make it the turboprop. I don't think the strip can handle a jet. Got it?"

"Got it," the radio confirmed.

"Good. We'll check in again at eighteen hundred. Same frequency." He hung the handset back in its slot, swung the chair around to face his crew as he pulled his fingerless sailing gloves over his hands. "Gentlemen, we're back in the hunt. I know where they're goin'."


**R**omer, Toni Johnson and Bub all huddled around Murphy and his chart of the waters northeast of the Little Bahama Bank. In the upper right was a penciled counterclockwise swirl with the notation "HH." An arrow pointed to the south-southwest—directly at *Mudslinger's* noon position.

"Crazy-ass direction for a hurricane to be going," Murphy muttered, shaking his head. When the wind had hit, all four had scrambled on deck, dousing canvas except for the staysail, which they left up, letting *Mudslinger* slide away from the storm at five knots while they figured out what to do. "Absolutely no reason for a hurricane at this latitude to be moving south. No reason at all."

"Goddamned Republicans," Romer fumed. "Bury their heads in the sand about global warming. Refuse to sign Kyoto. Well, this is what they bought us. Dumb, greedy bastards."

"That's not fair," Toni Johnson said. "Not all Republicans are like that. I'm not, and I'm a Republican."

"Big deal. So am I," Romer said.

"Me too," Bub chimed in.

Murphy threw his hands in the air. "Wonderful. We're all four Republicans. Great. We'll form an enviro-PAC later. Raise some soft money for the Sierra Club. In the meantime, we need to figure out where to go." He pointed on the chart. "Florida's out of the question. With this norther, the Gulf Stream's going to have forty-, forty-five-foot waves shaped like apartment buildings. Not to mention the folks Farber has looking out for us at the ports."

Bub pointed at a curved string of islands on the chart. "What about these here? The Abacos?"

"Can't," Romer said. "All the channels face north or east. The swell from this storm will be breaking right at the reef line."

"Rage on the bar?" Bub asked, eyes wide.

"You got it." Romer nodded.

Murphy blinked, studied the chart. "Except for one channel. . . . Hah! Who ever said it's not a small world?"

"Whatcha talkin' about?" Bub asked, pushing himself upright as the boat leaned hard over.

Murphy took his dividers, spread them to a width of ten nautical miles, walked off the distance on the chart, then turned to Bub with a smile. "So. You wanna have dinner with your son?"


The swells had grown to eighteen, even twenty feet, with five- and six-foot wind waves tumbling down them in great sheets of white water.

Percy Billings stared, transfixed by the sights and sounds, gripping with white knuckles the stainless tubing surrounding the steering compass. "O wild West Wind, thou breath of Autumn's being! I suppose it's only appropriate it would come to this, a storm of Shakespearean, even biblical proportions. The only question is, which side are we on? Are we Lear? Or his daughters? Angels? Or devils?" Percy sighed as another sapphire wave crashed into the hull, sending a shower of sparkling droplets over him. "History will judge, Farber. History will judge."

Farber LaGrange rolled his eyes and checked the compass course. *Soft Money* charged eastward now, aimed at a point a quarter mile north of Walker's Channel. Flying only a high-cut yankee and the storm main, she was still making eleven knots through the water and just over twelve over the ground with the boost from the current.

He leaned toward Clyde Bruno as he stood behind the wheel. "Bub's boy is there. And the nanny."

"What?" Clyde Bruno said.

Farber grimaced, patted his pockets until he found the notepad and pen. He scribbled on a sheet and handed it to Clyde Bruno. Clyde Bruno nodded, said, "I'll take care of it."

Farber wrote on a new sheet, handed it over. Clyde Bruno read it, asked, "Kill everyone on the island? How many?"

"Probably only a dozen," Farber shouted. "They've evacuated all the guests. It shouldn't be too hard. There's no cops. With the storm and everythin', just load all the bodies on a boat, sink the thing in deep water."

"What?" Clyde Bruno said.

Farber LaGrange shook his head and waved a hand. "Never mind."


The sun shone through occasional breaks in the cloud, offering up a miniature rainbow each time a wave rolled down one of the mammoth swells, slapping into *Mudslinger*'s hull and sending a shower of spray up and over the boat.

Toni and Bub sat side by side on the cabin top, taking each wave with shouts of delight as the droplets hit them square in the face. Murphy stood instead in the cockpit, one foot up on the starboard bench, one hand on the dodger frame to steady himself, a scowl of worry compressing his lips as he watched the knotmeter sit at six-point-seven, then drop to six-point-one, then touch seven-point-four on the faces of the bigger swells.

They were flying a high-cut jib, staysail and double-reefed main as they drove eastward. To the south a few miles was the edge of the Little Bahama Bank, an expanse of shallow water sixty nautical miles long and forty wide, bounded on the south by Grand Bahama island, to the east and north by the Abacos chain and a long, largely continuous coral reef.

A dozen potential catastrophes swirled inside his head: The wind would strengthen too quickly and drive them on the reef. The waves would grow so big as to make even Walker's Channel an impassable maelstrom. Hilda would pick up forward speed and crush them where they were. Farber would, somehow, figure out where they were going and chase them, catching them before they reached the sanctuary of Walker's with its radio and telephones and nonmurderous people. . . .

With a thud, Romer dropped down off the boom, then down into the cockpit. "We need more of these," he said, nodding northward, where the horizon was a sickly thunderstorm-green. "Good, honest storms to cleanse our reefs, our shores. Our souls."

"Great. Cleanse them after we get our asses tucked into one of Gary Knowlton's slips."

Romer thought about that, finally nodded. "Yeah. That works for me."

A low rumble caught their attention: a breaking wave tumbling down the face of what looked like a twenty-five-foot swell, crashing into *Mudslinger*'s side and throwing an enormous splash up over the cabin and into the sails. The boat literally jerked sideways, heeling over and dipping her starboard rail in the water before coming back upright. Toni and Bub, T-shirts and shorts drenched to the skin, whooped with joy.

"That was not good," Murphy said.

"It's only going to get worse," Romer agreed. "The longer the wind blows this hard locally, the bigger the wind waves get. The more momentum they carry rolling down the face of the swells. The further they knock us over. If we put the stick in the water—"

"It'll snap," Murphy finished. "And we're S-O-L. On a lee shore, with an advancing hurricane, with an hour and a half's worth of diesel."

He craned his neck as *Mudslinger* sat momentarily at the top of a swell. "Did you see anything from up there?"

Romer shook his head. "Nothing. Walker's has a radio mast, doesn't it?"

"It does. Two hundred fifty feet. It'll be impossible to see in the daytime though, with all this spray in the air. We'll probably see the island first."

"How high?"

"About fifty feet on the main hill. They've got a good, solid concrete-block supply room for a shelter, built right into the coral, if Hilda doesn't head back north. We'll be okay there."

Romer squinted off the bow, then nodded at Bub and Toni Johnson, who were now lying back on the cabin top looking at the bands of cloud overhead. "Those two don't look too worried."

Murphy watched and listened to their laughs as yet another wave showered them with spray. "Well, I don't think Bub knows enough about small boats and hurricanes to be worried. Plus he thinks we've escaped Farber. He's going to see his kid. Life's good."

"Thinks we've escaped Farber," Romer said after a pause. "*Thinks* being the operative word."

Murphy stood on the curved bit of cockpit coaming by the tiller and strained his eyes at the ocean behind them. "On the one hand, they've got weatherfax and all the fancy-schmancy communications gear. They must've known about this storm for a while. The logical thing for an engineless boat to do is get the hell back to Florida as fast as possible." He lifted himself on tiptoes at the top of a swell. "On the other hand, they've already committed a capital crime on the way to stealing an election. They can't let us live."

Romer nodded. "In which case, they'll have figured out Walker's is the only possible destination for us. They must know that, thanks to Toni, *we* know they've got Florida's ports covered. And Walker's is the only all-weather inlet in the northern Abacos."

"So say our trick with the dinghy won us a thirty-mile head start," Murphy continued. "Once the wind starts honking, they get a five-knot speed advantage on us. The wind started at around noon. Which means they'll catch us at six—"

"Which is pretty much our ETA at Walker's," Romer finished.

Murphy stared as the knotmeter dropped down to six-point-zero for a few long moments before bouncing back up to six-point-eight. "We're still not at hull speed a hundred percent of the time." He glanced up at the mainsail, "reefed" with a series of hooks and reinforced grommets so that only half of the full area was catching wind. "If we shook out one reef in the main, I bet we could pick up two-tenths of a knot."

"Might mean getting there ten or fifteen minutes sooner," Romer agreed. "Might make the difference."

Murphy stood on the cockpit bench and cupped his hands against the wind: "Bub! Toni! Come help us with the main!"

## ★ ⑩ ★

**P**ERCY **B**ILLINGS **S**TO**OD** gripping the binnacle, eyes narrowed against the wind, staring off toward the horizon where the layer of cloud became almost black.

"It takes a storm like this to remind us of our place in the cosmos, doesn't it?" he said to Clyde Bruno. "A hurricane of this magnitude puts out in a single day as much energy as the entire nation uses in three years. Awe-inspiring, no?"

Clyde Bruno had a while ago stopped saying, "What?" to the movement of Percy's lips and now just stood silently at the wheel while he philosophized. Farber LaGrange, appreciating the success of Clyde Bruno's tactic, likewise ignored him, instead scanned the seas ahead of them for any sign of their quarry.

"Our entire history as a species has been shaped by storms. Think of our literature. *The Odyssey. Lear,* of course. *The Rime of the Ancient Mariner.* Think of the epic battles. Remember the Spanish Armada? Drake didn't beat them. A great storm did. Imagine if that storm hadn't happened. Why, we might all be speaking Spanish right now. My brother, of course, would still speak it badly and with an accent. . . ."

Bravely, he took a burst of salt spray in the face, wiped his eyes with the sleeve of his dress shirt. "I guess it's fitting, then, that the final battle come to this. Only: Am I King Philip? Or is he? And who wins this time? Philip, or Drake?"

With a groan of disgust, Farber LaGrange took the Steiners from around his neck and set them in the teak holder mounted under the steering compass. He shouted at Clyde Bruno at the top of his lungs, "I'm going below to check the radar!"

Clyde Bruno nodded, and Farber stepped down the companionway as Percy commenced a monologue on *The Tempest*, which he declared to be one of the Bard's most underrated plays: "Sometimes, honest to God, Clyde, I feel as if I *am* Prospero. . . ."

Farber slid up beside Link Thresher, who stood hunched over Grant Hanson's shoulder staring at the radar monitor. "Anything?"

Grant Hanson shook his head in frustration. "I can't see anything in this."

All over the little display were dark splotches, most of them shifting, fading, spreading. "It's clutter, 'cause we got such big waves. We can't get a good, clean shot at the horizon, goin' up and down so much." Farber squinted at the screen, finally pointed a finger at a dark spot in the upper right corner. "This is Walker's right here."

Grant leaned his one good eye closer to the monitor. "That? How can you tell?"

"For one thing, it ain't changin' much. That tells ya there's somethin' really there, that it ain't just a false echo. Plus I rec'nize it. I only been in a dozen tournaments there." He pointed at a longer, thin shape above and to the right of the first. "That there is Tea Table Cay. And this is Tom Brown Cay. And this speck here is Jump Off Rocks."

"Who's Tom Brown?" Grant Hanson asked.

Farber ignored him. "Just match it up with that display." He pointed to the GPS chart plotter on the opposite side of the nav table. "See these shapes? They correspond to what oughta turn up on the radar."

"Oh, yeah!" Grant said. "I see it now!"

Link Thresher straightened, removed his horn-rims and wiped salt spray off the lenses with the front of his undershirt. "Time is it?"

Farber reached to pull off the latest weatherfax. "Five-thirty. Gonna be gettin' dark soon."

"What happens if we don't find 'em?" Thresher asked, grabbing the nav table seat for support as a sudden wave knocked them over.

"They gotta go somewhere," Farber said. "We'll go in to Walker's. I don't expect to see much of a crowd there. We'll look for his boat. If it ain't there, then, well, we mighta overtaken 'em gettin' here. I'll post Clyde as a lookout at the harbor entrance, in case they show up later."

"And if they *are* there?" Thresher asked.

"Well, then we gotta take out everybody on the island. My people tell me that the phones are already down 'cause of the storm. That makes it easier. Clyde can round 'em all up. Get rid of the bodies offshore. Sharks'll take care of the rest." Farber twisted his mouth into a grimace. "You start out just needin' to kill one person, and then that becomes two, and that gets fucked up, so you gotta do two more, then three more on top of that. It ain't ever simple, is it?"

Link Thresher shrugged. "No one ever promised us simple."

"Easy for you to say," Farber said. "You been havin' Ay-rab potentates and Eskimo agitators knocked off for years. Me, I'm just used to bribin' and extortin'. Ain't exactly sure I got the constitution for this, but what the hell. You do whatcha gotta do."

"Excuse me," Grant Hanson interrupted. "Which island's this?"

He pointed at a faint smudge on the radar display, and Farber leaned forward, gripping the edge of the table tightly as the boat rolled far to starboard, suddenly popped back up, then rolled again.

"I've been watching it awhile now. It hasn't changed shape or disappeared, like those others," Grant Hanson reported.

"That's because," Farber announced, standing upright, "that's them!" He mussed Grant Hanson's hair. "See? Gold star for you! I'll make a navigator outta you yet!"

Link Thresher leaned toward the radar. "*That's* them? You sure?"

"Yup. They're movin' slow. They're headin' for Walker's. Plus who the hell else's gonna be out in this shit?" Farber glanced at the radar, then the GPS, then back at the radar and allowed himself a smile. "And lookit that! I think we're even catchin' a break. See that big gap in the reef? That there's Walker's Channel. Guess who's gonna get there first? We got position on 'em, boys! Let's see if we can avoid fuckin' it up this time. Grant? Go take the bag o' guns up top."

The island appeared seemingly out of nowhere. One moment they were in mid-ocean, next there was a blob of green dead ahead.

"Hey!" Bub shouted, standing tall on the cabin top. "Hey! I see it! Land ho! Land ho!"

"*Yes!* We made it!" Toni Johnson cheered, jumping up to hug first Bub, then Murphy.

"We haven't made it yet," Murphy Moran cautioned, but despite himself felt relief start to melt the wad of fear in his gut. Somehow, it looked like they really had made it. Walker's meant Gary Knowlton, Bub's son and safe harbor, and they were almost there. "Nobody let their guard down yet."

Bub reached over to squeeze Murphy's shoulders. "You did it, man. You really did it. I owe you, big time."

"You really did good," Toni agreed. "Thank you."

Murphy heard the words, but searing into his awareness was the sensation of her hand on his upper arm, casually holding him, not letting go. . . . "Hey, it wasn't me. It was all of you. Toni, it was your idea to send out the dinghy as a decoy, and Romer, shoot, without you we wouldn't of even known about Hilda and would've blithely sailed right into her on the way to Bermuda. And, Bub, you've become a hell of a sailor in your own right."

The island seemed to grow closer by the minute, bigger and safer each time a swell lifted them up high for a view. Murphy acknowledged the aw shucks from Bub, felt himself start to relax, just a touch. They really had made it. He could even make out some of the bright yellow bungalows on the northern slope overlooking the water. They would be empty, because of the hurricane, and would remain so for at least a couple of days. Gary would offer them their choice of the island's accommodations for the night, he knew, and he found himself wondering which one Toni would stay in, and how far it would be from his own—

"So what do we do, Hoss?" Bub asked. "Just head on in?"

"God, no," Murphy said. "This place is lousy with reefs. But once we're past 'em, they'll protect us from Hilda's waves. In another mile or so we turn south through Walker's Channel, then east around a sandbar, then up through the dredged cut into the harbor."

Bub thought about that awhile. "What about 'rage on the bar'? I thought when there were big waves like this they made the inlets dangerous?"

"They do." Murphy nodded. "But that's because the water gets so shallow so quickly. Walker's Channel is different. It carries forty-five feet clear through the reef line. That way the waves spread out after getting through, and therefore just get smaller without breaking."

"Wave diffraction," Toni Johnson said. "Think about how waves bend around obstructions."

Bub scratched his head, studied the massive blue swells all around. "Waves bendin' 'round obstructions. Well, can't say I've spent much time thinkin' on that in recent years. Maybe after we get in, get some nice hot cheeseburgers and some nice cold beer, you can explain it to me. Me and my boy, both."

"Amen to that," Toni agreed. "Hot cheeseburger and a cold beer. And maybe some conch fritters. And grouper fingers. No offense, Murph, but I'm about Hormel-chilied out."

"Well, you guys can have cheeseburgers," Murphy said. "Might I remind you all that this is November? So guess what season started in August and runs through March. Anyone? That's right: lobster. I'm havin' lobster. About ten of 'em."

"Lobster?" Bub asked. "They got lobster? Screw cheeseburgers. I'm havin' lobster, too!"

"Uh, Houston," Romer said, pointing at a sail on the horizon behind them. "I believe we've got a problem."

Clyde Bruno sat beneath the shelter of the companionway spray hood and, one by one, removed assault rifles from his bag and wiped the moving parts with a rag soaked in WD-40. Grant Hanson sat beside him, watching in respectful silence, while Link Thresher and Percy Billings stood beside Farber at the steering wheel.

"I don't need to remind y'all that this is our last clean shot," Farber shouted over the roar of water and wind. He turned his face away from a splash of spray, then continued. "If we let 'em get to the harbor, things get considerably messier."

Percy squinted against the spray, at the other boat still a good two miles ahead. "What if we don't catch them in time? It looks like they're closer to the island than we are to them."

"We'll catch 'em," Farber said. "It ain't a straight shot to the harbor. You gotta go all the way around the reefs and the sandbars. He's just about even with the channel entrance now. You turn right, and then it's three miles due south before you clear the sandbar and turn left. That's where we'll get 'em."

"Jesus," Link Thresher whispered.

A low rumble announced the arrival of an enormous swell, easily thirty feet tall, which lifted *Soft Money* high into the sky before racing past toward the reef. They watched as, to leeward, the wave became an iridescent blue wall before crashing down in an explosion of white mist.

"You ever been in anything this big?" Thresher muttered.

Farber swallowed hard, tried to find some spit to moisten his suddenly dry mouth, and consciously eased his grip on the wheel. "We just stay away from the reefs and we'll be fine. Walker's Channel's a good, all-weather entrance. Carries deep water way past the reef line."

Percy Billings watched the next wave as it approached, then as it passed beneath them, then as it reared up before crashing onto the coral. "If we were a quarter mile closer to that reef, that thing would have rolled us, wouldn't it have?"

Farber saw both Thresher and Grant Hanson awaiting his answer with eyes wide. "But we ain't a quarter mile closer to the reef, are we?" he said confidently. "We're right where we oughta be. So quit worryin' 'bout the fuckin' waves, all right? We gotta pay attention to what we're doin'. Grant: When do we turn?"

"After we hear that GPS thing beeping to tell us we can," Grant recited.

"That's right. And when I say, 'Ease the jib sheet,' what do you do?"

Grant's brow furrowed in concentration. "Let it out. Taking care to keep my hands clear."

"Very good. And if you feel yourself slippin' or fallin' down, what do you do?"

"Take my finger off the trigger," Grant said sheepishly.

Farber nodded, spun the wheel hard to port to keep the bow from sliding down the face of yet another thirty-footer. "Very good. All right, everybody know what they're doin'? Okay, then: Battle stations!"

From below, the GPS started its plaintive beeping. Murphy ignored it, instead remained hunched over the waterproof chart he held clamped between knees and forearms. He glanced up for a peek behind them, saw *Soft Money*'s white sails now less than a mile back.

"Don't that beepin' mean it's time to turn south?" Bub asked.

"We can't," Murphy said. "They'll catch us."

"What if we shot off flares?" Toni suggested. "Maybe someone on the island will see 'em?"

"Even if somebody did, they can't possibly help us in time," Murphy said.

The sun poked through the clouds behind them, turning the approaching wave from slate gray to a brilliant cobalt. It barreled into them, dipping their starboard rail deep into the water before setting them down on its backside and continuing southward.

Romer watched it reverently. "Some of these must have forty-, forty-five-foot faces when they break. Once many years ago, I was in Oahu, north shore, I saw stuff this big. It was from a winter storm, from way up in the Aleutians. Thirty-foot swells became fifty-foot breakers in Waimea Bay. Unbelievable."

Toni Johnson tugged at Murphy's sleeve. "Hey, we need to turn. The longer we go, the better angle we give them."

"Good angle, bad angle. Doesn't matter. They'll still catch us," Murphy said, squinting at the chart, at the little black bumps signifying coral heads that dotted the water north of Walker's like a minefield.

"Hey, Murph, don't mean to sound like a naysayer here," Bub said, pointing out toward the bruise-colored sky to the northeast, "but I just thought I'd remind you of ol' Hurricane Hilda. Now I seem to recall your sayin' that a thirty-foot sailboat has pretty much zero chance of survivin' a cat-four storm out here, correct? And I also recall your sayin' this here channel's the only way through the reef—"

"It's not. There is *one* other way." Murphy clutched the cockpit coaming as yet another wave lifted them high into the orange rays of the sinking sun, then hurtled past them and onto the reef surrounding the tiny green island. "Hey, Romer, say you had your longboard and had to surf your way in. How would you do it?"

I t's beeping! It's beeping!" Grant Hanson sang, pointing down the companionway. "Can't you hear it?"

Farber heard it but ignored it, his attention instead locked on the beige boat ahead of them that, having passed the channel entrance, continued eastward. "Where in hell they goin'?" he wondered aloud.

"I thought that was the only way in. Walker's Channel," Percy Billings said. "Isn't that what you said?"

"It is," Farber said.

"Well, they're obviously not taking it," Link Thresher said, cradling a Heckler & Koch submachine gun in his arms like a baby. "They must know some other way in."

"Well, there ain't none," Farber insisted. He recalled the fishing tournaments where a few of the boats, those with local skippers, would get in and out using some shortcut just to the east of Walker's. He'd always spent the time schmoozing or rigging his gear, never paying attention to what the other boats were doing.

"Well, if they're not going in to Walker's, they must be going somewhere else. Obviously," Percy said. "Surely there are other places in the Bahamas to go?"

A steep wave lifted Murphy Moran's boat up, tipping her nearly onto her side before sliding beneath her. Farber let out the breath he'd been holding, with a dry swallow checked the depth sounder. Wandering into the shallows now would be fatal. No matter what course the other boat took, he had to watch his depth and stay in deep water, where the waves would pass harmlessly beneath them rather than tumbling them over and over, crunching their hull onto razor-sharp coral . . . crunching their *bodies* onto razor-sharp coral. . . .

"No, there ain't," Farber said with authority.

He recalled again the fishing tournaments. How, despite having left the docks first, his boat would often be out on the ocean well behind the local boats that had taken the shortcut. . . .

"Not with a hurricane bearin' down, there ain't," Farber continued. "Lookit these waves. As deep as Walker's Channel is, it's still gonna be hairy gettin' in. Every other inlet clear 'round to Cherokee Sound is gonna have this shit breakin' on the sandbar across the entrance. The locals call it 'rage on the bar.' It's just as nasty as it sounds."

"Okay, so where are *they* going?" Percy Billings demanded, then, getting no answer, stomped down the companionway. He called up a minute later: "Farber! I found it. I found where they're going!"

Farber handed the wheel off to Clyde Bruno and went below, moving in beside Percy at the nav table. The chart plotter, he saw, had been centered over a square that included Walker's Cay and the surrounding area.

"Dark blue means deep, does it not?" Percy asked. "Yes, I see from the key here that it does. More than ten fathoms. What's that, sixty feet, correct? And light blue is, let's see . . . at least two fathoms. And yellow, less than one fathom."

Once Farber had watched in amazement as a pair of the local boats had run in right toward the surf line. He had been certain they would end up on the reef. But, a half hour later, they were tied up at the docks, most of their dolphin and wahoo already cleaned and filleted. Christ, he wished he'd paid more attention. . . .

"Here. Here it is." Percy Billings pushed a thumbnail against the LCD display. "See that? That little strip of blue?"

Farber squinted at the indicated spot. There was indeed a thin blue line, no wider than a piece of string, running through a yellow barrier speckled with the small dark hash marks that symbolized coral. "That? That ain't no channel. Hell, for all we know, it's a software glitch. A mistake when they scanned it in or somethin'."

"How can you assume that?" Percy asked. "This appears to be an expensive, high-quality instrument. Dark blue means dark blue. A deep-water channel through the reef."

On the radar display, Murphy's boat continued eastward, now less than a half mile ahead. "It don't mean shit. It means a random line of blue on a computer screen." Farber's eyes moved back to the chart plotter, then immediately away. He didn't even want to look at the damned thing again. "Plus, see? We're almost there. Another five minutes and we'll get 'em."

Percy punched the plus-symbol button with his thumb repeatedly, but to no avail. "Can't this thing zoom in any closer? Don't you have a paper chart for this place?"

"No, it don't zoom any closer, and no, I don't got paper charts. The fuck's the point of havin' a ten-grand 'lectric chart plotter if you still gotta have paper charts?"

"They're doing something! They're doing something!" called Grant Hanson.

Farber clambered back up into the cockpit, where Link Thresher held the Steiners to his face. Off the bow, the crew of *Mudslinger* worked like ants on the little boat, the details of their activity still obscured by the distance. "Well, what?" Farber demanded. "*What* are they doin'?"

"Keep your shorts on," Link Thresher said. "Thing's a bear to hold steady, with all this— Ah, there. . . . Huh. You know them long poles? Spinning poles, or whatever—"

"Spinnaker poles," Percy Billings said from the companionway. "Used to increase efficiency of headsails on downwind headings. Limited by racing rules to the J-length, the distance between headstay and mast."

"Thank you, Dennis Conner." Farber's brow furrowed in thought. "What in hell they need spinnaker poles for?"


Murphy stretched at a forty-five-degree angle over the leeward lifeline, clinging perilously to the deployed spinnaker pole with his arms, the cabin trunk's teak handrail with his toes.

"Hold on!" Toni shouted behind him as a wave rolled *Mudslinger* hard to starboard, dipping the outboard end of the spinnaker pole into the frothy water. Murphy winced, waiting for the pole to break in two and send him tumbling overboard, dragging beside the boat at the end of his tether.

But it didn't break, and instead rose up and out of the water as the wave passed beneath them. Quickly he grasped the snap shackle he held between his teeth, reached out for the stainless ring on the underside of the pole and snapped it home.

"Done," he breathed, and three pairs of arms pulled him inboard.

He allowed himself two deep breaths, staring intently toward the reef line. They had passed Walker's now, and were coming up even with Tom Brown Cay. Another half mile or so, if he was remembering Gary Knowlton's instructions properly. He turned to his crew. "Okay, we're rigged to run downhill. Everyone understand what we're doing?"

Toni and Bub nodded, and Murphy glanced at Romer. "All right. So explain to us again how we have to do this."

Romer held his hands six inches apart, palms toward him. "Think of those reefs as a wall. The only place the wave can get through is this little gap, where the water is deep enough so the wave doesn't completely break. That's the gap we've gotta hit, dead-on in the middle."

"What happens if we ain't exactly in the middle?" Bub asked. "Just hypothetically, of course."

"As it goes through, the outside edges of the wave are going to spill out onto the reef. If we're over by the side, we spill out onto the reef, too." Romer shook his head somberly. "Not good. Now, in terms of catching this thing, it's just like surfing."

Romer made a big wave shape with his left arm, moved his right hand along it to simulate a surfboard. "The top of this wave will be breaking, so that's not a good place for us to be, unless for some peculiar reason we want to be tumbled end over end."

Toni Johnson shuddered at the thought, peered anxiously toward the reef. Another big breaker thundered toward it, reared up into a towering blue crest, then obliterated itself in an explosion of mist.

"What we need to do is stay right down here, on this part of the face." He patted the bottom part of his arm. "That way, the part of the wave that breaks will do so behind us."

Bub watched yet another breaker, then asked, "What if the whole thing just curls up and crashes down on our heads?"

"It won't," Romer said. "Check out the chart. The water we'll be running through is deep enough so that won't happen. It's seventy feet deep on this side of the reef, sixty feet on the other. The top of the wave will break, like I said, but the whole thing won't. It'll get steep, and I mean *scary* steep, but as soon as we get through, it'll dissipate out into nothing."

"Well, that's comfortin'," Bub said. "So as long as we stay exactly in the middle, and don't get too high up the face, shoot, we won't necessarily die!"

Murphy stood on tiptoes on the next swell. Tom Brown Cay was still overlapping Tea Table Cay. They weren't there yet. He glanced aft, saw big white sails now barely a quarter mile behind them. "We're not going to die," he said firmly, and to Romer: "Go on."

"The key is catching the wave properly. We have to go fast enough to end up on that bottom part of the slope. Too fast, and we'll end up in front of the wave and it'll break on top of us. Too slow, and it'll pass under us, leaving us way up close to the reef where the next one could roll us." He pointed off to port, toward the next advancing swell. "We only get one shot at this, folks. We gotta pick the right wave, and hit it just right."

Bub followed the wave as it lifted them up and set them back down. From the top, he could clearly see a figure standing on the foredeck of *Soft Money* holding a rifle. "I don't mean to sound like a spoilsport or nothin', but how in hell are we supposed to catch one of these? Look how fast they're goin'! Murph, no aspersions intended against your yacht, but we're slower than a three-legged turtle!"

Murphy peered out over the reef line. He could see most of Tea Table Cay now, but a piece was still covered up. "That's why we've got these sails rigged. A one-eighty cruising chute to starboard, the one-fifty drifter to port. On top of that, the engine right up at red line. Romer, how far in you wanna be?"

Romer studied the waves, watched how the one that had just passed them was starting its curl. "About a hundred fifty, two hundred yards further in ought to do us."

To starboard, a sliver of daylight finally appeared between Tea Table and Tom Brown cays. "All right, folks. We're here. Toni, drop the main. Romer, you and Bub get the genny down. I'll go crank the engine."

They're droppin' sail," Farber LaGrange said in amazement. "What in fuck . . . they're motorin' in toward the reef!"

"I bet they're going in through that gap I found," Percy said beside him.

*Mudslinger* crossed their bow, now barely three hundred yards ahead. From the foredeck, Grant Hanson shouted, "Can we start shooting?"

"No!" Farber yelled. "I don't want you runnin' outta ammo! Hold on till I say!"

He turned the wheel slightly to starboard to put *Mudslinger* just off their port bow again. He glanced at the depth sounder, saw with a swallow that the display had gone from blank, which it was whenever the depth was greater than two hundred feet, to flickering between one-fifty-five and one-forty.

"Now?" Grant Hanson shouted again.

"*No*, goddamnit!"

At *Mudslinger*'s mast, Farber could see Toni Johnson, the traitorous bitch. He would have to fire her, once they got back. Retroactively, as far back as her last paycheck. Not another goddamn Republican dime for her. Or her heirs, actually, if she had any.

What the hell was she doing? Something . . . waiting . . . now she was uncleating a halyard, wrapping it around a winch. Then he saw the billowing, red-and-yellow nylon on their foredeck. . . .

"They're goin' in!" he realized aloud. "They're goin' in! Shoot 'em! Shoot 'em! Open fire! Open fire!"

A series of *pops* and *braaaps* echoed from their foredeck as *Soft Money* closed the gap toward their prey. Farber watched spellbound as *Mudslinger* moved slowly backward, keeping her stern toward the waves, water and soot coughing from her exhaust pipe.

"For God's sake, shoot 'em!" Farber exhorted, as yet another wave rolled beneath them. "Can't y'all fuckin' aim?"

Grant Hanson turned, the black barrel of his Kalashnikov pointing toward the cockpit, and Percy and Farber dropped down behind the wheel. "Watch how you're holdin' that!" Farber LaGrange screamed.

"Sorry," Grant Hanson said, lowering the barrel. "It's just, moving around so much 'cause of all these waves, it's *hard* to aim!"

"Stop talkin' and keep shootin'!" Farber yelled.

Grant Hanson turned forward, then back again. "Hey, did you save some ammo someplace, you know, for the island? For the boy? Or do we need to save some of what we got up here?"

Farber gave a sidelong glance at Percy, then yelled at Grant, "Shut up and shoot!"

He concentrated on steering, stared fixedly forward at the smaller boat, before finally giving in and acknowledging Percy's questioning scowl. "The, uh, island," Farber began. "My people found out that Bub's former aide's waitin' for him at Walker's."

Percy narrowed his eyes. "Boy?"

"The aide's black. That is to say, African-American," Farber said. "If I told that Grant once, I told him a thousand times: We ain't got no room for that racist shit in our party no more. We're a big tent now, for Chrissake." He cleared his throat and shouted, "Come on! *Hit* somethin', dammit!"

They're shootin' at us again, the bastards," Bub reported, squinting.

In confirmation, Murphy heard a *snap* in the air, above and to the right. He ignored it, instead watched the wave rushing toward them from behind. He held the tiller in both hands, played the throttle with his toe.

"All right, I think I see the one we're gonna take," Romer yelled, climbing down off the boom. "Everybody set?"

Toni nodded rapidly, her fingers clutching the port foresail halyard. In the cockpit, Bub held a slack genoa sheet in each hand and said, "When you gimme the word, I pull like hell on these till they're full, then cleat 'em off."

"Good," Romer said. "Murph, the hardest job falls to you. You absolutely, positively *cannot* allow the bow to wander off course. And it will want to. Badly. But you can't let it."

"I know," Murphy said. One at a time, he unclamped his fingers from the tiller to wipe the sweat from his palms onto his shorts. "Everybody got their tether off? If the boat's upside down and getting dragged onto the reef, the last thing you want is to be attached to it."

A sharp *ping* resounded off the mast, and Murphy winced against a possible ricochet. He allowed himself a single glance to starboard, saw *Soft Money* now within two hundred yards. Three figures lay on her foredeck, flashes of orange erupting from their rifles.

"Remember: If you end up underwater and disoriented, follow your bubbles. Your bubbles will always go up," Romer advised. "Also, get in behind the reef to catch your breath. Don't stay out in the channel. The tide's rushing off the bank right now, and it'll sweep you right back through."

Another bullet tore through the air with a loud crack, and Toni yelled out. Romer put a hand on her shoulder, continued staring at the approaching waves. "It's all right. Two boats on a rough sea, there's no way they can aim. These are random shots. The odds are on our side."

He climbed onto the bottom winch on the mast for a better look, quickly hopped back down and grabbed his halyard.

"Okay, folks, on my mark. Let's do it!"

**B**arely a hundred yards separated them. Now eighty. Farber could see them all clearly: Murphy Moran in a torn yellow T-shirt at the tiller. Bub Billings on the cockpit winches, sporting a buzz cut and a beard. Toni and a strange, thin man at the mast. Romer, that would have to be.

"I thought we ascertained," Percy said from beside him, "that Murphy Moran's boat had no working radio. That if they had had one, they would have called for help at the very start."

Farber squinted at Percy, annoyed. "Yeah. Your point?"

"Well, if they had no radio . . . then how was Byron able to call his aide to tell him to meet him at Walker's?"

Farber growled and shook his head. "The fuck should I know? What am I, a mind reader now? Look, you wanna go to jail? Or you wanna be gov'nor? Them are the options, so quit—"

He heard the wave before he saw it, an enormous indigo wall rumbling as it approached. The last rays of sunlight turned the thin part of the crest a translucent turquoise and the foam that tumbled over the lip a brilliant orange.

The wave pushed *Soft Money* onto her side, sent Link Thresher, Clyde Bruno and Grant Hanson tumbling into a heap against the starboard lifelines on the foredeck. Farber clawed at the wheel, forcing the bow back toward the wind.

The wave passed and Farber stood. He listened absently to Percy Billings's explanation about the physics of a breaking wave. Then he noticed that *Mudslinger* was gone.

Murphy clenched his teeth as he leaned backward into the mountain down which his tiny boat was careening, the muscles of his arms cramping as he held the tiller centered.

Sensory information flooded his brain, everything happening in slow motion: off the bow, an enormous red-and-yellow sail billowing out to starboard, a slightly less enormous white one to port . . . the engine tachometer needle pegged in the red . . . Bub clinging onto the dodger frame for dear life . . . the knotmeter holding steady at nineteen—*nineteen!*—after momentarily hitting *twenty-two* . . . spray flying aft in sheets as the bow planed out and over the surface. . . .

And above it all, water roaring like he'd never in his life heard it before, a low, throaty rumble that just went on and on. . . .

He struggled to keep his focus, to steer so there remained the barest slice of daylight between Tea Table and Tom Brown cays even as *Mudslinger* hurtled down the perpetual first drop of a roller coaster, the spray stinging his eyes. . . .

And then the wave rose up, like in the surfing movies, a green tunnel going off to right and left, just before the water came crashing down on them.

Farber and Percy searched the water all around. The spot the other boat had been. Ahead. Behind. Even off to windward.

"They're gone," Farber said finally.

"How could they just go?" Percy Billings demanded.

"The wave prob'ly rolled 'em. Came damn near rollin' us. Thing musta been forty feet tall. Even higher when it broke."

Percy scanned the water some more. "There'd have to be something," he insisted. "Debris. Fuel. You said so yourself, last time."

"In an explosion, yeah. There won't necessarily be nothin' in a plain ol' sinkin'." Farber cast a nervous eye at the depth sounder. "Put enough water down that companionway hatch, she'd a gone down like a rock. Like ol' Sec'tary Highbeams." He looked up to Percy's still-unbelieving face, reached a hand out to pat his shoulder. "I think Mother Nature mighta done our dirty work for us. Congratulations, Mr. Governor-elect."

Percy put his hand to his cheek, his gaze fixed on the bit of water where *Mudslinger* had last been. "So he really is gone," he murmured with a sigh, then grimaced.

"What now?" Farber asked.

"It's nothing," Percy said quietly. "There was a certain . . . something that went down with that boat, I think." An idea came to him, and he glanced at the depth sounder. "I wonder how deep it is here. If we oughtn't mark the spot, the latitude and longitude."

Farber grabbed Percy's arm and spun him around. "Now, you listen to me: It's just a fuckin' ring, okay? It ain't some sorta magic charm. The last thing we need is for anyone to ever find that boat, understand? She's in a hun'red and ten feet of water. That's a damn good place for her, if you ask me. My only regret is it ain't a thousand and ten. You come out here on some scuba junket, don't think the whole damn press corps won't follow. It's done, it's over, it's gone. Understand?"

Percy nodded weakly and sat down, then remembered something, looked back up at Farber and opened his mouth just as Grant Hanson, eye patch soggy and loose, came running back to the cockpit as he pointed toward the island. "Mr. LaGrange! I found them! Look!"

Farber looked, his jaw first dropping, then clenching tight as he ground his teeth. For there, on the other side of the reef line in calm waters, sat *Mudslinger*—her sails torn and hanging overboard, her spin-naker poles now broken stumps. But she was in one piece, afloat. And on her deck, even from a half mile away, he could clearly see four figures, dancing and hugging in celebration.

"Motherfuck," Farber said, frustration becoming anger, then: "Pre-pare to come about!"

Link Thresher, Percy Billings and Grant Hanson looked at him in disbelief, and Clyde Bruno shook his head helplessly.

"The fuck's wrong? Y'all deaf or somethin'? Well, I know you are, Clyde, but the rest of you: Come on!" Farber exhorted. "What, y'all wanna go to fuckin' jail? Prepare to come about, goddamnit! And then help me get that goddamned spinnaker pole up!"

Toni Johnson, soaked to the skin and dripping wet, was hugging him, hard and long. That much Murphy could understand as he stood drenched and shivering in the total mess that his boat had become.

The mainsail hung from the boom, ripped and flapping. The spin-naker was completely shredded, as was the drifter. The life raft had been wrenched from its bracket, and half the stanchions on the port rail had been torn away.

But they were, amazingly, alive and, even more amazingly, unhurt.

"Can you believe it?" Bub kept repeating. "*I* can't! Can you? Romer? Can *you* believe it?"

"That was something else," Romer agreed.

Bub moved in beside Toni and Murphy and included them in a huge bear hug. "Can *you* guys believe it? God*damn!* That was the most awesome thing I ever experienced. Scary as hell, yeah, but awesome! God*damn!*"

Toni broke free, squeezing his hand as she drew away, and Murphy savored the adrenaline that continued surging through him for another moment, then with one eye saw the approaching squall line from the north.

"That was amazing. Everybody did great. And maybe if this ol' tub had been a half-knot faster, that crest wouldn't have come down on our head like it did—"

"Tub? You can't call this boat a *tub*," Bub protested. "Not after gettin' us through a hundred-foot wave like that."

"Hundred is a bit of a stretch," Romer interjected. "At least fifty, maybe sixty. On the breaking face, I mean."

"Hundred. Sixty. Still the biggest goddamn wave I ever seen in this or any other lifetime. Biggest wave I *wanna* see in this or any other lifetime, too, for that matter," Bub laughed.

Murphy glanced nervously off the bow, where a brown patch of water indicated coral, then to the orange and pink western sky. He moved toward the bowsprit, removed the safety pin from the shank of the main anchor. "All right. Agreed. I won't ever call her a tub again. Point is, we've got a lot of work to do and about a half hour to do it before it's dark. We're not in the clear yet." He lowered the anchor into the water, let the drift of the boat start taking chain through his hands. "This oughta keep us put while we get things sorted out. We have to get all the lines and sails back onboard before we restart the engine."

Toni Johnson said, "I'm on it," and began hauling torn, yellow nylon back onto the deck.

"We lost both foresail halyards to the masthead. We need those back." Murphy dropped the chain over the windlass sprocket and put a wrap around the cleat. "Plus the engine died when the wave broke."

Bub said, "Hey, Murph?"

"If water got pushed back through the exhaust manifold, we may have to pull the injectors to get it out, then bleed everything. Romer, can you start on that while I go up the stick? One way or another, we need to get into Walker's harbor. Don't forget there's still a category-four storm bearing down on us."

"Murph?"

"What is it, Bub?" Murphy said finally.

Bub nodded toward the channel they had come through, a narrow path of blue surrounded by whitewater. A quarter mile beyond, *Soft Money* sailed across the wind, as her crew wrestled with a long, black pole sticking outboard from the base of her mast.

Bub said, "I don't think they're givin' up yet."


No, goddamnit!" Farber screamed. "I said *port* rail genoa turnin' block!"

Grant Hanson stared at him with one eye wide, then scampered to the starboard side, the end of a thick jib sheet in one hand.

"No, *other* port," Farber said, stomping after him to yank him back across the boat by his ear. "All right, see this? This is a turnin' block. This here round pulley contraption. It's what lines go through. And this whole halfa the boat," he indicated with a wave of his hand, "is the port side. Got it?"

Grant Hanson nodded and Farber released him, then walked back to the cockpit to wrap the three new lines on three separate winches as *Soft Money* rolled over the top of a swell on her charge back westward.

"Listen up, and listen up good. We're gonna get one chance at this, and only one." He peered south, at the gap between the two small islands just east of Walker's. "There's a nat'ral range created by them two islands right about at the same point where they went in. It also matches up with a deep-water channel Percy here noticed on the chart."

Percy stood silently, a told-you-so smugness momentarily pinching his face, then disappearing as he raised a hand. "Farber, I wanted to ask—"

"It's gonna be hairy, and we gotta do everythin' exactly right," Farber continued. "Or we'll more than likely die horribly, if that's any incentive for y'all." He pointed at the new lines they had rigged. "We got here, in this order, foreguy, afterguy and sheet. The first two control the position of the spinnaker pole. The last one the tension on the sail. Everybody got that?"

Link Thresher nodded. Grant Hanson saw him nodding, after a pause nodded himself. Percy said, "Farber, about that aide. On the island? How do *we* know he's there?"

Farber scowled. "Now's not the time, Percy."

Off to port, the two islands grew closer together. Farber clapped his hands and pointed to the mainsheet winch and the genoa winches. "Okay, everybody to your stations. When we get to the spot, I'm gonna yell, 'Bearin' off!' Grant, I need you to let out the main as far as it wants to go. Percy and Link, you guys work that big winch to deploy the chute." He pointed at the spinnaker hanging like a long, blue-and-white sausage from the top of the mast. "As soon as the tiniest bit of air gets in, it'll pop right open. Remember, you guys do that when I yell, 'Pop the chute!' Everybody set?"

The islands were almost touching as, from starboard, came the rumble of an enormous wave.

"This is it, folks. Stars are in alignment." Farber moved back beside the wheel to take over from Clyde Bruno. "Here we go: Bearin' off!"

Murphy hung upside down over the engine block through the hole where the companionway ladder and a series of sound-insulated panels ordinarily went, flashlight in one hand and thin crescent wrench in the other.

Beneath him, Romer worked a second wrench with restraint, trying to loosen the injector assembly without breaking it.

"More WD-40?" Murphy asked, adjusting his weight slightly to ease the pressure on his ribs.

"Can't hurt," Romer said, reaching for the can and giving the area another squirt. "Can't afford to crack that sleeve. Totally screwed if that happens."

"What's going on with *Soft Money*?" Murphy called.

"Still out there, sailin' back and forth. Like some kinda big, evil shark or somethin'," Bub said. "They got their spinnaker hoisted, but they ain't opened it yet. Murph, I got one of them halyards hooked up to that yankee sail, if you wanna try and sail to the island."

"Go ahead and run the sheets, then. We might end up having to do that."

"Hey, Murph, they can't possibly get through that gap, can they?" Bub asked. "Ain't they too big? Won't they hit bottom?"

Murphy said nothing. The channel was plenty deep enough for *Soft Money*. Instead he shook his head to fling away the drops of seawater and sweat that had collected on his forehead, glanced into the cabin where Toni was fiddling with the radio. With sunset had come a whole new world of AM stations. "Any word on the storm?"

Toni Johnson blew out a breath in frustration. "Nothing. Getting some election results though. About half the precincts counted and Ramsey's up by nine hundred votes."

"Nine hundred in which county?" Murphy asked.

"Nine hundred *total*. As in statewide."

"Perfect. Puts us in recount territory. That's always fun."

"The Democrats are already complaining about the ballot design in Palm Beach County," Toni said. "They're calling it a boll weevil ballot. Apparently it's arranged like some curled-up caterpillar, if that makes any sense. Anyhow, the entire Nautilus Gardens retirement community in Boca Raton got it wrong. Thirty-two hundred votes for the Reformed Nazis of Florida candidate instead of Ramsey MacLeod."

"Terrific. That'll make it even more fun." Murphy squinted at the locking nut his wrench was holding still. "Oh, hey, Romer! I thought I saw it move!"

Romer examined the injector intently, shook his head. "Why don't we just sail her in from here before we lose the light?"

"Because there's coral everywhere, and the motor lets us move directly into the wind, which we definitely have to do to get into the harbor." Murphy shifted his grip on the flashlight. "Plus if the storm turns the other way, we could ride it out right here tonight, if we had the engine to take slack off the anchor rode in the squalls."

"What about our friends chasing us? You remember. The ones with the guns?" Romer asked.

"If Farber's got any sense, he won't try coming in. He's got a fin keel, spade rudder. Steering down a big wave's gonna be skittish as hell. He's got an incompetent crew—"

"He's got Death Row looking him in the face if he lets us live," Romer finished, then gave another tap on his wrench with a plastic mallet. "Yeah! I got it! It's loose!"

"Hey, guys, they're doin' somethin'," Bub called from the cockpit. "Aw, nuts. Here they come!"

Farber couldn't keep the grin from taking over his entire face, it was so amazing:

*Soft Money* raced toward the gap in the reef, propelled by the downhill slope of a fifty-foot wave added to forty knots of wind filling their spinnaker to the bursting point. The knotmeter pegged at twenty-seven, which was nearly as fast as Farber's big, twin-diesel sportfisherman.

Spray flew away from the hull from as far aft as the mast, and Farber let out a long, loud whoop. "We got 'em, boys! We got 'em this time! Hang ten! We're surfin' now!"

Which was when Percy Billings stepped in front of the wheel, hands on hips. "Byron's got a six-year-old son?"

The grin disappeared from Farber's face. "Now, don't go leapin' to conclusions, all right? I ain't got no earthly *eye-dee* where you pulled that one outta, but let me just tell you, here and now, no joke, man-to-man—"

"Grant just told me," Percy said.

Farber eyed Grant, standing at his assigned station, clapping with joy. "Why that dumb, good-for-nothin' moron. . . . I could strangle the twerp. Hell, maybe I *will* strangle him—"

"And so you were planning on *killing* him?" Percy shook his head. "A *six*-year-old boy? *My* nephew?"

Farber clung to the wheel as the boat hurtled toward the gap in the reef, the rumbling behind them growing even louder as the wave began to crest. "Yeah, well, I will concede it ain't 'xactly the most honorable thing I ever had to do."

Percy crossed his arms. "No. That's way over the line, Farber. Killing Byron, that was wrong. But *this?* This is downright evil. We're not doing it. Any of it."

"Oh, don't start gettin' all moral on me now, asshole. Look at it this way: You wanna make an omelet, you gotta bust a few eggs. Sometimes, it turns out you gotta bust a few more eggs than you thought you did. But you know? That's Florida politics. And it's a little late now to be—"

He heard the mechanical *creak* of a line under heavy load slipping on a winch drum. "Uh-oh," he muttered, and noticed the spinnaker now luffing at one edge, pulling the boat to starboard. "Link! Trim on! Trim on!"

Link Thresher first pushed the button, then inserted a winch handle into the top of the drum but still couldn't gain a notch. "Can't!" he yelled over the roar of the water. "Too much pressure on it!"

Farber felt the tug of the wheel as the force on the big sail pulled the boat off the straight and narrow. He studied the sail, the control lines, finally realized what had happened. The afterguy had slipped a few inches.

"Grant! Trim the afterguy!"

Grant flashed through wide-eyed bewilderment, then triumph as he remembered what Farber was talking about. He moved to the drum that held the foreguy and pushed the button. Instantly, the great, blue-and-white Southern Toyota sail wobbled farther to starboard, dragging the bow with it, and Farber gripped the wheel even tighter.

"Damn it all."

He turned to Clyde Bruno beside him, motioned him to take the helm, then cupped his hands to shout in his ear, "Don't let it turn! Hold it steady!"

Clyde Bruno flashed a thumbs-up, widened his stance on the sloping cockpit sole and tightened his hold. Farber moved out and forward to the row of winches with the spinnaker control lines. Ahead, the bow surged toward the gap in the reef, a thin blue path amid a field of white foam.

"*This* one is the afterguy," he yelled, slapping Grant Hanson's hand away from the foreguy winch. "You ease that one while I crank in on this one. Got it? Remember how I taught you. Keep your fingers clear."

Grant nodded, with one hand pulled the tail of the green-and-white foreguy out of the locking groove, put his other hand on the wraps of line around the drum . . . and immediately lost control of it, the line peeling off the drum, catching his thumb in a loop, shearing off his thumb. . . .

Grant Hanson held his hand up, his face pale, as bright red blood spurted from an artery. But his building scream was drowned out by a new noise from the spinnaker, an uncontrolled flapping as it wobbled now over to port, yanking the bow with it as the afterguy, without any opposing tension from the foreguy, drew the pole aft until it clanged against the shrouds.

"Aw, fuck," Farber LaGrange said as the spinnaker finally exploded into a shower of blue and white scraps and *Soft Money*'s bow veered around to port, into the wind. He turned toward the steering wheel, cupped his hands as he began stumbling toward it: "Turn, Clyde, turn to starboard! To starboard!"

Clyde Bruno held the wheel rock steady, said, "What?"

"Goddamn, deaf," Farber muttered, as he scrambled back to take control of the wheel, managed to manhandle the boat back downhill under mainsail alone . . . and then he felt the pressure of the wheel, first tugging, then dragging him to windward . . . which was when he noticed Percy Billings at the mainsheet winch, his index finger on the button, the sail cranking in.

"No!" Farber yelled. "You crazy son'bitch! Let it out! You'll kill us!"

Percy kept his finger on the winch, the line kept winding in on the drum, the sail kept coming inboard. "Sorry, Farber. It is a far, far better thing that I do, than I have ever done."

The wind pressure on the main continued building, continued tugging the bow, until it was too much for Farber and Clyde Bruno to resist. The wheel broke free from their grip, spun madly as *Soft Money* swung clear around until she was broadside to the wave she was riding, then rose up the face toward the crest, and the last thing Farber saw was a pale blue overhang of water falling toward them from the sky as the big yacht began rolling sideways down the wave.

"Aw, fuck," Farber said again, just before everything became white, bubbly water.

★

Sweet Jesus," Bub whispered finally.

The four of them had watched from the cockpit, soaking wet, Romer and Murphy grease-stained from the engine, as *Soft Money* had begun her final charge. They had stood, awestruck and speechless, as the boat raced ahead of the wave that reared up behind her. Only Toni Johnson had said anything, a quiet "Oh, God," when she suddenly broached, then came tumbling down the wave and onto the reef.

Five more waves had rolled onto the coral barrier, until not one recognizable piece of wreckage was visible.

"Jesus," Bub repeated. "It's gone. It's completely gone. You suppose after the storm, it'll all wash ashore?"

"I doubt it," Romer said. "The tide's at maximum ebb right now. Everything's getting swept off the bank into deep water. Most of that debris will sink in eighty, hundred feet."

"What about," Toni breathed, "what about the . . . bodies?"

Romer waved a wrench matter-of-factly. "The Bahamas have one of the healthiest shark populations in the world. By morning, I don't think there'll be any bodies."

Bub squinted out into the gathering gloom, watched as the next wave rumbled onto the reef. "So it's over. It's finally over."

Toni first put an arm around him, then wrapped that into a hug. "Oh, Byron . . . I feel awful. If I'd thought for an instant they'd go this far, I would have called a press conference right there at party headquarters, laid it all out—"

"Hush, now. It ain't your fault. It's their fault. They're the ones who— Whoa, there's somebody in the water!" Bub pulled free and climbed up onto the cockpit coaming. He pointed at the near edge of the channel. "There, see? Oh, my God. . . . It's Percy!"

Bub stripped out of his T-shirt, kicked off his boat shoes. Murphy grabbed his wrist as he stepped over the stern railing. "Hold on, you don't know that."

A hundred yards away, the body drifted toward the channel, only to be buffeted back by a low wall of whitewater. Bub pulled his hand free. "Yes, it is. I'd know that big head anywhere."

Murphy grabbed it again. "No! The currents out there are deadly. They could suck you under, then right through and out."

"That's why I gotta hurry."

"Wait!" Murphy yelled. "Stop and think. He tried to have you killed, for God's sake. Now you're gonna risk your neck to save him?"

Bub shrugged, the decision out of his hands. "Man, he's my brother," he said, and dived in.

They watched from the cockpit as he stroked toward the reef, the current helping him along, until he reached Percy, slipped an arm beneath him, flipped him over onto his back, then awkwardly frog-kicked against the current.

"He ain't gonna make it," Murphy said, watching as the pair drifted closer and closer to the gap in the reef. "No way."

"We have to do something," Toni Johnson said.

But Romer already was. He'd stripped down to his underwear and had opened the Velcro flap atop the Lifesling container mounted on the stern rail. He pulled out the horseshoe buoy, slipped it over his head and shoulders and shook out the coils of polypropylene line into the cockpit.

"Make sure that runs clear," he said, and then dived in himself, one hand holding the buoy to his chest, the other outstretched ahead of him. He swam with a powerful kick, a fast, steady stroke.

Wordlessly, Toni and Murphy teamed up to manage the pile of yellow line in the cockpit, Murphy pulling up armfuls to break the kinks and loops, Toni tossing it overboard as Romer swam. The pile got smaller and smaller and soon Murphy saw the bitter end just a few yards away.

"Uh-oh," he said, and wrapped it around his hand twice to make sure he wouldn't lose it, then searched the cockpit for a suitable line to tie to the end. He chose the jib sheet that Bub had coiled and draped over the starboard winch, and then stood there, trying to remember how to tie a sheet bend, when he heard Toni Johnson breathe, "He's got 'em."

A hundred and twenty yards away, Romer took the yellow horseshoe off himself, slipped it beneath and around Percy, then flashed a thumbs-up back at the boat. He and Bub took hold of the rope as Murphy wound the line around the port winch, inserted the handle and began cranking.

It took Romer and Bub pushing from below, Toni and Murphy pulling from above to get Percy Billings up and under the starboard lifeline. Bub followed him up and bent over him, stroking his face, as Romer climbed in and went immediately to the companionway.

"I'll go bleed the engine," he said. "We're losing light fast. He'll be all right. Pulse is a little weak, but he's breathing on his own."

Murphy stood on the cockpit bench as Bub continued stroking Percy's cheeks, talking to him softly: "When you were little, and you were havin' a tantrum, this used to calm you right down. You remember that? 'Course you do. It's gonna be all right, Bro. It's gonna be all right."

Which was when Percy Billings coughed, once, twice, then opened his eyes. He looked around to see where he was, looked up at Bub, and he began to sob.

Bub put his head on his brother's chest. "It's gonna be all right, Bro," he repeated, his own tears streaming down his face. "Shhhh. It's gonna be all right."

# Epilogue

★

Murphy found Governor-Elect Bub Billings on the pebbly beach beside the seaplane ramp, teaching Lamont to skip oyster shells into milky blue water.

"Like this," Bub said, laying his index finger along the edge of a shell. "Then, sidearm. Like the way ol' Dennis Eckersley used to do it. Except without all the cussin'."

The boy left his father's side to find a suitable shell, slung it awkwardly into the water, then turned to his daddy, eyes wide and bright.

"There you go!" Bub clapped. "You got it. We'll get you that baseball scholarship yet."

He walked over beside Murphy as Lamont searched for another shell. "Plane ready yet?"

After finally getting into the marina at around nine, after a tearful reunion with his little boy, after introducing Percy to his nephew, they had used Gary Knowlton's single side-band radio to get a phone patch to call Florida and Ramsey MacLeod. One of the state's Kingairs had been dispatched at first light for Walker's, given the Hurricane Center's most recent update that Hilda, as expected, had turned back toward the northeast.

"Another half hour," Murphy said. "Mr. Winner-of-the-Closest-Election-Ever-Even-Though-You-Were-Supposedly-Dead."

Bub smiled and turned back to watch his son. "Ain't that the damnedest thing—oops! Excuse me. Gotta watch my language around Lamont—I meant: Ain't that the darnedest thing? Three hundred and fourteen votes, outta four and a half million cast. What are the odds? Anyhow, I talked with Ramsey for a good bit. You were right about him, I gotta say. A darned fine man. First words outta his mouth, he's offerin' me his office, his staff, the shirt off his back, pretty much anythin' I wanted for the transition. I'm sorry now I was so mean to him in the campaign."

Murphy gazed silently at the laughing gulls and pelicans standing sentry atop the creosote-coated pilings. The marina was empty, for a change. The big, multimillion-dollar sportfishermen had all cleared out on the coming storm and had not yet returned. They would, though, and soon. The sky was clear, and a crisp November wind blew from the northwest. Within a day or two, all the sand and silt in the water would settle back out, returning the seas surrounding the island to their normal, crystalline perfection.

"And your brother?" he asked finally.

Bub took a deep breath and nodded. "He's gonna be okay. Coupla cracked ribs, I think. He's gonna have a pretty impressive shiner for a bit. Doesn't remember how he got it. Suppose he musta whacked it on somethin', when they rolled." He took a deep breath. "I talked to your friend Gary. Thanked him, of course, for takin' such good care of Lamont and Marlita. It's amazin', really, how this place has, like, I don't know, pulled him outta his cocoon. Shoot, I'll come live here, if it'll help him. Fill air tanks and sweep the floor for Gary."

He dug into the rough coral sand and broken shells with the toe of a Walker's Cay sneaker. Shorts, shirt, cap, his entire ensemble, in fact, sported the resort's logo. Compliments of the gift shop.

"Anyhow, remember that little research station you told me about out on Rat Snake Cay? I asked, and he says he's still lookin' for somebody to do it." Another sigh. "Which gets me back to Percy. He woke up this mornin', bright and early. Me and him had us a good, long talk. Walked out on the beach just over that ridge, in fact. Watched the sun come up. We talked about . . . stuff. About the campaign and Link Thresher and Farber LaGrange. Like I suspected, it was him who set me up with that oil drillin' question, knowin' full well how I'd answer. Had his gofer tape the whole thing. Passed the tape along to Thresher. And he admits to goin' along with the plan to bump me off." Bub paused to watch his boy lay two shells on top of each other and toss them both.

"He's bawlin' like a baby, tellin' me this. I think I told you once, he ain't evil, or anythin', at his core. He's just selfish. Plus he figured it was only me, nobody else. Once he found out about Lamont, and that they were after him, too, that put it in a whole new context." Bub shook his head. "I don't know. Maybe it's some ego, superego thing. Yet another class I goofed off in."

Murphy said nothing. He had a feeling where this was headed, and was wrestling with what he would say.

"I don't expect you to buy into that," Bub continued. "I'm just tellin' you what I honestly believe to be true, is all. Anyhow, the point of all this is, despite everythin' that's happened, he's my brother. And I love him. He swears up and down on Daddy's name that he had nothin' to do with Spencer Tolliver, and I believe him. So we're left with him tossin' me in the drink and leavin' me for the sharks, and what I'm sayin' is, me personally, I forgive him."

He raised a preemptive hand against Murphy's raised eyebrow. "Now, hold on, Sailorman. Let me finish. I'm not suggestin' my forgivin' him means he's free and clear with society as a whole. I don't think he is. But what I'm proposin' is this: What if he spends the next, say, five years or so on Rat Snake Cay, countin' birds and surveyin' fish and recordin' water temperatures?"

Murphy blinked. "By himself?"

"By himself," Bub nodded. "He's always fancied himself as havin' a scientific mind. This'll let him develop that to his heart's content. The mail boat'll bring him food, water, writin' paper, books, so on. Think about it, Murph: Far as society's concerned, it's gettin' the same thing it woulda gotten if he was behind bars. Plus he'll be doin', well, at least somethin' of value. And plus," Bub took a deep breath, and when he continued, he did so with eyes moist and voice cracking, "and plus, I can't even bear to think of my baby brother in prison."

Murphy folded his arms, walked back and sat on the low seawall. "So what do you want from me?"

Bub came and sat beside him, waited until he could look him in the eye. "I want your blessin', is what I want. As the politicians say, you're a stakeholder in this. Him and Farber and Thresher, they were tryin' to kill you, too. Your say is more important than mine."

"What about Toni?"

"I already talked to Toni. She's okay with it. You and Romer are the only ones left who got good reason to object. And Romer, well, somehow I get the feelin' he ain't got a listed number."

It was only as *Mudslinger* was approaching Walker's, Toni and Murphy scrambling to get bumpers and dock lines ready, when it occurred to them that they hadn't seen Romer in some time. They'd panicked, Murphy throwing the engine into neutral and drifting until a search of the boat had found that Romer's wet suit and weight belt were no longer in the little cubbyhole where he'd stowed them.

"I expect you're right. We've likely seen the last of Randall Romer, eco-terrorist, for some time." Murphy stared out at the horizon beyond the breakwater, where pale turquoise water met winter blue sky. It was forty-five miles across the bank to West End, Grand Bahama, and a commercial airport, and he wondered idly how Romer would get there. "What's to keep Percy from just hopping on the mail boat and wandering off?"

"You're gonna have to trust me on this one, Murph," Bub said. "When he's promised somethin', that's it. His whole self-esteem is wrapped up in honorin' his word. Believe me, he will not leave that island."

"And Gary's okay with this?"

"Yup." Bub opened his arms as Lamont came to sit on his lap. "Gary and Toni, both. Ain't that right, pardner?"

Murphy watched Bub and Lamont in silence. The boy was studying the water intently, eyebrows narrowed in concentration.

Murphy took a deep breath and let it out. "All right. If Toni's okay with it, and Gary, then I'm okay with it, too."

Bub smiled wide, reached around Lamont to squeeze Murphy's shoulder. "Once again, man, I owe you."

"He's going to be lonely out there," Murphy warned.

"He understands that," Bub said. "He also understands he's gettin' off easy. Anyhow, me and Lamont, we're gonna come visit at least once a month, regular as clockwork. Ain't that right? And Daddy'll teach you how to fish and swim and snorkel and all that good stuff, and Uncle Percy can teach you about *ther*-mo-clines and salinity and all that other book-learnin' stuff."

Murphy listened to that, then replayed it in his head. "Hold on. Explain to me how you expect to pull *that* off? The governor of Florida takes a monthly trip to a deserted island in the Abacos?"

Bub scratched his head. "Now what's this got to do with Ramsey? What are you talkin' 'bout?"

"What are *you* talking about?"

Bub blinked rapidly, then smiled. "Didn't Toni tell you? I'm sorry. I thought she'd tell you."

"Tell me *what?*" Murphy shouted.

"I conceded. This mornin'. Well, to Ramsey, anyway. I'll sign the 'fi-cial papers in Tallahassee this afternoon. I thought for sure Toni would tell you."

Murphy's mouth hung open for a good minute before he recovered his ability to speak. "You've got to be kidding."

Bub snorted, set Lamont on the ground and stood. "After everythin' I put into that campaign over the last five months, I wouldn't kid about somethin' like that."

Murphy shook his head helplessly. "Why?"

"Mind if we start walkin'? I don't wanna keep the pilots waitin'." He held Lamont by the hand and led him up the seaplane ramp. "Well, for one, you gotta admit it makes a coupla things a whole lot easier. For example, now I don't gotta spend months tellin' half-truths about what happened. You know, explainin' how you fished me outta the water, and then how we sailed here just ahead of the storm, but leavin' out all the stuff in the middle, includin' what all happened to Farber and his boat.

"Then there'd be the issue of how Governor Bub suddenly came to have a six-year-old son when *Candidate* Bub hadn't exactly volunteered that fact. And, as you point out, it makes my goin' out to visit Percy a whole lot simpler, without havin' to mislead the Tallahassee press corps every time." He bent to lift Lamont onto his shoulders. "But you know what? At the end of the day? The thing that really made it simple was that boll weevil ballot. I looked at it every which way, includin' sideways, and there's just no gettin' around the fact that three thousand old Jewish folks did not vote for a Nazi, reformed or otherwise, on purpose. If that elections supervisor had designed a normal ballot, Ramsey wins by twenty-nine hundred votes. End of story. And I'll be damned, sorry, *darned*, if I was gonna wake up every mornin' for four years knowin' I was the accidental governor. Hey, Marlita, *buenos días!*"

They had reached the plateau where the little airstrip stretched off a half mile, to the very edge of the jagged coral rocks that constituted the island's western shore. To the north, a leftover swell continued to pound the barrier reef. Lamont wriggled to be put down, then ran into his nanny's arms with a loud, "*¡Hola!*" She picked him up and gave him a hug and a kiss while a dark-suited Florida Department of Law Enforcement agent helped the copilot load up the cargo hold of the six-seater.

Murphy stood, alternately studying Bub, then the State of Florida seal on the side of the plane, shaking his head the whole time.

"I know. You think I'm nuts," Bub said.

From behind them, Toni Johnson put an arm around both their shoulders. "I swear to God, Bub, Lamont's the cutest punkin' I ever seen. After breakfast this morning, he gave me the biggest hug. Oh, hey!" She shook Bub's arm. "Did you tell him? Does he think you're nuts?"

"Certifiable," Bub said. "Hasn't been able to say a word. Don't think I've ever seen him like this."

Toni laughed. "Well, you have to remember the culture of the political consultant. Scorched earth. Take no prisoners. Destroy the village to save it. And here, you win and then throw it away? *Heresy!*"

"I don't think it's nuts," Murphy said finally, reaching out to shake Bub's hand. "It's, well, the most decent thing I've ever heard of in a political campaign. Bub, I'm honored to have been a part. Truly, I am."

A wry smile twisted Bub's lips. "Hah! You're just sayin' that 'cause your original client ends up winnin'!"

Murphy shook his head again. "What did Ramsey say? When you told him."

"Said it was decent and honorable and thanked me." Bub shrugged. "Then he offered me a job. Chief of staff. Told him I didn't think I had the experience. Said he didn't care. He would teach me. Said a man's character is more important than his experience." He nodded to himself. "Darned fine man, Ramsey is. Make a good governor."

"So you're going to work for him?" Murphy asked.

"No," Bub said. "I got my own row to hoe. What I'm gonna do is show the world that I can make Bub's Fine Lawn Furniture work, even without Petron oil subsidizin' me out the wazoo. It's gonna be a lean coupla years, but you know what? I'm gonna make it. I got fifty-seven good people countin' on me, and I ain't about to let 'em down. You watch. And once I get that goin', I'm gonna run for the Brevard school board. I think parents of learnin'-disabled kids need a voice, and it may as well be me."

"*I'm* working for Ramsey," Toni said.

"Oh. Naturally. *You* are," Murph said, nodding. "But you're a Republican."

Toni shrugged. "He said any friend of Bub was a friend of his. He gave me Environmental Protection. Know the first thing I'm going to do? Sue Petron's ass. Next, I'm revoking all the exploratory leases. Heh, heh, heh!"

Murphy smiled. "Remind me to dump my petroleum stocks."

Bub punched him softly on the arm. "So how about you, Sailorman? You gonna head out into the deep blue?"

Murphy grimaced, peering back toward the harbor. "I've got just a *little* bit of work to get done, first. New stanchions on the port rail, new drifter, new spinnaker, repair the main, new depth sounder, bunch of bullet holes to epoxy over. Oh yeah. And install the *radios*. Ol' *Mudslinger* does not so much as leave that slip without working radios. So, no, I think I'll be right here for the next few weeks."

He turned to Toni, who was outfitted in a white tank top, blue shorts and white canvas slip-ons. Over a dark tan, it looked stunning, even with the little Walker's logo on all of it. "However, I could use a hand getting *Mudslinger* back home. Probably in late December. It would just be a day or two, depending on the weather. I promise: no armed goons chasing us."

Toni's eyes went to Bub, and she struggled for words. Murphy saw the interplay, immediately knew where things stood.

"Well . . ." she began. "Well, Ramsey kind of wants to get started right off with the transition, and—"

"Actually, now that I think about it, let me offer you a rain check on that," Murphy said. "I think I'll just hang around here in the Abacos for a little while. After all: What's the rush? It's lobster season. I'll drop you a note when I'm getting ready to bring her home, if that's all right."

A tall man in dark Ray-Bans and epaulettes on his shirt approached with a nod. "Excuse me, sir. We're all set."

"Well, let's get a move on, then. I got an important election to concede and some lawn furniture to sell," Bub said, corralling everyone toward the white-and-blue plane.

At the doorway, Lamont moved over and clung to his father's leg as Marlita climbed up the stairs. Toni Johnson turned to Murphy and gave him a hug, then squeezed his hand.

"Thank you," she said. "For following up on my anonymous tips."

"It was nothing."

"It was not nothing. It was a lot of work. I just want you to know I appreciate it." She flashed a grin. "And don't think I'm not envious about your impending adventure."

"I'll send postcards. To lord it over you," he said, suppressing his desire to renew his offer. "Give Ramsey a hug for me."

She smiled at Bub, then tousled Lamont's hair and took his hand. "Come on, sweetie. Let's go grab some window seats."

Bub and Murphy watched them climb into the plane, then waved at their faces through an oval window over the wing. Murphy glanced at Bub as he smiled at his son and Toni. Despite the lack of sleep, his eyes were bright and his trademark dimple going strong.

"So you lose the election but win the girl," Murphy said softly.

Bub smiled wider. "She fell in love with Lamont. I'm just part of the package. I don't wanna jinx anything, but I think GOP Gal and I, well, we might be seein' a bit of each other in future." He reached out and squeezed Murphy around the shoulders. "Hey, I'm sorry, man. I know you were interested in her, too."

Murphy shrugged. "Don't sweat it. Losing the girl, that's sort of becoming my specialty. But listen, you all have a safe trip home."

Bub grabbed his hand to shake it, pulled it in for a hug. "Sailorman, I don't know the words for this, so I ain't even gonna try. But I appreciate everythin' you done. I mean it."

"I think your pilot's leaving."

Bub pulled away, started climbing the stairs and turned. "If you see Romer, tell him thanks. And give him my regards."

The propeller on the opposite side of the aircraft started its noisy whir, and Murphy held up an OK sign and covered his ears. Bub flashed a thumbs-up, then climbed in to sit beside his son.

Murphy backed away slowly, stopping by the tin-roofed shack that served as the island's Customs and Immigration Office. He nodded a greeting at the uniformed officer leaning against the door, and they both watched as the Beechcraft spun up its second propeller, rolled to the eastern end of the runway, then revved both engines and shot past them and up into an expanse of Arctic blue.

"Dat mon, he da new guv'nor of Florida or sumt'in?" the customs man asked.

Murphy watched the plane diminish into a tiny speck, then not even that. "No," he answered finally. "Not yet, anyway. But eight, twelve years from now? He'll be back. You watch."

"He a good fella?"

Murphy peeled his eyes away from the sky and nodded at the customs man. "The best. *I'd* vote for him." He glanced at the sun, then his watch. "You think it's too early for a cold beer?"

The customs man offered a wide, toothy grin. "Mon, you in da islands now. It *never* too early for a cold beer."

Murphy returned the smile and nodded. "I'll see you around, huh?"

He crunched over the shell path down the hill between clumps of buttonwood and sea grape toward the harbor. A hundred images floated through his head as he fought exhaustion. The view from the face of the wave they had ridden in, a narrow blue seam through a wall of solid coral. *Soft Money,* her sails ghostly white, chasing them across a moonlit sea. Toni, her skin soft and brown, in her fresh new summer clothes. . . .

He forcefully pushed her from his mind. Two weeks earlier he'd never even heard of her. He had no cause to mourn losing her. Losing her, hell. He'd never *had* her to lose her. And yet . . . the way she knew how to coil a halyard and hang it from the cleat, not a single kink in any of the loops. The way her log entries were succinct and accurate, lettered in a perfect hand. The way she stood on the cabin top, legs stretching from shorts down to bare feet as she reached on tiptoes for a mast fitting above her head. . . .

Murphy shook his head to clear it, turned onto the path that bordered the seawall. He had a lot of work ahead of him that day alone. At a minimum he needed to pump the bilge, wash the bedclothes, mop the cabin sole and hose down the topsides and deck. Plus make a list of all the parts he would need flown in from Lauderdale. Plus borrow a grinding tool to get to work on those bullet holes.

But before any of that, he decided, he would nap. If he wasn't going to get the girl, then at least he was going to get some sleep. That much he deserved. That and some conch fritters and a nice, cold Kalik.

Yes, he decided with a nod: a cold Kalik, hot conch fritters, nap and then work.

He felt better, the decision made, and began walking with a purpose toward the restaurant overlooking the marina, which was when he noticed the commotion on the little floating dock where local guides from Grand Cay tied their flats skiffs.

A thin man in plaid shorts and a faded blue safari shirt was dancing around, hoisting a black, diver's weight belt above his head. His buddies were clapping him on the back and laughing.

"What's going on?" Murphy asked an older fisherman as he climbed up the ramp from the celebration.

"Most crazy t'ing, mon," the man laughed, pointing. "Some dude steal Li'l Johnny's ol' Aquasport. Johnny all upset at first, but den he coilin' up the dock lines the tief left behind, and it turns out the tief left sometin' else, too. You know dem South African coins, mon, dem Krugerrands?"

Murphy began to smile. "I've heard of them."

"Well, dis crazy tief, he leave Li'l Johnny 'bout twenty *t'ousand* dollars' wortha dem coins, and the boat he take only worth about ten t'ousand!" The man laughed. "Hurricane come, ev'rybody go crazy!"

The man clapped Murphy on the back and continued on his way, laughing. Murphy thought about it, then he began laughing, too, as he climbed the steps toward the restaurant.